MISS BRANDYMOON'S DEVICE

a novel of sex, nanotech, and
a sentient lava lamp

Rune Skelley

To the two best kids. Thank you for not eating the Declaration of Independence.

CONTENTS

Chapter One

TALISMAN

Re: Reverse-Engineering the Device
  Now that we've seen its innards, it's clear we will not be able to copy it. So, we need to procure more. The nanotech is incredible. The thing looks like ordinary body-piercing jewelry, yet there's so much crammed into it.
  We managed to figure out a few things. The device doesn't need a battery because it's powered by the wearer's bioelectrical field. The wearer's body also acts as an antenna, which is how such a small device can send and receive over such great distances.
  Side note of interest: PierceX, the company covertly distributing the jewelry, is a front for Shaw Ministries, and is willfully ignoring the concept of informed consent in regards to both the piercers and the end-user.
                  internal TEF e-mail, 08-02-2000

FRIDAY, SEPT 22, 2000

Fin Tanner searched the dank alley for the tattoo parlor Booth mentioned yesterday. Specifically, his friend said, "Go to Talisman," and, "The piercer there is a hot babe."

Of course Fin didn't have an umbrella and the rain had started again, dampening both his soviet surplus trench coat and his mood, and lending a soggy ripeness to the stench seeping out of the dumpster cave. The trucks making afternoon beer deliveries to the service entrances of the bars and night clubs splashed through oily puddles, turning the narrow sidewalk into a test of skill his sleep-deprived body had trouble passing.

A rank splatter of puke confronted Fin and he cursed the amateur revelers who overran Webster. It was a college town, not a real city, and as such had an anemic bar scene. Not that the bars weren't plentiful, they were just garishly lit, mock-edgy and pathetic. Buckminster students hit their 21st birthdays and flocked to these pretentious kiddie-rides, quickly achieving alcohol poisoning. On any given morning, a few of them turned up scattered around town on lawns or even rooftops, sometimes not in their own clothes. Referring to a night of excessive partying as 'getting abducted by aliens' was the new hip jargon, especially when you couldn't even remember you'd been drinking.

The fall semester had just begun, filling Webster once again with a fresh crop of students desperate to prove how grown up they were by behaving like spoiled children. The only good thing about the situation was that when Fin's band Nicotine played a gig, they got a cut of the cover charge. But, even splitting the rent six ways, he had to moonlight in order to maintain the poverty-line lifestyle to which he'd become accustomed.

"Already late for work," Fin mumbled. He was about to admit defeat and grab a cup of coffee at Magic Beans. He would sorely need it if he expected to make the layout for The 100th Anniversary of Homecoming "fresh and snazzy." *Sycamore*'s dutiful alumni readership wouldn't fork over hefty contributions for anything less.

A Molson truck came barreling toward him. Fin dodged behind one of the massive utility poles prevalent in the alley and almost fell down the flight of stairs hiding behind it.

"Shit!" He checked his black cargo pants for splashes and found none. When he looked up, a slow smile crossed his face. Booth neglected to mention the place was subterranean, and the neon sign was on the fritz. Instead of TALISMAN TATTOO! it read IS TOO!

Fin ground his cigarette out under his boot and started down the steep, concrete steps. The scarred wooden door at the bottom was propped open to emit the smell of coffee, and some extra-crunchy noise rock.

My kind of place, Fin thought, trying to smooth his unruly hair with both hands as he slipped through the opening into the dim interior. The only light came from a work lamp on the counter to Fin's right as he entered. To his left the cramped room was filled with a huge green velour sofa and a battered coffee table spilling over with photo albums and copies of *Tattoo Biker*. The cement floor was partially covered with a blood red carpet. A wall-mounted TV played *The Road Warrior* with the sound off.

Fin looked back to the counter. He recognized the big, well-muscled guy sketching shirtless there, but didn't know his name. The sheer abundance of aboriginal and Native American tattoos was hard to forget, as was the tribal look of his piercings which included his ears, septum, the bridge of his nose and, as Fin now noticed, his nipples.

This better not be Booth's idea of a hot babe, Fin thought blackly.

The artist looked up and brushed a long strand of black hair out of his dark eyes. "With you in a minute," he said, and added a few more strokes to the tattoo he was designing.

Fin amused himself by making up dialog in his head for *The Road Warrior* until the music got quieter and the overhead lights came on. Both men blinked for a few seconds.

"I'm Marcus Savage. What can I do for you?" He gestured toward the design samples covering the walls.

"Hi. Fin Tanner," said Fin as he failed to spot the babe body piercer. "I'm not looking for a tattoo today. I wanna get my eyebrow pierced I think."

"Not my department," Marcus said, then bellowed, "Rook!"

Fin looked around, startled and confused.

"ROOK!" Louder and impatient.

Movement in the shadowy depths of the sofa became a girl sitting up. "What?" she complained.

"Customer," Marcus said serenely, and went back to work at the counter.

Rook, apparently, yawned and stood up. After pulling her houndstooth miniskirt down to cover the tops of her bare thighs, she stretched and ruffled her hair.

Catching a glimpse of her black panties did wonders for Fin's mood and he felt a smile threatening. Her shaggy, shoulder length hair was mostly blue-black, except for her chin-length, cherry red bangs. He couldn't hold the smile back when she finally got all that damn hair out of the way and he could see her face. Light freckles dusted her nose, but otherwise her skin shone flawlessly pale, accentuating full lips tinted a red so deep it was almost black. Cinnamon colored brows drew together in puzzlement above the most striking eyes Fin had seen since the last time he fell in love with a stranger, a luminous snow-shadow blue. Fin realized with a start they were burrowing right into his brain. He dropped his gaze to her chest and admired how the clingy gray henley showed off her proportions. Impressive, but not so large as to be off-putting. Not that that was really possible. He knew he was grinning like an idiot and thinking nonsense. *I really need that coffee.*

"Hi. Should I come back when you're done napping?" He tried for sarcastic nonchalance.

Sliding her feet into a pair of goofy Cookie Monster slippers, she said, "You'd be waiting a while." Her voice was slightly husky, like dark beer. Fin shivered.

This is ridiculous, he thought. I gotta get some coffee.

Rook brushed past Fin and walked to the counter, hopped up, scooted across it on her bottom, and dropped down on the other side. Fin took the opportunity to check out her ass. After glancing at Marcus's drawing, she reached under the counter and pulled out a coffee pot. She filled a mug, crossed back over the counter and sat down on the sofa, cradling the mug in both hands.

"Well?" She patted the spot beside her. Around her right ankle a flock of tattooed black birds soared above the blue muppet pelt of her slipper.

Fin shrugged off his coat and sat down, a little closer to her than would generally be considered polite. He was as drawn to the heavenly fumes rising from the mug as he was to Rook herself, hoping that being so close to the coffee he would get some second-hand caffeine and straighten out his head.

The coffee smelled great but, instead of helping, it made his need more palpable. Rook took a sip and sighed happily. Fin was about to do something rash when she placed a green vinyl photo album in his lap.

Relieved to finally know what to do, Fin opened the album. The first page held an elaborate certificate from The Society of Professional Piercers, dated nearly two years ago and made out in the unlikely name Rook Brandymoon.

Rook ran a finger under a black silk cord encircling her neck and pulled a pendant from her cleavage where it had been hiding. Fin swallowed a mouthful of lust.

"Rook Brandymoon?"

"Yes."

"That's familiar for some reason." Fin was still trying to get his brain in gear.

She twirled the pendant, a glossy, dark green castle tower, between her slender fingers, disturbing the steam from her coffee and mesmerizing Fin. "I write for *Conspiracy Theory Press*. As Brandy Moon."

"That's it," Fin agreed. "Rook. Brandymoon. Is it your real name?"

"Yes."

Emboldened, Fin reached out his left hand and held the pendant steady to get a better look at it. It radiated her warmth. "Are you named after the bird or the chess piece?" He indicated the rook he still held.

"Are you named after Huckleberry or a fish's ass?"

"Touché." Fin dropped the rook and turned to the next page in the album and saw a female nipple with a barbell through it. "Hey, how'd you know my name?"

"You sound paranoid." Rook sipped her coffee and let him wonder for a moment. "I've seen Nicotine play a couple times."

"You like our music much?"

She considered while savoring another swallow of coffee. "You should knock off the whole Nine Inch Nails homage and play more originals."

"You think?" Fin let the criticism slide because he was compelled to stare into her uncanny eyes, and was both unnerved and aroused when he found her staring back.

"Yeah. But I'm not a music critic anymore. I gave it up for the lucrative and exciting life of a Professional Body Piercer. Nothing can compare to the thrill of sticking needles into the genitals of complete strangers and having them pay you for the privilege," she said. "So are you gonna look at the pictures and make a decision, or do you want me to pick a spot at random and go for it?"

Fin could tell she was fully awake now. The caffeine was doing its job and he wished he had some so they would be on equal mental footing. He forced himself to look down at the photo album.

The next five or six pages showed various ear ornamentations including cartilage piercings of all sorts. After these were several pages of nose and septum piercings.

Between sips of coffee, Rook offered helpful comments. "When you get your nose pierced you need to be careful about what color stone you choose. Red and onyx look like zits. Green and yellow look like snot. So do opals." Fin noticed hers was a small sapphire that matched her eyes. It didn't look like any sort of unfortunate body product.

Next were eyebrows, anti-eyebrows, cheeks, lips and tongues.

"Did you do Marcus?" Fin asked.

"Yes. And my own nose, nipple and navel." She finished the coffee and set the mug down on the floor when she couldn't find room on the table.

"Your own? Ow."

"Well, duh."

Fin flipped past the vulvas, penises, clitorises and labia. He lingered for a moment over more nipples and finally got to the last page.

"Decided?" she asked.

"Yes. I want a hoop in my right eyebrow. A black hoop."

"Step into my office." She indicated a door opposite the sofa. Trailing behind her, Fin entered the piercing room.

His eyes watered as he looked at the hallucination-inducing pattern painted in black and white on the concrete floor.

"Sit on the bed-thing," Rook said, motioning toward a lozenge-shaped table cushioned in forest green leather, with several foot pedals underneath. "Is this your first piercing?"

"Except for my ear."

Fin sat on the edge and found to his chagrin that his feet dangled an inch or so off the floor. He caught himself swinging them while watching Rook open an accordion door in the back corner and disappear.

She came back carrying a small white box with *PierceX* emblazoned on the top in gold lettering. She slit the shrink-wrapping with her thumbnail and pulled out a plastic insert cradling a dozen black metal hoops.

"You're the first with a black one," she said. "They're new. You like?"

Fin dragged his eyes away from her smile long enough to confirm what she held was, indeed, the piece of metal he would like embedded in his face.

At the counter along the wall she pushed up her sleeves, washed her hands and put on rubber gloves. Fin glimpsed bold black tattoos on her inner wrists, but couldn't make out what they depicted. She opened a fresh needle and gathered the rest of her supplies on a small cart that reminded Fin he hadn't been to the dentist in quite a while. Rook sat on a stool in front of him and reached for her tool tray, giving Fin a partial view of more black ink on her collarbone, then used the foot pedals to adjust the height of the table. Fin gazed up into her auroral eyes, his caffeine-starved brain struggling to come up with an excuse for kissing her, when she suddenly poked his eyebrow with a marker and handed him a mirror.

"I think I know when someone pierces my eyebrow," said Fin. "Don't tell me. You've always wanted to be a lumberjack."

Rook laughed. It was a deep, musical thing. Like raw honey.

"Just check and see if that's where you want it, jerk," she said.

When Fin concluded it was a good spot, Rook swabbed him with an alcohol prep and placed a clamp on his eyebrow. She moved in close, and Fin could smell her, and she smelled wonderful, like cloves and something darker, and she brushed against his arm and her nipples were standing up, and he could tell it was her left one she had pierced and...

"Fuck! That hurts!" Then he smiled.

"I love my job." She unclamped his brow.

To tune out the needle still impaling him, glinting, right there in front of his fucking eye, Fin kept his gaze on Rook's face. He felt a tug as she threaded the hoop through, evicting the needle. She lingered over popping the captive bead in place, then smiled. "It looks good."

Inspiration struck. Fin placed a hand on the back of her head and kissed her. She nipped him, but relaxed and kissed back, her tongue sliding over his. She tasted like Kahlua, and she made a throaty little sound. After a few fleeting seconds of this heaven, she pulled away and looked at him like he was crazy, but in a good way.

"I wanted to see if your tongue was pierced too," Fin said with an impish grin.

"You could have just asked." She sounded like she felt she ought to be mad but wasn't.

"Where's the fun in that?"

Rook rolled her eyes and started swabbing his eyebrow with iodine.

"Shit that hurts!"

"So sorry darling. Just want to be sure you don't get an infection." She finished up and slapped on a bandage. "Should I kiss it and make it better?"

Fin was in love. "Yes."

She kissed it lightly.

"Maybe I should get my nipple pierced too."

"Don't push your luck."

Rook opened the door and they walked out to the counter while she explained the daily cleaning regimen. After hopping over the counter again she punched a few buttons on the cash register.

"That comes to 55 dollars."

Fin took out his wallet. "If you're not working too late, maybe we could get together. Get a drink? Play some chess? Read some Twain?"

Marcus looked up from his sketch predatorily. Fin suddenly didn't feel good about this at all, especially after he noticed the shotgun under the counter near Marcus's knees. He and Marcus both looked at Rook.

"Marcus and I have plans tonight," she said, putting an arm around Marcus's bare shoulder. "Maybe you could bring a chess board here sometime. He won't play with me."

Fin felt trampled. He was about to leave when Rook handed him his change along with a business card.

"The cleaning instructions are on there. Be sure to read them carefully when you get home." She smoothed Marcus's hair and started braiding it.

Fin pulled on his trench coat and left the shop with Marcus eyeing him darkly. On the steps he could hear sharp words, but couldn't follow what was said. The rain had picked up again and another truck rumbled past. Now he was really late for work and someone important might notice.

Fin was utterly depressed by the time he got to Magic Beans, and ended up having an Irish coffee and a black cherry tart because the color of the fruit reminded him of Rook's lips. His tongue ached where she'd bitten him. When he drank his coffee too fast, the heat and the alcohol burned exquisitely and took his mind off his broken heart. After two more Irish coffees, he saw Dan and Elise on their break and remembered he had to go to work, so he ordered one more and another tart to go.

At the magazine office, he stashed the tart in his desk drawer and sipped the coffee while taking out the instruction card she gave him. After reading the front, he turned it over and couldn't suppress a whoop of delight. Right after ROTATE THE RING TO WORK THE OINTMENT INTO THE PIERCING there was a handwritten note:

M Beans 4:00 Wed

*** *** ***

Reverend Brian Shaw watched the monitor as the technician, Gregory, explained what it displayed.

"There, that's a new subject coming online. Serial number puts it at Talisman Tattoo over in Webster. This number is the signal ID, and beside it is the frequency. Being brand-new, it has listening priority set to High."

"Why is that?" Shaw asked. Gregory quailed. Shaw smiled at him. "I'm not criticizing, I'm interested. Why does being new cause it to get higher priority?"

Gregory turned back toward the screens and said, "The number of devices in the field is currently 178% of our available bandwidth. That means we get 1.78 times more signal than we can take in at one time. So, there's a schedule, and priorities. Until we gather some data about a new subject, we don't know how to fit them into the schedule. They start off as High priority so we can get data quickly."

"Well, that seems very sensible."

"What we really need," Gregory said, handing a set of earphones to Shaw, "is more equipment. Then we wouldn't need to have the signals in a rotation, because we could just listen to all of them all the time."

"I'll see what can be done," the reverend replied, still smiling. "They don't exactly sell these things at Walmart."

He put on the earphones, and heard, "I wanted to see if your tongue was pierced, too." He handed the headset back.

Listening in was of only secondary importance to Shaw's plans, but it did vex him that a glaring logistical gap like the equipment shortage wasn't mentioned earlier. He might never have known about it if he hadn't insisted on being briefed about the nuts and bolts. The irony that he gained this valuable insight from a traitor amused him.

In his youth Shaw let it trouble him that God made him so strong, yet not strong enough to do it all by himself. Such foolish pride had long ago been replaced by pragmatism. Just as a carpenter needs a hammer, Shaw came to realize that he needed tools as well. First television, transmitting his words to millions. And soon, with these marvelous devices, he would transmit divine grace itself.

"Thank you for the demonstration, Gregory. I'm quite impressed." Shaw gestured and said, "Could one of the others take over for you for a few minutes? I'd like to speak with you up in my office."

Gregory said, "Wow, I don't know about that. I mean, without a little advance notice it might be awkward…"

Shaw waved over one of the other technicians while Gregory tried to stall, and ten seconds later they were in the elevator together.

"It's a long ride up," Shaw remarked, and Gregory nodded nervously. The reverend mused aloud on the subject of the expansive Shaw Ministries compound, notably the large portion located below ground. So many tunnels twisting and turning through the darkness, interconnecting most of the above-ground structures. As Shaw spoke, Gregory grew drowsy. Shaw let himself ramble about the cthonic maze, and the parallels between its physical nature and its convoluted and hidden purpose.

The words weren't important. The reverend's voice carried the hypnotic power.

Shaw reached into Gregory's mind with his own and overrode his volition, paralyzing him.

"I know about the little notes you've been passing to your friends," Shaw said. "You're quite clever, Gregory, but you're in way over your head here. I don't know what made you think you could pull this off, except you obviously don't know enough about me. Well, now you do know. But it's too late."

The elevator doors opened, and Shaw glanced out to make sure the anteroom was empty. He could feel a bleak and tremulous kind of feedback from Gregory, who wanted to panic but no longer knew how.

"You deserve to understand my interest in the jewelry." Shaw flashed his on-air smile. "What I'm doing to you now, it only works in person. And it's devilishly tricky to apply to more than one target at a time. The marvelous technology hidden in those baubles is my key to widening my reach. I like you, but you're a threat to my great works, Gregory. I wish it weren't so." As he shut off Gregory's heartbeat, the reverend said, "I hope you understand that I never kill without an excellent reason."

Chapter Two

PARTY

09/22/2000
New Subjects
Talisman Tattoo [6] InkWell [3]
Males [2] Females [7]
Ear [1] Face [1] Tongue [1] Nipple [3] Navel [3] Genital [1]
Notes*: Subject T358~ft~18C, male w/facial piercing from Talisman Tattoo, is our first example of type* $\wedge\Omega\wedge$*, and therefore tracking protocol 2 will be in effect until such time as the lab techs have completed the diagnostics and signal mapping, and new surveillance protocols can be developed, if necessary.*
from TEF listening post daily report

The party had already reached cruising altitude when Fin got home from work at 10:30, still giddy from the prospect of his upcoming date with Rook.

Parties happened frequently in the run-down house where Fin and five other guys rented rooms. A lot more frequently than, say, mowing the lawn. This smelled like a good one, the blend favoring pot and beer over sweat and vomit. The green bulbs in all the lamps labeled this as one of Booth's parties, and made the whole thing feel like it was happening inside an aquarium. Techno flavored music thudded out of the speakers in a blatant attempt to get girls dancing.

Fin filled a plastic cup at the keg, handed the tap to the next person in line, and turned toward the kitchen to scrounge for food. The song cut out abruptly, a dozen gyrating bodies freezing in mid-dance. As their collective "Aww!" rang out, Fin put on his best dancer-face and spun around twice, bobbing his head like a pigeon and not spilling a drop of beer. Someone over by the stereo called out, "Sorry!"

Fin shimmied his shoulders, and moved with a zigzagging swagger through the forest of sweaty mannequins, keeping perfect time to the nonexistent beat. His efforts drew little reaction.

The music returned midsong, and everyone simultaneously resumed pumping and swaying, like they hung from the same set of strings. Fin stopped as abruptly as the music had, waiting for traffic to clear so he could cross the remaining distance to the kitchen. He finished his beer in three quick gulps before that happened, so he got back in the keg line behind his heavily tattooed black housemate, Booth. They exchanged nods.

"You went to Talisman!" Booth said, pointing at Fin's bandaged eyebrow.

"Thanks for the tip. You were right about the piercer." Fin grinned.

The line for the keg crept.

A man in a sleeveless black t-shirt with a ring in his nose sat at the foot of the stairs, talking to a hipster goof in a puke green cardigan. They were preoccupied with dreams, trying to describe a dreary one they'd both had. They called it "the green spaceship dream." Fin rolled his eyes for Booth's benefit and spotted Kyle coming in the front door. He had three of his muscle-headed cronies behind him, and as they filed into the house the party shrank back like a kicked dog.

That's when the heavy self-medication started. Fin needed something stronger than beer, so he absconded with a half-empty bottle of tequila and went to the kitchen for lemons. Or limes. Or anything citrus. An orange maybe. He found none, but encountered a motley assortment of revelers seated around the formica table, sharing a joint.

Booth tagged along, steering Fin into a private conversation. "You okay, man? You don't seem like yourself."

Fin was almost offended. "Who do I seem like?"

Booth laughed. "Fin. Mostly. Maybe it's just me."

"I seem like you?"

Booth smirked. "No, man. It's not that bad yet."

"Well, you can't be yourself without someone else."

Booth blinked, and shook his head again. "What?"

"How else are you going to know if you're doing it right?" Turning his back on his friend, Fin snagged the joint and took a deep drag.

***

Something hideous was trying to climb in through Fin's ears and let the air out of his brain.

He sat up and looked around. He wasn't really at the party anymore, inasmuch as he was alone in the third floor bathroom. Lint, grit, and a bad-smelling tacky residue clung to his shoulder and cheek where he'd been in contact with the floor. He pawed at them disinterestedly and ran his hand back over his lawless hair.

Fin's only sensory input that didn't keep dropping below the threshold of perception was his hearing. The irony was not lost on him as the melodic lobotomy twittered through the floorboards. If he nodded a bit, which he couldn't prevent, his eyes went below the surface of a rainbow Kool-Aid swimming pool and everything had dripping edges for a minute after he snapped his head back up. He couldn't tell if both his eyes were open.

His shirt lay in the sink, wet from the ever-dripping faucet. Fin pulled it back on. It smelled like beer and cigarettes. Comforting. He didn't bother to button it. Water trickled down his flesh, tiny cold snails heading for the waistband of his dilapidated black cargo pants. The phosphorescent slime trails helped him focus.

He had been having a good time until Kyle and his friends showed up. That would be Kyle's music doing violence to his brain, then. Kyle always slipped into wedding DJ mode when he got trashed, and Fin always slipped into misery mode when Kyle started having fun. No amount of drugs could dim the glare of Kyle's personality.

In this house, Fin had seniority. He wasn't going to leave his fucking home just because some entitlement prick moved in. Soon enough Kyle would realize he wasn't welcome.

Fin began the process of standing up and achieved it by stages, leaning on the toilet and the radiator. Slouching against the wall, he started to move along the short hallway to his room before he was entirely upright.

How did he get upstairs? Maybe it was a new drinking game, and the loser had to carry him to the bathroom. He chuckled, which made him dizzier.

By the time he unlocked his room, he couldn't retrace his mental steps to account for his silly grin. Kyle's so-called music was still present and accounted for, so the smile melted and formed a shimmering puddle on the floor. In the reddish glow from the lava lamp, the smile took a linty hairball hostage and scuttled behind the TV. Fin blinked and switched on the overhead light. Dingy off-white walls, avocado shag carpet, black garbage bag covering the only window — no feral facial expressions in evidence.

If only stupidity were painful, Fin thought, as Kyle's sonic assault renewed itself. He flipped the power switch on his amp and hefted his bass. He could taste a bit of throb coming through the amplifier.

With all the knobs all the way to the right on the bass and the amp, he dropped the instrument on the floor in front of the speaker.

When Fin got downstairs to the living room he was the only one smiling. The squeal of feedback shook the tired old house, making bottle caps and shot glasses skitter around on the coffee table down here. It didn't cover the awful music, but guaranteed nobody could really listen to it. Kyle's customary smirk had vanished. He was trying to be goth in a black turtleneck, so the scowl fit pretty well. Booth banged his head maniacally, dreadlocks flying.

Bishop stopped the stereo. Kyle's friends stood around like sheep with drinks. Kyle was no longer in sight, so Fin congratulated himself on his victory.

The feedback stopped. Premature congratulations.

On the way back upstairs, Fin startled Kyle on the second landing. Fin glared and grasped the bannister to steady himself.

"Nobody goes into my room," said Fin.

Kyle tried several faces, and settled on wounded pride for unintelligible reasons. He met and held Fin's gaze with his algae-colored eyes, but took too long preparing a retort.

"You went into my room," Fin continued.

Kyle squared his shoulders, wanting the full effect of the half-inch height advantage his combat boots afforded him.

"That makes you Nobody," Fin concluded.

Kyle pushed Fin's shoulder, trying to send him down the stairs, but Fin let go and melted to the side. Off-balance, Kyle stumbled down the next few steps. He stomped down to the first landing where his toadies could see him and yelled, "Asshole!"

Fin climbed the rest of the stairs and made the walk down the hall to his room with more grace than the last time. The only evidence of an interloper's presence was the unplugged amplifier. Fin placed his bass back on its stand and reset the dials on the amp so it would be less likely to detonate upon being powered up again, then sprawled on his threadbare recliner with a cigarette. Ordinarily, bringing about the untimely end of a party's life would be cause for shame and reproach, but in this case Fin regarded it as a mercy killing.

"Uh, Fin?"

Vesuvius sounded somewhat concerned. Or he could be seriously ticked off. Fin couldn't tell by the tone of voice, a quavery monotone he found soothing, usually.

Vesuvius continued, "I have a question, Fin."

"Yeah?" Fin lolled back on his chair and shifted his gaze to the nearby lava lamp. "And what might your question be?"

The lamp was quiet for a few moments. "Why are there express checkout lanes at the supermarket, but the deli is all one speed?"

Fin laughed until he choked and sat up, causing his skull to fill with marching band collisions. He curled up and tumbled onto the floor croaking, "Fuck!"

At length the environment inside Fin's skull returned to something approximating its normal grime and clutter and he slowly sat up, chuckling. "That was not nearly that funny," he observed.

"You were," retorted the lamp.

Fin stood. He said, "Want to discuss the game?" Vesuvius occupied a privileged place in Fin's pantheon and a prime spot in his room, right beside the chess board on the tall cafe table. He occasionally coached Fin during a game. Chess was evidently not his calling, but it was fun to 'cheat' anyway.

"I said you should attack with the knight. You still should."

"That's it?" It was unlike Vesuvius to show disinterest in the game, even when it had been discussed to death already.

Guilt swept Fin. The feedback. Poor Vesuvius had been trapped in the room with it.

"Hey, 'Suvius, I'm sorry." He stooped and checked the glass capsule for cracks. Languid crimson clouds rose and fell in the self-contained amber sky.

"I moved about an inch toward the edge," the lamp stated.

"Shit, I didn't even think." Fin ran his left hand down the warm surface.

Everything seemed okay, but Fin felt stupid for being so cavalier with such a good friend, and moved him back toward the center of the table.

"Come on, let's figure out what Bishop's up to."

"You're about to find out."

Fin didn't understand, until he looked toward the doorway. Tom Bishop towered there, about four inches taller than necessary. His perpetually friendly face was rimmed with dark hair, and he sported a mane that reached his waist even in a braid. How long had he been standing in the hallway, smiling and infuriatingly patient?

*** *** ***

Bishop was relieved when Fin finally spotted him in the doorway and stopped mumbling and fussing with his lava lamp. Fin blinked his bottle green eyes a few times. Because his eyelids were not behaving in a coordinated manner, the effect was that he winked rapidly and spastically several times with both eyes. He told Bishop, "I know. And of course you're right, so go the fuck away."

"Up for some chess?" When Fin got really far gone, like tonight, Bishop knew to ease into conversation, and give him some extra personal space. Fin was not likely to harm anyone, not intentionally, but at times his threat displays could be a little emphatic. Bishop's accumulated expertise in dealing with Fin in this state was put to the test more often these days.

Bishop settled onto one of the cafe stools and waited.

It was always Fin's move, whenever the game resumed. Fin managed it that way, always playing black and always stopping on his turn and taking about a week to decide his next move. Bishop suspected he always had the move figured out right away but insisted on taking a week to decide if he liked it.

Fin climbed onto his seat across from Bishop. The blank stare he gave the board was deceiving, as he invariably found and used the absolute sneakiest tactic available. His was the game that undermined traditional games. Blind to anything more than two moves ahead, he never had to think about his opponent's third move, being always about to perpetrate something illogical, foolhardy, and exasperating that would foul the most elegant deployment and force his adversary to retrench in desperation.

Fin toyed with his knight, giving Bishop covert glances to see if he could get a rise out of him with the implied threat against his bishop. Bishop kept his face pleasantly calm. Everyone he played chess with learned quickly that his favorite weapon on the board was the piece that bore his name. Adept at deploying the two of them as a team, he preferred them over even the queen as offensive tools.

Fin always hunted down the bishops, quite cheerfully burning off half his own armada to get them. The move with the knight would not be a bluff. Still, he tried for a reaction before going ahead with it. Bishop glanced at the board to make sure he hadn't forgotten anything and shifted his bishop back two spaces to keep it out of the knight's path for a while.

Bishop said, "Party ended a little suddenly. Not too subtle, you know."

Fin replied in a mocking singsong, "Wasn't it miraculous?" and reached for his cigarettes.

Bishop declined the offered pack. "You might want to perform some miracles that are less easily mistaken for sheer gleeful obnoxiousness. Most folks can't make the distinction."

"Well, if I only attracted disciples who are smart enough to learn, I'd be the most effective messiah so far." His Zippo sparked.

"No, you just wouldn't have any disciples." Bishop sat back and watched Fin exhale smoke through his nostrils.

"You know what? I'm sick of talking about it." Fin made a show of searching for an ashtray.

"Look Fin, I'm not trying to say you need to take responsibility for the way people interpret your actions. I am saying you could capitalize on it, instead of shooting yourself in the foot. Which, by the way, brings up my real concern."

"My limp?"

"You don't remember what you did." It wasn't a question.

Fin's expression went blank.

"Look at your right arm."

On his forearm Fin discovered a crude bandage, held in place by adhesion to whatever was underneath more than by the tape wrapped around it. He quirked one eyebrow as he tugged experimentally on the gauze, pulling more boldly until he'd peeled the whole messy pad from his skin.

Congealed blood partially obscured the design, a solid black circle surrounded by undulating shaded bands. An eclipse. All blackwork.

"What the?" Fin's eyebrows moved in opposite directions as he held his arm up and twisted it for a different view. "Who did this?"

"You did."

Fin pondered. "It looks good."

"Certainly does, considering. I thought you'd rather have a finished tattoo in any case, so I didn't interrupt you. You wouldn't let me clean it up, though. You have Bacitracin?"

Fin nodded. "Got some today for the eyebrow." He examined the new ink for another few seconds, and cocked his head to look at the game. He pulled the knight away from its pursuit of the bishop, then resumed admiring his tattoo.

The knight move stunned Bishop. Such a change in Fin's tactics was unprecedented. While Fin picked at the dried blood on his arm, Bishop analyzed the new direction of the game. Shortly he concluded he was toast. The game was Fin's to lose.

But Bishop had known Fin to snatch defeat from the jaws of victory before. His feud with Kyle being the prime example. In the short time since he'd moved in, the rest of the house learned to ignore Kyle. That seemed simple enough. Of course, none of them had known that Fin and Kyle had a history. This obsession, in Bishop's view, caused the entirety of Fin's misery. He squandered his resources, and when he did capture a piece, such as the pawn tonight's disrupted party represented, it came at too high a cost. Kyle was an unworthy opponent, so all the better to play with skill and have done with it.

Bishop moved his queen, a desperation maneuver but his best choice. Then he remembered that the game had been intended as a pretext to get Fin talking. Fin seemed hypnotized by his new tattoo.

"What do you think it means?" Bishop asked.

"Probably something like, 'I'm really cool 'cause I did this.' What do you think it means?"

"It doesn't matter what I think. You should be asking better questions."

Fin rolled his eyes.

Bishop sighed. "A month ago you were a grimy hedonist. Now you're thoroughly squalid. The fun is gone."

"Squalid, and no fun. Ouch. At least I have a cool tattoo and an eyebrow ring."

"I'm dead serious. The change is alarming. You need to spend some time with Fin, Fin." He saw Fin's distaste at the idea. "You've been avoiding him, when you're not sticking needles in him."

"So, a good heart-to-heart will fix me right up?" Fin sounded amused.

"No, it's just a start. There are some things a person needs another person for. Even you."

Fin made eye contact properly for the first time in days, and smiled. "Relax, Mom. I have a date on Wednesday. With a girl." Fin moved his rook. "Checkmate."

Chapter Three

SURVEILLANCE

The universe has a purpose, which gradually technology allows us to see. Creation lies not in the past but in the future. The universe is unstable because it isn't finished. It is a means, not an end. Most importantly, there is no God -- yet. The patterns of chaos have a purpose. You have a purpose. These are not the final days -- this is only the beginning! Technology leads God ever closer.
from TEF recruitment pamphlet

The silence is heavy, salty, and cold.

The bleak, colorless terrain is dunes, undulating, pocked with craters of all sizes. Occasional crags of black rock protrude from the sand. The grayness above darkens into impenetrable night, filled with fear and secrets.

Alarming and tingling, like lightning on the skin, comes the low vibration. Felt but not heard, like a signal using silence as a carrier wave. Sand dances to this tune in Byzantine patterns. Ripples stay behind, like crop circles, like writing.

Somewhere under all that sand is an important item, lost. Something small. It might be a charm of protection from darker mysteries. It might be a key.

Now, as the not-noise grows in strength, an enigma of ghostly pale green lights appears high overhead in circle formation. Descending. The disturbance becomes a maelstrom of sand as the illuminated visitor moves lower still, leaving its home darkness and entering the faint gray. The sand churns and swirls until only the ring of green lights can now be seen. The droning power of this invader numbs, overwhelms.

All becomes still. The sand settles slowly, softly. The massive invader hangs above the sand by a slender line, tethering it to the blackness. The verdigris metallic hull could be an enormous bulb of phosphorescent garlic, but for the limbs. Several delicate multi-jointed legs are affixed at its crown, and reach almost to the ground. Its sheer presence feels heavy. Its size is terrifying

One leg stirs about in the sand for a moment and finds a glinting prize. It offers this trinket, extending that menacing leg.

***

Fin rose early in the afternoon, which gave him ample time to stroll before the start of his shift. Before he was expected, at any rate. But he couldn't enjoy playing hooky under the bland gray sky. It unnerved him, which in turn annoyed him.

At the store next to his workplace, he stopped short. He regarded the window display with a blank face and smoldering mind.

Marilyn Monroe languidly licked a lollipop made from a stop sign, except that it said POST. Armadillos of steadily diminishing size were frozen in asynchronous wobble as they passed by her, striving to reach the antique telephone and Victrola to the right. These relics were captioned 'Modern' in carved old-fashioned lettering. The background was something crude but not quite indecent entitled 'Sistine Men's Room Wall,' consisting of a section of institutional-white ceramic tiles covered with faux Renaissance graffiti and a stick-figure parody of the famous God's Index Finger portion of the Sistine Chapel Ceiling.

The Michelangelo rip was witty, in the way that works pretty well as a notion to describe indulgently at a party, but not as something you would actually carry out. The art lay in the threat of such tastelessness. Something so crass collapses under its own weight. Still, the artist's audacity might have gotten a smirk out of Fin except that he himself described the piece in great detail about a month ago. Indulgently. At a party. Right down to which finger Adam was displaying to god, and the phone number for Gabriel to blow your horn.

He pissed on the mental coals to cool them and entered the store.

Olaf's was the best-stocked art supply shop for fifty miles. Sure, the prices were high, but in addition to being a supply store the place housed a veritable museum of objets d'absurd. Also, it was next door to *Sycamore*'s offices and open late most nights.

Fin's interest in the merchandise at Olaf's was itself a little absurd, since he did all of his artwork on the Mac. He had no use for a Rapidograph or X-Acto, or Pantone markers, or rulers with inches on one side and picas on the other. But he loved them, touched them, occasionally shoplifted them.

A quick recon told Fin there was nothing new among those treasures, so he wandered into the other half of the store. Olaf's stocked arguably the most useless selection of greeting cards and postcards in town, but by far the most entertaining and educational.

While Fin was reading the caption on a postcard to find out what the hell the picture was, Dan walked in the front door. Could it be break time already, or had Dan been sent on a Fin-hunt? That chore traditionally fell to the newest employee. Dan was a good kid, but so painfully naive. He would mix better with the morning shift, whose personalities were free of rough edges. In fact, they were free of any edges whatsoever, and Fin couldn't understand how they remembered all their own names.

Dan was no zombie, just earnest and non-combative and unable to fathom the night shift's tribal bent. Fin had to evade him. Dan would gather that Fin was loafing, and he'd try to understand.

Fin melted through the framing area at the rear of the store, while Dan asked the clerk the standard polite questions. The back room and workshop were accessible via a closed door only a few feet away. Fin froze, watching as the clerk gestured. *Yes, tell him I looked at the sketch pads and textured paper, and you saw me over by the greeting cards.* Dan looked around as if listening to Fin's thoughts.

You're a smart guy, Dan, you'll head right for the cards, Fin guessed correctly. As a large tier of t-shirts and portfolios came between their positions Fin put his hand on the knob of the workshop door and discovered it locked. He still held the semi-obscene postcard, and slid it between the door and the frame. The door opened with only a slight noise, masked by Jane's Addiction playing over the store's sound system, and Fin slipped through and pulled it shut behind him.

It felt like being backstage at a play about museums. Canvases and enlarged photos and frames occupied over a third of the room's floor space, set up on sawbucks and tables and hanging on the walls, mostly festooned with c-clamps and straps. He wasn't sure which was a worse firetrap, this workshop or the basement studio he worked in next door.

There were people back here going about their jobs and so far not noticing Fin. Moving steadily so as not to attract their attention, he looked for the back exit. He spotted an open door with stairs going down.

Downstairs turned out to be the storeroom, and unoccupied. Turning back now would mean trouble well beyond talking to Dan, and while Fin and trouble had a more than passing acquaintance, they didn't really get along. Fin scanned the room for his next move. Behind a huge overstock of metallic markers a vestigial window lurked near the ceiling. Fin stood on a box and tried to look through the glass. All he could see was a little bit of masonry.

The corroded metal window frame opened with a squawk. With the smudgy glass panes out of the way, Fin could see a coarse steel mesh grille mounted outside. It was bolted on, but the crumbly cement did not hold the bolts well. He had no more trouble with it than with the window. He contorted himself to pass through feet-first.

This nefarious, undignified shimmy would lead him into Dogstar, a used book and CD store specializing in blues collectibles and golden age sci-fi. No doubt there would be a treasure trove of a storage room somewhere, but the dampness indicated it wouldn't be down here.

Lowering himself an inch at a time, Fin was eventually able to stand on the other side, but with one foot up higher than the other. Stairs. He could reach up to the ledge of the window, but doubted it would be possible to lever himself back through from this side.

The staircase ran down between the two buildings, and had been roofed over at some point. The floor joists above his head were full of spider webs. As he got used to the darkness, Fin saw the railing and the door at the bottom. He hesitated to try the knob. As long as he didn't try to open the door, it could be considered an option. Fin felt a lot like Schrödinger's poor cat, neither alive nor dead, or both. The finer ethical aspects of Schrödinger's treatment of animals had never been clear before this.

In any event, he need not panic. Someone would hear him sooner or later if he started yelling. He could even be optimistic about the door being open, since it was not exposed in the alley. If it were it would definitely be locked. This way it was just probably locked.

His logic, sound or not, was vindicated. The knob turned. He opened the door and found an office set up on the other side. Four metal desks, a few cabinets, cheap carpeting, fluorescent lights. A map of the state on the far wall, bristling with pushpins of various colors. No steps going up to Dogstar. Three men looking like they walked out of a fifties hygiene film, but wearing headset phones. One of the men winced and yanked his off. Fin heard faint feedback. When did Mormons start telemarketing?

"Hey," Fin began casually, "did Dogstar move their bathroom?"

They slipped each other sidelong looks. One of them was older than the others, mid-thirties. He spoke. "How did you get in there?"

Fin rapidly needed to decide between telling the truth and making something up. The truth had one major thing going for it. It was ready to be told, whereas a fabricated story would require fabrication. Also, the truth was he hadn't been sneaking around in this office, which it occurred to him was one possible explanation the men might themselves happen upon, if left to make guesses.

Unfortunately, the truth had gotten Fin into trouble before. Also, the truth was he had been sneaking around, albeit in a different office. Showing them the damaged window wouldn't prove anything, except that he'd been breaking stuff.

"There's a window out here. I came in through it because I was looking for a leak." The illogical sentence began to grow stale the second it left his mouth. "Dogstar never pulled the ancient pipes and conduits when they remodeled and now something is giving them a problem." The men remained impassive. Fin continued, "So I'm looking for the old vent traps, which are not anywhere in the finished space upstairs. I thought this area was unfinished space and I'm pretty sure the traps are in the ceiling down here." All eyes flicked upwards for a second. A good sign. "And since I don't see any water-damaged tiles, the traps are probably not the problem." Doubtful, semi-credulous looks. Less openly suspicious. Time to put the cherry on top. "Do you ever notice any odd smells, like coolant or perhaps a sharp musty odor?"

The men looked at one another. The eldest drew a breath and spoke without looking directly at Fin, his brows pinching together. "No, no odd smells. There is no problem down here." He stood, revealing himself to be even taller than Bishop, and motioned with his left hand, indicating the main entrance. On the back of the door hung a poster entitled 'Public Appearance — Respect the Organization.' It displayed two photos of Junior G-Mormons: one labeled Summer Attire, in shirtsleeves — the other, Inclement Weather, in a puke green Mr Rogers cardigan, holding a large fur hat in one outstretched hand, an oversized yellow umbrella in the other. Beside the door was a row of four pegs, three of them neatly holding hideous green cardigans.

Fin forced his eyebrows down and glanced back at the spokesman who finally made eye contact and said, "I ask you to leave now."

Fin tried not to grin like a maniac, tried to maintain some semblance of nonchalance. He had just persuaded these three grown-ups he was an HVAC serviceman despite his ratty Hawaiian shirt, soviet army trench and the bawdy stolen postcard in his right hand.

Crossing the room, Fin noticed something that shocked all the sugar out of his buzz. A deflated basketball, with the skeleton of an umbrella stuffed inside, hung by a string over the desk of the missing fourth man. The umbrella ribs protruded at the top and drooped around the saggy ball. The whole thing had been sprayed with something to give it the sickly gray-green look of a glow-in-the-dark toy.

Fin lifted his feet and placed them back on the carpet mechanically until he got outside. The model dangling above the unoccupied desk made him incredibly uneasy. A moment later he remembered the spaceship from his dream the night before.

Who the hell were these people?

The door slammed.

No identifying sign, not even a street number. From the outside, the door was easy to miss. It didn't face the alley and the only way to get to it was to sidle between the building and an eight-foot cyclone fence.

Fin glanced nervously at the flat, leaden sky and shuddered. Even the glowing retrospective of past homecoming parades awaiting his attention at *Sycamore* held more appeal than this incipient dread.

He hurried out of the alley.

***   ***   ***

Shaw stood gazing out his office window as his inner-circle functionaries dutifully filed in for the regular Monday afternoon meeting and took their seats at the large conference table. The weather was dreadful, giving the distant cathedral's many facets only dark and drab tones to reflect. Shaw's mood was much the same, but he marshaled an energizing grin before turning to face the group and take his seat at the head of the table.

"Reverend, would you begin please?" Shaw addressed Declan Spitz, seated to his right.

Spitz smiled, piggy face broadening. He closed his eyes and bowed his balding head. "Gracious Heavenly Father," he exclaimed, each word expelled as if he were being kicked in the abdomen.

All other heads bowed around the table as Spitz recited a prayer, brief and glib, for wisdom in this important meeting of the board. Shaw's was the last head to dip, and the last one to rise as Spitz pronounced, "Amen."

"As per our usual Monday agenda," Spitz steamed ahead, "I'd like to offer my congratulations to Reverend Shaw for another magnificent program yesterday."

Shaw affected a bashful look as those assembled hastened to agree with that critique. He raised a hand as if to wave off the approbation, but with a subtle shift of his posture transformed it into a gentle command for silence.

"Let us fix our minds upon the future, friends. This week I will be in Webster to meet with the Buckminster University religious studies department about a new program, and to interview finalists for next year's scholarship award. Declan shall keep the home fires burning in my absence." A pause to nod warmly at Spitz. "He will now reveal to you what he has in store."

Reverend Spitz addressed the group, leaving Shaw to contemplate the next few days. The Buckminster engagement was a nice publicity move, but mainly it served as a pretext for spending a block of time in the vicinity of Webster. The unpleasantness with Gregory forced the exodus of his entire covert staff and all the marvelous jewelry to a new, less civilized locale, and he'd taken the further step of expanding his security force. Now it was time to review the troops.

If only that operation was as easy to manage as this one. Spitz was telling Miss Chatham the quarterly financial summary would be needed by Wednesday afternoon for the meeting to compare allocations for operating expenses to donation requests. Everything Spitz mentioned so far was one form of monetary issue or another. Typical Monday.

Shaw inwardly rehearsed his planned motivational talk with the research technicians out at the secret workshop. He'd expected the program to be farther along by now and would use his unexpected appearance at the previously abandoned factory to give his mad scientists some incentive to accelerate their progress.

Deciding where to hide the operation had been far easier than Shaw would have dared to hope. A huge, untenanted, isolated building on the outskirts of a college town. Not too distant, yet far enough. Provident, truly, that one of those shirking technicians attended a rave there and divulged the location to Shaw.

Keeping other ravers away was now a bit of a concern.

More important was for Shaw to be vigilant during his travels to and from the facility. Gregory's people, the TEF, would be watching him, would plan to tail him. Well, let them try. Gregory's mission turned out to be a failure, in the end. For at the end he'd unwillingly divulged many valuable facts. Shaw now knew all of their faces, and he knew all their tricks. There was nothing to be worried about as long as he took sensible precautions.

Eventually Spitz reached the end of his list of chores and the assembly dispersed to their own offices, and Shaw stood and gazed out the window, planning.

*** *** ***

Fin stood at the bus stop in front of the library, wearing a Buck U ball cap and matching gray and green varsity jacket he'd borrowed from Kyle without asking. His trench was bundled up in his backpack, and when the next bus pulled up he would retreat into the library to remove the cap and switch coats. Thus re-attired, he would resume his stakeout.

He had been unable to stop wondering about the setup in that basement office. In particular, the fourth member. Having the same spaceship dream again last night cemented his resolve. Now he stood across the street watching the alley. Man number four had better "respect the organization," because otherwise how would Fin know it was him?

Booth had agreed to ride the 11:45, get off at the library with a spare leather bomber jacket, and run over to Magic Beans for a cup of Ironsides. Fin recalled being less than specific that the coffee was to be for him. He looked up at the clock on the front of the library.

10:32, well before reveille for Fin and too damn long to wait for his next cuppa. Deciding the guy was unlikely to show up in the next five minutes, Fin resolved to go to Magic Beans before his withdrawal symptoms started to register on seismograms in Buckminster's geology department.

He removed the ball cap in the coffee shop, releasing his dark unruly hair. The dampness gave it even more attitude than usual. Fin lit a cigarette, said a polite 'Go to Hell' to the six people who wrinkled their noses at him, and paid for his coffee. He didn't try to act unhurried returning to the bus stop. People are always dashing to the bus stop.

The gray morning steadily became a drizzly gray morning over the next hour. The library offered an overhang for shelter, but it was set back too far to give him the best vantage on the alley across the street. He spent some of his time keeping dry and most of it getting wet when Kyle's jacket displayed a startling lack of waterproofness.

Fin stifled a sneeze. Someone said, "Bless you," anyway, and Fin grunted and snorked the mucous back to create a suitable projectile, which he lobbed into the middle of the street. This performance earned him a few more inches of space along the curb. Watching the alley, his eyes started to droop but his mind focused on the mystery of the spaceship.

He rehearsed his inquiry: "Why the hell am I dreaming about your spaceship?" The question would sound pathetic but it would inspire no violence. He hoped it wouldn't, anyway.

At 11:36 on the library's clock, his target appeared. The fourth man was a woman. Fin gave no thought to the possibility she could be anyone else. Yellow umbrella up, ridiculous hat in place, she approached from the other end of the block, giving Fin just enough time to intercept her near her doorway.

Fin slouched across the street, allowing cars to miss him by inches but not provoking any horn blasts from the jaded townie drivers. Straightening up a bit, he turned into the alley.

His quarry was not alone. A short, bearded man with long, graying hair and a black peacoat shared the umbrella, in animated conversation with the blandly pretty Miss Greensweater. Fin held his course, feigning apathy while straining to pick up some of what was said as he passed.

"...at the University. The reverend is coming to us this time," Miss Greensweater said.

"Fortuitous."

"Yes. Perhaps we can track him to the devices."

Fin stepped around the corner at the far end of the alley and stopped. Although he'd been unable to ask his question, the mission wasn't a total loss. He made a mental list of things that could be called 'devices.' Would 'the reverend' know about the spaceship, too?

The idea that going to church might be the only way to find out quelled much of his curiosity.

Chapter Four

DATE

*Missionaries invade foreign countries and wage spiritual warfare
on the natives. Televangelists are simply domestic missionaries.
Brian Shaw's recent cryptic comments about soon reaching the
unreachable - presumably those who don't watch his show -
should frighten those of us who like to think for ourselves.*
    from *Useless Artifacts* opinion column by Brandy Moon,
CTP, 07-21-2000

"This won't hurt more than my tongue, will it?"

Rook shook her head. "Has the swelling gone down?"

Rainbow proudly stuck out her normal-sized tongue and wiggled it.
The silver ball in the center clacked against her teeth.

Rook nodded her appreciation and pulled on a pair of latex gloves.
Rainbow giggled and lifted her gauzy blouse, exposing her tummy. A
vine of tiny blue flowers encircled her navel and trailed down under her
waistband. Marcus's work. Rook could tell by the shading on the stems.
How well had Marcus gotten to know this particular blonde client?

Rainbow chattered on and Rook half-listened as she opened a sterile
needle pack.

"It's really weird, you know? Cos my dreams are usually really,
really colorful and beautiful and cosmic. So it's, like, really weird cos
this one's not. Except for the green UFO, it's all, like, gray. It must mean
something really heavy, doncha think?"

"I guess." Profound deja-vu washed over Rook. The glowing
spaceship hovered clearly in her mind for a moment, then vanished.
Her hands shook and she dropped the needle. Swearing, she threw it

away and got out a clean one. The spaceship was gone, but it left an afterimage throbbing behind her eyelids. The anxiety faded with the image and left Rook wondering if the deja-vu was for the spaceship or the anxiety attack. To hide her confusion, she began prepping Rainbow's navel, all the while supplying noncommittal responses at random intervals.

Her repeat customers all spouted about their dreams lately, and they were all about green spaceships. It wouldn't have bothered her as much if it weren't a reminder she wasn't dreaming anymore. She'd thought it was because of all the peyote Marcus fed her, but when his stash ran out there'd been no change. Even so, she blamed him. His craziness seemed to be on the upswing of late, his behavior more erratic. The relationship had soured and he made a convenient scapegoat.

***

Wanting to avoid Marcus out front, Rook sat at the counter in the piercing room and booted her Mac. She opened the folder for this issue's assignment, 'Behind the Scenes at Buckminster U — Where Does Your Money Go?' but couldn't even feign interest. *Conspiracy Theory* was supposed to be more cutting-edge. She closed the folder and sat with her eyes shut for several minutes, letting her mind wander. It wandered to a green spaceship. Rook's breath came faster as her muscles tensed and she broke out in a sweat. Biting back a moan, she willed something to happen, but nothing did. Rook's sense of foreboding grew. She opened her eyes and took several minutes to slow her breathing. Once calm, Rook opened a new word-processing file and named it Bullshit.

I DON'T BELIEVE IN ALIENS
I DON'T BELIEVE IN ALIEN ABDUCTIONS
I DON'T THINK I'VE BEEN ABDUCTED
I KNOW I HAVEN'T BEEN ABDUCTED
I HAVE NOT BEEN ABDUCTED
WHY DID I HAVE THE DREAM?
WHY IS EVERYONE I KNOW HAVING THE DREAM?

Then it came to her. The perfect story for *Conspiracy Theory Press*. The University was researching mind control. Or dream control. They obviously had a government grant and were doing something sinister to the citizens of Webster. Water? Air? Radio? Subliminals? Pattern of traffic lights? Something. Her editors at *CTP* would love it. The readers would eat it up and salivate for more. It couldn't be more perfect. All she needed was some proof, or something that could be called proof if you looked at it sideways in bad lighting.

She had two hours before she was supposed to meet Fin at Magic Beans. Plenty of time to scare up a source or two. Anonymous of course.

***   ***   ***

Marcus could tell Rook was up to something as soon as she came into the waiting area. Sparks leapt from her formidable blue eyes as she searched the counter for her keys. He remembered a time, not too long ago, when her eyes were the thing about her that excited him most. Now they were unsettling and he tried to avoid them when she was fired up like this. He acted like he wasn't watching as she packed her computer, micro-recorder, and wallet into her snakeskin backpack, pulled her leather jacket on over her crimson dress, and picked up her skateboard.

She would turn more than a few heads skating through town in fishnets and such a short skirt. Marcus enjoyed his intimate knowledge of what little remained hidden. Let the rest look. She would come home to him. Talisman was closed tomorrow and he would use the free time to expand her collection of markings. It had been too long, weeks, since she'd submitted her skin to him. She thought she had enough ink, but Marcus knew better.

"Raven," he said. She took a moment before lifting her gaze to him. It hit him like a storm wind, but he didn't flinch. "Come to me."

She took deliberate steps over to him. She didn't blink. Her strength excited Marcus — no one could keep her. But ritual must be observed.

There was a sewing needle affixed behind one of the end pieces of the counter. Marcus wound his left arm around Rook. While crushing her to him and kissing her hard on the mouth, he pressed his right middle finger against the needle's point, drawing blood. He ran the small droplet through her hair before releasing her. She was marked.

She still had her eyes open.

"Bye." She swept out the door before he could reply.

*** *** ***

Outside, Rook wiped Marcus's kiss off. He thought he could mark her so easily. She took the stairs two at a time up to street level. Heedless of the petroleum-rainbow puddles lingering from yesterday's rain, she skated down the alley. After dodging her way through the traffic on Linden Avenue she reached the tree-lined Buckminster University campus and quickened her pace. 1:30 classes were in session, so the sidewalks were nearly deserted and Rook made good time to the north end of campus.

At the library, she found an unoccupied carrel on the fifth floor. Her Doc Martens thunked on the dull green linoleum as she paced the stacks, pulling books at random. After making the carrel look lived-in, Rook put her feet up and waited for her informant.

***

"What do *you* want?"

The informant was hostile. Probably because of the incident at Donovan's party.

"Just some information. Maybe a quote." Rook smiled.

Lara glanced at her watch, looked around to see if they'd been observed. She sighed.

"I can give you ten minutes, I'm overdue for a break anyway." She parked her half-empty book cart behind the carrel and perched on the windowsill, her iridescent plum saddle shoes on the desktop. Rook started the micro-recorder and set it on the ledge where Lara's black and green fingernails drummed restlessly.

CTP wouldn't notice or care if she wrote her articles in her sleep, so long as the spelling came close, but she had a work ethic. Not a

Protestant work ethic, but it worked for her. And she wouldn't always work for them. When given the time to investigate, she would go through the motions. To keep in practice.

Rook began the ritual as she did every time. "You are an employee of the University, are you not?"

"You know damn well I am." Lara reached around and cracked the window open. She lit a cigarette and took a long drag. Exhaling, she ran her thumb over the chrome stud protruding below her bottom lip.

"And you are involved in many of the major research projects?"

Lara looked around at the books on her shelving cart and filling the library and snorted, "Yeah."

Rook tried to sound serious. "So you are, no doubt, aware of the University's involvement with dream control?"

Lara choked on her cigarette smoke trying to suppress a laugh, coughed, then said, "Who told you about that?"

"So you're aware of it." Rook sat back. "Are you involved?"

"Not personally." Lara watched Rook intently.

"But your co-workers are?" Rook prodded.

"Undoubtedly."

"What does the University hope to gain?"

"What does the University ever hope to gain?"

Rook thought for a moment before replying, "Money."

"Precisely." Lara looked at her watch and pushed up the sleeves of her baggy black sweater.

Rook took another minute to consider before asking her next question.

"How are they doing it?"

"The dream control? How do you think? There aren't many viable options." The informant clearly enjoyed putting the reporter on the spot.

"How do they hope to make money by having everyone dream about spaceships?" Rook wondered aloud.

"Green spaceships?" Lara was suddenly interested. She stubbed her cigarette on the windowsill before tossing it out.

"Yeah." Rook decided to act cagey to see what her faux informant might really be able to tell her.

"In the dreams, what does the spaceship do?" Lara tried to hide her nervousness.

"You tell me."

"Bitch. Tell me what you know about the dream!" She stood and stared down at Rook, trying for menace but managing only desperation.

"The University is using its own employees as guinea-pigs. Was this with or without your consent?"

"Rook! Tell me what this is about. I don't want to play your stupid game anymore. If this is some sort of weird payback for me hitting on you, you can go fuck yourself!"

Rook turned the tape recorder off. She felt rotten for pushing the act this far after it stopped being fun for her friend. "Shit, Lara. I didn't mean to piss you off. This was just another fishing expedition. I didn't expect to catch anything. You've had the dream too?"

"What do you mean 'too'? What's going on?" She lit another cigarette and started inhaling.

"I don't really know what's going on," Rook said, thinking how smoothly she screwed that up. "I'm supposed to be writing about what Buckminster does with tuition money and thought this would be an offbeat twist." Rook took a drag from Lara's cigarette. "Calm down, would you? You're starting to make me nervous."

"Have you had a dream about a glowing spaceship?"

"I had a recurring one, but not recently. A lot of people I talk to mention similar things. I figured it was because of the whole UFO culture. Now I don't know. I guess I'm just paranoid from working with all the nuts at *CTP*."

"Yeah? Well I'm completely freaked. This sucks." Lara tugged on her lip stud and paced.

Rook said, "Hey, look, we can pretend this interview never happened."

"Maybe you can."

Rook sighed and said, "I'm sorry." She ejected the tape and offered it to Lara.

Lara handed the unfinished cigarette to Rook in exchange for the tape and started down the aisle with her book cart. A few yards away she yelled back, "If this is some sick joke, I'll kill you."

"Oh great, a death threat. That helps with the paranoia," Rook muttered. After finishing the smoke and tossing it out the window, she booted her computer and began typing.

A source at Buck U who spoke on condition of anonymity confirmed...

One hour and two files later, Rook shut down her Mac, packed her bag, and found the nearest bathroom. She spent a minute applying more black eyeliner and mascara, ran a brush through her hair, and made sure she didn't have anything stuck in her teeth. She gave herself the once-over in the mirror. This red satin minidress with its embroidered dragon was perhaps a bit obviously flirtatious, but it looked damn good on her, which was why she'd chosen it. Time for her coffee date with her pushy piercing client while her boyfriend waited at home. With a smile Rook hurried out of the library and skated through the crowds as quickly as possible without running anybody over, arriving at Magic Beans five minutes early.

Fin was already there at a table in the back, near the abstract sculpture which pointed the way to the restrooms. He glanced at the wall clock and looked around furtively as she watched through the window. Rook smiled. Such a doof. Why had she made this date? She didn't know, but looking forward to it helped her through the week. That he'd shown up made her inordinately happy.

He wore jeans, clean ones, and an endearingly peculiar shirt. Short sleeved, shiny and made of an entirely unnatural fiber, it was covered with a confusion of stylized tigers in shades of green, purple and blue, and unbuttoned about halfway to expose a gray t-shirt. His shoes were matte black leather loafers with rounded, dull metal caps over the toes. He had dressed up.

A gray wool trench coat hung over the back of his chair. His hair looked recently brushed and was almost behaving itself. The thick, dark curls hung well past his chin and he didn't seem to mind when they fell in front of his face. Too bad. His features were fine, but sturdy. He had shaved, presumably on her account. His eyes were deep green and very expressive. They told her a lot the other day at Talisman. She liked his voice, too. Low, but not menacing the way Marcus's so often was.

Rook watched Fin fiddle with his brow piercing and his lighter. His hands were large. They worked well on a bass player. She wondered how calloused his fingertips were and how they would feel on her skin, laughing quietly at how she was getting ahead of herself, even as she regretted leaving her diaphragm at home.

The door beside her opened, its little bell jingling, letting out a customer and the heavenly aroma of roasting coffee beans. Fin looked up expectantly and his face brightened when he saw Rook. She caught the door before it closed and walked to the back where Fin stood to greet her with an awkward half-hug that made them both blush.

*** *** ***

The tattoo on Rook's collarbone was a four-inch long black feather so detailed Fin was tempted to reach across the table and claim it, then caress her pale skin with it. The ones on her wrists were matching chess rooks, solid black on her left, an outline on her right, and not so prone to inspiring lustful thoughts. A fourth image spanned her right arm from elbow to shoulder. Fin sensed a theme. This one was a black quill in a rook-shaped inkwell, stippled and crosshatched like an Edward Gorey illustration, utterly fascinating down to the ink drops splashed around its base.

Fin smiled as Rook reeled off an elaborate justification of *Blue Velvet* as her favorite movie. The smile broadened as he listened to her saying all the things he thought about his own personal favorite, *True Romance*. He basked in the freedom to be himself.

"The best thing is," Rook confided, "I can really be myself around you."

Fin shook his head, then quickly nodded instead when Rook's expression clouded. He downed his imaginary last gulp for the third time, to get his bearings. She'd been reading his mind for much of the past hour, apparently without knowing. What would it be like to play chess with her?

"Listen," Rook said, "if I have any more caffeine I'll start vibrating, and we both know how difficult it is to play chess under those conditions."

Fighting the urge to hold her hand, Fin led her the few blocks to his house. On their way to the third floor, Fin and Rook met Bishop. Of all his housemates, this was the one Fin trusted not to make a pass at Rook, so he introduced them. "This is Tom Bishop. He's in the room next to mine. Bish, this is Rook. We're gonna play some chess."

"Is that what the kids are calling it these days?" asked Bishop with a laugh. He bowed to Rook, kissed her hand and continued down the stairs.

Fin hurried Rook to his room before they could run into anyone else.

"Cool lava lamp," Rook said.

"Me and Vesuvius — we go back a long way." Fin cleared off the two cafe stools. "Why don't you set up the board while I get the beers."

"You're in the middle of a game."

"Bishop will remember where everybody was. Always does." Fin unlocked his nightstand mini-fridge. Rook, busy with the chessboard, wouldn't notice him hide a bottle behind the milk carton. "Last one. I guess we'll have to share," he said holding up a lager.

"You don't have cooties do you?" she asked.

"No, but I do have this." He held up a baggy of weed.

"Cool." Rook had the board set up and claimed the seat farthest from the door, Fin's favorite, but he decided not to kick her out of it.

Fin handed Rook the beer and began a search of the floor near his mattress. By the time he located the pocket bible under the ottoman, she had the beer uncapped and had made her opening move. One delicate eyebrow arched when she saw what he held.

"They're always handing these out on campus. Cheaper than rolling paper."

"I suspect they'd hope you soothed your soul some other way."

Fin tore a page from Genesis, the only part of the bible that he knew featured naked people, and moved a pawn out.

Rook took a swig of beer and contemplated the board while Fin rolled and lit the joint.

***

"Who taught you to play so well?"

Rook glowered at him before speaking, and with the voltage her gaze could generate it had the same effect as a raised club. Her eyes twinkled though, as she saw she had scared him. "I read the inside of the box. You know, under the lid. The rest I managed to figure out myself, despite being a girl and all."

Fin made his move sullenly. "I didn't mean it like that."

"I know. I take it as a compliment, really." She glanced at the board.

"Really," Fin said flatly.

"Guys usually try to take it easy on me and... well, I'm used to a wee bit of condescension."

Fin sat up straight. "Please don't tell me you think I'm going easy on you!"

"You'd like to kick my ass, I can tell. And you still might. But your surprised tone must have triggered my latent feminist streak." She was staring at him, but smiling.

"You don't go in for having a big strong hero around to protect you?" Fin relaxed back into a slouch.

"Oh please. I get enough of that shit from Marcus." Rook leaned forward to make her move while she spoke, "If you ever try to rescue me, I'll tear you a new one. Babe." She held Fin's gaze and he was helpless to fight it. "Check."

Fin yanked his eyes down to the board and saw she had pulled a knight out of nowhere. He sighed and gave a rueful half-grin as it dawned on him why her playing style was so exasperating. It was like playing against a mirror.

He had no choice but to move his king, and she would just check him again with the same knight. After that, hard to say. Fin brooded for a few moments, plotting unrelated counterstrikes.

"Do you mind me doing all the talking?" Rook asked.

Fin made the king move. "You're not. I mean, sorry I'm not saying much."

She checked him as expected, and he moved his king another space before she could say, "Check." To continue with the knight now she'd be sacrificing it.

"Well," she cooed, "what is it you might say, were I to encourage you?"

He reflected for a moment. "I guess first I'd say I admire the integrity of your monologue. I don't get tired of your voice, or weary of your wit."

"Your fault. You listen. You get sick of your own voice when you don't think anybody cares what you're saying."

"Mr Hero isn't attentive?" Fin made no effort to disguise the opportunistic nature of the question.

"He has his hands full with himself." Rook moved the pesky knight again, but this time in retreat. "Check."

Fin laughed, because he had no idea what she was talking about.

"It's her rook," droned Vesuvius, and Fin saw she'd suckered him into a reveal.

"You stay the hell out of this!" Rook growled and pointed at the lamp.

Vesuvius bubbled furiously for a moment and squeaked. The lava all settled to the bottom and quivered.

"How'd you do that?" Rook asked in a flustered voice. "Are you a ventriloquist?"

Fin laughed, a too loud thing that ended abruptly. He tried to collect himself. Mostly succeeded. He looked to the lamp for help, but

Vesuvius remained impenetrable. "You heard Vesuvius speak," he said with wonder.

"Well, yeah." Rook looked concerned, eyebrows drawn down. "Where'd the lava go? How are you making it do that?" She picked up the glass capsule and peered down into the base, causing Fin a moment of nigh-parental anxiety that she would break something. Not finding anything suspicious, she reassembled the lamp and looked back at Fin, accusing.

Fin stammered, "He doesn't like to be yelled at."

She eyed Fin shrewdly, the icy blue smoldering through her thick black lashes. "Sorry. I'm sure I didn't mean to offend your lamp."

He could tell she thought he was playing some sort of practical joke when in reality he was stunned. No one else had ever heard Vesuvius. No one but this remarkable woman. Fin was both afraid and aroused. He couldn't let her get away, had to make her see this connection they shared.

"Say something 'Suvius," Fin said. He pressed Rook's hand to his mouth so she would know he wasn't throwing his voice. She tensed, but allowed it. Her fingers were hot.

"I would prefer not to," Vesuvius said, quoting Fin's favorite Melville character.

Fin watched Rook's eyebrows rise and her eyes widen. She looked around the room, searching the corners for cameras or who knew what. Keeping her right hand clamped over Fin's mouth she gave the lamp the finger and said, "All right Bartleby, how many fingers am I holding up?"

"One," said Vesuvius, unfazed. "But my name is not Bartleby."

Rook looked back at Fin. "Is this a trick?"

Fin shook his head.

"Your lava lamp talks?"

Fin nodded. She studied his eyes for almost a minute before deciding she trusted him enough to remove her hand from his mouth.

"Can other people hear him?"

"They've never let on. I'm pretty damn sure they can't."

She shrugged. "I am aware talking light fixtures are not part of consensus reality, and you could easily have a little speaker hidden somewhere and a friend with a Mr Microphone, but I don't see how you could possibly be controlling the lava like that, so I'm inclined to accept this. For now. I reserve the right to decide you're full of shit later, or flip out."

"It remains an option."

"I'll keep it in mind. Did you freak the first time he talked to you?"

Fin felt sheepish. "No." He thought back. "I got Vesuvius when I was into my own little late-60s world. You know, Hendrix, the Doors, acid. I suppose I had been assuming Vesuvius was a residual pharmaceutical effect." The glow from the lamp became notably redder, but he said nothing. "I thought I was insane," Fin concluded.

"You are, I'm sure, but your offended friend here is something different." She reached for the sullenly undulating Vesuvius. "He's quite special."

Fin felt a surge of jealousy as Rook approached the lamp.

"If I rub him, will a genie come out?"

Vesuvius erupted in a series of embarrassed plumes, his glow modulating into its customary gold. Fin ground his teeth.

Rook smirked. "Okay, then," she purred, "you are still in check."

Fin rolled his eyes and hunkered down to study the board. Rook slunk over to his side. "Unless," she exhaled into his ear, "you want to distract me from the game for a while... think up some moves... since you can't cheat now..."

Fin looked at her sidelong while interposing his bishop, backed up with a knight, to get out of check. "I never take his advice when it comes to chess."

"Or anything else," Vesuvius deadpanned.

"Now, you can plot your next move," Fin said. He slid down off the tall chair and snaked his arms around her waist. She looked up at him with a sardonic expression and swayed a little, then extricated herself and twirled over to the stereo to peruse a heap of old CDs.

"Can we put this on?" Rook asked, handing him Talking Heads' *Remain in Light.*

"Sure." Fin inserted the disc, adjusting the volume to a modest level so they could converse over the lush jungle foliage of the opening track.

Rook rolled her eyes back in her head, her mouth partially open, head lolling from one shoulder to the other.

"Always nice to meet someone with a true appreciation for music," Fin quipped.

She smiled and made her eyes return. "Certain albums feel like they were found, not written. You know? They're too perfect." She turned back to the chess game, standing with her back to Fin and one knee on her chair. This pose tilted her hips quite far to starboard.

Fin nudged the volume up a notch.

Rook began to sway slightly. Fin resisted the impulse to reach for the volume control again and leaned on the edge of the table. "So anxious for endgame?"

After a few seconds of focusing on the game pieces, she made a move, and looked at Fin.

Her gaze caused a jump in his heart rate, but he couldn't read her. He glanced at the board, while Rook slid fluidly up onto her chair. Fin's attention moved to her crossed ankles and the most thoroughly broken-in pair of Doc Martens ever. Her shiny red skirt had ridden up on her thighs. An embroidered black dragon ran from the square neckline to the hem, which crept higher yet. Her collarbones were delicate, fragile-seeming. Fin wished to brush his fingers along them, kiss them, taste the feather tattoo. The pulse throbbed gently in her neck. Fin watched her tongue slip across her slightly parted lips. Finally he met her eyes again. She appraised him, seeing what his next move would be.

At each turn in the game, energy passed across the board. They baited each other, surrendered pieces to one another; feeling a tingle, a shiver, when the other would make the anticipated move.

They reached a point of diminished options. Many pieces had fallen, and neither player held a strong strategic position. They spent long stretches of time looking at each other's eyes. The CD's closing track cast deep, hypnotic shadows. At last Rook bit her lower lip and made a move.

Check, with the queen, but no backup. Fin could capture the piece with impunity. A sacrifice. Something told him to look deeper, the outcome of the game suddenly important again.

By moving the queen she left her rook unprotected. Of course, he was in check... Fin took the rook with his knight and watched Rook for a response. She voiced no objection.

They were locked on each other's eyes again.

The stereo advanced to the next disc. A bright and jaunty drum riff snapped the tension, and Rook let out a long-pent breath. Smiling slowly, she slid her queen onto the square with Fin's king and leaned across the table. He met her and they kissed.

Fin stood, still kissing Rook, and moved around the table. She was warm and pliant as he slipped his arms around her waist and lifted her. With her fingers twined into his hair, she pulled him ravenously into the kiss.

Rook landed in Fin's lap as they fell into the armchair. He kissed her neck, throat, smooth shoulders, collarbones. Rook arched her back and breathed in slow, shallow gasps. Her hands roamed along Fin's shoulders, arms and neck.

Fin came up for breath. Rook looked at him and smiled. She wiggled her hips and her skirt rode higher, displaying green panties under black fishnet stockings.

"Oops," she said, but made no move to cover them.

Fin leered.

Rook's left hand crept under Fin's shirt and slid across his belly, exploring, leaving a tingling trail across his skin. Eyes closed, he relaxed and enjoyed her touch.

After a short time the need to kiss her again overwhelmed Fin. He held her face in both hands and drew her to him. As they kissed, she straddled him, rocking her hips and running her fingers over his chest.

Finally she pulled back and smirked. She slipped his tiger pimp-shirt off and yanked his tee over his head leaving him naked from the waist up. She licked her lips, but didn't touch him. Fin relished the feel of her gaze as it swept over him.

He lifted her by the hips and stood, placing her before him. She looked up at him and locked eyes. The blue was so bright, like something from a drug trip. Fin moved stealthily to the right, stalking her. She turned her head to follow him. Pouncing from behind, he wrapped his arms around her and nuzzled her neck. Pressing against him, she sighed.

Fin ran his hands over the slippery fabric of her dress, cupping her breasts. His hands glided over the smooth, bare skin of her arms, over the quill tattoo, up to her shoulders. He moved her hair off her neck. She had another tattoo there. It excited Fin to think about what other surprises awaited him.

He got a better look at her neck and whistled low through his teeth. A tower, like from a tarot deck, starting at her hairline and extending the length of her neck. Black flames leapt from the arched window. It was both intimidating and arousing. Fin licked it.

Slowly Fin unzipped Rook's dress, his eyes devouring each inch of flesh he uncovered. His cock throbbed when he discovered another tattoo in the small of her back. He slid the straps off her shoulders and let her dress drop to the floor to get a better look. But she twirled and pressed against him, flesh on flesh. They kissed.

Fin unhooked Rook's bra. Stepping back and smiling devilishly, she shimmied out of it and dropped it with the dress. They embraced again, kissing each other's mouths, necks, and moving down. Gracelessly they tumbled onto the mattress on the floor. Rook took off her boots while Fin kicked off his steel-toed loafers. She pulled off her fishnets, then helped Fin with his pants while he took in her body art, all of which fit the theme he'd detected earlier. The girl was obsessed. A flock of tiny ravens encircled her right ankle. The top of each foot sported a large chess rook, exquisitely shaded, one light, one dark. Most impressive, though, was the masterpiece that started on her left hip and continued all the way up her side to her underarm. It depicted an entire parliament of rooks erupting from a dark stone castle tower, reeling up and away across her slim waist, soaring over her ribs, and continuing up, a few boldly swooping onto the voluptuous swell of her breast. While removing her panties, Fin discovered no unexpected piercings and one more tattoo. A small raven silhouette just above her pubic hair.

They both grew impatient with tender attentions at the same time.

"Do you have any fun condoms?" Rook asked.

"Men don't buy the fun kind."

Rook slithered to her belongings and dug into her backpack. "So who's supposed to buy the fun ones? I never do."

Later they lay exhausted on the bare mattress and compared tattoos in detail. Rook was the clear winner by every criterion Fin could think of, but she was nice about it. She complimented the linework on the Janus head in the center of his upper back, and was impressed by the precision of the four rows of Escher's tessellating horsemen encircling his left biceps. She liked the Hokusai-style willow on his chest, but claimed her favorite was his self-inflicted eclipse. For Fin, the drove of black birds on her side was incredibly erotic. He kissed each one as he counted them, and lost track somewhere around 75. He rolled her onto her stomach and finally got to see the spread-winged raven spanning the small of her back, every fiber of every feather as clear as the intelligent glint in the bird's eye. On her right shoulder blade was one final tower, easily eight inches tall, composed of dozens of interlocking black birds. A rook made of rooks.

Fin did have a couple of boring condoms strategically yet casually mixed in among the unwashed mugs, overflowing ashtray, and other lifestyle artifacts atop his mini-fridge, a fact he was glad of now.

***

"Will you pierce my nipple now?" Fin asked.

"Not right now. My stuff's at Talisman," Rook said as she dabbed black nail polish on his left baby toe. "Hold still or you'll make a mess."

"It tickles."

"You act like nobody's ever painted your toenails before."

"Nobody has."

She smirked. "Some rebel you turned out to be."

After his toenails dried, Fin pulled on his jeans and went downstairs to order a pizza and try to bum a few condoms.

Bishop wasn't home.

Booth said his girlfriend took care of that sort of thing.

No one would ever want to sleep with Quent, so he wasn't even worth asking.

Max claimed to be fresh out.

Which left Kyle.

So, Fin asked Quent and got the anticipated result.

Normally Fin would avoid asking a favor of Kyle, but the alternatives in this case were either no more sex with Rook tonight or going back upstairs, getting fully dressed and going to the store. He knocked on Kyle's door.

No answer, so Fin knocked again, louder. Still no answer. Even pounding brought no response.

"Shit."

Fin debated with himself for almost a minute before trying the knob. He rationalized the trespass by blaming Kyle for not locking his door, and also reminded himself Kyle had invaded his space at the party. And he really needed some condoms.

The door swung open under his push.

Fin stepped through the doorway. A quick glance around confirmed his suspicions. The room was, by Fin's standards, compulsively neat. Kyle apparently kept his clothes in the closet, because they weren't all over the floor. "Freak." The liquor cabinet was well stocked and unlocked. "Idiot." Fin liberated a bottle of romantic-looking red wine, then continued toward the neatly made futon. He thought of Rook in the room directly above this one and hurried past the sports trophies. Feeling eyes following him, he looked around. The blonde nymphette sprawled across the hood of the Ferrari on the wall looked back at him. "Typical."

Beside the futon sat an end table where Fin intended to start his condom quest. He opened the top drawer and rooted through the Altoids, loose change and weird remotes. After staring for a moment in puzzlement at the electronics bits filling the middle drawer, he moved on quickly to minimize the chances of an altercation with Kyle. Fin didn't think Rook would be too impressed if he ended up scuffling with a silver-spoon alterna-wannabe over condoms.

Pay dirt. In the bottom drawer, Kyle had an impressive collection of prophylactics. Fin gleefully pilfered a handful of the more interesting ones.

He returned to Rook triumphant, bearing pizza, wine and condoms.

"Kyle buys the fun ones," he explained. "Must be overcompensating. I took some regular ones and a couple others in case we feel adventurous."

"*I* sure do."

Chapter Five

DINER

Event Report W0011a:
The outpost was breached today (09-25-2000). An individual
calling himself a ventilation system repairman entered by a
previously unknown access point. This security deficiency has been
rectified and the individual has been identified. He is not a
ventilation system repairman. Response protocol two was
followed. There is therefore little danger that he saw the outpost
for what it is. Consensus among outpost staff is that he was
surprised to find the space occupied. We do not believe he was
seeking us, nor do we think he was attempting to learn about the
goings-on in the outpost. Since he could be expected to be curious
after this encounter, and he lied to us, we will monitor him in
accordance with Guidebook follow-up procedures, protocol two.

Midmorning at The Shamrock Diner, Fin poured maple syrup on
his second order of French toast. Rook, content with a single breakfast,
carried the conversation while Fin's mouth was full.

"Technically, I belong to a nature cult."

Fin's eyebrows lifted, causing a twinge in his piercing.

Rook explained, "They're called The Threshold. My mom was a
member for ages, so I'm in. Kinda like citizenship." This morning she'd
pulled a change of clothes out of her backpack, and the icy blue color of
her retro minidress accentuated her eyes to almost fever-dream status.

Fin gave her a thumbs up and a smirk as he swallowed. "Speaking of
cults, I saw something strange..." he looked at the ceiling while counting
back on his fingers, "three days ago." To rid his mouth of the syrup
residue, Fin reached for his coffee mug. Empty. Where was the waitress?

He turned and scanned the back of the restaurant.

"Good for you," Rook prompted.

Trying to reboard his train of thought, Fin turned back toward her as a large man took a stool at the counter. Not enough tattoos to be Marcus, but it reminded Fin of the risk they were taking.

"Rook. Is Marcus going to kill me?"

She looked puzzled. "I don't think so."

Good news, so why the plummeting sensation behind his solar plexus? He lit a cigarette. Even better than coffee for removing the taste of Vermont. "You're going back to him."

"I live with him." Taking the cigarette, she inhaled.

They contemplated each other in silence.

"I don't want you to think I'm straitlaced or domineering or anything, but we won't be able to have a relationship if you keep living with him."

She seemed surprised. "Is that what you want? A relationship?"

Seductively strong and novel feelings neutralized Fin's habitual detachment. The truth wouldn't get him in trouble this time, would it? He didn't even care. "Yes."

A warm, hesitant smile lit Rook's azure eyes and Fin felt its twin spreading across his own face. A girlfriend. This was good. Right?

Rook broke eye-contact and looked down at the greasy remains of her mushroom omelette. "There's still Marcus."

Fin exhaled.

"I can quit Talisman," she hastened. "I'll need to find something else to supplement my meager journalistic income, but my skills are marketable, right?"

"I still want you to pierce my nipple," Fin affirmed. "And you can poke other holes in me if it'll make you feel better."

"Thanks. But there are the sleeping arrangements to think of."

Several awkward moments passed, the two of them toying with their silverware.

"Well, just leave him," Fin said.

"Are you offering me a place to live?"

Fin didn't even need to think about that one. "Yeah. If we're loud enough, maybe Kyle will move out."

"Okay." She smiled.

He shoveled in the last of his French toast. A live-in girlfriend. His pulse raced as he rode the thin green line between giddiness and nausea. Bishop was right. He'd only just met her and already he felt different. Like he might not get the full customary use of his breakfast. He wiped his palms on his jeans.

Too much maple syrup, he diagnosed.

The waitress came over with a smirk and asked if they were still hungry. Fin, mouth stuffed full, picked up his mug and clunked it on the table several times. "I take it," the waitress ventured, "he wants more coffee. How 'bout you?" Rook nodded. The waitress departed.

Fin swallowed. "She's cute."

"She's gay. Hits on me sometimes."

Fin didn't have a reply for that. Should he be jealous?

"I agree, by the way," said Rook. "She's cute."

Well, that was uncalled for. "Do you mean exclusively gay? Or bisexual?" Fin asked without inflection, leaving his options open.

Rook laughed. "I don't know. Women hit on me all the time," she purred.

Fin didn't have a reply for that either, and knew he should. Something was definitely amiss.

"You think I'm bi now, don't you?" Rook asked.

Fin grinned. "Hadn't occurred to me 'til now, but…"

Coffee flowed into their mugs. Fin was still grinning. Time to be assertive. "So," he directed to the waitress, "my girlfriend here tells me you're gay." Girlfriend.

"And she's a lousy tipper who smokes too much. What about it?" She put their checks on the table and left.

Rook didn't look amused anymore.

"Did I just screw up my chances for a ménage à trois?" Fin ventured, hoping to milk a sort of class-clown vibe.

Now she seemed downright hostile and her eyes were starting to freeze him. Fin realized he'd gone too far. Rook was waiting for him to say something. Something not stupid or sexist. Something boyfriendy.

"Ah, sorry. That all sounded a lot funnier before I said any of it. Sleep deprivation."

"Are you apologizing, or making excuses?" she asked.

"Making excuses," he proclaimed with an impish grin, then knew he'd made another mistake. This was going to be the shortest relationship on record.

"It's not like we're talking marriage here," Rook muttered. "Relax."

"I'm sorry. I am." The thought of her going back to Marcus because of his own rampant, knee-jerk isolationist tendencies gutted him.

It must have shown on his face, because she looked ready to accept his apology. Her eyes were less flinty.

However, he did feel entitled to an honest answer from his new live-in girlfriend. "I'm just asking this for informational purposes, not being opportunistic. Are you? Bi?"

"NO!" Rook shouted. The whole place looked their way. Rook grimaced and waited for the crowd to lose interest before continuing. "I'm not gay, Fin."

"Well, okay. But you're loud."

Rook narrowed her eyes and sat, rigid. "Sorry," she intoned icily, "sleep deprivation."

"Actually," Fin said, happy to change the topic, "I once went three days without REM sleep. I got really strange, or so I'm told."

He thought Rook was on the verge of forgiving him. She wore a small, bemused smile and relaxed her ramrod posture. "How exactly did you do that, and why?"

"With help, and for money. Psych department experiment. They have a drug that blocks REM sleep," Fin explained, glad she was allowing the conversational diversion.

"They do? Of course!"

Safe topic! "For a week or so after comedown, I would sometimes enter a REM cycle when I was awake, sort of. Major, astounding hallucinations."

"What lab was this in?" She began to clear a space on the table in front of herself, shoving her plate aside.

"Fuller. What's the weirdest dream you've had lately?"

"I don't remember my dreams."

Fin considered that. "Mine have gotten bizarre. There's this one I've had a few times now, very odd. I don't even know if I'm in it, really, and it's very drab. But there's this thing..." Fin trailed off because Rook was bending her spoon. She looked panicky.

"Go on," she said. She blinked brightly.

"Well," Fin hesitated. "It's a thing I need, but I lose it. Like in sand or something. The only other part I remember is a big, bioluminescent green spaceship."

Fin thought the spoon would end up in a knot. "Are you all right?" He reached across the table and gently removed the utensil, enfolding her hands in his.

"You aren't the only one having that dream. We aren't the only ones."

Fin started to feel some of the panic he'd seen on her face. Quite unlike his rush of syrup-and-commitment anxiety, this felt metallic and unnatural. Easier to fight. Whatever was going on, they were in it together, and she needed his help.

He looked her in the eyes. "Tell me. Explain it. What's going on?"

"It has to be the University..." she said vaguely, looking at a micro-recorder she'd pulled from her pack and popping it open. It was empty.

"C'mon, from the top. Explain it."

She took a weary breath. "I couldn't tell you how long it's been since I had a dream I can remember, but that's the last one I had. The one you described. I had it a bunch of times, then nothing."

"Since the first time, I don't remember any different ones either. But it's just this week." And there was the whole secret office thing. "You know Dogstar, right?"

She nodded absently and said, "It gets better. People love to chit-chat while I'm puncturing them, and they all keep droning on about the same fucking dream."

It was so far removed from reality, Fin loved it. One of the sweaterguys in the office must also be having the dream. "This is outstandingly strange."

"Well no shit," she said. "I'm working up a piece on it for *CTP* right now. Pinning it on Buckminster. With government money funding it of course. Kind of combining therapy with journalism."

"Sounds like Pulitzer material."

"It's utter crap. Or, it was. Now, with your direct experiences added to my irresponsible speculation it's better than *CTP* deserves." She still had a slightly unhinged look in her eye. "The photos and secret documents will put it into Pulitzer territory."

"You have this evidence?" Fin asked in surprise.

"We will."

"We?" Fin's lust for the paranormal was suddenly sated. "When exactly did this become 'our' exposé?"

"When I found out about your involvement, Muffin."

Fin wrinkled his nose.

Rook pulled out a silver flask, took a swig and handed it to Fin. He raised it in mock toast, sipped, and handed it back. Southern Comfort. Not his drink of choice, too sweet. If Rook liked it, though, he supposed he'd get used to it. After pouring the remainder into their mugs, she put the empty flask away. Fin took a slow sip of coffee. "What makes you suspect the University?"

"What makes you not? They have a budget literally the size of Peru's, but they don't publish it. What are they hiding?"

Fin was puzzled. "I heard they put the budget on the Internet now."

"It's 400 pages without the supplements! But it tells you nothing. There are no specifics. There aren't even page numbers. They put this enormous beast of a document on their web site, but it's just lip service.

They do this so they can say it's an open budget, but it's not. If you call them and ask them how much it costs to plant flowers outside the student union, or how much the football coach makes, even they can't tell you! They say that's not the purpose of a budget document!"

Her passion for the subject and her knowledge of the details astonished Fin. He paid little attention to the news, and never got riled up by it. He'd always fancied himself cynical and jaded, but began to wonder if he wasn't just apathetic. Rook's enthusiasm was infectious and Fin suddenly needed to know how much it cost to plant those damn flowers every year.

"Okay. Certainly, Buckminster's fun to slag. And they have it coming..." he paused to sip his coffee, leaving an opening for her to continue.

"But..."

Shit! She thought he had opinions, or views, or something. Something more substantial than attitude. If he disappointed her now, they'd be back to glaring.

"But why is the University doing this?"

"Because they can," she said.

"You can do better than that."

She looked peeved. "They obviously have some huge government grant."

"Why's the government want everyone dreaming about spaceships?"

"They probably want to use it for propaganda. Here or overseas. It's the first step toward mind control."

Fin sat back and regarded her. "I noticed you have *1984* in your pack. You don't suppose you've got Big Brother on the brain do you?"

"Like Cobain said, 'Just because you're paranoid don't mean they're not after you.'"

"I can't tell whether you believe all the stuff you're saying."

"Neither can I. I get this way when I'm working on a story. I still half believe the government is using radioactive cobalt in blue M&Ms to track people through their dental fillings."

"Um... I must have missed that issue."

"The world's a scary place," she concluded.

"You ever think it might be aliens invading our dreams? In their spaceship?"

She looked at him like he'd grown an extra head. "What on Earth for?"

"You think it's more likely Buckminster's got a space fleet?"

She thought for a moment before replying. "What I think is, the University is a lot more accessible to us." She pulled her laptop out of her pack and booted it up. "I want to make a few notes here, then we'll get going."

"Going where?"

"Campus." She typed as she talked. "I have a contact in Fuller lab. A technician. I'm nice to him when I need a quote from a scientist."

"You have contacts?"

"I have sources everywhere." More typing. "I take my work seriously."

Something she said gave Fin pause. "Oh shit! I was supposed to work last night!"

"You have a job?" She sounded more surprised than he would have liked.

"Yeah. I do graphics." He tried not to sound too apologetic about his employer. "For *Sycamore*."

"Graphics. Cool. Are you gonna get fired?"

"Nah. I'll do some work at home today and upload it."

She typed for a while. "I didn't notice a computer."

"I keep it in the closet. That way I don't spill beer on it."

She smiled. A few minutes later she shut down the computer and handed it to Fin. "I want you to wait for me in the library. You can write a firsthand account of your experience in the drug trials. I'll go talk to Steve."

"I'll go with you."

"No offense, Muffin, but it'll be kinda hard to flirt with you along."

Desperate to keep her, Fin blurted, "The other day, I was trying to avoid a coworker and I ended up in this weird basement office below Dogstar."

She blinked at him.

"Well, they had a model of the spaceship. From the dream."

"What?"

"And this place is almost impossible to get to. I found a way in from Olaf's, entirely by accident. Well, I was looking around in their basement..."

"Fin."

"Huh?"

"The spaceship?"

"Right! They had it hanging over the one guy's desk. I thought they were hapless telemarketing geeks until I saw it. Cue Rod Serling. And they had a map. With pins in it. Some kind of color-coded geographic voodoo..."

Rook glanced at her wrist, where there was no watch. Fin paused. She said, "I really need you to write this down for me."

"I think you'd get a kick out of these guys. I mean, you should see the way they dress—"

"Fin," she interrupted. "I'm on a deadline. If there's time, maybe you can show me. After I talk to Steve."

Fin gave in. They'd had enough tension this morning. He rolled his eyes and sighed. "Must sleep."

"As soon as you're done typing."

"Just no more pet names, okay? I'm not Muffin."

Rook winked at him.

They gulped the remains of their coffee and paid at the front. Fin was exhausted. Why was the cute waitress with the crew-cut shooting him dirty looks? He'd left a tip.

Rook slung her backpack over her left shoulder and picked up her skateboard by the trucks. Hand in hand they walked outside.

Traffic looked heavy on Linden Avenue, the one-way main drag. Getting across would take a minute or so. They stood on the curb, waiting for a chance to jaywalk.

There came an unexpected lull. Fin glanced to his right and saw a forest green mini-van double-parked in front of the bakery, its driver's side sliding door open. Quicker to take advantage of the break, Rook hurried between two parked cars. As Fin stepped out to catch up, the van leapt forward with a squeal of rubber. A dark-haired man in a green cardigan reached out and grabbed Rook. Her board skittered across the pavement as she yelled, "HEY!" and was hauled inside. The door slammed as the van sped off.

Too late, the adrenaline reached Fin's muscles. He lurched into the street. The van turned left on Beech Street and was gone.

She was gone.

"Hey shithead! Get the hell outta the road!"

Fin looked around dumbly, then scooped up Rook's pack from where it landed. He retrieved her skateboard from under a car.

Hunched over on the sidewalk, he stared at her belongings for several minutes, numb, playing the scene over in his head.

Green sweater. The guy who'd grabbed her wore an ugly green sweater.

Chapter Six

CINEMOPOLIS

Citation - Drunk & Disorderly
Dec. 19, 1999, 4:20 A.M.
Fin Tanner
Happily provided urine "sample," some of which did go in the cup. Defied me to figure out what all is in it. Lab gave us four unknowns, nothing matching a controlled substance. Had to release him. Ninth time this year. Merry fuckin' Christmas.
from the notebook of Webster Police Officer Larry Campbell

Fin looked like hell when he arrived at Cinemopolis, carrying a skateboard and backpack Bishop recognized as Rook's. He also had a bag from the liquor store which he opened immediately. Bishop was the sole projectionist at the old two-screen theatre, so they were alone in the booth. Good thing, since Fin had already puked in the garbage can and now slumped against the projection booth's steel lining, swigging 'Comfort but not feeling any.

Bishop could tell this was not the usual bullshit and monitored his friend while threading the film for the left house. The previews were running on the right side, so shortly both shows would be in progress and there would be no real demands on Bishop for almost two hours. So long as Fin wasn't sliding too steeply toward coma, they could talk then.

Fin opened the backpack and started to cry before he even reached inside. He pulled out a small mass of shiny red fabric and buried his sobs in it.

Bishop kept about his job until the projector was ready, then sat beside Fin and gently took the party dress away so they could talk.

"Should there be police involved with this?" Bishop knew Fin didn't

want to think about that, and could see the panic flare up in his friend's
eyes. He spoke quickly to head off the torrent of objectionable words.
"Is that what normal people would do?"

Fin broke down again and could only nod. Bishop sighed. Fin had a
reputation with the police, had been taken into custody several times.
Probably more traumatic for the officers than for Fin. Bishop took a sip
of the liquor himself and said, "Tell me everything."

"They yanked her off the street, right in front of me. Dragged her
into the van and bugged out. I don't know what they want."

"How could you?"

Fin blinked at him. "There was this place," he started, but it was too
much. "I think it's me they want."

"Back up. Where was this place? Who are they?"

Fin told him about the hidden stairway and the office. Talking his
way out. Rook. Breakfast at The Shamrock. Recognizing the man in the
van.

Bishop stayed silent for the entire story. He said a case could be
made it was Fin they wanted, except for the simple fact it was Rook
they'd taken. Not knowing what they wanted with her made any further
guesswork problematic.

Fin didn't agree. "They either want something from me in exchange
for Rook, or it really is Rook they want. In either case, she's what they
have. If they want her, she needs help. If this is about me, they think
they know what I'll do. They don't think I'll try anything stupid or
heroic."

"I gather," said Bishop, "they're wrong."

Fin smirked, then grew solemn.

Bishop pursued. "What do they think you'll do? What will they
expect?"

Fin had to reflect a moment. "I'll avoid the police. They know that.
Wait for demands?"

"Did you give somebody somewhere the impression you own sports
teams and oil fields?"

"No," Fin said defensively.

"Then these people are not in the kidnapping business. They're blackmailers."

"Either way, they want something. Don't they?"

Bishop waited a three-count before continuing. "You were the audience for their little show, grabbing your girlfriend. It could be a threat. They might expect you to stop doing something, and if you don't stop they'll think you're calling their bluff."

Fin was destroyed. "I have no fucking idea what you're talking about," he wailed. "I don't do anything! How can I stop?"

Bishop had been less than tactful there, he realized.

Fin stood and ranted. "What if somebody else is doing something they don't like? How the fuck should I know?" Bishop reached up and dragged him down by his waistband.

"Please don't get me fired today. I don't want to have any conflicts over helping you."

"Sorry."

"S'alright. We still don't know what this has to do with you."

Fin looked at the floor.

"Do we?" Bishop prompted.

"It doesn't make much sense."

"I'll try to keep an open mind."

Fin opened his mouth, then grimaced. He shook violently with suppressed sobs.

"I want to help. You have to tell me."

"My fault!" Fin croaked.

"We haven't established anything of the sort."

"But I told her. I told her I saw it. She told me about the dreams, and I told her about the place, the men..."

Bishop waited a full minute, but Fin didn't say anything further. Standing, Bishop crossed to the projector for the left house, and said, "You're right, it doesn't make much sense."

Fin looked hopelessly at him.

Bishop started the projector. "So, you obviously need help. I'm in."
He walked back to Fin and sat. "First, we'll need to make a plan."

As he spoke, he watched the wheels spinning to a blur in Fin's mind.
Fin said, "I know where there's a gun."

*** *** ***

From the business card Rook gave him, Fin knew Talisman was
closed Thursdays. He had her keys, so there wasn't a large amount of
planning involved in the mission. Bishop took a sentry station at the top
of the steps while Fin unlocked the door. He opened it and slipped
inside saying, "Be right back."

The place was even darker than it had been during business hours.

Fin leaned over the counter and reached underneath for the
shotgun. It was heavier than expected, and he was afraid he might drop
it.

He did, because Marcus landed on his back. The gun clattered to the
floor behind the counter as Fin and Marcus collapsed in front of it. The
attack startled Fin far more than it hurt.

"Shit! Take a day off!" he grunted, grinding his middle knuckle into
Marcus's sternum and shoving — the only fighting maneuver he knew.

It dislodged Marcus enough for Fin to throw a few kicks and start
getting up. Marcus retreated out of reach, got his balance in a squat, and
landed a jab. Fin managed to kind of roll with it, since he'd already
begun a sloppy shoulder roll to his left. The added momentum sent him
completely over and onto all fours. Marcus stood. Fin charged ahead
without bothering to rise.

He caught the larger man around his knees, toppling him into the
ponderous door. Marcus landed a clubbing blow with both hands and
continued to fall, as the door drifted shut. Fin scrambled to get into a
more advantageous position, clambering up his opponent's body and
trying to pummel it at the same time.

A forceful knee to the ribs stunned Fin, followed by a driving blow
to the nose. His head rocked back, and an elaborate bouquet of agony
unfolded through his face.

Marcus caught Fin by his hair and left arm and dashed his head against the front of the counter, leaving him to fall to the floor. Fin heard rather than felt his jaw striking the cement. A spray of red stippled the baseboards in front of his face as Marcus kicked him in the stomach.

Fin was quivering and barely conscious with pain, but could tell another boot was coming. He convulsed his body where he lay, swinging his legs toward Marcus as he wound up for the kick. Marcus fell again, swearing. He attacked Fin with both fists, cursing and hammering.

The door swung open. Marcus sprang up to go over the counter for the gun, but Fin tangled him up and he fell.

Bishop loomed like a bear. He nearly stepped on Fin's head as he lunged into Marcus with a right to the body.

Fin dragged himself around the counter to where the shotgun lay. He heard dull thuds, labored breathing, and occasional grunts. Marcus's boots scuffled, Bishop's squeaked. As Fin sat up holding the gun all the noise stopped.

He sat trembling in the dark for several seconds.

"Let's get moving," Bishop said at last.

Keeping to the alleys, they quickly covered the three blocks to the mystery office.

Fin leaned against the cyclone fence and tried to push all thought of his spectacular near-failure at Talisman from his mind. He leveled the barrel of the shotgun and waited for Bishop to kick in the door.

His nose had stopped bleeding, but Fin couldn't breathe through it anyway. Breathing itself hurt like hell and he assumed he'd cracked some ribs. Or, rather, Marcus did the cracking, but they were definitely Fin's ribs.

Blood from a gash near his hairline trickled into his right eye as Bishop landed his kick and the door flew inward with a bang, almost closing again on the rebound. Ignoring the impulse to wipe away the blood, Fin lurched into the opening and swept the room with the muzzle of the gun and his good eye.

Empty.

The momentary relief Fin felt gave way to helplessness and fury. He stomped into the room, roaring in frustration and overturning the nearest desk, kicking it repeatedly.

*** *** ***

Bishop followed Fin inside and closed the crumpled metal door behind him as best he could. It shrieked in protest and didn't latch properly. It was imperative to calm Fin down. Bishop didn't want a passerby or someone upstairs to be drawn by the racket.

"Fin."

It took several tries, but Fin finally ceased his attack on the desk and looked over. In his rage, the wound on his forehead started bleeding again, raining drops of blood on the dark gray carpet.

"Let's see if they left anything behind. Then we can get you to a doctor. You look like shit." Bishop knew Fin would object to medical intervention, seeing it as a needless delay as well as a sign of weakness. He wouldn't have brought it up at all, except he was certain Fin needed it.

"No doctors!"

"I think you have a concussion," Bishop said. *And a broken nose, and a cut that needs stitches.*

"Fuck it. It doesn't matter. Not if I can't find her." Fin's naturally low voice came out rumbling and choked. He coughed, spat some blood on the carpet and wiped his eye on the sleeve of his trench coat, wincing. After setting the shotgun down on one of the other desks, he started yanking open drawers. Bishop sighed and began to help. The quicker they got out of there, the better. Bishop was prepared to use his knowledge of pressure points to get Fin to the hospital if necessary, but the threat alone should be adequate persuasion.

The room was cleaned out. The filing cabinets were empty, even the drawers gone. The desk chairs were missing, the desks bare. Nothing on the walls except four matching coat hooks.

Bishop pulled the drawers from the desks and checked the bottoms. Fin climbed up on a desk and moved aside a couple of ceiling tiles, tried to hoist himself up. The framework buckled and he had to settle for poking his head in and looking around. They came up empty except for a roll of heavy-duty aluminum foil Bishop found in the bottom drawer of the desk Fin attacked.

Bishop could tell Fin was about to lose his temper again and tried to think of something to say that would calm him, but it was pointless.

"Trash the place." He picked up the gun and stepped back. "Maybe you'll feel better."

Fin punched the wall, discovering he'd injured at least one finger in the fight. Howling, he kicked instead until his boot went through the plaster. He knocked over two of the filing cabinets and started stomping on them, all the while cursing gutturally.

Bishop watched for signs of fatigue. He planned to stop Fin before he needed to be carried home.

In the four years they'd been housemates, Fin had never reacted this strongly, even to Kyle. Bishop was ill-prepared to handle this situation with his usual grace and it bothered him. He would need to find a way to make it up to Fin.

Then he did.

Bishop crossed the wreckage-strewn office to the back wall. In the spot once occupied by the pair of filing cabinets, he knelt and picked up a CD-ROM that lay flush against the off-white molding behind the left cabinet.

Fin stopped rampaging when he noticed what Bishop held.

Bishop turned the CD over, but there was nothing written on either side. He handed it to Fin.

Fin grabbed it and checked for a label himself, but didn't find one either.

"Well, it's not much to look at, but there might be something interesting on it," Bishop suggested.

"I'm not sure it was theirs," Fin said. "They didn't have any computers. Now that I think about it, that's really strange. They were doing some kind of telemarketing thing. I don't know. They were all wearing headset phones anyway. But there was no computer."

"Maybe one of them had a laptop?" Bishop asked.

Fin brightened a bit, his scowl now less likely to peel paint. "Yeah. That could be it."

Together they moved the last filing cabinet away from the wall and found three green pushpins and a single paper clip.

The cyclone fencing outside rattled. Fin shoved the CD into his inside jacket pocket and reached for the shotgun. Bishop saw Fin's green eyes darken and the little hope he'd had fade as if someone flipped a switch.

"We're too late," a man's voice said through the mangled front door, followed by the sound of automatic weapons being readied, a sound Bishop knew well from his six years as projectionist at Cinemopolis. Fin, perhaps, didn't watch enough movies, because he didn't register the sound as a threat.

Bishop kept the gun and grabbed Fin. They ducked into the stairwell and Bishop closed that door as the outer door banged open for the second time in fifteen minutes.

*** *** ***

During the commotion that followed, Fin stood with Bishop in the near complete darkness and listened. Fin had difficulty breathing quietly, but the heavy door effectively muffled his wet noises. He longed for a cigarette, but didn't think Bishop would approve if he lit up under these circumstances. His head throbbed.

When Fin caught himself mentally complaining about his own petty physical discomforts, he felt like a traitor. He had forgotten about Rook. No one else would try to rescue her, because no one else knew she was gone. If he died now, he would have let her down in the most complete way possible. If there was an afterlife and they met in it, she wouldn't speak to him. He couldn't risk that. He had to act.

He reached for the gun, but Bishop shifted the weapon to the far side of his imposing frame and whispered into Fin's ear.

"You'll get us both killed. You'll help her more if you just listen."

Fin didn't want to just listen, but didn't want to be responsible for Bishop's death either. His karma would really suck then. So he gritted his teeth in the blackness and listened to the conversation of the interlopers, muted and distorted by the metal door.

"Tango-November-Hotel."

"No fuckin' shit."

"Cut the chatter. Of course 'They Not Here.' We didn't come for them."

"This can't be their HQ. Too small."

"I said cut it!"

A moment of queasy quiet.

"You morons all forget how to do your jobs?" drawled a fourth voice.

Fin heard a brief flurry of footsteps, and clattering furniture.

"Blood."

"Looks fresh."

Moments later the doorknob rattled beside Fin. He and Bishop placed their feet against the wall and braced their backs against the door, which flexed ominously.

"Doesn't matter what's in there," announced the insufferable leader. "It won't be if they come back."

A brief quiet, then sloshing and splashing, the odd ping.

"Get the lights on your way out."

"No problem."

Fwoomp.

Bishop and Fin were calm for a few seconds before panic set in. Fin grabbed blindly for the doorknob. Bishop stopped him.

"The whole room's on fire, Fin! You heard how much juice they splashed around. We can't go out that way. They may even have posted a guard or a lookout."

Fin pressed his forehead against the door and felt it growing hot.

"Sorry, dude," he mumbled, "I didn't mean to get you killed."

"We're not dead yet." Bishop sounded unconvinced.

The door was becoming unbearably hot. If only this damn door had been locked the first time.

His head jerked up.

"The window."

Fin scrambled up the bottom steps and ran his hands along the rough concrete wall above his head, heedless of his injuries.

Seconds later his fingers found the spot where the window should have been.

"Shit! They would have to be efficient."

Bishop stood beside Fin and followed his arms to the window frame which was expertly boarded over. He pulled the Zippo out of Fin's coat pocket and scraped the light to life.

Together they examined the heavy plywood and the masonry screws holding it in place. Fin tried to jiggle it.

"You didn't leave the house today without your utility belt, did you?" he asked.

Bishop searched his pockets, but came up empty.

Fin looked through his own pockets, but didn't even have an obscene postcard to rely on this time.

In desperation he scooped the shotgun off its bed of dog-ends and aimed the barrel up at the window. Bishop looked skeptical, but, failing to think of anything better to try, turned his back and clapped his hands over his ears.

*** *** ***

The blast was deafening. Bishop turned to find Fin looking dazed. The smell of gunpowder started creeping into Bishop's accelerant-clogged nose. His eyes watered from the smoke seeping under the door in acrid tendrils.

The blast blew a hole in the board near the lower-right corner and broke the glass on the other side. Bishop yanked the loose bits free and tried to pry the board off, without luck.

It was getting hard to breathe.

Fin motioned Bishop back and blasted the board again, this time in the center. The blaze in the office behind them roared loud enough for Bishop to hear, even with his overloaded eardrums.

Both Bishop and Fin started frantically pulling on the remains of the board. Somewhere above and behind them an alarm started to scream.

Using the gun as a bludgeon and a pry, they cleared the rest of the obstruction and shattered glass.

"Okay. GO!" Fin shouted.

"I'll follow you!"

"NO! I'll need to push you. GO!"

Bishop hefted himself into the opening and promptly got stuck.

Fin supported Bishop's legs as he wiggled into a better position and slipped his shoulders through one at a time. Fin shoved hard and Bishop landed gracelessly on boxes and broken glass. A loud hissing coming from the ceiling drew his attention. Fin's shots had done collateral damage.

Bishop turned to help Fin. As he grasped Fin's hand, the door at the top of the stairs opened and the lights flicked on. A nervous voice cut through the hiss and pop.

"It's probably something at Dogstar. It's their alarm."

Fin's head appeared in the opening as the employee started down the stairs. Three steps later, he turned and ran back up shouting, "SHIT! Get OUT! I Smell GAS!" The door slammed and Bishop heard pounding footsteps overhead as Fin fell through the window into his arms.

Bishop gestured at the hole in the ceiling and ran for the steps.

Upstairs, music blared but there was no one to be seen.

Bishop couldn't run full-out because of all the displays he had to knock out of the way. Fin stuffed a handful of art supplies in his pocket as he ran.

"This is no time for looting," Bishop hollered.

Fin looked wounded. "I'm not looting, I'm saving them!"

They burst through the door onto the sidewalk and kept running.

Peripherally, Bishop was aware of a crowd forming. People from the *Sycamore* building milled around.

Fin and Bishop made it across the street before the explosion threw them to the ground. As they picked themselves up, they heard the first sirens.

Fin insisted on climbing to the top of the nearby parking garage to survey the damage. Dogstar blazed. *Sycamore* was half-collapsed and aflame. Olaf's was gone.

"So, should I have waited 'til now to do my looting?" Fin asked ruefully.

Chapter Seven

HOSPITAL

My unit found the office already empty, but there was some evidence left behind: blood on the carpet, damaged entryway. My assessment is that another interested party beat us to them, and now represents a threat. On another point, I want to state on record that the quantity of accelerants used was within guidelines.
from Samaritan Security Agency internal briefing #KT1515

Rook's brain was fuzzy. A metallic, sickly-sweet taste filled her mouth and her feet hurt. Wherever she'd been, it couldn't have been much fun. She felt queasy and was walking slowly down a street she only vaguely recognized. Blinking didn't help her dry, itchy eyes.

Shaking her head to clear it brought an extended bout of nausea and a throbbing in her sinuses, so Rook stopped and leaned on the nearest object for support. The rickety handrail shifted and she landed on her ass on the bottom step. Rook rested, head on knees, eyes closed. When the nausea subsided, she looked up and discovered she was sitting on the front steps of Fin's house, blocks and blocks from the apartment she shared with Marcus.

She made her way up to the top floor. Damn, there were a lot of stairs.

By the time she made it down the long hall to Fin's door, her head cleared somewhat and she could stand unsupported without wobbling. Knocking brought no answer.

"Fin?" she called, her voice hollow and quavery. She cleared her throat and tried again. "Fin? It's me. Rook."

No response.

Even as she tried the doorknob she remembered he kept his room locked. If she was going to live here, too, she'd need to get her own key. She could recall her backpack falling on the street when she was grabbed, and started to check her pockets for something to pick the lock with. But she couldn't find her pockets.

Her leather jacket was inside out. She started to take it off and noticed her blue dress was also inside out, all the seams on display. Confusion turning to fear, she looked down her dress. Bra too.

Head spinning and legs rubbery, Rook darted back down the hall to the bathroom and locked herself in. With violently shaking hands she pulled off the jacket and dress and threw them across the room, where they lay in a heap beside the overflowing trash can. She could not steady her hands to unhook the inside-out bra and ended up pulling it off over her head with a shout of triumph and a few strands of hair. As she flung it across the room, it caught the light and sparkled. Rook studied it from where she stood. The cups were lined with foil.

Now desperate to know what else happened to her, Rook untied her boots and discovered they were on the wrong feet. That's why her feet hurt. She kicked the boots off and yanked her inside-out black stockings down, snagging them. As they joined the growing pile near the trash she got her first good news and started calming down. Her panties were right-side out and frontwards. As she'd left them. Everything felt right down there and she relaxed a little, concentrating on breathing so she wouldn't faint.

Rook shut the toilet lid and collapsed onto it, sobbing.

*** *** ***

Fin stood with Bishop atop the parking garage and watched the unfolding chaos below until fire engines invaded their vantage. By the time they reached the elevator, Bishop was already talking about the emergency room. They argued as they rode to the ground floor in the urine-scented glass box. Fin doubted he had health insurance having just blown up his employer. He wanted to go home and see what was on the disc. Bishop insisted stitches and X-rays were more pressing. Fin remembered Rook's computer and they reached a compromise. They would retrieve the laptop from Cinemopolis, Bishop would drive Fin to the hospital, and Fin would hope Rook's Mac could read the disc.

At the hospital they encountered a huge crowd. Due to the fire and explosion, they had a long wait ahead of them.

The waiting room was sprinkled with photographers, reporters and a smarmy individual Bishop recognized from one of the local news shows. Fin saw a few people from *Sycamore*'s front office. Bishop and Fin sat in a corner and put on their best surly looks so the media would leave them alone.

Fin studied Rook's laptop setup while turning the unlabeled disc over and over in his hands.

"What are you waiting for?" Bishop asked.

"What if there's nothing on it." Again not knowing anything felt better than being sure of something bad.

Bishop took the CD and popped it into the drive slot. Fin held his breath. The Mac hummed and an icon appeared on the screen.

Fin let out a long sigh and double-clicked. A file called 'recruitment' caught his eye and he opened it. Bishop read over his shoulder.

```
            TEF Manifesto
     All religious systems include a creation
story. These systems invariably also
include a prophecy of the world's end, when
some ultimate battle will sort all the
inhabitants according to their deserved
rewards. This is an explicit encoding of
causal relationships onto the moral realm.
All of these stories are thusly grounded in
the "common sense" paradigm of beginning,
middle, and end.
     The generally accepted scientific theory
explaining the universe also assumes this
linear structure. Creation at the Big Bang
and inevitable entropic attenuation. The
```

universe is just the stuff in the middle.
Even with the advent of ideas like special
relativity and route-dependent time, this
theory keeps the universe "overall" safely
wrapped in the conventional "beginning,
middle, end" causal chain. Unlike religious
systems, the scientific one posits no means
to influence the final outcome.

The common sense world view, the one
based on the dim and fleeting information
supplied by our physical senses, is of a
stable world. The continents don't move,
common sense would tell us. The world is
flat, as anyone can plainly see. All
assumptions are doomed to one day seem so
quaint, and to be replaced with ever more
powerful new ideas like the ones we now
cling to - plate tectonics and oblate
spheroids.

Stability is an illusion. The universe
is a collection of dynamic phenomena. It is
filled with paradox - patterns of chaos.
The central question for any religion must
be, "Would God create an unstable
universe?"

No.

The universe has a purpose, which
gradually technology allows us to see.
Creation lies not in the past but in the
future. The universe is unstable because it
isn't finished. It is a means, not an end.
Most importantly, there is no God - yet.

The patterns of chaos have a purpose.
You have a purpose. These are not the final
days - this is only the beginning!
Technology leads God ever closer.

"What the hell's that supposed to mean?" Fin asked.

"Makes sense to me," said Bishop. He frowned. "Sort of, anyway."

"But what's it got to do with Rook? Why'd they take her?"

"Maybe another file will tell you more."

There were four more files with recognizable icons: 'black,' 'silver,' 'gold,' and 'profiles.' Fin opened 'black.' It was a plain text document. He studied the short list of columns.

^Σ^	black/black	35%	1000	25
^∏^	black/silver	25%	1000	27.3
^Ω^	black/none	10%	500	29
^Δ^	black/gold	05%	1000	29.2
^M^	black/other	25%	500	23.6

The next two files held nothing more useful. He looked to Bishop who again read over his shoulder. Bishop shrugged. Fin opened the last file, 'profiles.'

Webster	22.4	B	Rook	±S66nkj~37F
Webster	29.2	B	Jennifer	Brie~23R
Webster	35	A	Kent	R355-da~48S
NewAlsborg	29.5	B	Chris	J382~rl~00O
Webster	27.2	A	John	C573-ji~29V
StoneDock	21.2	A	Jerry	B511~mo~17S
GamblersMill	31	B	Danny	R255~ax~19F
Webster	29.2	C	Carrie	Mohawk~46S
Webster	32	B	Lara	K655-ui~88H
Cheddarly	25	B	Rose	Lungfish~32p

Fin pointed out Rook's name.

"What does it mean?" Bishop asked.

"I don't know," Fin admitted. "But it has to be her. There aren't many Rooks around."

Fin studied the rest of the list, but had no clue what it meant. Rook's was the only name that stood out. He scrolled through several pages.

"They can't all have been kidnapped. We'd have heard something, right?"

*** *** ***

Rook exhausted her tears. Looking around, she discovered no tissues or toilet paper. Fin kept a roll in his room, she now recalled. She splashed her face at the sink and dried it with the rough olive-colored curtains.

On the back of the bathroom door hung a spotty full-length mirror. Rook stood in front of it to examine herself. She saw a puncture mark and bruise on her neck where they jammed a needle into her in the van.

She had no idea who 'they' were, just that there'd been two of them in the back with her, both in dorky, pea-snot sweaters. They had a big sheet of aluminum foil which they started to wrap around her before she lost consciousness. With a shudder she remembered the foil in her bra and began to examine herself again. Another bruise on her left upper arm. No memory of that injection. How long had she been gone? It was late morning when she and Fin left The Shamrock and it was now starting to get dark. She wasn't hungry enough to have been gone overnight.

Rook studied herself in the mirror. No other marks. No bruises, bite marks, rope burns, writing, new tattoos. No implant sites. The more she thought about the situation, the more puzzled Rook became. During the course of her work for *CTP* she'd had occasion to talk to alien abductees and many of them said they'd had their clothes turned inside-out, buttoned wrong, whatever. The jerks who'd abducted her certainly weren't aliens. They weren't even Men in Black.

Her makeup was a bit smudged, but mostly intact. Like she usually looked the morning after sleeping in it. After breakfast, she remembered, she'd applied a fresh coat of lipstick, and there it was, more or less. Fin's scent lingered on her, so she hadn't been washed to remove evidence. With much relief Rook decided she hadn't been raped. She was now more puzzled than ever. Why was she kidnapped, if not for rape or ransom?

The only other explanation she could come up with was that the conspiracy she'd made up was real, and the people behind it discovered her investigation and kidnapped her. Perhaps they wanted to frighten her, but this just proved she was on the right track.

Rook retrieved her clothes. The foil was glued into her bra, so she decided to go without. As she turned the dress right-side out, her arm brushed against her left breast, bumping her nipple ring. It sprang open and snagged her skin. She looked down at the silver hoop, puzzled. The ring in her belly button should be the wonky one, not the one in her nipple. Tugging on the hoop in her navel proved it to be secure. The rings had been switched.

*** *** ***

An intern checked Fin's eyes, then gave him a shot. Left alone on a gurney in his briefs and hospital gown, Fin tried to relax. The shot helped, but the curtain walls did nothing to muffle the sounds of hospital staff and the injured. Based on what he heard, there had been no fatalities so far.

Fin opened Rook's Mac again and started looking through her hard drive. He hoped to find something to comfort himself, something to cling to. Realizing he didn't know Rook well at all, he was looking for ways to remember her, justification for his irrational actions and what he understood now as love.

Fin learned to cope with loss at thirteen when his mom disappeared. He'd gone to live with his father, Brad. And Brad's family. The repertoire of coping skills he mastered under that roof included denial, distance and repression, but Rook deserved better.

The doctor finally came in. She looked tired as she examined Fin, but had enough energy to question him on how he sustained his injuries. Fin didn't want to tell her he'd been in a fight because he didn't want the police involved, so he told her he worked at *Sycamore*.

"That doesn't explain your injuries," she noted.

"The building blew up."

"That still doesn't explain what happened to you. These injuries aren't from an explosion or a fire. Believe me, I know. I just finished treating seven of your co-workers. The police are taking their statements now."

Fin didn't want to talk to the police, especially about his whereabouts during the fire.

"I do work there, but I wasn't there today. Not inside. I was outside when it happened. I was late. Ask anyone. They'll tell you I'm always late. I was late because I was in a fight."

"Now that I can believe. Would you like to file a complaint? About the fight? I can get an officer for you. They're all over the hospital."

"No. No, thanks. They're busy enough, wouldn't you say? It was my own fault anyway. I'm an asshole sometimes."

"That I can also believe."

X-rays were ordered and Fin received another injection. His sprained left index finger was taped to his middle finger. His nose was set and bandaged. Two ribs on the left were cracked. The cut on his forehead required four stitches.

Most of the explosion victims had either been discharged or admitted and the emergency room became a lot emptier. Fin got a real room, with walls and a door. Dressed in his bloody, smoky clothes, he sat in a wheelchair with Rook's computer, exploring her files. Her words on the screen reminded him of her voice, of their night together and the conversations they shared — over coffee at Magic Beans, over the chessboard in his room, over breakfast at The Shamrock, and, most intimately and vividly, over their intertwined naked bodies in his bed. Her voice filled his memory so thoroughly that he could hear her reading to him in a sort of nostalgia-fueled emulation. Occasionally a nurse or aide would interrupt him to check his vitals, but otherwise Fin was left alone to listen to Rook tell her story.

*** *** ***

Rook was in the shower, full blast, hot, before she thought about the possibility of destroying evidence. Too late now. Probably nothing useful anyway. Rook reached for the soap. There wasn't any, so she stood under the scalding deluge until it ran cold. She took her green panties off, wrung them out and tossed them over the shower-curtain rod. She stood under the cold water for another five minutes, until she started to shake again. Fin's towel must be in his room, too, because there were none to be found in this hole of a bathroom. Rook had been in plenty of public restrooms that were better appointed. A quick search of the medicine cabinet while she dripped dry provided her with a nail file, a straight razor and some used dental floss. She left the floss, but took the other things to try to pick the lock on Fin's door.

It took a few minutes, and she felt self-conscious standing naked in the hall, her clothes in a heap at her feet, but she managed to get the door open without being seen. She locked it behind her.

"Hi, Rook."

She whirled around, frantically searching the corners.

"So you can hear me without Fin here."

With great relief she remembered the lava lamp. "Oh, Vesuvius! You scared the shit out of me." What kind of life was she now living that the existence of a talking light fixture was comforting?

"Sorry," the lamp said in his characteristic monotone. "No one besides Fin has ever been able to hear me."

Fin's dingy towel hung on a hook on the back of the door. Drying her damp skin, Rook took comfort in his smell, even overlaid with must.

"Have you seen Fin? Has he been here?"

"He could have been here while I was sleeping."

"You sleep?" There were so many better questions she should be asking, the reporter in her said, but the idea of treating Vesuvius as anything other than a new friend felt exhausting. She longed to warm her hands on him, but thought he might react badly. Instead she laid her boots and jacket on the recliner, and threw the rest of her clothes in the garbage with all the used condoms.

"Usually at night, but you two were distracting. I was unable to sleep soundly last night."

Rook couldn't quite justify her embarrassment. Vesuvius was only a lamp, even if he could talk. She hoped he wouldn't start asking questions.

Oblivious to her discomfort, Vesuvius went on, "Fin often keeps me awake all night."

Rook tried to open the fridge. Locked. She reached for the nail file, but Vesuvius said, "He keeps an extra key under his amp."

"Thanks." Rook found the key, opened the freezer and looked behind the empty ice cube trays.

"Eureka." A half-empty bottle of vodka. After taking a swig, she set the bottle down beside Vesuvius and located a coffee-stained mug among Fin's clutter. She removed her navel and nipple rings.

"Rook, what are you doing?"

"Sterilizing them." She dumped the hoops into the mug and drowned them with vodka, swirling the mug as she told Vesuvius what happened to her after breakfast. Having to backtrack repeatedly to explain details of human behavior to the lava lamp frustrated her a little. She concluded her tale by explaining she couldn't get new hoops yet because they were at Talisman, and her keys were in her backpack which she hoped Fin would have.

"I think they should be pretty clean by now." She fished the jewelry out, blotted them dry on Fin's pillow and inserted them in their proper holes.

"Fin sprouted one too," Vesuvius deadpanned. "On his eyebrow. You probably noticed it."

Rook laughed. "Yeah, I noticed. It didn't grow though. I'm the one who put it there."

"On purpose?"

"Yes."

"Wasn't he upset?"

"No. He paid me to do it. It's my job."

Vesuvius grew quiet for a minute. "All people aren't like Fin. Are they?" Rook thought he sounded worried.

"No. Fin's rather special. Unique. That's probably why he can hear you when no one else can."

"Except you. You must be unique, too."

"I suppose I must be. But in a different way than Fin. Otherwise we wouldn't be unique. So where's Mr Unique keep his clean clothes?"

"Fin has no clean clothes. That's something else that makes him 'special.'"

After digging around, Rook selected the least offensive jeans in the room. She couldn't remember the last time she'd worn pants of any sort. They were too long and felt strange with no panties, but they'd do. A Space Ghost t-shirt which hadn't been worn on stage didn't smell too rank, and she discovered a clean pair of socks behind the radiator.

As she sat on a cafe stool and tied her boots someone knocked on the door. She looked up at Vesuvius, but he didn't say anything.

Another knock and, "Rook?" A voice the same pitch as Fin's, but clearer. A non-smoker's voice.

"Rook? Are you in there? Hey, this is Kyle. From downstairs."

Hoping he wouldn't ask for his condoms back, she opened the door.

The clean-cut guy in the hallway stood about six feet tall, the same height as Fin. Dark blond hair, neat and short under a denim and corduroy ball cap. At least the cap wasn't backward. He wore chinos, a dark green rugby shirt, combat boots and a salesman smile.

"Rook?" he asked, looking her up and down.

"Yeah." She felt uncomfortable in jeans, but tried not to look it.

"Hi. Hey, Fin just called. He asked if I could give you a ride."

"Oh great!" She was relieved to have some news. "I've been looking for him. Is he OK?"

"Uh, yeah. He was glad to hear I thought you were here. My room's right downstairs," he explained. "Are you ready to go?"

"Let me grab my coat."

"Rook?" Vesuvius said.

Rook glanced at the lamp. Kyle obviously didn't hear it. She shrugged and started pulling on her jacket.

"Where is he?"

Kyle pulled the door shut and led her toward the stairs. "The hospital."

*** *** ***

The room slid slowly toward the floor, but never quite made it. This painkiller was a lightweight drug by Fin's standards. After enjoying the vertigo for a short while, he refocused on the computer screen.

Rook's low, melodious voice filled his imagination as he read her files. He relished the sarcastic tone she took on when reading her college papers, mostly communications, a smattering of psych and one marketing opus.

She had some decent short fiction, but Fin could tell she wasn't proud of it by the halting, embarrassed way she read it. He longed to encourage her.

In with all the school papers was a file called 'DREAMS.'

The dreams made Fin smile. He wondered about the people mentioned, and how they got lucky enough to frolic in Rook's head. Skipping ahead to the most recent entries, he checked to see if he made an appearance, sure he would remember it if he had.

The most recent entry, six weeks old, said simply, "Again Dammit."

Fin remembered the spaceship dream. Pensively he scrolled back through her entries. He went back through a week's worth to the first mention.

She whispered the details as if recounting a ghost story around a campfire.

> *Setting: Desert, or possibly ocean floor.*
> *Rocks and sand everywhere. Something important is hidden.*
> *Everything starts to vibrate. Terrible subsonics. A greenish*
> *spaceship (bathysphere) shaped like Cinderella's carriage hangs*
> *there. It's got spider legs. It finds a key. I don't think I want to do*
> *this.*

Fin shuddered as he closed the folder.

The returning pain in his head and fingers annoyed him, so he tucked the computer under his arm and stumbled out to find a nurse. He found an unattended pharmacy cart first though, so he gave himself a shot of Demerol, he thought, and went back to his nest.

After settling back down and reviewing some of Rook's old articles for *Conspiracy Theory Press*, he started poking around in the folder called 'Bullshit.' She read him her anti-affirmations in a somewhat strident voice. Well, she was right about one thing; she hadn't been abducted by aliens.

Reading her article about dream control and Buck U depressed Fin because it wasn't finished. She might never get the chance to finish it.

Those thoughts nauseated him and he clicked that window closed. Tears trickled down Fin's cheeks. Clicking randomly, he opened folders, looked at her monitor settings, checked available RAM.

His head swam with painkillers. He studied the striations and flecks of color of the Mac's hypnotic desktop pattern. Letting his eyes relax, he achieved a rudimentary 3-D effect. He floated through it for several minutes, until something in his peripheral vision distracted him. When he tried to focus on it, Fin came crashing back into himself. It took several seconds to locate the cause — a stray period in the lower right corner of the screen.

Thanks to his injuries, Fin was using the trackpad right-handed. Occasionally at *Sycamore*, he would race one of the other artists to see who could finish their work first. To make things interesting, he would sometimes handicap himself by using the mouse with his off hand. He never thought it an especially useful skill, until now. Clicking on such a small target required fine maneuvering. A folder containing over fifty text files opened.

Some of the files had titles such as 'fall-out,' 'schmuck,' and 'gamesmanship,' others were titled with dates.

Though it wasn't fool-proof, Rook went to some trouble to hide this folder. Why? From whom?

Fin justified reading the first file by hoping it might contain something to explain her current situation.

It wasn't about the organized crime gang threatening her family, or the international terrorists who wanted to kidnap her and sell her to the Sultan of Brunei. It was about some guy named Dagan.

Her journal.

Fin knew he ought to stop reading it, but didn't. Rook seemed to want him to know what it said, because she read to him again. He took comfort in her voice, wrapped around him like a blanket, as she told the story of Dagan and how she'd left him for Marcus. He'd given her the computer and asked her to meet his family. She claimed he wasn't emotionally supportive, but Fin could tell that really she was scared.

To make the break from Dagan, she moved in with Marcus immediately. It made Fin's heart and stomach ache to hear how happily she described the early times with Marcus, and the joys of their animal sex. She'd been with him for close to two years, judging by the dates on these entries.

Reading on, he heard her tell of feuding with her mother. Mom refused to call her Rook, insisting on her given name, Brook. Mom didn't approve of Marcus, thought the twelve year age difference too great. She didn't think Brook should get serious with anyone while still in school. Rook thought it hypocritical for a woman on her seventh marriage to lecture anyone about relationships. Mom thought Brook should call her newest stepfather Dad instead of Bill. Rook decided not to talk to Mom anymore.

Marcus led her down the path of tattoos, body piercing and drug experimentation in the name of spirituality. Marcus claimed Lakota blood. He wanted desperately to be a shaman, took peyote on a regular basis. Rook at first thought this interesting. At first. During one vision quest, he 'discovered' he was an incarnation of Coyote, trickster par excellence, and she was Raven, a trickster as well as a creator. After that he took to calling her Raven, and liked to role-play as Coyote, especially during sex. As tricksters they had a duty to rebel, break taboos, create chaos. This was very meaningful for Marcus, but Rook thought it all rather silly. She concluded Marcus's spirituality was a massive overcompensation for some inadequacy he couldn't face. Fin had to agree with her.

She graduated the previous May and had begun trying to figure out her next move, away from Buck U, Webster, and Marcus. So far her lack of savings and legitimate job offers stymied her.

Fin wasn't sure how he felt when Rook told him about Marcus cheating on her, and her own cheating in retaliation. From that point, Rook's tone grew gruffer. The entries became less frequent. Mostly they were about Marcus being a shit.

When Fin came to one called 'fish parts' Rook fell silent.

*** *** ***

Marcus was in a mood. Actually, he'd been in several. At first he burned with rage. He would have destroyed all Fin's things after breaking in, except he didn't know when the whelp might return.

His anger cooled a bit, slowly, while he waited motionless in Fin's chair. The waiting had gone on much too long. Emptiness over the loss of Rook gave him a few pangs, but he kept his heart hard. He wasn't ready to give her up, needed to let his spirit animal stay in charge. A long, deep breath stoked the coals of his black meditations, summoning power.

> *Coyote lurked in the crimson dimness, the jet plumage of Raven his great war-bonnet. The dual tricksters, unstoppable agents of disorder. Together they would unmake the world so a new one would be born. His eyes glowed, and he grinned. But he was alone, with no wings-of-night companion.*

The smile soured into a grimace. Marcus recalled meeting Fin, the day he came in to get pierced. He remembered the way Fin looked at Rook, and her acting flaky. Fin brazened his way into Marcus's sanctum and entranced Rook. Now she was gone!

The next encounter festered in his mind. The mangy animal barged right in again, and with Rook's keys. Marcus almost had him, but the Bear came. They tricked him.

Now he was on Fin's turf. He would dish out some rude surprises, like the one he had right after he got here. Rook's clothes.

Panic and bafflement had swept him. Completing his search left him still grappling with why her clothes were in the trash. The lock on the fridge had caught his eye, even though it was disengaged. He doubted her entire body would fit into it, although some ingenious configuration of the pieces might make it possible. The tangle of blankets and numerous used rubbers didn't tell him anything he wanted to know. He had convinced himself he would find something by the time he opened the locked closet, and was scarcely reassured by his uneventful investigation.

***   ***   ***

Fin considered reading 'fish parts' to himself, but Rook took up her narration again, her imagined voice filled with false cheerfulness. She didn't like what she was about to tell Fin.

> *What do I know about this Fin guy?*
>
> *He plays bass in some second-rate bar band. He's a good kisser. He's bold, reckless. Or stupid. He smokes. He's intimidated by Marcus.*
>
> *Being wary of Marcus is generally a sign of intelligence, but I can't decide if he's dumb, a druggy, or reasonably intelligent but with no concept of reality.*
>
> *I'm gonna have to find out more before I meet up with him. Well hell, I am a journalist, after all. I shall investigate!*

Next came 'more fish' and Fin wasn't sure he wanted to hear any more. His hand had its own agenda and clicked open the file. Once it opened he had no choice.

Everybody knows Fin Tanner. He's fond of pulling crazy shit at parties. According to some otherwise reliable sources, at a party at his house the other day he gave himself a tattoo while on a massive drug binge. Without benefit of training or proper equipment, just stuff from around the house. He ended the party with a huge feedback solo that shook everyone's fillings loose.

I hope he's not a performance artist.

The important part is nobody thinks he has a girlfriend (or a boyfriend). He seems to have had some in the past (girlfriends), but he's pathologically uninvolved and it drives them nuts. He doesn't care what anyone thinks, as long as they don't give him shit. If they try to change him, he either blows up and spews a torrent of 'pseudointellectual clap-trap' or just laughs and sends them on their way.

Why am I doing this? Who really cares what Fin is like? He's cute. He's a good kisser. It's always nice to get a break from Marcus's penis studs. If Marcus finds out, he'll complain. But that's what he gets for screwing my sister. And if I have to hear one more time how she and the other chicks are deer women, I'll scream. Why should I believe anything a self-proclaimed trickster tells me anyway?

I can't believe I'm playing by his rules! He's just a man. Just a great big raving loony who thinks he can stake a claim to me because I fit into his personal fantasy world pantheon.

I NEED OUT!

Fin closed his eyes, but Rook's voice echoed inside his head. She wouldn't let him rest. She told him since he'd gone this far, he ought to read the last entry and be done with it.

Reluctantly he did, and found Rook less hesitant to read to him. It was called 'twain' and dated yesterday.

I'm supposed to meet Fin in half an hour and am horribly nervous. I don't know how much is because of what Lara told me and how much is about Fin.

Things are over with Marcus. I need a way out. Maybe I can move in with Fin. If that's not jumping the gun, what is? I've only kissed him once. I get butterflies when I think about that.

A week ago I thought Marcus and I were going through a rough patch, but we'd go back to the status quo. Now even the sex seems stale. And what do we have besides sex? When Fin asked me out I wanted to say yes, but couldn't because Marcus would have killed someone. I'm sick of that reaction.

From what I hear about Fin Tanner, that shouldn't be a problem.

Fin turned off the computer.

Normally, having a beautiful girl want him for sex would be a good thing, but Rook should have been different. It wounded Fin to know she was just using him to get away from Marcus, the way she'd used Marcus to get away from Dagan. Thinking back over their time together, he dared to hope she felt something more. He did, and it scared him. But sitting in the hospital, broken and nearly killed because of her, he didn't regret it. Would do it all again. No matter how she felt about him, his love for her was real. Overwhelming. He hadn't loved anyone since his mom went away.

Fin broke down in sobs, but soon recovered and requested more painkillers. The nurse offered something non-prescription. Fin decided he had better stuff at home and would go get some.

Bishop had gone back to work, but left cab fare and word that he wanted to see Fin after he'd cleaned up.

Once he had more drugs, Fin didn't think he'd bother.

Chapter Eight

AMBUSH

Divided Seed shall a Divided Child Beget
who shall grow into a Divided Man
from *New Revelations* by Reverend Brian Shaw, unpublished

Marcus felt he was losing his edge, like he'd been tricked again and Fin was already far away, howling gleefully at Mother Moon.

He shook his head. Way too much fucking thinking. Fin would show. Things would soon be right again. Marcus ran his thumb over the .357's knurled pommel. Gonna put everything in its proper place.

Finally, a shuffling approach in the hall. Someone limping. Marcus stood and moved to a position of ambush near the door. He raised the pistol like a club as the lock shunked and the door creaked.

"What? Where?" Fin exclaimed, turning his head and almost finding Marcus as the blow landed.

Marcus paced a few times back and forth in the cramped, dark room trying to burn some adrenaline before hoisting his wilted victim into the armchair. The anticlimactic attack left him with copious unspent anger, and he struggled against the urge to demolish Fin. He picked up the laptop from where Fin dropped it and noted with grim satisfaction that it was Rook's.

Fin's eyes opened unsteadily. They weren't focused, but the left one did track the muzzle of the gun pointed at his face. He showed no indication of his feelings about the situation.

Marcus loomed over him and growled through clenched teeth, "Where is Rook?" Fin remained impassive. Marcus rolled his eyes and chuckled. "Dipshit. What I'll do to you if you don't spill is supremely unkind. I'm looking forward to it."

"My head fucking hurts," grumbled Fin, patting his pockets for a smoke.

Marcus cocked the pistol's hammer and glared.

"I heard you," Fin muttered. He'd located a pack and a lighter. After drawing the cigarette to a bright glow and exhaling a fog of slow death, he proffered the pack and Zippo to his assailant. Marcus did not acknowledge.

"Where is she?" Marcus gave the chair a rough shove with his boot for emphasis.

"Well, I've been better, thanks for asking. And you? Anything broken?"

"I hope you keep holding out on me. I have major issues with you."

Fin lolled his head back. "I thought I knew where she was." He saw the effect this revelation had on Marcus and smiled coldly. "That reminds me, I forgot your gun. Your other gun, I mean. The big one. I was in a hurry because of the fire. Maybe you heard the explosion."

Marcus's only outward response to this additional tidbit was a tic near his right eye.

Fin gave his lava lamp an incredulous look. Marcus applied the gun barrel to Fin's bandaged nose none too gently to swivel his head back. "Fucking lying freak! I found her clothes, asshole!"

"Congratulations. Why are you in my face?"

Marcus whirled, grabbed the garbage can, and dumped its contents in Fin's lap. "That's why!" Marcus shouted, thrusting the gun into Fin's cheek. "It's eating me, not blasting you! This is what's keeping you alive," he said pointing to the green panties, "so get one last good sniff! Where! Is! Rook!"

Fin was dumbstruck. His bafflement seemed genuine and he looked quizzically back to the lamp.

"Kyle?" Fin barked. The heat in his eyes made Marcus drop back a step. Who the fuck was Kyle? The lamp? "Kyle!" Fin bellowed, holding Rook's stockings and bra in quaking fists.

He stopped. Plucking at the foil in the bra, he started to laugh.

Marcus paced. This was not going the way he'd planned. His head was buzzing and Fin seemed to be hypnotized by the lava lamp. The thought of this whelp defiling his Raven made Marcus try again. He slapped Fin and shoved the gun back in his face.

Little bubbles of laughter kept welling up from Fin. He shook his head in disbelief then grabbed Marcus's gun hand and locked eyes with him. "Hey!" Fin said. "Would you like to know who you should point this thing at?"

***

Marcus took a position at the edge of Kyle's door, by the latch. He cocked the hammer on the gun as Fin leaned against the door, listening. Fin shook his head and said, "No, dickhead, stow the cannon for a minute." He opened the door and stepped inside, gesturing to Marcus to follow. Marcus wasn't ready to forgo the reassuring solidity of the weapon in his hand, and so held it bootlegger style behind his thigh as he crept into the room. Fin shut the door.

Light filtering up from the street was enough to locate furniture in Kyle's uncluttered room. Fin turned to the liquor cabinet while Marcus scouted the shadowy areas. Fin slumped onto the futon with a bottle of imported Scotch and two tumblers. Marcus stalked over, sat at the other end, and accepted a drink.

"He's a total shit, but he buys good hooch."

Marcus tossed his off. "Whatever. Do you know where he is?" They were keeping their voices low.

"Normally, I'd say some poser night spot." Fin refilled their glasses. "Tonight, you don't want to hear my guesses."

"Maybe I should anyway."

"Well, you aren't gonna. Not now." Fin took a gulp of the whiskey.

A minute of silent tension passed.

"So," Marcus ventured in a low tone that was not quite a whisper, "how much do you know about this Kyle?"

Fin chuckled. "He's my half-twin."

Marcus was about to ask a rude question about Fin's mother when Fin spoke again.

"We have the same father, same birth date, different mothers."

"Okay," Marcus groped for relevancy, "what about it? I mean, what's he like?"

"An asshole. He's the evil twin. As Booth likes to say, we're a transporter accident made flesh."

Fin looked wistful. "He has a pathologically screwed-up value system. Well, look at his stuff," Fin gestured broadly. "He is just what this room implies. Would rather seem than be, 'cause being is a lot of work for him.

"Of course," Fin's voice took a somber inflection, "maybe I've underestimated him. We don't get along, but I can't fit a kidnapping in with all the other shit. He'd do something to fuck up anything that made me happy, sure, but this feels weird."

The door opened, so Marcus didn't reply.

The first thing Kyle saw when he turned on the lights was the gun pointed at his face. With a weary sigh he shut the door and swung his gaze to Fin.

"Like I told you before, paying off your suppliers is your responsibility. Maybe if your pathetic excuse for a band had a manager you wouldn't have these problems."

"Shut up!" Marcus bellowed. He was sick of people not taking him and his gun seriously.

Fin stood up, smirking, and Marcus steered Kyle over to the futon. When Kyle was sitting, Fin said, "I don't want your money, Kyle. I know how hard Daddy works for it."

Kyle ignored the jibe. His attention wandered over to the gun again. With his eyes on it, not Marcus, he said, "I guess I better let you tell me what it is you do want."

"You know," Fin said.

Kyle made a sour face. "What the fuck is that supposed to mean?"

"It means, you arrogant prick, you fucked up somewhere. It means you have two pissed off individuals controlling whether you'll stand up to pee tomorrow. We know you're the one. You know what we want. The rest is easy math." Through clenched teeth, he said, "As you can see, my composure is fucked. Score one for Kyle. Now end it."

"Oh," Kyle said, "I remember. Geez, you don't need a gun to get an apology from me."

Fin made a pained face.

"I'm sorry I went into your room, even if you were being a shithead."

Fin buried his head in his hands, digging his fingers into his hair. Either sobs or laughter escaped him in strained clumps.

Marcus kicked Kyle in the gut.

*** *** ***

Kyle couldn't even gasp yet, face-down in a tight ball on the floor in front of the futon. Fin fell silent and watched with interest.

"My turn now," Marcus said. "Today has been altogether too full of you two and your bullshit. You tell me right now where Rook is and I never see either of you again. No games, no sibling rivalry, no stalling."

Fin checked his critique of Marcus's interrogative approach and concentrated on watching Kyle now that the cat was out of the bag. Kyle warily pushed himself into a sitting position and placed his hands fitfully in his lap

"Where what is?" he managed to wheeze. Nice touch, thought Fin.

Marcus was about to boot him again, but the way Kyle flinched was good enough. "Where is she!" he demanded.

"I don't have any idea what you're talking about," Kyle muttered. His eyes locked on Fin. "Still using me as your excuse, I see."

"Why, Kyle?" Fin shook his head. "Actually, answer his question first, but I really do want to know why."

Kyle's gaze once again shed all semblance of guile. He looked scared, a look Fin had seen him summon up in front of parents, teachers, and police. The puppy-dog eyes that always deflected full blame onto Fin. "I can only say 'I don't know' so many times." He licked his lips, his eyes darting between the two men standing over him. "I'd like to know why, too. Why are you dragging me into this? It looks like you're in some kind of trouble, but why involve me?"

"There's lots of trouble left where that batch came from," Marcus interjected.

Fin showed no emotion. "You didn't realize there was a witness. Your surprise is perfectly understandable."

He noted with satisfaction the definite indications of startled terror in Kyle's face, the way the pupils dilated and the jaw clenched. Fin kept his own face impassive. "So take your time. Consider your response, all your options."

Marcus pressed the muzzle of the gun against Kyle's left temple.

Fin sat on the coffee table and rested his boots on the pale sage futon cover. "Now, we have a clear, logical path before us. We won't get discouraged, because we know you have what we want. You get to decide how hard we work in getting it from you. The harder you make us work, the worse off you'll be."

Now Kyle was truly afraid. Fin could see the difference from the affectation of fear earlier, the sweat. Kyle looked at Marcus, whose burning eyes didn't appear very compassionate. He glanced at his watch.

Marcus gave the gun a shove to indicate he preferred Kyle's eyes up.

Fin said, "At the tone, it will be time to tell us where she is — BEEP!"

"Whoever told you they saw me, whatever they said, they're lying. I don't know what's going on!"

"That's getting old. Maybe a few broken ribs will help you understand..." Fin signaled Marcus with his eyes.

"No matter what you do, I don't fucking know!"

Marcus grabbed Kyle's wrist and twisted the arm up and forward, exposing his flank to a cruel impact from the pistol's grip. Kyle yelled, and Marcus knelt across his back. Barely able to breathe, Kyle whimpered.

Fin was conflicted. He both enjoyed watching the torment and longed to stop it. This was serious shit. He sat storm-tossed while Marcus told Kyle he should save his breath for answering questions, and shifted his weight so Kyle could inhale with a sharp wince.

Marcus chuckled. Fin felt a bit sick.

"Sit up," said Marcus, gesturing with the gun.

Kyle complied meekly, looking from Marcus to Fin and back again.

"Fin, come on," he wheedled. "Are you gonna let him do this to me? We're brothers. I don't like you, you know that, but I wouldn't sit back and let someone kill you."

"No, you'd help," said Fin, quickly getting over his squeamishness. Kyle, the consummate manipulator. He deserved this and worse. Rook was in real danger, or had been. This stunt was ill-timed.

Kyle dropped the wounded brother angle and smirked. "Yeah." He shrugged. "It was worth a shot."

Fin stood and glared down at Kyle. The asshole still wasn't taking this seriously. What the hell did they need to do to get his attention?

Kyle began to rise. "If we're done, then…"

Fin and Marcus lunged at Kyle at the same time and ran into each other. Kyle sat down gracelessly, but grinning.

"You know, Fin, you ought to hire better muscle. You two seem at cross-purposes. You need to be able to rely on your team."

"Enough fucking football metaphors," Fin spat. "Tell us where she is and let us work the rest of it out."

Kyle's eyes took on a malicious glint. "You aren't friends. That's clear. He's not professional muscle," indicating Marcus. "So what's left?"

Marcus glared at Kyle, then Fin. His nostrils flared.

"Shut up," said Fin. He didn't like what Kyle was up to, trying to turn them against each other. Like they needed any help.

"She didn't mention there were two of you." Kyle smirked.

"If you've touched her, this is going to get so much worse." Marcus sounded like he hoped to make it worse.

"Well, I had to find out what all the fuss was about."

Marcus and Fin both cocked their heads. Kyle continued, "The noise from upstairs last night was unbearable."

"You weren't even here!" Fin protested.

Marcus was stonefaced.

"I know," Kyle said wickedly, "but I also know you stole my condoms."

Fin gave Kyle the finger and looked at Marcus with a sneer. "Get some backbone, *partner*. We're kinda busy right now to be moping about a breakup."

Marcus's face had a reptilian calm, like a hungry croc. He pointed the gun at Fin. "There's no breakup."

Kyle continued, "She kept making this one sound. Sort of a whimpering moan."

Marcus cocked the gun, still pointed at Fin. "Shut up!"

"I figured if Fin could make her sound like that, I ought to be able to make her howl."

Marcus pointed the gun at Kyle.

"I haven't yet," Kyle said hastily.

"What did you do to my girlfriend?" Fin asked.

The gun swung back to him.

Kyle looked smug. "She went with me willingly enough. She is cute, but not exactly my type. Nipple ring would have to go, for one thing."

Marcus belted him with the gun.

Kyle shook off the blow and glared at them. "She's a good kisser, once you're past the biting stage. Smells good, too."

Marcus raised the gun to strike again but Kyle quickly said, looking at Fin, "Maybe we can have a three-way, since she's moving in with you."

Marcus hesitated, but only because he couldn't decide which one of them to whack first. Fin was impressed by the depths to which Kyle had sunk. Kyle watched alertly to see what the next move would be. The gun again pointed at Fin.

"She's not moving in with you," Marcus said with barely contained anger. "We're not breaking up."

"Sure aren't getting back together until we find her." The gun didn't move. Fin sighed. He addressed Kyle. "Let me show you how to avoid being shot."

He sat on the coffee table again and said to Marcus, "Besides me, how many leads do you have? Now you've already beaten me savagely, and heck, let's set a date to do it again. Why not? But if you don't stick with our agenda right now it's rather pointless."

Marcus growled. He struck Kyle across the face, knocking him flat. He placed the muzzle of the gun against Kyle's head. Kyle didn't move. Fin couldn't tell if he was conscious.

Marcus said, without looking back at Fin, "I can do this without your help. Leave now if you want to."

Fin studied Kyle with detached fascination. He said, "I'm none too thrilled about teaming up either. But," he looked at Marcus, confident he was being regarded in the other's peripheral vision, "I think it's her best chance."

The door crashed in without warning. Before they had time to react, Marcus and Fin were surrounded by men in dark body armor and gleaming visors, pointing high-tech small arms at their heads.

Marcus set the pistol down and placed his hands on his head. Fin sat absolutely still. Marcus's wrists were grabbed and he was shoved off of Kyle, who stood up with minimal difficulty. He gave Fin a look that deserved a good whack with a crowbar and tapped his watch.

"At the tone, you're utterly fucked. Beep." Kyle drifted out of the room.

*** *** ***

Shaw sat at his battered steel desk after they'd taken the girl away. The old factory was furnished entirely in battered steel, which crystallized for Shaw why he preferred the warm glow of fine wood. He laid both hands on the blotter and tried to achieve calm.

Useless.

He stood and paced. At the window he stopped and looked down at the work floor. The technicians sat at their table, headphones clamped on, fingers tapping away on their keyboards. On the platform there were only two men at the production stations, soldering the tiny angel pins and pendants. Shaw's mind wanted to turn to managerial concerns, but he refused it. The girl held more importance right now.

He needed to know who she was, really, to determine whether she represented a threat, but how could he when even she didn't know?

Her name should have been the easiest answer to get.

She'd furrowed her brow for a long time and Shaw thought she wasn't going to reply. Slowly she chanted, "I am Rook. I am Raven. I am Brook. I am Bramble. I am Brandy. Moon. Brandymoon. Brook Bramble Brandymoon. I am Coyote's Raven. Rook. Raven. Brook. Rook. Black tower. Black bird. Tower bird. London Bridge is falling down..."

He had silenced her. Too much and too little information. Unprecedented. Delving deeper into her mind to untangle things, Shaw encountered a landscape unlike any he'd ever seen. False structures and abandoned facades dotted the tangled, black forest. Shaw realized this poor creature had built herself an elaborate defense system, and he wanted to know why. Some searching uncovered the core structure of her mind which was further evidence of over-zealous self-preservation. It had no portal. This girl was overprotected by her mother in certain aspects of her childhood, but woefully underprotected in others. She had tried to protect herself and overreacted, desperately wanted to be in charge of her own identity. Shaw knew somewhere nearby would be evidence of discarded personae. If he could locate them, he might be able to help her.

Unfortunately, this was not the time. Shaw had an agenda and it did not involve resolving an identity crisis.

This pathetic creature was brought in because the intelligence division claimed she had knowledge of the program, an assertion Shaw now saw was laughably overstated.

Through the lengthy interrogation, he determined she was a reporter of some kind, though her 'real job' involved creating chaos, saving humanity, and poking holes in people. She was investigating something at Buckminster University involving dream control, spaceships, and the budget, but she was just making it up. The great irony was, in her day job as a body piercer, she played an integral part in Shaw's plans to disperse his wondrous devices to the unwashed masses, and yet her suspicions were turned in entirely the wrong direction. She had personally done enough to advance Shaw's holy agenda that, by rights, she should be named employee of the month, and yet she blamed Buckminster University for her paranoid delusions.

His people would explore the few names she mentioned. He didn't expect to turn anything up, but needed to be thorough. The program was moving along nicely and he didn't want to overlook anything that might jeopardize its implementation.

Returning to his desk, he turned his thoughts to the girl's first kidnapping, if that was indeed what it had been. She'd been drugged and her recollections were suspect. Shaw felt all but certain he knew who did it, but was baffled as to why. She clearly wasn't a member of Gregory's coterie. Were they perhaps trying to recruit her?

His intercom buzzed and he received the first good news of the night. Perhaps these two his ambitious squad leader was bringing in would explain everything. It seemed that someone else was in the running for employee of the month.

Chapter Nine

Sandcastle

*In researching this work, I traveled to Blessed, Missouri and
interviewed the few remaining residents who remember the day
the charismatic, pious young man named Brian Shaw first arrived
in town. With the help of a Forestry Service map of the area, I
found the site of Shaw Oracle, several days' hike out of Blessed in
a rocky, inhospitable valley. Nature has all but reclaimed the
original twelve cultivated acres, but there is evidence of the past.
Charred foundations remain from one large and several smaller
buildings. And there are many graves.*
from *Brainwashed* by Julie Rome, ©1998 Futhark Press

Fin came around in a shaking and leaning room. There was a loud,
low, growling noise and several sudden bumps. He was in the back of a
panel truck, bound in some sort of straitjacket, with a bag over his head.

Sitting up took a determined effort. The truck's engine reached a
steady note and the ride became smoother. They were on a highway.

The injection had been a fast-acting sedative, a synthetic to judge
from the dizzy residual high and metallic taste in his mouth. Probably
would have kept a normal adult under for several hours. Fin's hunch
was he'd been out for five or ten minutes.

"Is that you, Fin?"

"Marcus?"

"This is ugly. Big time ugly shit. If you know what any of this is
about, you need to tell me. Probably makes no difference, but I can't
stand wondering."

Fin shifted over awkwardly to lean against the side of the truck. He
wanted a smoke. "Why do you think I would know what my brother is

up to?"

"I sure as hell don't."

Fin wished he knew enough to affect a cavalier attitude. The attitude remained an option, of course, but with no inside knowledge to back it up, it wouldn't carry well. "We need a plan. Knowing something about Kyle's agenda would be great, but we'll have to make do with my intuition."

After a long pause, Marcus asked, "Would I be better off sticking to my own devices?"

Fin snorted. "You broke in."

"What?"

"You entered my chaos stream, and now you think I might not be the key to your survival."

"Good point."

Fin was a little nonplussed.

Marcus continued, "There must be some patterns you can see here. Alright, so now there's some type of mercenary twist on those patterns. Granted. But, if we're trusting your intuition, can you at least give me a taste?"

"Marcus, I really have no fucking clue. I fucked up."

"No, no." Marcus sounded eager to keep Fin talking. "You were right all the way. You knew he'd taken Rook. The fireworks were my department. We're not dead yet." Fin smirked at that, thinking it wouldn't be long now. Marcus went on, "Does this situation remind you of anything? Even way back? He's your brother."

"Half-brother." Fin scanned a rapid flash of teenage memories, all with Kyle doing things he couldn't, or wouldn't. Sports, shallow friends, trophy girlfriends, sucking up to teachers and egging their cars with his buddies later. Definitely a pattern. "The knee."

Marcus prompted, "Kyle's? Yours?"

"His. Took him off the scholarship fast-track, which effectively negated his social existence for a while. Pruned his network."

"Does it still hurt?"

Fin scowled. "Yes, but you're missing the point. He found a surrogate for football. One thing Kyle understands, it's toadies. He is one himself, instinctively, and he needs his own little troupe."

"Okay..."

"This GI Joe shit is how he gets his fix, now that he can't get it on the field. Or off for that matter." Fin enjoyed putting Kyle under a microscope. What did Kyle want, besides lots of uncritical acquaintances? "He wants to move up. Wherever he is right now isn't high enough, so we're most likely to be some kind of offering to his dark master. He brings in everything, simpering for approval."

"Everything?"

"Rook."

"You're sure?"

Fin shouted, "No! How the fuck can I be sure about any of this?"

"You sounded sure a second ago!"

"Then why did you ask?" Fin retorted.

"He knows we know, I mean he'd be taking us right to her."

"I notice you didn't say, 'I miss her.'"

That one found its mark, and they were both silent for a time.

Marcus finally sighed. "What should I do?"

Fin narrowed his eyes and pursed his lips, noting that his shrewd expressions were going to waste at the moment. He said, "You're letting me call all the shots?"

"I'm just looking for ideas here. Can't say whether I'll stick with you once the shit hits."

"You won't. But you don't have a clue what to expect."

"Well bring me up to speed."

"Play it cool. I'll improvise."

"Christ!" Marcus sounded disgusted. "Okay. Today is the day. You're an asshole."

"What day?"

"The day somebody calls your bluff. Do you think these people are gonna fuck up and let you waltz away? Maybe they'll be so entertained by your yammering that you can trick them? Wake up. I thought I saw signs of something, a spark of true knowledge. I was thinking you put on an idiot act to keep people guessing."

"Guess again."

"Yeah, that's the incomparable wit of Fin Tanner that'll get you out of any mess. Boy, are these guys in trouble now!"

"Fine. Don't listen. Make your own luck."

"I'll take mine over yours."

"You still don't know what I plan to do."

"Neither do you. That's what 'improvise' means."

"No. Improvisation is deeply informed, not random. To improvise is to create, making something out of nothing. Do you think making up the notes as you go is the easiest way to play? Does the name Miles Davis mean anything to you?"

Marcus chuckled. "I never said you don't put on a good show. Hell, I can't wait to see what you end up trying. I just don't want my life depending on it."

"Too bad."

"Let me tell you what I plan to do. I plan to play 'possum, and listen for them to leave me unguarded. Then I'll take my chance."

"Sounds reasonable."

"So you still don't have any idea?"

"Oh. Sure. I'm going to mess with their brains when they question me. Just a stall tactic, of course. I'll make my move when the commandos storm the building."

"Commandos?" Marcus said sarcastically. "I've obviously underestimated you."

"Never underestimate chaos."

The truck slowed and made a tight right turn, crept along. Vibrations shook the vehicle as it drove over an uneven surface before stopping. Fin laid back down.

The back of the truck opened, introducing new acoustics. After a brief pause a voice piped up, "Put 'em in number two?"

Fin got an icy jolt — Kyle's voice, right beside him, "Let's not waste any time. We'll take the 'possum here up first. As soon as Shaw finishes with him, send the other one up."

The disembodied voice of his evil half-twin echoed in Fin's head, trying to connect with something important.

"You morons all forget how to do your jobs?"

Connection made. The men who'd torched the office. Fin felt ill.

"Get this one upstairs," Kyle continued. "Keep the other one quiet and wait until Shaw is ready for him. Don't fuck up. Simple enough?"

Unseen hands dragged Fin to the tailgate and left him to droop over the edge and slouch with a graceless thud onto the concrete floor. He heard muffled thrashing and cursing as Marcus was unloaded.

∗∗∗   ∗∗∗   ∗∗∗

Kyle ascended the staircase to the third floor. At the top, he rapped on the door. Two henchmen lugged Marcus along behind.

The door opened. "Welcome, and hello. Bring him in," Shaw said.

Kyle hadn't met the reverend before, and had not formed any ideas about what he might be like. He entered, stepping aside to let the others bring Marcus in. "Here's one of them. I doubt it's worth your time to question him."

Shaw beamed at him and brushed off all this shop talk with an effete gesture. Looking over at the guards, he said, "Make yourselves comfortable. I'll be ready to start in a few minutes." The guards shrugged and moved to a large brown sofa, where they sat and dumped Marcus on the floor. The spacious room had a huge window overlooking the old work floor. Recessed lights created pools of brightness in the dim lair. An imposing desk sat somewhat forlornly in the center of the room, and two austere black chairs faced it. Shaw stationed himself behind his desk, and stood there leaning on it as if at a pulpit. His suit didn't bunch up at the shoulders, which Kyle knew meant it wasn't off-the-rack.

The lighting gave Shaw an aura, or at least Kyle assumed it was the lighting. He sported a substantial quantity of gold jewelry, but it worked. Kyle remembered hearing Shaw was a TV preacher, and decided he looked the part. With a start he realized Shaw had been speaking to him for at least a minute. He couldn't tell if the man was self-absorbed, or just supremely patient and polite with inattentive underlings.

"Don't let it worry you," Shaw said. "My message has a way of sinking in."

Kyle blinked.

"Sit in that chair," Shaw said calmly. Kyle was appalled with himself for the undignified way he scampered to take a seat. He sat fuming.

"Now relax," Shaw soothed. "I brought you here because I'm interested in you. Your recent exploits are almost too good to be true and I simply can't take any chances."

Settling primly into his enormous chair, Shaw signaled to the guards, who brought Marcus forward, struggling. The guards unhooded him when they'd reached a position in front of the desk. He looked frenzied, eyes bulging and teeth bared like a cornered dog's.

At a subtle shift of Shaw's dispassionate gaze, the two men shoved Marcus down into the available seat. Kyle watched, blank-faced, as Shaw began to speak. The evangelist started with a standard summary of his captive's situation, underscoring the futility of plotting an escape. He worked outward, mentioning Marcus's restraints first, then the guards, then the locked door, then the many more armed personnel, and the remote location of the factory. Shaw was a natural orator. His voice alone held power. Marcus now looked merely wary.

Shaw continued his monologue, describing the immenseness of the continent, and the greater immenseness of the Earth's mantel. He spoke of the elegant ballet of rotation and revolution performed by the planets, condensing all their graceful curves into a single web of meaning. Impressed, Kyle wondered if anyone else noticed how far off-topic the boss had wandered.

Dismissing the guards, Shaw stood and stated to Marcus, "You cannot lie to me, and you cannot refuse me."

"Fuck you!" Marcus said, flashing an unsteady grin.

"Sure, you can swear at me. No problem. Now let's have some fun. How did you trace your little sweetmeat back to Kyle?"

Marcus's sneer turned into an agonized grimace. He took a sudden deep breath and looked almost imploringly at Shaw. He worked his jaw like he was choking or about to be sick. In a retching voice he said, "Fin just knew. Fucking slippery... persuasive... little shit..."

With an expression of minor offense, Shaw said, "Excellent, thanks. Save the editorials for another time, and for God's sake relax. You'll have a stroke."

In another two minutes Shaw confirmed the dirty details of Fin, Marcus and Rook's little triangle, so far as Marcus understood them, and satisfied himself that seeking the girl was his sole motive for ambushing Kyle. Marcus never did relax his will against answering, and at times his words were interspersed with shrieks and screams. These sounds didn't produce any visible response in Shaw.

The preacher once again seated himself, and used the intercom to summon the guards to remove Marcus. He looked at Kyle appraisingly.

Kyle found the state of hypnosis Shaw had imposed on him easy to adapt to. His alertness was boosted, because the choice of what to focus on wasn't his. He was glad not to be used like Marcus. Thinking how helpless he would be to prevent it scared him, but his personal choices about how to feel were also made for him. He remained perfectly calm.

The interlude while the prisoners were swapped lasted about three minutes, time Shaw spent in prayer or meditation. Kyle spent it trying to think about resisting Shaw's control, which proved quite difficult. He could consider hypothetical escapes involving hypothetical people, but not himself.

Two guards entered the room, with Fin between them, bound, hooded, and cooperating meekly. Kyle knew the meekness masked a low cunning. Moreover, he knew Fin's eyes were open.

The reverend nodded and the hood was removed.

Fin was staring into Shaw's beatific face, his own features blank but a storm lurking in his eyes. A second passed, and Fin cracked an incredulous grin. He convulsed with suppressed laughter, shaking his head. Kyle struggled with a silly smile that kept climbing onto his face despite his determination to look professional. Shaw sat patiently while Fin got the giggles out of his system, but his serenity seemed forced.

Fin composed himself and said, "It's an honor to meet you, Reverend."

Shaw replied guardedly, "Thank you, young man. Please take a seat."

"I didn't know you had moved on to guerrilla evangelism. Only us few, sad wing nuts left, and the show doesn't reach us? Makes sense I guess..."

"Please do have a seat." The guards leaned on Fin, pressing him into the chair. "How did you know Kyle was involved in the girl's disappearance?"

Fin shot a hostile look at Kyle who sat in his chair like an attentive lap-dog. "Lucky guess."

Kyle felt a bewildering flash of anger, directed at himself.

"You're lying," Shaw stated.

"Not really." Fin smiled. "I gave him the impression there was a witness. It worked." The smile slid away. "Sort of."

"Yes. And now here you are."

"In the clutches of the Holy Carnival Barker."

"I'm doing God's work," Shaw said.

Another reptilian smile appeared on Fin's face. "You wanna know what I think? I think god gives you menial shit jobs to do, to keep you out of his hair. He doesn't have the heart to tell you you're not as cool as his other zealots."

"You can't shake my faith. You must realize that?"

"Don't tell me what I can't do. Besides, faith, insanity. Tomato, toe-mah-toe."

"Let me tell you what I see," said Shaw calmly. "I see a bitter young man. His bitterness makes his world a dark, loveless place. Because the world is dark to him, he assumes it is also dark to everyone else. He thinks the darkness is truly real."

Fin smiled easily. "You only have me here right now because I risked my life for Rook. Who you kidnapped, by the way."

Kyle felt unaccountably worried about Rook. He knew perfectly well where she was, but the feeling persisted regardless. Shaw flicked him an irritated glance.

Fin went on, "I see a violent old man who projects his self-loathing onto younger people and feels compelled to interfere in their happiness."

Shaw didn't mind being judged. It seemed he might smile. "I refer to God's love, of course, not your addiction to sin, your lust." The guards stepped back and exited the room like sleepwalkers. "Recklessness is no proof of love, and you obviously aren't happy."

"Confinement makes that tough. I'd be very happy, fucking ecstatic, if you'd let me go."

Shaw held his impassive expression and continued to stare at Fin. "Release is what we all seek, but right now, you couldn't possibly escape. You are bound, and under guard. This building is well-stocked with mercenaries. And remote. Where will you run? Miles of empty countryside lay in all directions. There is no urgent reason to flee, anyway. The continent still drifts no matter where on it you might be. The —"

Fin crossed his eyes and sneered. Shaw's eyes widened slightly as he stopped speaking. He blinked and swallowed. Fin smirked. "You were saying? Something monotonous and pedantic."

"Cooperate. You will in the end anyway."

"Uh, I think your prophetic faculties have let you down on that one."

"Have they." Shaw's face and voice were icy. He didn't move or blink, but he became a crushing, smothering presence all over Fin. A coiling constrictor, heavy, oppressive, insinuating.

The world capsized, plunging Kyle into howling chaos. He couldn't scream. He was drowning. The undertow lashed him upon the bottom

and wrenched him through an invisible fissure. Lacerated and wrung
dry, he gave a start at the sudden eerie silence.

What could be worse than the inside of Fin's head?

It looked every bit as unpleasant as Kyle expected. Steam vents
hissed all around the landscape of barren rock and twisted lifeless trees.
The heavy sky glowed an ominous overcast orange. As Shaw focused his
attention on different aspects, Kyle's was focused also. He picked up on
Shaw's interpretation of their surroundings. An alien planet. Shaw
thought he understood what it meant, but Kyle feared he was wrong.
Whatever things might mean somewhere else, they surely wouldn't
mean here.

A vicious, hot wind buffeted Kyle. Shaw glanced back and chuckled.
"This is a lesson I never meant to give you, but I can always wipe your
memory later."

They traversed a spine of oily black rock with a steep drop on each
side. Kyle paid meticulous attention to every step he took on the slick,
uneven surface. To the left a tar pit roiled, inimical and glossy. To the
right were several glimmering pools of water, their bottoms coated with
brightly colored minerals and their surfaces reflecting the glare of the
sky.

Shaw muttered distractedly that some of the pollution was drugs,
but not all of it. He concentrated on something for a moment and his
grasp on Kyle weakened. Horrified, Kyle envisioned himself left behind.
Shaw might not know as much as he thought he did, but he remained
Kyle's best chance of survival. He followed Shaw like a wary, distant
shadow.

The first order of business would be to locate the center.

This thought felt so reasonable and natural that at first Kyle
presumed it had been his own. Shaw halted, as if waiting for Kyle to
show the way, and Kyle realized Shaw had provided that knowledge as
part of this tutorial on ransacking someone's mind. Kyle looked in every
direction, but it wasn't obvious to him that this bleak place would even
have a center. The reverend smirked and suddenly Kyle could feel which

way to go.

The second order of business, thought Shaw, is the shortcut. With that, their surroundings fast-forwarded away, leaving Kyle with flickering half-seen impressions of a rugged journey. Shaw didn't share how to do that trick.

Kyle's initial disgust at the idea of entering Fin's mind had given way to eagerness to learn all Shaw's secrets. If he learned enough, maybe he could hang on to some of it when Shaw tried to erase it later.

The landscape went to dunes, every direction uphill. Glassy outcroppings hindered their progress and Shaw stopped to survey. Kyle felt the sand shifting under them. The valley deepened and steepened. The dunes rose and merged with the orange sky. Kyle looked to Shaw for an explanation or reassurance. Shaw gave neither.

The gully continued to deepen, becoming a ravine and then an open mine. The deeper the hole became, the darker it got, and the wetter the sand.

Kyle could feel it under his nails, could see the mound growing beside the hole, felt the summer breeze stirring childhood memories. Soon he would reach packed soil and clay, elementally cool to the touch. He could smell it already.

As they sank deeper into the pit, Kyle sank into Fin's memories. He realized that some of Fin had been bleeding through even before Shaw dragged him in here. In here, it was far more intense. Kyle recognized the park, remembered walking up to that sandbox. He recalled meeting Fin for the first time, unaware that they were brothers. Fin's memory engulfed him.

The hole was big enough to sit in now. He was happy inside his hole. Digging was satisfying. The hole need serve no other purpose.

He looked up at the boy beside the sandbox. A stranger, really. They were the same size, but didn't go to the same school.

"Fin," the boy said, "my dad says you have to leave soon. He asked where you are."

The damp mixture of clay and sand binds exceptionally well. At the bottom of the hole is the magic spot to build a castle with this magic mud. There is also magic in words, so as he sits in the hole, building, he speaks. He speaks Fin's words.

"Here is the tower. It's where my dad lives. He's a wizard, and he keeps everybody safe. He can't leave the castle or the dust trolls will win the war."

The sandcastle responded to all this magic. Mysterious flickering lights moved about in the scratched-on windows. The tower had a proper flat top ringed with lumpy battlements. The spell of building and speaking was nearly complete. He spoke the final words, "This is my daddy's house."

The other boy smiled dully and jumped down into the hole. Evil sneakers annihilated the beautiful castle.

The hole became utterly black.

Kyle's pulse raced. The bleed-through left him trying to shake off lingering hatred for the 'other boy.' Actual anger at himself for being vulnerable to such a juvenile grudge mingled with the borrowed animosity, and he got mad at Fin. Such a prick, still pissy about something that happened when they were five years old.

Before him loomed a slouching fortress of mud and sand, revealed at the bottom of the mineshaft.

Shaw surveyed the structure. He approached it slowly, dragging Kyle along and sending him reassuring vibes as he explained what they were looking at.

"At the core of every mind is a structure, its architecture showing the fundamental nature of the personality. It is the personality." Shaw paused, and among his good vibrations Kyle picked up that this was the first sandcastle he'd encountered. "No matter its appearance, there are rules about these things. Rules I know how to break. And because the core structure also houses the main repository of a person's knowledge and beliefs, this is where I will get the answers this prisoner refused to give up willingly."

They passed through the doorway.

Chapter Ten

LAVA

Abel and Seth Shaw married their cousins, Mary and Rebekah, and fled the influences of society. Intermarriage between their offspring being encouraged, the population grew. Shaw Oracle is remote now, 50 years after it was abandoned by its sole surviving inhabitant. I can only imagine the world unto itself it would have been to him, let alone when it was founded in 1851, eight years before Blessed.

My extensive on-site research has provided me invaluable insight into the previously unexamined early life and religious education of Brian Shaw. In a setting so isolated, any aberrant interpretation of scripture would be carried, perhaps amplified, for generations. It is unclear what the exact beliefs of Shaw Oracle were, but they were definitely as inbred as the inhabitants.

from *Brainwashed* by Julie Rome ©1998 Futhark Press

As Kyle followed Shaw into the sandcastle at the core of Fin's mind, a portcullis of interwoven steel thistle leaves engaged to block their escape, ringing like swords driven through solid stone, not the cell-door clank Kyle anticipated. Why had it closed behind them?

Shaw kept moving forward, into the center of the single circular room that made up the ground floor. The walls and floor were basalt, and only the cruel latticework of the portcullis let any light into the chamber.

A length of thin rope lay strewn on the floor. The ceiling was rough beams and the planks of the floor above, with dust sifting down through the copious gaps. A trapdoor near the opposite side of the room drew Shaw, and a rope ladder unspooled upon his arrival. They proceeded to the second level.

This circular chamber had less illumination, gaining light only from a single arrow slit and the pittance that filtered up in exchange for dust through the cracks in the floor. A massive wooden table sat alone in the center of the room. It had exquisite carved dragons running up the legs, hideous talon feet, and sculpted folds and tassels like a rich, heavy cloth thrown over it, all fashioned from a single piece of wood. A sorcerer's table.

Upon it rested an unfurled scroll, a tall, slender candle, and a layer of dust over an inch thick. Shaw approached the table. He shook the dust off the scroll but couldn't read it in the dim light.

Before Shaw could light the candle, the swirls of dust he'd disturbed coalesced into a ratlike creature about four feet long, which lunged onto the table and made off with the candlestick. As Shaw checked that there weren't more popping up, the beast dove through the trapdoor. "A mental antibody of sorts," Shaw said. "We're foreign to this psyche, so we're triggering its immune system." Shaw took the scroll to the minuscule window.

Low panic crept over Kyle. Through his newfound symbiosis with Fin he had gained more autonomy and could decide for himself where to stray. A growling horde of dust trolls swarmed on the lower level, visible through the cracks in the floor. Shouldn't Shaw be trying harder not to trigger the immune system, given what a self-destructive fuck-up Fin was?

Shaw read, "Away too long, and the land is lost. Dust trolls take the castle too, as I've no longer any taste for war."

He snapped his full attention onto Kyle, gouging for an explanation. "How do you know what those creatures are called?" Kyle didn't understand either, something Shaw was reluctant to accept. Crushing pressure forced Kyle onto his knees. His limbs sagged and an invisible elephant stood on his chest. "Tell me what you know about this prisoner, and how much he knows about you," Shaw demanded. Kyle could only shake his head. That made Shaw look even more cross, so

Kyle nodded instead. The pressure in his chest slacked enough for speech.

"He's just a druggie," Kyle gasped. "He's always been a shit. If you think I'll try to protect him, you're wrong. So what if he's my brother, I work for you."

Shaw released him, smiling. "I knew there was something, felt you absorbing knowledge from your surroundings. I knew you were exploiting some secret connection. I don't blame you for keeping it to yourself, but nothing remains hidden from me." Turning, he added, "I'm not concerned about this mind's defense measures because I have an escape plan. You don't."

Shaw walked off to study one of the four massive chains that extended up the wall toward the distant ceiling, blending into darkness. Shortly he moved counterclockwise to the next one.

Kyle went to the scroll and spread it out flat. A second message, clearly Fin's handwriting, read, *Pardon all the childish fantasy melodrama down here. Head up to the roof for some real Revelations.*

Kyle checked on the dust trolls again, and saw some making a fuss over the candlestick while others did something with the rope. Light flashed up through the floor as a dust troll applied the lit candle to the frayed end. The light of the flames drove the dust trolls to the edges of the room, showing Kyle the rope's tortuous loops. The other end was inserted into the center of the floor. It burned with an angry, hissing shower of sparks.

Shaw reached the fourth chain. Whatever he'd done at the other three he did there as well, and a convulsion shook the floor. With loud ratcheting sounds, the floor began to rise.

The ride up was slow, bone-shaking and dusty. As they neared the top, another trapdoor presented itself, with a rope ladder waiting.

Kyle and Shaw climbed up onto the tower's flat roof.

Battlements like massive tombstones loomed all around. Like tombstones, they were inscribed. Kyle approached one of them with Shaw. It read, *Divided Seed shall a Divided Child Beget, who will grow into a Divided Man.*

To Kyle, the verse sounded like something from the bible.

Distress emanated from Shaw. Kyle, bathed in the reverend's confusion, began to see its cause. The words did not come from the bible. Shaw had written them.

Finding his New Revelations being excerpted here obviously rocked Shaw. Kyle looked at a few other stones. One laid out the mothers' journey into shadows, the next described the father's trials and punishment for dividing his seed, and the next told of a 'Completer' who could heal the Divided Man. The tone implied strongly that this healing was significant to the fate of the world.

Kyle recalled the trolls below, and went to the trapdoor. Straining for some clear impression of how much of the fuse remained, he caught a glimmer of its combustion near the center point.

"It's you!" Shaw cried. "You and your brother! Just as it was shown to me!" The reverend's face was an ecstatic grimace. He spun around with arms uplifted, weeping and laughing.

Kyle couldn't make sense of Shaw's words, and right then he didn't care. This was the worst place they could possibly stand, so he fled the roof in the most direct way — out between the battlements. As he reeled and tumbled beside the tower he felt a shockwave. An instant later, searing molten rock shot up in a glowing shaft that obliterated the roof. Geysers of lava spewed out the arrow slit and raged over the ledges between the battlements.

Kyle fell, and the bright stream of lava shot up and out of sight into the heavy clouds like some infernal beanstalk. Cracks radiated from the base of the tower, and lava seethed and splashed in them. Large chunks of ground broke free and capsized into the orange melt. The fissures extended in a throbbing web to every horizon.

Something different fell too, limp and broken but somehow alive. Kyle didn't know what it was, but he knew it was not of this place. He latched on.

A dove.

It struggled, but Kyle gripped it tenaciously. They spun downward together and as they met the churning surface of the lava the dove found its strength for a moment. It gave a twisting spasm and seemed to unroll. It vanished in a burst of white flame that left a circular mark on the lava's surface, through which Kyle plunged.

***

Kyle heard faint church music. He hesitantly surveyed his surroundings. No lava. Bright blue sky, rolling green hills, a quaint little country church perched on a nearby rise, but mainly no lava. No searing, no choking, no blinding. A pleasant spot.

The diametrically different settings and their conformance to Christian doctrine were not lost, even on Kyle, and he spent some time musing on the possibility he had died and gone to heaven, with a stopover in hell.

The music came from the church. Kyle approached the small building warily. Something about the idyllic scenery didn't look right. A moment of reorientation showed Kyle that was because it wasn't real. It was painted on a screen. The bottom edge mated imperfectly to the ground, and he could trace that edge in a complete circle about one hundred feet in diameter. Now he lifted the edge a bit and looked behind it.

Foreboding and dark, a gray world filled with tombstones. He could see the side of the church, a soaring stone wall with severe narrow windows, and buttresses like a spider's legs. Its entrance jutted up against the barrier.

Kyle lowered the scrim back into place and went to the door of the cutesy little church. The door was real — weathered gray wood. He opened it.

The music was immediately louder. Inside, the church was far larger than the clapboard structure on the little hill. It was the mammoth cathedral hidden by the scrim. Kyle felt some uneasiness about entering.

He'd crossed from Fin's mind into Shaw's. Pausing now in the doorway to this imposing place, his thoughts raced. The cold stone was ominously reminiscent of the core structure in Fin's mind.

Emboldened by the notion of Shaw stranded in that hellish wasteland, Kyle entered the building. Moving deeper into the stillness of the cold church, he wondered if he would find anything worth stealing.

A central aisle the length of a football field led down to the altar, and the illuminated ceiling soared about the same distance overhead. Paintings of gleaming cloudscapes inhabited by sternly bearded men in robes covered the whole ceiling. Gold leaf and hidden candles gave the vaulted structure a lavish glow.

The pews were an orderly sea with motionless wooden waves. They made Kyle feel like an intruder. It wasn't hard to imagine acres of deathly pale disapproving faces tracking his movements. He kept his attention fixed ahead.

Beyond the pulpit and the altar rose a loft twice the area of any church Kyle had ever been in. The choir, had there been one, would have been up there, with the organ.

The pipes defied numbers, the largest big enough for a couple to dance inside of, the smallest as fine as a hair. The music playing now was soft and soothing, but the console displayed more than a hint of menace.

He passed the pulpit. Upon it rested a bible, in outlandish proportions suitable for this place. Kyle began flipping pages at random. Whatever inconsistencies might exist between this bible and the version Gideon put in all the hotels would be telling, but he would have no idea if there were any differences. He wasn't even sure he'd notice modified commandments, basic stuff. Ten of those, right? Are they even listed out in the bible itself?

After glancing at pages in various parts of the good book, Kyle noticed where he stood. The view over the pulpit woke some part of him. He'd been keeping off to the side, but now boldly assumed the position on the riser and surveyed the ranks of vacant pews. From here they didn't look so scary. From here, some of the stuff in the big book made sense. Arrayed down either side of the chamber he now noticed the windows. They were set slantwise to the sweep of the outer wall, so only from the front of the sanctuary could they all be seen. They were sumptuously colorful, a tapestry of light spread across the whole church. Certain characters recurred in nearly all of the twenty-four windows. They told the Divided Man's story. Kyle could almost decipher it.

He flipped to the inside front cover of the bible. He didn't know what one would traditionally find there, but probably not an organizational chart. That's what was here, with names and titles handwritten into pre-printed spaces, connected like a family tree.

Now that was holy scripture for which Kyle could see some practical value. There at the top sat Brian Shaw, with the core of his empire explained in relation to him. The chart illustrated also how Shaw held control, in part by keeping the right hand from knowing what the left was doing. A unique and powerful document.

Kyle peeled the chart from the backing of the cover and tucked it away for safekeeping.

Kyle surveyed the gaudy immensity of the place, getting better at reading it. It all meant something, like the organizational chart in the bible. All of it related to Shaw's life in one way or another.

An elaborate candle rack off to the left — locations of other hidden facilities in five states. The baptismal font on the opposite side — financial resources of the television ministry. Hanging on a peg inside the pulpit, a real find — a string of beads with a cross. The beads were talismans to illuminate the powers of the mind, powers Shaw spent many years learning.

Upon the cross Kyle discovered something disturbing.

There, where even a heathen like Kyle knew to expect Christ in his agonies, he saw a small effigy of himself.

The impact it had was unaccountable, but overwhelming. Revulsion over the blasphemy, or heresy, or whatever, competed with a profound sense of elevation. Toward the part of himself that lay there helpless he felt only ambivalence. It was weak, like a quivering organ, something unfit to touch in its vulnerability. It allowed Shaw to control and bind him. Kyle knew, had he not found it, he could never have left this place.

Kyle was unable to act, unable to find purchase in the quicksand of his mind. Suddenly, the hideous little doll rolled its eyes up to stare right at him, pleading, and he had a moment of clarity. He might not need this aspect of himself, so long as no one else held it either. It was repugnant, all the things he'd worked hardest to eradicate anyway.

Using the effigy as a mallet, he pounded savagely against the pulpit. Smashing, scraping, grinding, until the cross was vacant. The agony of the process brought a twisted comfort, like scratching open an infected sore.

Handling the beads filled Kyle with shadowy hints about his own latent mental abilities and made him impatient to experiment with them. He moved purposefully toward the exit of the church.

The wall switch looked glaringly mundane in this place, but its symbolism was clear to Kyle now. On and Off, Life and Death. On his way out, he flipped the switch, snuffing all the candles and plunging the cathedral into blackness.

*** *** ***

At least this time she hadn't been drugged or undressed. So far.

This would be a hell of a story if she lived to write it. First the weirdoes with the sweaters and the foil, now this nut-case TV preacher.

Rook's prison crate was stuffy, and Fin's jeans were a suffocating reminder of why she'd sworn off pants years ago. She refused to take her leather jacket off and risk losing it in the dark, which meant she was stuck being uncomfortable in addition to being a prisoner.

This predicament had something to do with the spaceship dream. That's what she'd been talking about with Fin at the Shamrock Diner, right before her first kidnapping. Someone must have been listening. She couldn't remember anyone with a cellphone, or leaving suddenly, or paying any attention to them. How could she call herself an investigative reporter? For all she knew, Fin had been grabbed as well. Maybe he was in the crate beside hers.

Why couldn't things be simple? Her first inclination had been to use Fin simply to escape Marcus, and it surprised her to find there was more to it now. They were the only people who could hear Vesuvius. That had to count for something, right? They had a lot of fun together, kidnappings aside. If only they could get away from the world, they could go on having fun and talking to light fixtures, see how long it lasted.

For that to happen, Rook knew, she needed to understand what was going on. The knowledge would give them power over their enemies.

Fuck, I sound like Marcus.

When exactly should she have caught on that Kyle was full of shit? He'd told her Fin called. Believable. He'd told her Fin was at the hospital. That's why she hadn't been very alert, worrying about Fin. She now chose not to believe that part of Kyle's story. Fin was fine, somewhere safe, worrying about her. Or possibly in the other crate, worrying about her.

In the Jeep, Kyle laid his arm casually across the back of her seat when he wasn't shifting gears. Rook had been relaxing a bit until a cop directed them onto a detour. Catching a glimpse of the rubble and fire engines where the *Sycamore* building should have been started her worrying again, close to tears. She didn't know why Fin might have gone to work after witnessing her kidnapping, but, well, what else could he do?

The Jeep's top and doors were off, the wind biting. Kyle acted jittery, glancing around a lot and drumming his fingers on the steering wheel.

"Hope I'm not making you nervous," she said.

"It's not you. I'm wondering what's up with Fin."

"I'm surprised. I didn't get the impression you liked each other."

"We don't. But we are brothers, after all."

That threw her. She sat in silence and studied him in the flickering illumination of the streetlights. "I can see the resemblance now," she said finally. "You have the same eyes. The same color," she added hastily.

"Fin didn't tell you. I'm not surprised. He's always resented me."
Kyle shifted gears roughly. "We're half-brothers."

They were entering a part of town unfamiliar to Rook, since she'd
never had reason to go to the hospital in Webster.

The traffic eased somewhat and Kyle continued his tale.

"We were born the same day and we have the same dad. Fin likes to
say we're half-twins. Anyway, Dad chose to marry my mom, not his. Fin
never got over it."

Rook didn't know what to say.

Kyle glanced over. "When we were thirteen, Willow — that's Fin's
mom — Willow disappeared and Fin moved in with my family."

"What do you mean, she disappeared?"

"Well, Fin doesn't talk about it, and I wasn't told much at the time.
Just, Willow went away. Left him with some hippie friends of hers.
Never came back. After something like two or three weeks these friends
finally reported her missing. Nobody ever found anything out."

"Oh, how horrible!" Rook told herself her tears were from the
freezing wind. Fin was at the hospital, but he was fine.

"So, he moved in with us and was a major disrupting influence. My
folks separated for a while. I hated him for that. My mom came back
though."

Rook thought hateful things about Kyle, staring at him. He kept his
eyes on the road, only occasionally glancing at her.

Eventually Kyle continued, "Fin refuses to believe Willow ran off.
He also refuses to think she died. He's in denial. I feel sorry for him."

Rook was about to tell him what she thought of his pity when Kyle
slowed and signaled a turn. She looked out the window, expecting the
hospital, but saw a factory.

"What the fuck?"

She had her seat belt unbuckled before Kyle grabbed her by the hair.
He got a solid fistful close to the scalp and yanked her back into her
seat.

"You've been so cooperative so far. Don't make it hard on yourself now."

A chain link gate rolled closed behind them. As they approached the factory, a garage door rumbled up and Kyle drove in.

Kyle relaxed his grip on her hair, produced a handgun, and ordered her out of the Jeep as the door clanked shut behind them. Looking out, Rook saw six or seven men, a few of whom wielded automatic weapons.

Mechanically Rook stepped out. This wasn't happening. Kidnapped twice in one day. Kyle walked around the Jeep and took her by the arm. He leaned in close and spoke quietly, but firmly, into her ear.

"Everything I told you is true. I want you to know what a loser my brother is. And I want you to know I can make it easier for you here."

Then he'd kissed her. She bit his tongue, her stomach fluttering with fear even as her nipples and crotch tingled. Ignoring the nip, he let the kiss linger. When he finally stopped, she spat on the floor and wiped her mouth on the back of her hand. Kyle, then his friends, laughed. She couldn't muster any resistance as they tossed her into the green metal cargo crate.

She'd been taken to meet Shaw. He was full of righteous bullshit, but did seem to mean it. Rook found it almost impossible to believe he would actually hurt her. She was not naive. She knew all sorts of horrible things were done in the name of religion, and that all sorts of perverts used the church as a cover. Shaw didn't strike her as that sort of zealot.

Maybe she was an experiment in the outreach program all the late night comedians were joking about. Shaw had made statements about his message reaching the unreachable flotsam of society: biker gangs, drug addicts, college students. He alluded to a breakthrough that would bring them the word of god. Nobody knew what the hell he was talking about, but it made great joke fodder. That coupled with the lump-sum payment to the IRS kept everyone laughing for weeks.

Rook had a hard time remembering specifics from her conversation with the reverend. That felt very odd, and got her trying to dig things up. The harder she strained, the farther out of reach it all seemed, dim and waterlogged.

Rook's speculation was interrupted when the crate suddenly started throbbing and vibrating. Horrendous subsonics made thought impossible. Her eyes thrummed. She stood and lurched away from the wall, into the center of the crate, but it didn't help. Shouting, and a few gunshots, terrified her. Who was shooting? At whom? What the fuck was the throbbing hum making her joints feel loose, like her period was coming early?

She thought about yelling, or pounding on the walls, but what good would it do? Would anyone hear her? Would she want them to? She didn't want to be remembered with the factory under attack, but she also didn't want to be forgotten.

Rook curled up in the fetal position as the subsonic pulsing consumed her.

Chapter Eleven

FACTORY

Technical Memorandum - Perceptual Disruption Field (PDF)
Field tests have been completed on the prototype PDF Generator.
Subject responses are summarized:
Confusion*: Subjects were unable to interact rationally with each*
other or their surroundings, due to the PDF's amplification of
pattern-seeking filters rooted in the limbic system.
Disorientation*: The PDF makes it impossible for inner-ear data*
to be integrated with visual impulses, and it severs the connection
between the right and left sense organs (eyes, ears).
Shielding*: The specially calibrated transceiver successfully*
protected subject #4, who reported it was possible to tell something
was going on, but there was no impairment. The transceiver's field
extends several feet, and more tests could determine the tactical
value of this.

Kyle gingerly reclaimed the thing he'd called 'self' and found it no longer entirely suited him. The realization that his mind contained layers and portents, that the part he was familiar with was merely a thin overlay, frightened him.

The external moment quickly engulfed all such introspection. He sat in the office of a powerful man he'd just murdered, with a catatonic miscreant brother for companionship, a skull full of stolen knowledge, and dozens of schemes to exploit it.

Reaching over to Fin, he confirmed the presence of a pulse. Good. Shaw had seen Fin as an important figure, and Kyle intended to go back inside and find out why. It would also be handy to have a familiar, if bizarre, mind to practice on.

He stepped up to the desk, where the reverend lay slumped with his eyes open. The body was obviously lifeless, as Kyle knew without checking. He'd assured that as he'd departed the cathedral.

The eyes were unnerving.

Could Shaw be trapped inside Fin's head? No. The plundered understanding, Shaw's own extensive research, indicated it didn't work that way.

Trying to sneak away from the corpse would be foolhardy, especially if he was going to drag Fin along. If he escaped, there would be awkward questions when he tried to make a claim as successor. Perhaps the best use for Fin was to frame him for Shaw's demise, although it seemed a waste.

The lights went out.

Brusque *what the fucks* from the mercs in the hallway switched, sans segue, to howling and screaming. The emergency lights flickered on and pulsed weakly as the building began to vibrate. Kyle knew instantly this was an attack, and by whom, because Shaw dreaded this very possibility. The TEF. These were Gregory's people. Gregory, a spy planted in Shaw's office, a man whose disappearance did less to discourage his organization than the reverend had hoped.

With darkened chaos reigning, Kyle felt sure he could in fact sneak out, and what's more when he resurfaced he could easily hold power. Shaw's death would be as much of a mystery to Kyle as to everyone else. Fin could come along, and they'd do some more brotherly bonding. For that matter, the girl could come too, and they'd all ride off in style in Shaw's big car. Executive privilege.

He picked Fin up by the armpits and dragged him to the door. Isolated gunfire punctuated the sonic goulash. Kyle set Fin down to check on conditions outside Shaw's office, opening the door. Nobody in evidence.

Kyle debated flinging Fin down the stairs, but decided not to risk catastrophic injury. No point dragging him out of the office just to toss him down a flight of stairs. Right? He kept the debate going for a minute and persuaded himself he wanted Fin intact, for now.

Kyle had to back down the steps to keep from tripping over his limp burden. This made him nervous, but he only encountered one person before he reached the bottom. One of the mercs, a career soldier of fortune named Hawkins, busted up and trying to stand. The twitching limbs and facial contusions were alarming, but Kyle fought panic and forced himself to study the man. The cause of the injuries was not a beating, but repeated falls down the metal steps. The panic backed off, but a nagging anxiety took its place. The knowledge he'd stolen from Shaw included little about how the psychotropic effects of the jewelry worked, what it was all these technicians were up to. Was this not an attack after all, but a meltdown?

At the bottom, Kyle turned toward the improvised detention area. Which, as luck would have it, was away from all the yelling and the gunshots. He was in no mood to see how long his apparent immunity to the chaos would last. He wanted to get the girl and get out.

Fin would be a liability in dealing with Rook. She would get flighty, and with Kyle encumbered she might jump him. Assuming she wasn't delirious or drowning in her own drool. He opted to leave Fin on the floor and go to the next chamber for Rook. With her under control, he could come back this way to collect Fin and exit the building.

Kyle paced from his brother, at the bottom of the stairs, over to the door. The mass of ugly noises worsened, and he thought he saw signs of stirring from Fin. Three times he went back and prodded the unresponsive body, getting angry at himself and at Fin. He couldn't afford to waste any more time.

Resolved to get moving, Kyle went to the door a fourth time. Movement in the shadows near some ancient shelves made him reach for his gun. He dropped into a crouch and scanned that corner of the room, seeing no one. Blinking sweat out of his eyes, he scanned the whole room. He couldn't find anyone other than Fin, but his peripheral vision was infested with lurking assassins.

Now desperate to escape this room, Kyle yanked open the door and staggered out into the cavernous garage.

Here, too, things were shadowy and saturated with caustic noise.

Christ, Kyle thought, this is like one of Fin's band's rehearsals.

Kyle lurched toward the hulking green container where Rook was imprisoned. The floor kept shaking, getting worse. It was all getting worse. Soon he had to stop because of the floor's violent pitching.

This couldn't really be happening. The building wouldn't withstand it, for one thing. He had to put mind over matter and walk to the crate.

It was like trying to walk on a sagging bed sheet. He fell, landing on the treacherous concrete with a sensation like being doused with ice water. Aware he could be seriously hurt, Kyle chose to crawl. The hard dampness against his palms tasted green in his left hand, beige in his right. The floor hadn't stopped its undulations, and even on all fours Kyle was unsteady. The room flipped completely and Kyle fancied centrifugal force splayed him on the cement.

He threw up, managing to lift his face first. The small puddle whispered in conspiratorial odors that it would go in search of a spirit guide for him. Then it left.

Kyle looked ahead. The container wasn't there. The thing was thirty feet long and green — how could he lose it? All he saw were shadows and darker shadows. When he tried to focus on anything, the vague areas of light and dark swam together into enormous faces. None of them looked happy. Ghostly Easter Island heads surrounded him, all shrieking and howling and gibbering. He was unable to rise because the floor wouldn't hold still.

Kyle remembered a time when he decided to be civil toward Fin in exchange for decent weed. Of course the bag was laced, with what he never did find out, and that was the end of civility between the Tanner brothers. Kyle was now glad that happened, because the harrowing effects of the augmented joint gave him some basis to understand how he might survive what was happening now. A narrow ledge along which he could skirt the abyss.

He made a decision. The container was that way. He would drag himself until he reached it. No matter that he couldn't see it. It was there. He would get there.

***

Kyle pulled himself upright, clinging to the cold, vibrating steel. It was solid and real, and the most comforting thing he'd ever felt, even if it was trying to shake his fillings loose. He leaned there, with his cheek against the crate, coming back to himself a bit.

Gradually, he remembered he had come there for a reason. Kyle felt almost steady now, so he pulled the lever and swung the door open.

The girl lay curled in a ball in the center. A second after the door opened, so did her eyes. She tilted her head up and shot a defiant look. Kyle now felt even better. He smiled.

She gave him the finger.

Well, given the manner of her arrival it was unlikely she'd be so easily charmed. Still smiling, Kyle extended his right hand and said, "Time to choose. Coming with me, or dying in here? And I'm in a hurry."

She scowled as she stood. Squinting in the half light, she walked toward Kyle, but stopped about four feet before his outstretched hand and said, "Where are you going?"

Kyle was proud of himself for not reacting angrily. "I'm heading to the top of the food chain. Taking a short cut I just learned about. You're invited."

"I wouldn't want to appear ungrateful," she replied, "but why? I barely know you."

"You know me well enough. I'm shallow. No mysteries."

"Now that's not true at all..." She looked away.

Kyle took a step into the crate and Rook retreated. He smiled and she glared. More than sibling rivalry, more than lust, was at work in him. The closer he drew to Rook, the less all the chaos and sporadic gunfire mattered. His disorientation abated the moment he released her. He moved another step and she held her ground, looking vulnerable and terribly unhappy.

"You're a puppet," she said, "and I don't like who's pulling your strings."

Kyle chuckled. "Not anymore. I got my wish, killed Geppetto, and now I'm a real boy."

"Fin's a real man. You should be careful what you wish for." She tried to push past. Kyle barred her way and tried to snare her. She tore away and sulked back to the recesses of the container. "Fine. I'll stay here. Fuck off."

"No," Kyle said, "you missed your chance to choose. And we really do need to get moving." He withdrew from the crate and took several deep breaths. Recalling the feel of the string of beads he'd found in Shaw's mental cathedral, he focused his will and said, in the most forceful voice he owned, "Come with me now!"

She advanced hesitantly. Her movements were robotic, her face drowsy. Kyle waited by the door, impatient to leave, eager to spend time alone with Rook.

At last she came within reach, and Kyle seized her wrist without a struggle. She continued to glide forward, then suddenly kneed him in the stomach, obviously higher than she'd planned, grabbed his arm in both hands and pulled hard. Kyle tumbled into the prison, thinking he'd need some serious practice with this mental shit. She shoved the door. It was heavy and moved slowly, giving Kyle time to brace a foot against it.

Rook lunged to the other container and pulled the lever, probably assuming any other prisoners would be her allies. The door unlatched and moved open about an inch. Kyle snagged her.

He had his arms around her from behind, and held his pistol in his right hand. Bending, he rested his cheek against her neck. She shuddered, but relaxed against his body.

"That almost worked, didn't it?" he asked.

"Not even close," she said, "but I felt... something."

Placing the muzzle of the gun in the hollow of her jaw, he smoothly turned her to face him. With the gun still in place he bent forward and kissed her. She made no reaction. He stopped and backed up a step, pointing the gun at her forehead. She licked her lips.

It might have been fear, but it looked like something different. Her hard little nipples poked through her thin, baggy t-shirt. Kyle stepped up to her and lowered the gun to his side. She didn't move. He kissed her again, and she still didn't kiss back, but she made a tiny noise.

The door of the second prison container had drifted halfway open. Kyle noticed it peripherally and rolled his eyes that way. He saw Marcus standing in the doorway, his restraints in a heap behind him and murder in his eyes. Rook, eyes closed, lifted her left hand uncertainly.

Kyle swung the pistol toward Marcus, who sprang and landed a powerful blow on Kyle's forearm, knocking the gun free.

Marcus's momentum bore him into Rook, whom he enfolded and carried a step with him. The gun skittered past the crates, sprouting crab-like legs. Kyle limped and stumbled after it.

*** *** ***

Marcus took Rook's face roughly between his hands and glared at her.

"Filthy slut!" he shouted, and kissed her. He was gone before she knew if she was kissing him back.

Kyle reached the pistol, and struggled to stand up with it. Rook stared in confused fear. Marcus crossed the distance to Kyle in three bounding strides and tackled him. Kyle's varsity days were fresh enough in his muscle-memory to save him from a skull fracture.

A short volley of gunshots echoed sharply from another room. Rook cringed and looked around for a way out.

The only exterior door she saw was the big garage door.

As the men rolled across the cement, they traded more-or-less ineffectual, though ruthless, elbow smashes and jabs. Rook backed quickly away in the direction of the closed receiving door. Who should she root for? Either way she was in deep shit with the winner. Best to make a break for it while they were distracted.

The feeble emergency lights along the far wall dimmed and the shadows all lurched to the left. Rook's heart thudded painfully.

Kyle and Marcus rolled to a stop. Neither one could land a punch, and it took them several seconds between attempts. What the hell was wrong with them?

Marcus turned away from Kyle and laboriously drew a bead on Rook. She struggled to keep her features composed. Kyle took the opportunity to get up, backpedal, and fall over. When Marcus turned back he was unable to relocate his opponent.

Rook felt exasperated with both of them. If they would keep beating on each other, she might be able to get away from them and whoever was doing the shooting on the other side of the building. She reached the huge overhead door, but couldn't lift it. It must weigh a ton.

Giving up on Kyle, Marcus picked his way over to Rook, avoiding most of the invisible obstacles but falling down twice anyway. As he crossed the last ten feet or so he straightened up and moved without difficulty. Rook shook her head in confusion.

"Hi, little Raven," he murmured. She wanted to defy him, but faltered. In all the chaos and turmoil Marcus was at least something familiar. The day had taken a heavy toll, and it felt like a direct response to her foolish desire for happiness.

Lesson learned, she thought, I'm fucking exhausted.

She permitted Marcus to lay her head against his chest and stroke her hair.

"You've been lost, wandering a land of poison dreams, but it'll be okay now. Your soul will wake up and the nightmare will fade away."

Rook winced at the pseudo-shamanistic bullshit, but maybe Fin was just a dream-being. Thinking about him, and her experiences of the past five minutes, made her feel punished and dirty. She bit her lip and blood welled at the corner of her mouth.

"Now," Marcus said, "we should leave this place." Rook sucked in the blood, and nodded. She half-wished she had surrendered like that when Kyle showed up.

Marcus was unable to lift the garage door either, so Rook felt less incompetent. Even working together they couldn't budge it.

"There must be a control box." Rook scanned the walls.

They were in a large open space with the two cargo containers, a black sedan, and a panel truck from Bud's Appliance Heaven. All the walls were bare cinder block with no windows. A tunnel-like opening had a cloudy, slatted plastic drape hanging across its twenty-foot mouth, making it impossible to see what lay beyond, but that's where the yelling and sounds of struggle came from. Beside it an interior door stood ajar, and let in to a dim room. Maybe the overhead door control was in there.

Rook entered the room and flipped the light switch, which did nothing. The room's single anemic emergency light provided enough illumination for her to make out the shapes of a few tables and chairs, and a shape on the floor by yet another doorway. Her eyes acclimated to the dimly pulsing light and she realized it was a person. Had someone been shot?

Rook rushed over and was simultaneously stunned and horrified to discover it was Fin. She called his name. He was unresponsive, zipped up in something like a cross between a straitjacket and a body bag. What the hell? The reverend must have interrogated him, too, and he had yet to recover.

"Let's go," Marcus said. He grabbed her wrist and pulled her to her feet.

"Carry this guy," she said, pointing to Fin. "He's my friend."

Marcus snorted and dragged her back toward the door they'd come in through.

"Let me go, Marcus." Rook tried to plant her feet, but he pulled her back into the garage area.

Towing Rook by the wrist, Marcus nudged aside the plastic sheeting at the tunnel entrance. The passage led into another, larger, open space. He began edging down the side.

No way was she going to just leave Fin laying there on the floor with all this nasty shit going on, and no way in hell was she going down that hallway to almost certain death. Rook leaned over and bit Marcus's hand. He shook her off, but let go of her wrist, too. She wanted to kick him in the balls, but needed him to carry Fin, so she had to be at least moderately civil.

"I'm not going that way," Rook said. "Let's go get my friend and find the controls for the garage door."

Marcus pounded the block wall with his knuckles, and said, "Fuck. You don't understand, we gotta go. We get out of this place and leave all these people — all of them — and things will be like before."

"Before? You mean when we only had sex to hurt each other? You mean..."

"I mean this is the doorway into our lives as they were meant to be, and you're trying to go the wrong way."

"...that you're full of righteous bullshit and all that matters is that I listen to you, always, and don't talk back. Gee, how could I tear myself away!"

Marcus raised his fist again. This time he was looking at Rook.

Her gaze didn't waver. "You know my real problem? Too many fucking heroes. Hit me, or don't, but don't feed me your warmed-over cosmology and hokey philosophy. Fin is important to me and I'm not leaving him."

"Rook," Marcus growled. He stopped, unflared his nostrils, continued in a softer tone, "I don't want you to lose your way."

"You don't want me to lose your way, which by the way, you don't even know yourself. Let the spirits open a door for you. Just leave me alone." Rook stepped back into the garage area and darted into the dim room where Fin lay in a heap. Marcus cursed under his breath, but didn't follow.

She rushed over to Fin and said his name a few times as she patted his cheeks, trying to bring him around. He had two black eyes, a bandage on his forehead, and another across his nose. She wasn't the only one who'd had a bad day — Fin had been to the hospital. That much of Kyle's story was true, then.

While waiting for Fin to recover from Shaw's hypnotism, or whatever the fuck it was, Rook removed his bindings and held his head in her lap, stroking his forehead and saying his name. After a few minutes she decided she would have to move him, get them out. She kissed his brow and stood.

He was so fucking heavy. Dragging him by his ankles, she moved into the next room, away from the garage. The far side offered two doors to choose from, both with frosted glass windows. One admitted a feeble light. Rook moved toward it.

It opened to the outside where a streetlight buzzed.

She'd have to drag Fin a long way across pavement and wasn't sure either of them would hold up very well.

"Rook..." came a rough voice. She stayed quiet.

"Rook, I came back." It was Marcus.

Rook tongued the swollen place on her lip where she'd bitten it. Marcus came into the room looking haggard.

"The spirits wouldn't lead me out. They led me back to you."

"Whatever. Help me with Fin and let's get the fuck out of here."

***   ***   ***

When Rook said, "Carry him," Marcus didn't object. He narrowed his eyes and weighed his options, but scooped Fin up without a word. Let her think it was the forceful tone of her voice or the icy fire in her eyes. It seemed petty to argue about transporting Fin. After all, his flimsy carcass slowed Rook down and allowed Marcus to find her.

They moved warily out onto the parking lot. Nothing much appeared to be going on outside. There were some dark-colored vans parked near the building, but no signs of life. Rook and Marcus looked around, then at each other to find their next move. Marcus shrugged and the icy fire leapt forth.

"Not this again. You gonna pout now that you can't be in charge? Those guys from *Tattoo Biker* were absolutely right. You can't even draw! You're a hack, and all your shit is," she groped for the words, "is pretentious neo-aboriginal dreck!"

Raven. So good to warm himself again by her fire. "Those *Biker* fuckers are tools! They don't know shit about power markings!"

"And neither do you!" Raven taunted. "You live in denial and bully anyone who points out the realities you ignore."

"Listen to our resident expert on the higher self," Marcus shouted, thoroughly enjoying his fury. "Neglecting her sacred duties, stoned or comatose, except when she's printing lies. I fail to see how your work gives you any basis to judge me."

"At least I realize my whole identity doesn't rest on my work." Her fierce blue eyes shattered the moonlight. "Which is, by the way, more creative and original than yours."

"Original? You're a goddamn tabloid wannabe!"

"My point exactly."

An intense flashlight beam hit Marcus full in the face and they both fell silent. Raven drilled into Marcus with her eyes. She wanted to do the talking. Before Marcus could stop her, she spun around.

"It's you," the man said in a surprised voice. Raven kicked him in the groin.

The man folded and dropped the light, which she grabbed. It was a hefty truncheon-style thing. She raked the beam over him and stopped, looking stunned. He wore a green sweater, not the black commando suit Marcus expected. Marcus could almost hear whatever snapped inside her. The blows she delivered were inefficient, but the man couldn't ward them off. Once he was sprawled on the pavement she paused, breathing heavily.

Marcus still held Fin over his shoulder and hadn't moved since the light appeared. He put his free hand on her shoulder. A calculated risk.

She almost hit him. She stopped herself and took a steadying breath.

"I think he came from the van right here. Come on." Marcus headed over toward the vehicle before he finished speaking and Raven tagged along. The side door was open, revealing a satellite dish aimed at the building.

"Let's take it and get out of here," Marcus dictated, heading around to the driver's side.

"Wait, I don't think that's smart. Too conspicuous."

"So we ditch it and improvise later."

"There are plenty of cars over there that would draw far less attention." She gestured toward the fence. "We should check them out first."

"No time. Let's roll!"

Raven gritted her teeth. "Marcus, look at what's here. Don't you think they'll track it? These are the guys causing all the chaos in there. When we escape, I want it to last more than ten minutes."

He scowled at the twinkling lights and humming electronics crammed into the van, and rolled his eyes toward Raven.

"Please stay with me right now." Her voice, desperate and pleading, was impossible for Marcus to ignore. Raven needed him.

By the third car tension was building again. The attackers had been thorough in disabling the vehicles parked outside. Marcus was on the verge of demanding they take the van when the garage door began opening. The black sedan squealed out when there was barely room for it under the door, its engine roaring as it sped by Raven and Marcus and out through the mangled gate. He caught a glimpse of Kyle in the driver's seat.

Without a word or a look, Raven ran into the garage. Marcus said, "Fuck," under his breath and waited to see what she was planning. She climbed into the cab of the truck and backed out. Marcus chuckled.

While she cut the wheels and fished around for low gear, he tossed Fin into the back and jumped up after.

Chapter Twelve

SANCTUARY

Down South there is a movement to endorse a so-called 'Covenant Marriage,' that would require counseling before marriage and make divorces harder to get. This proves marriage is useless. If it were worthwhile and desirable, would so many people plan for its demise? Covenant Marriage is just the flip side of prenuptial agreements. Both plan for the end, one financially, one emotionally. If you trust your partner, there is no need to plan for the day he or she will stab you in the back.
        from *Useless Artifacts* opinion column by Brandy Moon, *CTP*, 08-25-2000

Marcus sat with his back against the wall of the truck and regarded his companion and rival. Surely he'd never get a better chance to dispose of Fin, and, just as surely would regret it if he passed it up. At the same time it would be unclean to move against his opponent now. Fin's present vulnerability was some other's doing. Besides, he was broken, and might die on his own.

Marcus thought about his last conversation with Fin, right here in this truck. The little shit had been cocky and defiant. He'd also been right. The place did come under attack, allowing the three prisoners to escape, but ironically helping Fin the least.

All of this created a fog around Marcus, rather than helping him see what to do. He could feel the full symptoms of the day's beatings, druggings and other mistreatments. The fatigue and the motion of the truck were pulling him into a physical fog as well.

He drew a deep breath, stretched, and willed himself to sharp attention to call for his spirit guide. He needed a vision. Pushing doubt from his thoughts, he concentrated on the enigma of Fin.

Was he an idiot, like he seemed? Had the clairvoyance been only a weird piece of luck? Or did Fin have powerful medicine and act foolish only so people wouldn't guess? Chaos surrounded him, but did he control it, or it him? Marcus couldn't write him off. There was a chance this was a genuine god, a trickster-god, helpless before him. What kind of trickster would Marcus be if he didn't steal a little of that medicine?

Interrogation at the hands of Shaw accounted for Fin's broken condition. Fin must have resisted, too. Marcus steadied his resolve as he reflexively recoiled from the memory of his own session. The pain was necessary, like the agonizing pangs of the fast while on a vision quest. Push through.

Marcus recalled the way his will had been bent aside and another's reached within his mind. Push. Live in the remembered pain. He bent his own defenses aside, making himself more receptive, listening for the hints to these tricks of the mind. In this state he didn't need to make excuses for being awed by Fin, could hate and admire him simultaneously. He rolled the strange sheath back a bit further, opening up even more than Shaw forced him to, and waited.

Things started slipping wrongward. A new pain terrified Marcus. He considered pushing through it, but only for a millisecond. Stretched like taffy, dizzy, he fell toward some seething gulf, a rip in space. He roused himself from his trance but the pain didn't stop.

Fin was a black hole. His vessel, now emptied, hungrily tried to refill itself. Marcus had reached too close and fallen within the influence of this psychic gravity.

Convulsions wracked Marcus's body, but he remained alert and aware of everything. The attenuation increased, his mind and spirit distorted and unspooling into the void.

Stopping the pull proved impossible. Marcus fought to keep from disappearing into the pit. He lurched to his feet and stared wild-eyed at Fin. He could shove him out of the truck. Maybe that would help.

Doubt froze him. Killing Fin now might be suicide.

Marcus wasn't accustomed to being assailed by fear and doubt. A warrior doesn't feel fear, only anger. A trickster doesn't doubt himself. He was Coyote, creator of the next world. He could not allow himself to falter. No unclean mongrel could sabotage his destiny! A blast of rage surged through him and along the tendril of himself dwindling away into Fin. It made the pain worse, further stoking his anger. Marcus felt on the verge of aneurysm when Fin let go.

Marcus slumped back against the wall, semi-conscious. He had burned off a portion of his mental taffy, but he was free.

The truck slowed and stopped. Marcus looked out and saw a quiet street. The driver's door shut and Raven appeared at the rear gate a moment later. She regarded the men warily. Not his fearless Raven, then. Rook.

"I think I wiped off all my prints up there."

Marcus blinked but didn't move. Rook tilted her head to the left a bit, and said, "How was the ride back here? Nobody fell out, I see."

Marcus let out a heavy breath and climbed down from the truck. Rook hoisted herself up and began wiping the interior surfaces with a balled-up newspaper while Marcus tugged one of Fin's legs. She speeded up her efforts, in order to get over to Fin in time to assist Marcus with lowering him.

They moved down the street, supporting Fin between them. Here in the fraternity district this was unlikely to attract any notice, especially at three in the morning. The cool air helped Marcus clear his head.

They paused to rest after five blocks, and Marcus asked where they were taking Fin.

"I think his place would be dangerous. So, what I had in mind," she gave Marcus a searching look, "was Talisman."

Marcus scowled.

She added quickly, "Just until I find some other place."

"Why don't we dump him on a well-lit corner and call an ambulance?"

"He doesn't need an ambulance," she said.

"Fine. Even simpler."

"Asshole." Rook pushed up her sleeves. "Fine. Go. I'll manage."

"Manage what?"

"You could try to pay attention. I'll get him someplace safe. Go away." Rook tried to take Fin, who had one arm draped around Marcus. As she struggled, Marcus pitched on turbulent waves of indecision. He could almost think that if he let Rook go now, called her bluff, she'd give up dragging her inert fling after two blocks and run right into his arms. Then again, she might not. He also didn't feel right about leaving her to fall into the gaping void in Fin's head, which she was certain to do.

There was no probability Rook could be persuaded to leave Fin, not right now. To her he was like a helpless lost kitten or something. Maybe the best thing would be to drown it, but if he did she would hate him for it. If she didn't kill him outright to prevent it.

Rook tugged on Fin's left arm, while Marcus listlessly held on to his right. Fin represented the power balance here, and all Marcus could do was stall and hope for some kind of insight. Letting Rook go was bad news. To hold on to her, he had to hold on to Fin.

With a dry mouth Marcus said, "You're right, this time you're right. Besides, he's too heavy for you to get far."

*** *** ***

Rook knew it was impossible for Marcus to give up control for more than a short time. Whatever inspired this sudden concession would grate on him until he snapped.

"There's a pay phone about two blocks from here. I'll call one of his friends to come pick him up."

"So you know his friends." Marcus sounded surly. "Are you fucking them, too?" He set off down the street, hauling Fin along. Rook hustled to match his longer stride and support her side.

"Well?" Marcus prodded.

"Oh, please Marcus. Not now. I've had a helluva day."

"I'll bet you have. Fucking is hard work, when you do it right. Which you do. I'll give you that."

"Fuck you!" She wanted to stop and give him an indignant look, but didn't want him getting away with Fin. It was dark anyway.

"Oh, Little Raven. Don't lie to me. Don't try to trick me. You know you can't."

"I'm—"

"You're my Raven," he interrupted, "You're my blessing and my curse. The gods sent you to me."

"No —"

Marcus didn't look at her as he said, "You're an untrustworthy little slut, but you are mine."

"Fuck you!" This was worse than his usual bullshit.

"No matter how many times you stray, you will always come back to me. You belong to me."

"Marcus!" She tried to plant her feet and stop, to get him to look at her, but he didn't even slow. "I don't belong to anyone! I choose who I want to be with."

"And?"

"And I choose Fin."

Marcus snapped his glare to her, but kept walking. "He's a trickster, Raven! Can't you see?"

"No one here is a trickster! He's —"

"He stole my shotgun," Marcus said, as if that closed the matter.

"What?" Rook groped for relevancy.

"He stole my gun from Talisman. He blew up those buildings downtown. To frame me."

"Oh, fuck off." Paranoia was a new wrinkle for Marcus.

"It's the truth. You know I don't lie. Not to you."

"I don't know any such thing." They were nearing a convenience store with a pay phone. Rook hoped she could get Fin there before Marcus lost it completely. With other people around, he would be less likely to toss Fin into traffic. She thought it best to keep him talking, but didn't have the energy to pretend she agreed with him, to participate in his role playing fantasy. "This is real life," she said. "You are not the embodiment of Coyote Old Man, or anyone else. Neither am I. Neither is Fin."

"He's blinded you! He's tricking you, Rook! You must see it. Don't let him fool you. He's a trickster." Marcus was nearly apoplectic.

"No." Rook shook her head.

"Rook, listen to me."

They reached the phone and Marcus dumped Fin against the wall. Fin's head fell forward onto his chest.

"No, Marcus." Rook sighed. "It's over. I'm moving in with Fin." She steeled herself for his angry reply.

Marcus glared at her, shaking his head. "Really. Well, tell me one thing before you go live your perfect life with this shitbag," he prodded Fin with his boot. "If Fin's so fuckin' great, why'd I catch you kissing his brother?"

Rook glanced guiltily at Fin.

"You know," Marcus continued, "when I tell him about that he's not going to want you anymore. No man could forgive that."

"Fuck you." Rook's voice quivered. Marcus would make it sound much worse than it was.

"Come home," Marcus said. "With me."

If only it were so simple. Marcus stared at her. If she could forget about Fin, and the televangelist, and the sweaterguys, and Kyle... Had she really thought he'd shoot her if she didn't kiss him?

Rook couldn't stand Marcus's black eyes penetrating her flimsy defenses. She closed her eyes, squeezing out tears. Maybe Marcus was right. Fin wouldn't want her, not anymore. The fact that Kyle was his brother made it much worse.

Marcus understood all of that, but how? "How did you know Kyle is Fin's brother? And what the hell were you doing there anyway?"

"Trying to rescue you, bitch."

Rook was stunned.

"Now, call whoever you need to call and let's get the fuck out of here. I want you, but first we need a cleansing ritual."

Rook had mental whiplash from trying to follow Marcus's moods. Even if Fin wouldn't want her, she had to get away from Marcus. He was toxic and slowly poisoning her. If she spent more time with him, he would start to make sense. This was her last chance to escape and purge the poison from her psyche.

Whatever Fin would think of her later, she couldn't abandon him now, not in this vulnerable state. She decided to speak Marcus's language. She opened her eyes and looked steadily at him.

"Yeah. Okay. Why don't you go start without me. Get things ready and I'll come right after Fin gets picked up."

"Now," Marcus growled.

"Marcus, I can't leave him. He could die."

"So?"

"I can't."

They stared at each other, waiting to see who would break first. Rook decided to cheat, although she knew it would come at the price of encouraging Marcus. He would listen if she played his stupid game.

"Coyote," she rasped. "We must do things in the proper way." She watched Marcus for signs he was buying this. He looked dubious. "You know without the full ceremony you might never rid me of his bad medicine."

Marcus glanced furtively to each side. He craned his neck forward and said softly, "Raven?"

Rook gave him a sultry smile. "It's me. But if he dies," she tilted her head toward Fin, "you'll lose me. Forever." This wasn't technically lying.

He straightened up. "Leave him. Come with me."

Rook scowled. She almost exploded at him again, but caught herself. Breaking character would lose her the game, and she needed to keep Marcus playing. Letting her annoyance come through in her voice, she said, "Your pride will cost you." More demurely, "I'm fading."

"Tell me what to do, Raven!"

"Go. Cleanse the lodge. I'll return this one to his people." She had to tell one lie. "Then, I'll come to you."

*** *** ***

Bishop heard the phone ringing, looked at the clock, and winced. 3:13 a.m. He must have been half awake if he was hearing it, two floors below. Worry-induced insomnia.

He bolted to the stairs. This call was about Fin. He didn't at all care for the swarming premonitions of tragedy, but was determined to reach the phone.

Downstairs, Booth huddled at the stereo with his back to the room, wearing headphones. Bishop came off the bottom step in an arcing leap and had the handset off the cradle before he hit the floor.

"Hello?" he said, skidding and fetching up against an armchair. Silence.

"Hello!" he reiterated, louder.

"This is Rook. Do you remember me?"

"Are you all right? Fin's worried about you."

She emitted a strangled laugh. "No. He's not..." She trailed off.

"I took him to the hospital —" Bishop started to explain.

"I have him. He's... he's not all here right now. We need a place to go before Marcus comes back."

"Rook, where are you?"

"On... the corner. Across from Bombay Take Out."

"I'll be there in five minutes."

"Vesuvius."

"Pardon?"

"Bring his lamp. The lava lamp. He might help."

The line went dead. She'd hung up. Bishop sighed and replaced the receiver. No reason not to grab the lamp. It might keep her calm.

"Hey Bish," Booth said over his shoulder, "I think the phone's ringing."

Fifteen minutes later Bishop was hoisting an unconscious Fin off the sidewalk.

Rook quick-timed it around Bishop and opened the rear driver-side door of the idling station wagon. Bishop placed Fin on the back seat, reminded of previous rescues, always saving Fin from himself. Rook clambered in with him and Bishop shut the door. With a furtive look around the dark alleyway he slid behind the wheel and put the car in gear.

"The lava lamp's in your backpack. Your computer too. We'll be at the hospital soon," he said to the dark backseat.

"The hospital can't help him. This is something else," Rook said. She sounded tired.

"Did he O.D.?"

"No." She sighed. "I don't think I can explain, but we just need someplace safe. Not the hospital. They might look there."

Whoever 'they' were. Who else had Fin pissed off?

Bishop drove toward the one place he was sure Fin would feel safe, gritting his teeth and recounting all the trouble Fin had caused. He reviewed his own participation over the years, especially the past couple of days, with clenching guilt. Over time he'd become conditioned to apply a different standard to Fin. With nobody else could he have been pulled along so far against common sense and his better judgment. Yet even unconscious Fin exerted his anarchic influence. Bishop was powerless not to see things through.

Bastard, he thought.

"Where are we going?" Rook's eyes found Bishop's in the rearview mirror.

Bishop said, "There's an old bomb shelter buried behind Fin's dad's house."

"Really?"

"I've never been there. I think Fin practically lived in it for a couple years."

"Does Kyle know about it?" She sounded worried.

"No. Fin went out of his way to keep it a secret."

"Not from you."

Bishop sighed. "He went back to it once, in spirit. I was helping him come down and he was there. I don't think he remembered telling me."

"I meant he must trust you."

"Yes, he does." *Did anyway.*

At the Tanner residence, Bishop cruised by to see that nothing was going on. He parked a short distance away and shut off the engine.

"Wait here." Taking Fin's keys, he moved off into the shadowed lawns, cutting along the shortest route to the densely wooded portion of the Tanner's lot.

Chez Tanner was among the largest houses in its upscale neighborhood. The streets all curved and snaked, leaving some irregular pockets of property undeveloped. Mature trees had been left in place wherever possible, and some of the larger orphaned parcels, like the one at the back of the Tanners', were almost forest primeval.

Bishop slipped silently in among the massive oak and maple trunks. From what Fin said, he'd know he was near the hatch when the leaning tree and its neighbor formed an 'X' through the Tanners' sliding doors.

To achieve that view he had to fight into the middle of a massive forsythia. Beneath its drooping fronds, partially obscured by dry leaves, waited the hatch. After determining which of Fin's keys would open the padlock, he went back to the car to get his friends.

*** *** ***

On the way down through the cement and steel shaft, Rook counted 18 rungs on the ladder, then she was in the fallout shelter proper. It was an enormous metal tube, like a drainage culvert. The walls were curved steel that met in an arch about eight feet overhead. The floor was also metal, made up of mesh panels with storage underneath. On her left stood a set of bunk beds, on her right, a desk with a bunch of clutter, surmounted by shelves. The narrow walkway led down to a tiny kitchen/dining/living room, about ten feet square. Hopefully the door at the far end led to the bathroom, or Rook thought she might regret her decision to hide here.

The decor tweaked Rook's love of mid-century modern design, apart from the gaudy mint color of the walls. Rebellious teenage Fin had done his best to obscure the cool, retro features with hippie trappings and pot fumes, so the overall effect was peculiar.

Bishop managed to get Fin's inert form down the ladder in a fireman's carry, and deposited him on the lower bunk. Rook thanked him, assured him they would be fine, Fin just needed to sleep it off, and locked the hatch from the inside after he left. She plugged in Vesuvius and curled up with Fin. "What now?" she said.

"I don't know. We can ask Fin," Vesuvius suggested.

"No, we can't," Rook explained. "He can't wake up."

"There was one time Fin hadn't been going to work, and Bishop kept him from getting fired. Gave him herbal tea to bring him around and told him what to say to his boss. I guess it worked. I was surprised Fin bothered because he hates his job, but at least he started getting up again."

Vesuvius went on. Rook let herself be lulled by his mild voice, not really listening, stroking Fin's face. Despite exhaustion, her thoughts buzzed.

Rook propped herself up on her elbow and looked at Fin. Obviously Brian Shaw was responsible for his current mental state, but surely not the physical. She ran her fingers over his forehead, through his hair, wondering what he'd run into that fucked him up. Had it been Kyle? Marcus? Maybe he'd been at work when the building exploded. She remembered telling him she didn't want him to rescue her, but was glad to think he tried anyway. Lifting his uninjured hand, she kissed the palm.

Rook was pretty sure she hadn't needed this long to recover from her interrogation. When the hell was he going to wake up?

She needed to look at his eyes, hoped they would show some spark of life. Gently, she peeled open his left eye. It stayed open, glassy, the iris a slight halo of green rimming the enormous black pupil. His right eye was the same. They weren't focused on anything in particular, but they were steady.

Rook straddled Fin and put her face right in front of his. If he was in there at all, he would see her. Her breathing slowed and her heart rate dropped. She stared into his eyes and felt herself disconnecting from her body. Letting go, she plummeted into Fin's mind, using his open eyes as a doorway.

Chapter Thirteen

Towers

A Completer, an Unknowing angel with Shadowed Wings,
Shall heal the Divided Man and restore Light upon the Earth
from *New Revelations* by Reverend Brian Shaw, unpublished

Rook took several moments to steady herself, and looked around. Ash everywhere. Like being inside an urn. It covered the ground as far as she could see. The gritty, gray ash and an overcast sky were the sum total of this cold world. Whatever had been here was gone.

A large black bird flew in wide, silent circles around her. Rook wasn't certain when it arrived, but knew it wasn't of this place so she tried to approach it. It landed to wait for her.

Rook edged closer to the raven, fearful of spooking it. The bird didn't act nervous, but when Rook came within ten feet, it launched itself. It circled, far out of reach.

The ash was too fine to even hold bird tracks. She looked up at the raven. Keeping a furtive eye on her glossy black guide, she moved on.

Her movement away from the spot distressed the raven. It swooped past her, over to the magic spot. Instead of landing, it hovered, beating up clouds of gray grit with each stroke of its huge wings. As soon as Rook moved back that way, it gained altitude and calmed.

Confident there was something special about that location, Rook tried to open her mind a bit wider.

The fine dust took a long time to settle in the stagnant air. Not that a little extra haze was notable with such breathtaking scenery.

The less she focused on this as Fin's remains, the easier it became to believe she could solve this puzzle. The ash, in such huge quantity, reminded her of Mount St. Helens, Pompeii, the surface of the moon.

Idle consideration of what strange artifacts might be concealed almost yielded to the next random thought when she abruptly realized it meant something. The raven had shown her where to dig. She dug, certain this was the solution. It had to be.

Her excavation was soon gigantic. A nice neat hole with sheer sides was out of the question — she flung the gray sand as far as she could, creating a sloping bowl with a dense cloud above it. The granules packed painfully tight under her fingernails. Her mind brimmed with grisly images of what she might unearth: bones, macabre statuary, gobbets of gray matter, pyramids, bedrock...

She stopped. She'd descended several feet and found nothing. The raven had gone higher to avoid the ash cloud, and she took its silence as approval. Rook was now concerned that her mood could be pivotal in locating anything, and worse, she might influence the nature of the discovery. She tried to center herself, calm down, and, above all knock off the morbid visualizations. She resolved to find something she wanted to find, although she couldn't be sure what it would be.

Another minute of digging, and a shape revealed itself at the floor of her pit, an object with tidy right-angle corners. A rectangular block of dark sandstone. Within seconds she exposed it completely, along with parts of several litter mates.

It made perfect sense. Building blocks are elemental and universal. Whether to take this experience literally or symbolically had no real effect on the interpretation, but what was she supposed to build?

"Maybe that too will become obvious, if I'm patient." She set to digging again, widening her work area until she had a few dozen blocks. That seemed to be the lot, so she began stacking them up at the bottom of the pit.

The process revealed that each block was in fact not rectangular, but slightly curved. They only fit together when set in an arcing wall.

Since there weren't many blocks available, Rook kept the first course short. As she placed the first block of the second course, she felt something akin to deja vu. As if she were ever so slightly more awake. She laid in the next stone, and it again felt as if an unknown fog began to clear.

She added more blocks, taking stock of the effects. By the time she began the third course images accompanied the heightened awareness. Jittery and unstable flashes, but more substantial with each stone added to the wall. They were connected, but too ephemeral to identify.

With half the blocks stacked up the impressions persisted well enough to form a flickering silent movie, and Rook could see what they showed: her. In the coffee shop, at the Shamrock, being kidnapped.

"Yes!" she screamed, "It's me! I'm here!" She increased the pace of her construction, feeling some glimmer of warmth now with the imagery, a contentedness at her presence. The wall was right. The goal came clearer with each added block, and she could visualize the finished structure. She could see the connection to an early, innocent sense of self. She could see the countryside that would surround the tower, lush and teeming. Painfully, she could also see she was out of blocks.

The wall was only five courses of seven blocks. The raw material was depleted already, along with her own reserves. She had worked furiously, whizzing from despair to elation and back.

She huddled against the wall, needing to stay in contact with it but needing to rest. She could sense a shift in the emotions emanating from the blocks. Fear, drawn from an awareness of vulnerability, mounting rapidly. Rook was too exhausted to help.

The bird landed atop the wall and cawed, frightened. Rook was despondent at her inability to continue, but she couldn't understand the bird's fear.

A quick look around cleared that up. Something moving fast below the surface of the dust, out near the rim of the large crater she'd made.

It followed the curve, not converging with her position, so her surprise didn't instantly crystallize into fear. The thump behind her caused the crystallization and also the shattering into razor slivers of panic.

She saw the next one form almost directly overhead in the lingering dust cloud, coalescing from the airborne particles into a matted, hairy animal, like a mutant opossum. It dropped onto the ashes.

She fled for higher ground, but remembered the unseen creature moving like a shark through the powdered ash and saw the hopelessness of running away. She stopped moving and tried to think. The two beasties near the wall had not pounced yet. When she glanced their way they slunk back. They looked hostile and vicious, but not bold.

Rook knew what they were. The dim knowledge lurked around her that these were dust trolls. They hadn't been present at first because they were part of Fin's juvenile subconscious. With the rebuilding underway, elements of his psyche were reappearing. These were a defense mechanism, like mental antibodies.

She whirled and backpedaled to keep from being surrounded as the ugly rat-tailed monsters rained down. "It's me! I'm trying to help!" she yelled, but nothing changed.

The creatures became much braver in groups. They closed in, too many for her to outmaneuver, coming up from the ground and shaking the dust off their whiskers. They fell from the sky, piling up four deep all around her.

She was about to be overrun. The sheer mass of trolls pushed those nearest to her ever nearer. The raven swooped on her and blotted out the chaos with its wings.

A twisting moment of vertigo, and she could see again. She was someplace else. The ground was a thick matting of dark pine needles and long black feathers. Tall evergreens pressed in from all sides, their green so dark it was nearly black in the moon-and-stars light. She could hear a coyote yipping in the distance, occasional calls of night birds.

The air was so much cleaner here without all the sand and ash flying around. Rook ruffled her hair, shaking the grit out of it. She brushed off her clothes as well, then sat on the ground to pull off her boots. They were packed full of the stuff like she'd been playing in a filthy sandbox. After thumping the boots together a few times to dislodge as much debris as she could, Rook slipped her feet back in and laced them up. She thought about scattering the little mound of pale ash, but decided to leave it as a landmark in case she got lost in this new place.

Rook threaded between the trees, avoiding the faerie circles of luminescent mushrooms. A sign nailed to the trunk of a dead tree caught her attention. The letters danced and shifted before settling down. NO TRESPASSING.

They could tell Rook didn't take them seriously, so they rearranged themselves and spelled, BEWARE SNAKES. When they saw she was undeterred, they tried one last message, RAVEN SEASON.

Rook left the sign scrambling to evoke a frightening warning and moved deeper into trees. A chilling fog settled on the ground and the woods grew noisier. Animals chattered and shrieked, twigs snapped.

This wasn't Fin's mind anymore, so it must be her own. Which confused her, because although presumably she spent a good deal of time in her own mind, this wasn't familiar. She was dredging up everything she could from Psych 101 when she came to the edge of a clearing. A gingerbread house stood in the middle, complete with candy cane porch railing, pancake roofing and lemon-gel windows.

A submerged part of Rook's mind jumped up and yelled that this was exactly what she'd been looking for. The perfect building material — lightweight, easy to work with and just as easy to replace — whip up a batch in the kitchen!

Rook wasn't sure there would be enough, or what it might mean to pull down structures within her own mind. She couldn't think of anything else though, and decided to give it a go. She would stop if it hurt or she felt like she was losing memories or forgetting how to do algebra, or any other overt signs she was harming herself.

The gingerbread was spongier than she would have liked, and smelled rancid, but she quickly tore down the roof and stacked the pieces in a pile. It didn't hurt at all.

Looking around for an obvious portal into Fin's mind got her nowhere, and depression slammed back. The swirling blackness she felt materialized as a swarm of ravens, circling and swooping, no sound but the rustle of wind in their wings. Untold numbers circled low out of the black sky, then swept around and were reabsorbed into it. The largest swooped down, snatched a block of gingerbread and flapped up and out of sight. Immediately the others followed suit and Rook shrieked, "No goddammit! Filthy scavengers! Shoo! Fucking crows!" She wanted to save some of her blocks, but the birds weren't easily spooked. She pressed among them and grabbed one, and felt vertigo again.

A moment later, Rook was back at Fin's wall. The ravens ferrying the gingerbread blocks here dropped them before melting away in heat shimmers. Rook regretted calling the birds filthy crows and mumbled a lame sounding thank you. She set to work, keeping an eye open for dust trolls.

Inevitably she ran out of blocks and needed to return to the cottage in the clearing for more. A raven transported her and sat patiently while she worked. When the ferrying began again, Rook went back to Fin, feeling she was making progress. She was horrified to see dust trolls swarming his wall, devouring the gingerbread and threatening to topple the other blocks.

Rook's fury was palpable. She raged at the dust trolls and grabbed one as it scuttled past her. A feeling more unclean than anything she'd ever experienced, worse than anything Marcus ever wrought, engulfed her and she gagged. The dust troll turned in her grasp and hissed. The raven pulled her away to safety again.

The cottage was torn down to its foundation. Rook knew she would have to obtain materials someplace else, but she was exhausted. Only the thought of the dust trolls ruling Fin's mind got her moving. The birds were gone, the forest quiet. She encountered more signs whose shifting messages warned her of everything from mudslides to land mines. The more dire the warnings, the thicker the woods, the more apprehensive Rook became. She took that as a sign she was on the right track.

Not at all comfortable with what she was discovering about herself,

Rook concentrated instead on what she was discovering about Fin. Obviously he was interrogated much more intensely than she had been. What did Shaw think Fin knew? Lost in reverie, Rook almost passed by the tower without noticing it.

Tall and octagonal, made of red brick, and covered with ivy, it was reminiscent of an academic building. She circled it twice but found no door. Looking to the top, Rook noticed a single small window, empty beneath the pointed slate roof. In the eaves she could see ravens nesting. Instinctively she knew the tower housed a princess. A weak, overprotected princess waiting around for a handsome prince to rescue her. Incapable of realizing he wasn't coming. That he was catatonic, trapped in the rubble of his own tower. All she had to do was climb down.

"Rapunzel, Rapunzel, let down your hair."

Of course it couldn't be easy.

"Princess!"

Still nothing.

"Brook!"

Rook knew she wasn't going to get an answer. The ivy formed a natural ladder, but she was suddenly certain she was afraid of heights. Although the thought of scaling the wall terrified her, she would have to do it. She reasoned she couldn't be safer than in her own mind, but knew how untrue that was. Standing at the base, she studied the best route up. No reason to rush, after all. Perhaps there was another tower nearby, with a more convenient entrance? The ravens gave her reproving looks, and she knew she had to quit stalling.

The ivy proved quite sturdy, but her progress was less than it seemed. The vines crept downward over the wall, erasing half her efforts. She speeded up, outwitting looping tendrils that caught at her wrists and neck. One coil grasped her ankle, but she kept pulling herself upward, dragging a length of the vine up with her.

Just below the windowsill, a handful of ivy crumbled in her grip and she was hauled down over a foot. All the vines above her were desiccated and fragile. She lunged and grabbed the stone ledge with both hands and hoisted herself over, the tendril finally releasing her ankle and slinking away.

Inside, the wooden floor was worn smooth and dark with age, a rounded-top trunk in the center. Against one wall stood a small table with a burning candle. A child's china tea set surrounded the candle in an intricate setting. On another wall, a shelf held mundane objects: a toaster, an iron, a diaphragm, some glossy fashion magazines. A full length mirror lay shattered on the floor near a camp stove and scuba mask.

Rook opened the trunk and stooped to see what it contained. Under several silk scarves and a pair of child's rubber boots lay the silent princesses. Six Barbie Dolls dressed in gowns of vibrant velvet and satin, four with crew cuts, one bald and the last headless. Rook set them on the table to enjoy the tea party, then continued looking through the trunk. Of course she remembered the dolls. Each of her stepfathers bought them for her and her little sister Junebug. Digging deeper, Rook found Baby Alive and Raggedy Ann. Mixed in with the dolls were doll clothes, shoes, furniture, even dress-up clothes and costume jewelry.

At the bottom of the trunk lay Ballerina Barbie, her favorite doll. The one doll whose hair had been spared. Once long and silky, it was now a frizzy clump. No wonder the prince never rescued these girls. They should have known the hair was their only hope. Rook rooted through the piles she'd made on the floor, searching for a brush or comb.

As she searched she discovered something unexpected — a hinge in the floor. Rook dragged the trunk to the side and pushed the doll paraphernalia over to it, uncovering a trap door. With no handle it was difficult to pry open, but she was determined.

The bottom of the tower smelled dank. Rook took the candle from the table and looked down. Water. No telling how deep. A rope hung from a pulley attached to the underside of the floor. She pulled up a large bucket and dumped the foul water out. Without thinking too much about what she was doing, Rook stepped into the bucket and lowered herself for a better look. The water was a few feet deep. Best of all, she could see chinks in the mortar and knew where she would get what she needed to help Fin.

But first she needed to go back upstairs and take care of something.

***

She felt foolish wearing the plastic tiara and rhinestone necklace, yet regal too.

Thus attired, the princess lowered herself and stood hip deep in the brackish water. The baseball bat stolen from her brother made a sturdy scepter. She hefted it and took aim at the weakest-looking section of the wall.

The first bricks were the most difficult to loosen, but as they landed outside, she had more room to work. When the opening was big enough to pass through, she went out and summoned the ravens. They seemed to bow to her before transporting her and the bricks to Fin's mind.

The dust trolls were nowhere to be seen, the ill-fated gingerbread gone. Rook inspected the wall. It had held. She placed bricks from her remodeling effort on the ground to finish the circular base for Fin's tower. As she connected the circle she felt a flash of remembrance and joy from Fin, and was filled with a ringing sense of victory. This would work. It was right. With renewed determination she completed the second and third levels, being sure to leave a doorway.

Back in her own tower the blocks were tougher to move now, the ivy greedily clinging to them. Rook worked downward and finally removed the bricks holding the stagnant water inside. It poured out and saturated the ground. As she removed the bottom-most layer and the last of the water washed out, Rook hesitated. Slowly she turned to see what the waters had hidden.

The skeletal remains of five or six girls lay scattered about the floor, all princesses of varying ages. Their empty eye sockets looked upon Rook piteously, accusingly. It was her fault they were dead, they said, her fault they spent years in their watery tomb, forgotten. It wasn't all her fault, she wanted to protest. Certainly her mother played some part. Tears stung Rook's eyes as she regarded these bones, the dregs of her childhood splayed out on the algae-slick floor. They reminded her of the Russian Grand Duchesses, Anastasia and the rest, who were all killed together and buried in the Siberian woods. Rook knew that her princesses, too, needed to be buried, but didn't want to waste the time or energy on it now. There was no worry of them going anywhere on their own. They could wait a little longer. She turned her back on their hollow stares and reaching hands, passed through the narrow doorway she'd made, and prepared to return to Fin.

After several more trips, Rook completed the excavation of a large arching doorway in her tower and topped off its counterpart in Fin's. She stepped back to survey her work and was startled by a loud thump behind her. Expecting dust trolls, she whirled around, but saw instead a block. One of Fin's. She looked to see who had dropped it, but the ravens had stirred up another cloud from the ashes. A second block dropped a few feet to her left. She studied the cloud and saw the next one form before it dropped. Fin was doing this! She gathered the blocks and struggled to lift them high enough to place them on the structure.

She finished another complete course but wouldn't be able to reach high enough for the next. A block fell onto the tower then, followed by another.

Rook stayed back and watched. The blocks came much more infrequently, but most of them landed in place. Some missed and landed outside, occasionally taking another with them. They didn't fit perfectly and there were gaps, but all in all, it worked.

The tower narrowed as it grew, and the ground under its foundation shifted upward. Rook's excavation disappeared like ripples in the sea, leaving behind a smooth, flat landscape. Around the base, grass crept out in slow fractals. Ivy climbed, velvety green and pulsing like a heartbeat, smelling like rain and electrolytes. A raven appeared and hopped in through the doorway. Rook followed, finding the interior

upholstered in moss. The raven moved into the doorway and took up a
guard position. Rook curled up on the moss and slept.

*** *** ***

Fin woke up slowly with a gentle, melodious hum in the back of his
brain. The warmth of someone beside him in bed reassured him. The
dull red light of Vesuvius on the other side of his eyelids, as always,
calming. He breathed deeply and exhaled, discovering something
unusual. He didn't want a smoke.

He felt content.

That shocked him to the core. He sat bolt upright and into a world
of pain. His ribs screamed, his head banged off... what? The bridge of his
nose throbbed and sent tendrils of eye-watering sinus pain radiating
across his cheek bones. Reaching up to cradle his head, Fin poked
himself in the eye with his taped fingers, setting off pain there too. Now
he wanted a cigarette. And a bottle of tequila. Maybe an aspirin or two
to wash it down. As his head cleared and he blinked the tears away, he
looked around.

The last thing he could remember for sure was getting duped by that
fucking weasel Kyle and meeting the TV preacher.

In all honesty, the last thing he could be sure of was getting his
eyebrow pierced. Everything that followed was just bizarre. A fever
dream or hallucination, except his own body gave evidence to the
contrary. And, the warm somebody beside him was Rook. He peered
through the womb-like lighting. They were both fully clothed, except
she was in some of his clothes. She slept the sleep of the dead, but she
was breathing. He checked.

If he was okay and she was okay, somehow he must have succeeded.
He saved her. The burgeoning pride he felt was tempered by not
knowing how the hell he'd done it or where the hell they were. Maybe
they were both captive and he would need to be a hero again. Only one
way to find out.

Fin swung his feet out and his boots immediately clanked on the
floor. The bed was only raised about six inches. Something about the

clanking jostled his memory. He stood and put out his left hand to steady himself. All he could see clearly was Vesuvius, bubbling on a table somewhere in front of him. The low light level was a comfort to his eyes. He took in his surroundings, but couldn't make sense of any of it. Metal bunks, metal mesh floor, tie-dye tapestries. The scents of incense, pot and stale air. All hideously familiar. Deja vu and dysnomia. He shook his head, trying to resolve the short in his wiring.

Inflatable Sally, ultimately, was what saved him. There she sat, in the kitchen chair, her big blue eyes wide and vacant, her mouth a perfect O of lustful surprise, the other, cruder, details covered by her seafoam green Donna Reed housedress and starched, white apron.

The bomb shelter. Somehow Brad and Melissa didn't know it was right there in their back yard, fully stocked. Kyle never stumbled across it. Fin never brought anyone here, not in high school when he practically lived here, not even a girlfriend. He'd never told anyone about it. Vesuvius knew, of course, because he'd lived here, too. This is where they'd met. When the box of his mom's things showed up, Fin brought it down here to go through it in private. Her lava lamp had comforted him, both figuratively and literally. Did Vesuvius tell Rook about this place? How would the lamp describe it or know how to get here?

Fin tried to clear the dust out of the unused corners of his mind. In addition to the gentle hum, he encountered much more debris than ever before. Things were missing, but he couldn't tell what. Like his mind had been ransacked.

He swayed gently in the narrow walkway between the bunks and the desk, trying to get his mental footing. A horrifying thought: maybe Kyle did know about this place. Maybe he'd locked them in here to die. Fin lurched to the ladder and clambered to the top where he was somewhat reassured to find it locked from the inside. Which didn't preclude it also being locked from the outside.

At least Kyle wouldn't get in.

Fin climbed down and began a search to refresh his memory. The gas masks were here. More important, so were the rifle and ammo, convincing evidence Kyle hadn't locked them in. The upright citizens who built this place in the 50s, 60s, whenever, thought of everything: Powdered eggs and milk. Canned veggies. Spam.

Gently, he moved his slumbering lava lamp from the table to the counter. As quietly as possible he lifted the table top, uncovering the bathtub underneath. Fin wasn't sure where the water came from, but when it ran hot he filled the tub and undressed. He was glad there was no mirror to show him what he looked like, because he was sure it wasn't pretty. Normally he wouldn't give a shit, but he didn't want to gross Rook out. They might be stuck down here for a long time.

Fin tried to make sense of the past few days, wanted to be sure of what happened before Rook woke up and maybe wanted to talk about it. He scooped up what memories he could, but they were like charred newspaper.

Reverend Brian Shaw. Kyle. Who knew Kyle had goons? Something about sand. Searing pain. Then he was here with more chaos than usual dancing in his head.

The tuning fork in his head modulated its tone as a gentle kiss brushed his forehead, and Fin's eyes fluttered open. Rook stood over him, naked and smiling. She kissed his mouth and climbed in the tub with him, spilling water out over the sides.

Chapter Fourteen

Underground

It is vital that your Peterson Fallout Shelter be as inviting and home-like as possible. You will be spending a lot of time there, possibly up to several months. In addition to such necessities as food, water, medicine, tobacco and firearms, you will want to stock up on the niceties.

Such things as cards, games, a Bible and other books will help pass the time. If you purchased a Peterson Royal Luxury model and have the space, a musical instrument or a phonograph would be a wonderful addition. And don't forget, little Johnny and Susie need their toys!

Even beyond entertainment, there are needs you should address. Store in your shelter plenty of soap and other toilet items. Father wouldn't appreciate running out of his shaving cream, would he? Or Mother her perfume? Of course the entire family will appreciate clean clothes!

Use the checklist on the back of this card, and when the time comes for your family to emerge from the safety of your Peterson Fallout Shelter and rebuild society, you're sure to make a great impression!

from Peterson Fallout Shelter owner's manual ©1956

Stepping into control of one of the world's largest religious broadcasting operations was effortless. Shaw had populated his staff with sycophants and blissed-out born-agains. Their reluctance to make waves accounted for their selection. They were lambs.

Kyle made contact with the covert layer of the Ministries while driving away from the factory disaster. Once his head cleared, he'd pulled over and started making calls. He dialed numbers only Shaw knew, and claimed to be relaying the reverend's personal orders. He knew who could send backup the fastest, who should run interference with the police. That Shaw was already dead didn't get mentioned.

By the time more mercs reached the building, the attack was over. Kyle orchestrated the cleanup and coverup on the drive to the Shaw Ministries headquarters in Donner. Shaw's remains were relocated to his residence.

Being in a position to give effective orders at a critical moment assured his unchallenged rulership. There were some near the top of command who might have thought to use Kyle's timely arrival and intimate knowledge against him. They kept their ambitions to themselves. Kyle knew more about the big picture than anyone else, which deterred potential rivals.

A major factor in Kyle's favor was that the paramilitary thugs viewed him as their kind of people. The reverend considered the mercs an unfortunate necessity, and they knew it. Spared the inconvenience of needing to learn everyone's names or any of the other particulars, and conforming well to the notions of leadership held by his troops, Kyle hardly needed to spend any time on the clandestine projects.

Instead, he forged and planted the necessary documents to guarantee his appointment to head the Ministries the moment Shaw's body was discovered. Sunday morning when Shaw didn't show up for the broadcast, everything went according to plan.

For his first three days in charge, Kyle mostly watched for opportunities to perfect his ill-gotten mind tricks. Little things, like making people agree with him, or lose control of their bodily functions for a moment.

Wednesday he decided it was time to try something more dramatic. Something had to be done about Travis.

Travis had attended Shaw's seminary college for three months and was interning at the Ministries office. He was young and charismatic, in denial about his homosexuality, and smitten with Shaw. His inner turmoil lent his judgmental zeal that classic brimstone flavor. He was a natural, and Shaw had taken him under his wing.

Now Travis was dangerous, deranged with grief. He openly blamed Kyle for Shaw's death. Taunted him whenever their paths crossed. So far no one seemed to be giving it any credence, but it was, to say the least, distracting. People in the biz were prone to take such fevered ramblings as some kind of message. Plus Travis knew his bible backwards. Forward too, and just that morning he deduced Kyle didn't.

The issue, as Kyle saw it, revolved around subtlety. His loudest detractor meeting a sticky end would only fuel new rumors.

When Reverend Lucas strode in unannounced, Kyle heard a heavenly fanfare. Here, about to shake hands, was the solution to his Travis problem.

Lucas was a crony of Shaw's, but not a friend or partner. Convincing circumstantial evidence implied his minions had tried to infiltrate Shaw Ministries, and that he funded an anti-Shaw website. It was distinctly possible he knew there was more than televangelism going on.

Kyle made nice with Lucas long enough to square him away in a conference room, promising to be with him shortly. At his office, he took delivery of an untraceable handgun. He struck out into the less-hectic north wing, trying to influence the chances of bumping into Travis. He felt silly, thinking over and over, "Come to me, Travis," but something worked, because they almost knocked each other down at a bend in the corridor.

Without an audience, the young man wasn't troubled to say anything. He just scowled. Kyle asked, "What do you see when you look me in the eye?"

Travis took the bait and tried to stare Kyle down. He also started to answer the question, but Kyle wasn't listening. He seized the man's intellect, shook it out like a rug, and spread it in a new shape. A much simpler shape. Charisma wasn't going to take Travis anyplace after this. Kyle walked the width of the sparse landscape, molding it into a plan of action and steamrolling anything extraneous.

It was nerve-wracking to give the man a loaded weapon. Kyle checked over his handiwork one last time, then practically sprinted back to the conference room.

He slowed up, and breezed in as Reverend Lucas was about to leave. He apologized for making him cool his heels for so long and asked, "To what do we owe the pleasure of your visit?" The energy expenditure of working on Travis suddenly caught up with him, and fortunately Lucas rather enjoyed the sound of his own voice. When Travis lurched into the room Kyle muttered, "Finally."

After shooting Lucas twice, in the face, Travis stopped moving. Kyle had to remind him to shoot himself.

Thursday morning was eerily calm and routine, as if the violence never happened. Tedious, in fact. By mid-afternoon, boredom made Kyle snappish, cornered in a meeting with a publicist from a religious magazine. He tried to behave, but as she droned on his attention wandered over to Denise, a blonde administrative assistant whose periwinkle suit, with a knee-length skirt slit up one side, inspired some ideas for a different application of his new talents.

He cut the meeting short and sidled up to Denise. He was spooling up his engines when she started cooing about yesterday, what danger he faced. Kyle almost holstered his whammy and did things the old-fashioned way, but a major goal here was to practice. Besides, he knew the type. This place was full of chaste women. No matter how genuinely she lusted for him, she was certain to halt things at first base if allowed to.

Kyle didn't allow her to halt anything.

Denise possessed a libido that reminded Kyle of an otter. He had seen them on television, and they were playful and lived in wild yet idyllic settings. This whimsical creature was silver, more serpentine, and liked to roll into a tight spiral and unknot itself again. And it liked Kyle. If he reached out to stroke it, the animal would dart up and quiver with joy. It would race around and around him. It emitted a lovely fragrance, slightly salty.

Denise also possessed a lovely body, and Kyle's mischief with her libido made her eager to be seen, to be touched. Eager to touch and taste.

Suddenly he couldn't partake of her. What should have been an enjoyable night, on into daylight, was marred by persistent thoughts of Rook. Her image filled his mind, and dim intimations of shame fell like a light rain. Confused, he sent Denise away tearful and disappointed.

He realized his blunder barely in time: she would have full recall. She would think her heat had been her own, wouldn't comprehend that she'd been coerced. Nevertheless, Kyle's behavior went far past what it would take to topple him from Shaw's throne.

She was about to enter the elevator when Kyle used the voice of command. Perhaps he had gotten better with it, or maybe Denise lacked Rook's strength to resist. He worked it so she would tell everyone he'd shared powerful insights about important things, and she'd believe it although she couldn't remember what they were.

After that, Kyle tried to keep things a little more low-key, but continued to sharpen his mental weapons. Occasionally a subtle, eerie loneliness reminded him of Rook. He didn't make any further attempts to bed comely staffers. His life was largely taken up by meetings, which were largely taken up with the prattle of functionaries. He found ways to diminish those he particularly disliked. Sometimes permanently. Most of the longtime clergy, who had known Shaw for many years, became increasingly convinced of Kyle's channel to the Divine.

They assumed he would give the sermons, but Kyle had neither the ability nor the desire to try. The idea was repugnant. He hadn't even bothered to plunder Shaw's vast Biblical knowledge while collecting security codes and business plans from the man's mind, seeing at the time no practical value. In any case, there was far too much he didn't know and any weakness in his pulpit performance would amplify his total lack of credentials. Without the sermons there would be no broadcasts, and therefore no money, so he had no peace until he announced that the new preacher would be revealed to him following

Shaw's memorial service.

He already knew who it would be. Declan Spitz was perfect. Politically inept and highly malleable, plus the loyal viewers already knew him. They would accept him, tolerate him, but he would bore them until changing the channel became a matter of survival. Spitz needed a little extra fire to maintain the standard for Ministries broadcasts. Kyle had a plan to address that need. He set up regular private meetings with Spitz, and a few people noticed a difference after the first one.

*** *** ***

Time passed in the bomb shelter. Whether it passed quickly or slowly was impossible to say. The laptop's battery died almost immediately, leaving the couple without a clock or calendar. Before it stopped working, the display read September 30, and Rook said, "It's almost my birthday."

Once Fin knew Bishop was responsible for hiding them here, nothing else was important. They were safe. Celebrating life in the most primal way was their only priority. They did little besides sleep and fuck. Conversation was unnecessary beyond the barest facts: they were alive, together, in love. They hadn't said the word yet, hadn't needed to. The omnipresent tingle Fin felt in his mind came from Rook, what else could it be but a manifestation of love? If it wasn't for their ordeals, their relationship wouldn't have lasted. While the physical side was spectacular from the start, they were both defensive, prickly. Or they had been. Their new bond had been forged in flame and danger and now they had nearly transcended the need for verbal communication. It was fulfilling and comfortable. From the little they did say out loud, it was apparent they were of one mind. They completed each other.

Fin's wounds were healing well, his black eyes and bruises all losing their tenderness and exotic coloration. His dreamlife was back to normal. No more creepy spaceships for him, or for Rook, from what she said. Rook removed his forehead stitches with a pair of tiny nail scissors from the shelter's antique shaving kit. For now his fingers were still buddy-taped.

When it seemed the time was right, Fin did his best to surprise Rook with a birthday party. The guest list was somewhat selective, but all those invited attended. Besides Fin and the unwitting birthday girl, there were Vesuvius and Inflatable Sally. An intimate gathering.

While Rook slept, Fin scrounged quietly about the kitchen. The best he could come up with was pancakes, without syrup. Since they were confined twenty feet underground and at least the food had 'cake' as part of its name, Fin thought he was doing pretty well.

The gift was going to be the more difficult thing. Fin considered his options. There was, of course, the purely physical, but they'd been naked the entire time down here, and already explored every play in the book. Didn't mean they couldn't repeat themselves, but he wanted something original to mark their first special day together.

So, nothing sexual.

He'd used the limited food supply and his likewise limited culinary skills to produce the 'cake,' and didn't want to push his luck by attempting anything more complicated in the kitchen.

He wanted to pamper her, but all he had was a half-case of Ivory soap and some fossilized Colgate. Long ago he'd finished off what liquor had been stowed under the floor.

What to give his lady love? A gas mask? A box of ammo? Old *National Geographics*? There was nothing suitable down here. If only he could go outside...

He could write something for her.

That felt perfect. Fin set to work on a song and produced several snippets which, though promising, ultimately led nowhere.

He was running out of time. Rook would wake up soon. Fin's eyes searched the limited confines of the shelter and came to rest on the ladder.

Outside?

Fin tried to work on the song again, but the ladder kept nagging him. They would have to go out eventually...

They were safe here. Who knew what surprises might be waiting outside? They hadn't started to grate on each other. Maybe they never would. Would the spell be broken once they left their cocoon? Why let outside forces spoil everything?

No. They were stronger than that. The hum oscillating gently in the back of his mind proved it.

Fin knew they couldn't hide forever and was suddenly eager to prove how indestructible they were, to vanquish any who dared try to part him from his bride.

He would be careful, of course. No need to walk blindly into an ambush.

Fin hung a wool blanket over the bunk to shade Rook. He had no way of knowing whether it was day or night outside. At the top of the ladder, he unlocked the padlock and eased the hatch open a crack. Nothing. No light poured in, but also no sound. No bullets. No fingers or pry bars. He swung the hatch open and peered out.

Night. Not much moon. The air was chilly, but not cold, and smelled of crisp leaves. So far, so good.

Hoisting himself out, Fin stayed in a crouch and peered around. The woods surrounding him were deserted. There were several lights on inside the big house where his father lived. The shades were drawn, the way Melissa liked.

Not wanting to be away from Rook for more than a minute, Fin crept forward toward the borderline between forest and lawn. Grab something quick and get back. A token.

What would she think if she woke up and he was gone?

He reached out with his unbandaged hand and plucked a fistful of blue asters that somehow escaped the wrath of his stepmother. She couldn't abide anything ornamental. Perhaps these were technically the neighbor's flowers. Perhaps technically it was the neighbor's bomb shelter. In any case, no one had ever challenged his squatter's rights.

The asters gave off a light floral fragrance as Fin hurried back to his haven. Hopefully Rook wasn't allergic.

Safely locked inside again, Fin pulled the blanket down and stuck the flowers in a glass of water, then hid them in a cupboard. He lit his Zippo and, lacking candles, stuck it in the middle of the now-cold pancakes before waking Rook.

When her silvery-blue eyes opened, he kissed her and sang 'Happy Birthday.' She smiled. He led her to the table where she laughed over her cake for a moment.

She closed her eyes, nodded, silently mouthed something, and blew out the flame. Fin wished along with her, for her wish to come true.

They dug into the cake with their fingers and fed each other. When the plate was clean, Fin told Rook to close her eyes and fetched the flowers. She opened her eyes on cue, and they kept opening wider and wider. They were filled with wonder when they turned to Fin. He nodded.

"You went outside?" She sounded awed and horrified at the same time.

"It's safe. There's nothing out there. No one."

She stared for a few seconds longer, threw her arms around him and pulled him close.

"Thank you!"

"We can leave anytime we want."

"Not yet. I'm not ready yet."

Fin kissed her.

She said, "I've only just gotten you. I'm not ready to share you."

"There's still plenty of powdered eggs..."

"Maybe I'm ready to share you with a grocery store cashier. We could restock..."

Fin laughed and kissed her again.

"Your next birthday will be better than this one."

"Not possible. Except I'll have a year with you to look back on." She paused and grimaced. "If you're sappy and you know it, clap your hands."

Fin clapped, and they both tried not to laugh.

"Call it sappy if you want to," Fin said, "but I feel so bonded. Connected. It's like I have a sixth sense for you." He tapped his skull. "I can feel you here."

She cocked her head and smiled. "It's amazing you say that. The whole time we've been down here my mental antenna has been picking up your signal, and my brain-radio has been tuned to nothing but WFIN."

"I love you, Rook."

"I love you, Fin."

They kissed.

"Let's get married."

They kissed for a long time.

"I've heard it's impolite to ask a lady her age…"

"But I'm no lady," Rook interrupted. "And if, in fact, this is October 3 or later, I'm 22. And you, good sir?"

"Turned 25 the first of June."

"Wow. You're old," she teased.

"But not grown up," added Vesuvius.

"All right, Mr Feverdream," said Fin, "how old are you?"

"Age is an arbitrary number."

*** *** ***

Sitting naked on the third rung of the ladder, Rook studied the hatch above her. Would she ever have the nerve to pass back through it? The real world out there contained Marcus. And Shaw. And Kyle.

Rook felt betrayed by her loins. She was pissed at herself for not being repulsed by Kyle's advances in the factory. That it was most likely a fear response or a primal drive toward the alpha-male — her rescuer — made it no easier to excuse. Rook knew Kyle was bad news, and she'd had enough of that shit from Marcus. Bad news was bad news. Still there was the nagging guilt. She should have done more to fend him off. Or, since he had a gun, at least not gotten all wet in the panties.

Whenever she thought about it she experienced the same illicit thrill, compounding the guilt, and she thought about it a lot since Fin went outside. Knowing they could leave the shelter put a fine point on whether they ought to.

If she could avoid Marcus long enough, he would find a replacement for her. He'd had no qualms about falling into other girls' crotches while they were together. Only a matter of time before one of the infamous 'deer women' turned his head again, and this time Rook wouldn't be there scowling at him. One female or other was bound to spark an obsession.

Reverend Shaw represented a nebulous evil. Obviously trouble, but what sort? Would he still be interested in them? He lay too far out of their scope of understanding to speculate about. There was simply no base-line with which to make comparisons. Rook decided not to publish anything about her encounter with him and hope for the best.

As she saw it, Kyle presented the most compelling reason for staying hidden. He was somewhat outside of their knowledge base as well, but had a personal connection. That made him more dangerous. Whereas Shaw could easily forget about them in the aftermath of the chaotic evacuation of the factory, Kyle might hold a grudge. The unknown side of him was much more terrifying, because it didn't fit with what Fin knew about his brother. There was no way of knowing how deep his evil might go.

Their escape from the factory was confused and confusing, so perhaps Kyle would have more pressing things demanding his attention now. Like that whole 'top of the food chain' thing he'd tried to tempt her with. A nice, perplexing offer to make to a girl you've just met.

He probably wasn't really interested in her, just wanted to get a dig in at Fin, to screw things up between them. Sometime in the future he'd show up and mention the time they kissed, just to be a jerk. Only that didn't follow, since he'd had a gun pointed at her.

Fin snored and rolled over, causing a guilty jump in Rook's pulse and a mild fluctuation in his slumbering mental vibration. She climbed stiffly down from the ladder and rolled her neck and shoulders while considering why she felt so guilty.

Meticulous review of the time she'd spent with Kyle confirmed she'd done nothing to lead him on. Therefore she had nothing to feel guilty about. Except, of course, all this obsessing.

Was she getting herself worked up over nothing? She probably wasn't even on Kyle's radar anymore. Except she knew she was. Which said something unflattering about her ego. She didn't want him to want her, did she?

Maybe a little.

And why would that be?

She and Fin were making plans for the future, so naturally the twisted, wrong half of her psyche looked for a way to screw it up. Her mother was the perfect role model for screwing things up.

What wouldn't Mom do?

Mom would never work to keep a relationship healthy. She would never confess. So, since Mom wouldn't, Rook would.

She would tell Fin that Kyle kissed her and for some inexplicable reason she didn't resist. She would trust him to understand. She had to tell him now, while they were in the protected environment of the bomb shelter. They couldn't leave until she was sure they were ready. Until they were strong enough again to withstand whatever the sun would expose.

Rook climbed into the bunk with Fin and spooned against his warmth. It wasn't often that she got to study his back and the odd tattoo he had there, a sort of yin-yang take on Janus, the two-faced Roman god of choices. Nicely rendered though they were, Rook found the twin visages a bit disturbing. They were part of Fin though, so she tried to make her peace with them. Before falling back to sleep she gave each of the stern faces a kiss.

***

Fin narrated his version of the events following her kidnapping with dramatic flair, doing much more than merely connecting the dots of what she'd already learned. He told the story as if it were a movie he'd seen, not something he'd experienced, and Rook's mind formed hyper-

real images of the action in glorious wide-screen Technicolor. The
security imparted by their surroundings and Fin's reassuring signal in
her mind made everything else unreal. All the movie lacked was a
satisfying ending, since the last thing Fin could recall before waking up
in the shelter was meeting Shaw and a smothering sensation in his
mind.

"It smacks of Deus ex Machina" said Rook. "Let me fill in some of
the gaps."

Her own narration went as smoothly as Fin's until she had to
explain how she'd escaped. They were lounging together on their bunk,
her head on his stomach, gazing up into his reassuring green eyes. She
fought the impulse to move away and adopt a more formal tone. Fin felt
her tense and stroked her hair.

He had no idea what was coming.

"I was sitting in the crate, feeling sorry for myself, and then there
were these horrible subsonics. It went on for I don't know how long,
then the door opened and everything got better. Except it was Kyle
who'd let me out. He wanted me to go with him. I kneed him and ran to
the other crate and opened it. Imagine my surprise when Marcus
stepped out."

Fin chuckled without humor.

Now the damning part. Rook took a deep breath. She'd already told
him about the kiss Kyle gave her when they reached the factory, and
how she'd bitten him. Fin had looked angry at first, then joked, "I
thought that was our thing."

"With Kyle I meant it," Rook assured.

With this second kiss there was no heroic defiance on her part,
unless she wanted to invent it. This time the hero mantle belonged to
Marcus.

Fin waited for her to continue. Even when she opened her mouth,
Rook wasn't sure which version of events she would tell.

"Kyle grabbed me. The door hadn't opened far. It was heavy, and I
didn't have time to open it all the way." Rook made herself stop stalling.

"Kyle grabbed me and held his gun here," Rook cocked her fingers like a gun and pointed to the hollow under her jaw. She felt Fin tense and his signal got louder in her head. She kept her eyes on his. "And he kissed me."

Fin's eyes were distant and angry, but the anger wasn't directed at her. Yet.

"Then he stepped back and pointed it at my forehead," she gestured again, breaking eye contact. "He stepped up, without the gun on me, and kissed me again. I didn't resist."

Moment of truth.

Through a welling of tears, Rook glanced at Fin. His face was stony. He looked down at her and saw her distress. His features immediately softened and he hugged her.

He said, "How can you blame yourself? I know Kyle. I blame him. I couldn't possibly blame you. I understand."

Rook wasn't sure he did, entirely.

From there her story was easier to tell. Her handling of Marcus sounded much more masterful in retrospect than it felt at the time. By the point in her narration when Bishop left them alone in the bomb shelter, she was feeling much better, and as a consequence much hornier.

"You seemed catatonic, and I was kind of worried, so I climbed on top of you so I could look into your eyes and let you see me." As she spoke, she straddled him again, only this time they were naked.

Fin put his hands on her hips and smiled slyly. "You're very kinky, aren't you?"

Rook laughed.

"You know it's not polite to take advantage of someone in an unconscious state," he said, trying to sound stern, but his erection belied him.

"I opened your eyelids and stared deep into your gorgeous baby-greens," she said as they locked eyes. Maintaining eye contact, she shifted her position and eased him inside of her.

He moaned, but didn't blink or look away.

Several minutes passed like that and Rook said, "I guess I fell asleep then."

"You're not going to fall asleep now, are you?"

"No worries." She squeezed him. "I dreamed I went into your mind and helped you somehow. You had a tower I had to fix."

"That's rather Freudian."

"I hadn't thought of that," Rook said with a laugh. "It didn't seem sexual at the time. I guess it worked, because when I woke up, you were in the tub."

"Healed by the love of a good woman and the promise of lots of sex."

Chapter Fifteen

Vagabond

Two weeks after the arson fire and explosion that destroyed three buildings on the 500 block of Spruce Street in downtown Webster, authorities are slow to release new information. Police Chief Harold Petroski denied the investigation had stalled, calling it ongoing. He reiterated that detectives are following lines of enquiry related to the tenant of the basement office where the blaze began, a dummy corporation called Salamander LTD.
     From the *Webster Daily Press,* 10-12-2000

Nothing was ever easy. Kyle had power and money, but he couldn't relax.

Shaw was lax with security measures at the factory, smugly certain Jesus had his back, and as a consequence the most important component of the program had been stolen.

Hell, it was the program. Without the spook technology hidden in that jewelry, Shaw would have been limited to the puny influence he could exert via television. Enough to make a certain type of person keep tuning in and sending checks, but not enough to really turn people around like Reverend Shaw envisioned doing once he could broadcast a hypnotic wave to millions on a closed frequency.

Kyle envisioned some remarkable uses for that carrier wave, himself.

The retaliatory strike to recover the goods would require a lot of planning, but it was going to be fun. Until the time came to wipe out the enemy, Kyle concentrated on the most important discovery among the spoils of Shaw's brain. The New Revelations.

When he wasn't prepping Spitz, Kyle cloistered himself to meditate on recent events, seeking to interpret them according to Shaw's prophecy.

Kyle first saw the Revelations during Shaw's excavations of Fin's head, and they also appeared as part of the enormous cathedral of Shaw himself. The stained-glass windows told the story, the whole of it focused on the idea of a Divided Man.

These Revelations nagged at Kyle, demanding his attention. If he could figure out what the hell they meant, they would guide his actions. The problem was, the images he took from Shaw were in bible-speak. Shaw hadn't needed to translate them in order to understand them. The same could not be said for Kyle. Certain things made sense, but mostly it was brimstone-tinged gibberish. After nine days he at least knew the wording by heart.

> *Divided Seed shall a Divided Child Beget*
> *who shall grow into a Divided Man*

The Divided Man thing referred to the Tanner boys. Shaw had been at a disadvantage, not knowing Kyle had a half-brother, but in the last seconds in Fin's mind he'd added it up.

> *A hidden Plague will Dream in Men and Blind their Hearts,*
> *and Black Dreams will descend for Twenty Years and Flood the*
> *Earth.*
> *And utter Blackness shall prevail over the Earth*
> *that the Hosts in Heaven not look back upon it.*

This sounded like conventional End-is-Nigh crap. Except the bit about the Hosts not looking back. Were they leaving? Already gone? Shaw hadn't thought so. He walked the talk. Why would he do that for a Celestial Host that had abandoned him? The stuff falling from the sky for twenty years, and the flood of darkness... What the hell was that about?

The Ministries' compound was waist-deep with bibles, so Kyle paged through a few of them for clues. According to those revelations, god promised not to use a flood next time. Shaw the heretic. Unless this flood wasn't supposed to come from god. Well, even then.

> *Those who go Forth in Chains will be called into the Firmament,*
> *but fall and be Minions of the Pretender*

Was Shaw the Pretender? Not according to Shaw, and why write that into your own manifesto? Kyle went to another fat book to look up 'firmament,' and pondered that line. Who's calling people up into the sky? No one good, apparently.

> *A Completer, an Unknowing angel with Shadowed Wings,*
> *Shall heal the Divided Man and restore Light upon the Earth*

Obviously Shaw saw himself in this role. He had been waiting for the Divided Man to show up, and recognized him too late. That was pathetic.

Well, if Kyle was the Divided Man, or at least part of him, he knew who he wanted to heal him. Unfortunately, she was occupied with the other part of the Divided Man at the moment.

Their first kiss was a pleasant memory, but the second, during the assault, burned behind his eyes and in deeper places. That's when they really connected. As foretold in the Prophecy. Whatever she might say to the contrary, she was drawn to him as well.

Of course, if he had left her in her box on his way out he would have her now. Fin too. Next time he wouldn't leave anything to chance.

In the past Kyle and Fin competed over many things, but female affection was not one of them. If they were going to compete for a woman now, at least the outcome of the apocalypse seemed like a good reason.

*** *** ***

Without sunlight Rook's birthday flowers soon wilted. That didn't bode well for the freedom they were meant to symbolize. She deserved something more.

Fin climbed up to the upper bunk and propped himself against the smooth, curving metal wall with a notebook and a pen while Rook lolled in the tub reading an antique issue of *National Geographic*. He intended to finish her song.

Inspiration came from the dream she'd told him about. Her mention of a tower had given him a strong jolt of deja vu, which combined with all the other strange events of late made him wonder if it really was a dream. Their connection felt fundamental, nigh-elemental. Perhaps she really had journeyed inside his mind.

It was slow going and his well quickly ran dry. After doodling for fifteen minutes, he sat, staring absently at Vesuvius. The blobs of lava began behaving oddly. They became smaller and more numerous, bouncing off each other in a near-frenzy.

"'Suvius?" Fin sat forward, concerned.

Vesuvius emitted a strangled sound, like a monumental note of embarrassment. Fin swiveled his head around, searching for the source.

Rook was no longer in the tub. Fin climbed down and found her writhing nude on the lower bunk with Inflatable Sally. Sally was also nude. Rook kissed Sally enthusiastically, kneading her crinkly plastic breast and grinding their pelvises together.

Fin was speechless. He blinked several times and cleared his throat.

"Join us, darling," Rook murmured.

Fin stumbled to the bunk and stared down, unsure what was expected of him.

"We're waiting," Rook breathed. She peeked at Fin and winked.

"Rook..." Fin began, but had no idea where to go with it.

"Sally told me she missed you," Rook sighed. "She was getting jealous just watching us."

"But we never... I never. With Sally. Never."

"Oooh," Rook cooed. "A virgin!" She straddled the inflatable doll and caressed it.

Fin was still uncertain how to proceed.

Rook glanced back over her shoulder and said, "This is as close as you're ever gonna get to a three-way, babe." She leaned down and licked Sally's nipple.

Fin shrugged, took a deep breath and tumbled into the midst of the sweaty, slick female forms. Rook moaned with anticipation and Sally made a sound like a happy inner-tube.

The condom-like smell of Sally and the musky, sweet saltiness of Rook blended and quickly stormed Fin's slight hesitancy. He abandoned all remnants of prudishness and plunged ahead with enthusiasm, relishing the unique and disparate sensations of living flesh and synthetic.

There was no one else he could do something so ridiculous with and still tolerate, with or without chemical assistance. Fin congratulated himself on finding his perfect mate.

***   ***   ***

Kyle sat alone in the greenroom, watching Spitz's debut on the monitor and swigging whiskey from the bottle. His chief impression of Reverend Declan Spitz was that he had an appropriate name.

The show was going well, though. With continued support from Kyle, Spitz would win over Shaw's audience.

After telling the Board he had 'been shown' who should guide the flock in praise, Kyle spent some quality time with Reverend Spitz. His goal was more challenging than controlling what the man said or altering what he knew. He needed to imbue Spitz with the old Shaw charisma. He needed to make sure people kept tuning in. And he had to do it carefully, so Spitz wouldn't be aware and so it didn't give him too much power. Best if it could be temporary.

He'd delivered a booster shot right before Spitz took the pulpit, and apparently it worked.

Working with Spitz, the subtlety and brevity, was a lot harder than disposing of rivals and scoring with bimbos. Kyle hoped, even let himself pray a bit, that it would get easier. He took a bigger pull on the whiskey.

In about an hour he would be downstairs to get an update on the search for Rook and Fin. Rook's frequency settings were among the files lost during the raid. Along with reinforcing everyone's standing orders, Kyle expanded the program a bit. There were terabytes of surveillance data and his brother and the woman would show up in it somewhere. He wanted anything within the last year or so on both of them, plus a fix on their whereabouts and present activities.

His tech-monkeys had given him some tidbits which, though tantalizing, led nowhere. The database had frustrating gaps. There was a technical limit to how many subjects could be listened to at once.

Rook and Fin weren't in the factory when the clean-up crew arrived, and ever since there hadn't been a recorded peep out of either one. It was like they vanished from the face of the Earth.

Kyle took another shot and tried not to slip further into melodrama. He capped the bottle, so he wouldn't pass out and miss the briefing.

Rook and Fin were almost certainly together in some protected location that blocked the transmission. Unless they knew about the jewelry? No. The last recording pertained to Rook's theories about the University's involvement.

Quaint. Way off.

*** *** ***

They dressed in hippie clothes Fin left behind when he moved out. He wore baggy striped pants and a tie-dye tee. Rook looked fetching in cutoffs and an oversized hemp shirt.

Fin climbed the ladder and opened the hatch an inch. Sunlight shot in, dazzling him. So, daytime. He opened the hatch all the way and peered out. All quiet. He helped Rook up and out. After locking the hatch, Fin led Rook to the Tanners' garage and looked in the window. No car. Brad and Melissa were probably at work, making this a weekday.

Using his key, Fin opened the back door. Not much had changed since he'd been here last, years ago. The walls were the same flat light-gray that erased all trace of shadow or depth, virtually unadorned. The dining room, seldom used, held the two pieces of artwork in the entire house — one large high-gloss square in yellow, one in purple. Not the most appetizing decorations, to be sure. The floors were endless expanses of blue-gray carpet, industrial in its stain- and wear-hiding abilities and ultra-short nap. The furniture had been upgraded, but held to Melissa's Shaker-like beliefs in simplicity. The sort of house that might look wonderful in a magazine, but was uninviting to a resentful teenage stepson. The sole addition to the decor was a small portrait of Kyle on the mantel.

Fin led Rook into the spacious, celadon kitchen. The clock on the microwave read 10:02. Rook found a newspaper on the breakfast bar. Thursday, October 12. They'd been in the shelter for two weeks, twice as long as he'd estimated.

Old newspapers were in a stack in the garage. Fin and Rook looked through the previous weeks' editions for mention of the factory, but found nothing. Good. It at least meant no one with actual legal authority should be looking for them.

A lot of ink was devoted to the explosion at Olaf's. The cops and fire officials were tight-lipped about details, but it didn't seem likely they would link anything back to Fin. The basement office was leased to a dummy company and efforts were focused in that direction.

All good news, as far as Rook and Fin were concerned.

Fin felt anxious to get out of the house. He kept expecting Kyle to walk in. Rook's sharp intake of breath startled him. He looked around, but Rook was reading something in the paper.

"Interesting," she said.

"What?"

"Reverend Shaw's obituary. In last Monday's paper. Two Mondays ago."

Relief flooded through Fin, followed by an uneasy sensation. "What's it say?"

Rook read: "Reverend Brian Shaw, father of Shaw Ministries, was found dead in his home yesterday of an apparent heart attack at the age of sixty-five. His body was discovered after he failed to appear as scheduled for the Sunday morning broadcast. He had been dead for several days. The future of the Ministries' works is unclear and a successor is yet to be named.

"'We look to the Lord in this time of sorrow and trust in Him to guide our decisions. Daily operations will continue as usual, after a brief period of mourning,' said a spokesman for the Shaw Cathedral.

"The broadcast this Sunday is planned as a memorial to the late reverend, whose involvement in such causes as..."

Rook looked up at Fin, her blue eyes sparkling with a mad glint. "Then there's a bunch of religious crap." She smiled. "We're in the clear!"

"A heart attack at home, huh?" Fin was skeptical.

"You're not suggesting it's not true, are you?" Rook asked in a mock-indignant voice.

"It doesn't say anything about Kyle in there, does it?"

"Sadly, no." Rook folded the paper and put it away. "Without the reverend to sign his paychecks, maybe he'll go away." She sounded hopeful.

Fin hugged her. "And I was so looking forward to all the family reunions." He sighed wistfully. "The market for mercenaries is pretty limited in a college town. He'll probably move to a city."

With their relief so fresh, their celebratory kiss escalated to a life-affirming fuck against the counter.

*** *** ***

Fin and Rook bought Bishop lunch at the Vagabond to thank him for his help. The three of them sat at a large round booth in the back under a map of wartime Paris, and shared a pitcher of warm Stout and a platter of nachos. Bishop ended up sitting in the middle, much to his chagrin.

Fin was more centered than Bishop had ever seen him. The hard rime of prickly nihilism had been scraped away. Bishop sensed this was the real Fin, the Fin who tried for years to express himself through drug abuse, searching for the chemical combination that would allow him to be.

Rook was bright, funny and a little neurotic. Bishop thought she had depths she was afraid to explore. He liked her.

Their waiter wound his way through the stacks of sticker-festooned steamer trunks and barrels decorating the restaurant, and passed out their slices of carrot cake.

Several minutes of quiet eating passed. Fin said, "What'll you do if Kyle comes back to the house?"

This Kyle issue was worrying for Bishop. He'd never particularly liked the guy, but hadn't disliked him either.

"Well, I'll get the lock changed today, and I'll box his stuff up. I don't think he's coming back. Not now that his cover's blown." He shook his head. "Now that life resembles an espionage film."

"Sorry, dude. We'd prefer a light romantic comedy..." Fin said.

"Or maybe an arty European thing with lots of symbolism and gratuitous nudity and subtitles." said Rook.

*** *** ***

Bishop excused himself at the end of the meal with a nod to Fin and a kiss on the back of Rook's hand. The couple sat and stared at each other for several minutes. Rook said, "You know, I need to file this story. Or, actually not this story. Some hastily-written piece of shit smokescreen."

"Sounds great."

"So I need to hastily write it first." She took out her laptop and a freshly charged battery. "Do you mind if I tune you out for a while?"

"We need to pick up that paperwork at the courthouse by 4:30," Fin pointed out.

"I said, 'hastily.'"

"Okay," Fin chuckled. "I'll meet you back here later. I should get an idea of my status at *Sycamore*. Find out if I still have a job or if they'll be pressing charges. It should only take an hour."

"An hour apart? It will feel like eternity." Rook batted her eyes.

"Soon, my sweetest, we shall be united in secular matrimony."

"Aw, that's such a pretty way to say it."

Fin kissed her, and said, "Not as pretty as you."

Rook smirked at him. He giggled, which made her snort trying not to laugh out loud.

Fin said, "We're this sappy now, what will happen to us once we're married?"

"Respectability," Rook answered. Fin looked aghast. "Sorry. It's mandatory."

"Well, I still want to marry you. Must be true love."

They kissed again, the kind of kiss that pushes out the whole world. Finally, Rook regretfully reminded Fin he was the one who was concerned about being late.

He kissed her another time, and left. Rook invented an absurd rant claiming Buck U's ultimate ambition was to use the dream control to program people into mindlessly loyal sports boosters. It took her ten minutes.

She left the Vagabond and headed for *CTP*'s office, four blocks over. After filing her story and sparring with her editor, Rook stopped at Goodwill and bought some clothes. She couldn't wear Fin's castoffs forever, and didn't want to deal with the hassle of cleaning all her stuff out of Marcus's apartment. The paper grocery bag of miniskirts, funky tops, and strangers' underwear would buy her another week of stalling once she hit the laundromat. On the way back to the Vagabond, she daydreamed, enjoying the outdoors after being confined underground. Fin's signal was a faint, pleasant caress near the base of her skull.

Dark eyes penetrated her reverie, and until she realized it was the wooden Indian in front of the Geronimo Sports Bar she couldn't breathe. He was weathered and beak-nosed and only two-thirds scale, but he stood on a pedestal which placed his chiseled visage about six feet above the sidewalk. The carved figure's exaggerated seriousness, its air of ludicrous nobility, reminded her of Marcus. She saw a connection between this caricature of a chief and his unintentional lampoon of a medicine man.

"Raven."

The voice behind her was like a knife. Rook whirled to face Marcus, her lungs again rigid. He seized her arm, his face stony. He squeezed.

Rook gasped in pain but didn't try to pull free. She met his stare and waited to see what he had to say. She wouldn't give him any words to twist.

With a faint sneer, Marcus asked, "Is he dead?"

She considered lying, thinking it might offer Fin some protection, but saw it couldn't work. Marcus would feel entitled to her all the more. "No. He's stronger than ever, I think." She tried to speak without inflection. Stick to the facts.

"Just as well."

Rook dared to hope Marcus had already replaced her, until he continued.

"His destruction is my duty. Bad if somebody else does it."

"He's strong now," Rook now attempted to sound concerned for Marcus. "I don't think you should try to destroy him."

Marcus smiled. Rook trembled with dread over what amusing thought he'd had, but he released her arm. Sensation invaded her hand like a swarm of carbonated bees. Marcus shook his head slightly and said, "Come."

"No."

"Now!" Marcus barked. He reached for her again, but she drew back.

"I can't! I can't and I won't! Marcus, please..."

He sneered and grabbed for her again, forcing her to retreat another step. A man emerged from Geronimo's and timidly asked if there was a problem. Marcus looked at him and he shrank back and closed the door. Please call the cops, Rook hoped. Marcus had her backed up against the building. His hard, cold eyes pinned her to the wall. Rook was scared, but a calm internal voice said, 'So much for sticking to the facts.' She let that voice take over.

"I can't Marcus. I'm trying to tell you he's very powerful."

"He's nothing."

"Oh, not true." She remembered how spaced-out Marcus was after their escape in the truck. "And you know it." He looked away. "His medicine is strange, and I cannot leave him."

Marcus looked stricken.

Rook pressed her advantage. "He has my magic now, too. You will need to seek another."

"No!" Marcus bawled.

"Yes," Rook said. She overcame the impulse to say anything further. It seemed like Marcus would collapse on the spot, and she'd be able to slip away.

Marcus suddenly grabbed her by the shoulders and peered into her eyes. He grimaced and looked away, wailing. "It's true! It's true!"

Rook blinked.

"I can see it, now. What he's done…"

"It really isn't that awful."

Marcus faced her again. "Yes it is. He can't have you."

"Well, he does," she said. "He's too powerful and tricky for you. You should forget me, forget the whole thing."

"He's bewitched your mouth. He controls what you say."

"Oh for fuck's sake," Rook said. Marcus looked hopeful for the moment. Presumably this sounded more like 'his' Rook. "Listen to me. We're all done here. Go away."

"I won't let go, Raven."

Let him call me whatever he wants, she told herself. Use his bizarre affectation against him. She smiled, gesturing with her index finger for Marcus to lean close, and whispered in his ear. "He thinks he's won. The only way to defeat him now is to out-trick him."

Marcus smiled weakly and rubbed his chin, which meant he didn't know what she meant but could tell he was supposed to. "Out-trick him."

Rook nodded.

"How?" Marcus looked suspiciously at Rook.

"Befriend him. Study him," she said, her voice pitched to ask why it wasn't obvious. Her game rested on selling him this idea.

A light came on in Marcus's face. "I can get him to give me his medicine, I can steal his knowledge!"

"Right," said Rook, wondering if this was really the best she could hope for. "But you'll need to be nice to him." She exhaled as his gaze softened. He looked confident, pleased. Seeing that expression on his face made her nervous, but it was better than the fury that was there before.

"Raven," he said again, "it's time for you to come home. We'll plan together how to break his spell and steal his power."

Now Rook was furious, at Marcus of course, and at herself for thinking anything good could come of playing by his rules. No, what he needed was a sharp dose of reality.

"Marcus, I am getting married. To Fin. Call some of the women you fucked while we were going out. Have fun." She held her breath, hoping she hadn't miscalculated the dosage.

Chapter Sixteen

WEDDING

Undergrounded
neural net is on the blink - sparks leap and collide
never know I'm here inside
undergrounded
no basis in reality - left of center, way off base
never know which way to chase
undergrounded
safety, warm and glowing red - you've been deep inside
my head
and now I've got you in my bed - what we share cannot be
shed
undergrounded
music and lyrics by Fin Tanner

Fin shielded his eyes against the sunlight streaming through the trees. He moved a block off the main avenue, to a quieter and shadier street. He breathed the clean air and looked up into the blue sky, happy he still had his job. *Sycamore's* temporary offices were in rented trailers near the bus station.

Something validating about a job, even a shitty one. He intended to quit without notice someday, hopefully soon, which he couldn't do if they canned him. The pay was better than nothing, especially for the stint he'd agreed to put in that evening at double his regular rate. It was mildly ghoulish, what with large-scale hospitalization of staff as the cause for his good fortune. Mildly.

"Mr Tanner?"

Fin stopped in his tracks. He didn't look at the person who'd said his name, just stood and weighed the relative merits of answering and fleeing.

The interloper spoke again, "Hello. I'm Leaf. I'm very happy, and honored, to meet you."

Fin looked at him. Young guy, puke green sweater. Shit. "What do you want?"

Leaf the Sweaterguy smiled a sheepish little grin and said, "We want you, actually." He looked like he needed to pee. "You are very special."

"And look how far it's gotten me. Leave me alone, okay?"

Sweaterkid looked stunned and appalled. He shook his head. "It's not that simple. You are needed."

"You'll figure out a way to get by without me, I'm sure," Fin replied. "Now toddle along and tell the Grand Poobah I said, 'Fuck off.'"

He shook his head again. "Not just us. I meant you're necessary. You don't have a choice in this. You do know how different you are?"

"Screw you and your fate-slash-destiny crap. I believe in free will. It's practically the only thing I believe in."

"And well you should. I'm not selling predestination here, Mr Tanner. That's superstition." He looked all around before continuing. "But like many superstitions, it grows from a hidden truth. Our actions are part of a larger pattern, and free will is limited."

The kid stooped and picked up a small stone. "Perhaps an example would help. Would you say I was talking about fate if I predicted this pebble will fall to the street when I drop it?" He dropped the pebble, which clattered on the pavement. He beamed at Fin.

"Wow. You're good," Fin said.

Leaf sighed. "Humor me."

"I am the pebble. I got it." Fin's words restored hope to the other's eyes. "But you can't have me. I don't belong to you."

"No! Of course not. You belong *with* us!"

Fin appraised the guy's clothing and demeanor skeptically. "Are you positive? I mean, what do you see here that makes you think for one instant your little club wants me as a member?"

"Nothing. Appearances are deceptive."

Fin scowled.

"You've read our manifesto."

Fin took a step back.

Sweaterguy stopped talking.

Fin took another step backward. They were spying on him. How long? Probably since he blundered into their office. Before that? And the model they had, from his dream. He felt dizzy, overwhelmed by the sudden pressing demand to take all this seriously.

Sweaterguy looked nervous now. He held up his palms and said, "I'm sorry. We expected you to be happy to get this invitation. We thought you were searching for the same things we are. Like the reason for the dream. There's so much we could learn from you. There is so much to be done. It's time, now. Please join us?"

"No way," Fin said with another retreating step.

"Mr Tanner, think. You know we're not the only group with an interest in you. You were taken to the factory. We had nothing to do with that."

"You fuckers got me into that when you kidnapped Rook!" Fin hissed. He furrowed his brow. "Hang on. You set up the whole thing. You sent her to Kyle!"

Sweaterpunk shook his head. "It wasn't like that. We were one step ahead. The reverend was already on his way, and our preparations gave her immunity to the Perceptual Disruption Field."

"What?"

"Oh. You were in a coma. Never mind. We didn't anticipate your presence, which is exactly the point..."

"What do you mean, your preparations? What did you do?"

"She wasn't harmed."

Fin exploded. "Answer me! What did you do to her!"

Sweaterdick calmly said, "I can't tell you about that unless you come with me. You must join first."

"Oh, you sick fucks."

"There is something I can show you. All you have to do is come over to the van around the corner. You won't even need to get in. No tricks, no strings. Just come and look."

Fin fought to control his trembling. "Why should I want to see anything you have?"

"You do, believe me. I don't blame you for being angry, but this is something you want to see. I think it will help."

"Help what?"

"I'll start to explain on the way. All we ask is that you see." The young man turned, keeping an expectant eye on Fin. As he took a few tentative steps, Fin sulked along behind him. "It's a reconstruction of visual stimuli. We have software that can handle still images in cortical format. Way too slow for anything in real-time, but neat. This particular image will interest you." They reached the intersection and Fin saw a dark green van with someone waiting in the driver's seat. They headed toward it.

Sweaterdouche opened the rear doors, revealing an enormous array of electronic components. A computer monitor stared out from the midst of it all, cursor blinking.

"Show him," Sweaterprick said, and the monitor flickered before displaying a grainy black-and-white image. The spider-legged bathysphere from Fin's dream, like the model he saw in the office.

"This image was captured by monitoring my brain waves while I visualized the dream. Does it look familiar?"

Fin stared.

"Show the other one."

The monitor flickered again, and the eerie image became a bit clearer. The angle of view also changed, but it was the same unearthly object and the same dismal sea-floor.

"This is an intercepted transmission. Strange frequency pattern, but not encrypted. Signals like this are detected almost nightly, and there's a definite correlation."

"To what?" Fin asked.

Leaf the Sweaterbastard blinked. He searched for words, as if this should be painfully obvious. "The abductions."

Fin didn't react.

"The alien abductions." He closed the doors. "That's as much as I can tell an outsider."

Fin reminded himself to blink, hoping it looked natural. He gazed off into the distance for a moment and said, "Well, that only makes sense. Tell ya what, I'll get back to you on the whole joining thing." He turned and resumed his trek toward the Vagabond to collect Rook and go get their marriage license. Over his shoulder he said, "Remember, duck and cover. Bye now."

*** *** ***

The intertwined lines swept gracefully, around each other and the tiny elongate rhombus they enclosed. Diamonds are forever. The pattern comprised a single line, knotted over itself into an intricate tracery with no beginning or end.

A pair of college guys entered Talisman, their jocularity and baggy shorts offending the tranquility of Coyote's den. Marcus sat motionless, tracking them with his eyes. They were startled to discover they were being watched, and one of them made a half-hearted greeting. They stayed for another minute, pretending to look at the walls.

Business as usual, lately.

Marcus resumed work on his spell, thinking about Raven, how she spoke to him. It had been difficult to hear her through Rook's bewitched words, but Coyote heard. He'd wanted to snatch her away, but Raven warned of Fin's new power. Knowing they could defeat him working together, and knowing that's what Raven wanted too, he said it was time for her to come home.

"Marcus, I am getting married. To Fin. Call some of the women you fucked while we were going out. Have fun." That was what Rook's mouth said. Marcus heard the words.

Coyote listened much more carefully. To him, Raven spoke of a powerful ceremony. She hinted it would be his last chance.

"You're right," he said with a sigh. She looked surprised. He did his best to look sad. "I guess this isn't working anymore. We had a good run, though, didn't we?"

"Sure. Whatever." Rook wasn't buying it yet, but Raven's voice told him to keep going.

"You and me, Rook, we've had our ups and downs." Marcus knew he couldn't address her by her true name right now, but Raven would hear him anyway. "Both of us fucked around a lot, but we always came back together. I thought we always would. No matter how many times you stepped out, you always came home. How was I supposed to know this time was different?"

Watching carefully, Marcus caught a hint of some unaccustomed expression in her brilliant blue eyes. Guilt, or maybe pity. With Raven's silent encouragement he pressed ahead.

"I took care of you because I thought we had something. I never made you pay rent. I never made you pay for any of your ink."

"I paid for the first one," Rook was quick to point out.

Marcus bit back the flood of expletives and said with a shake of his head, "I gave you a big discount on that."

"Because I sucked your dick."

"Because you sucked it well. Hell, Rook, we had so much fun together. You can't deny that."

She didn't, but she also didn't agree. Raven had fallen silent, too. Coyote had to let Raven know that he would not fail her. He had to tell her that he understood.

"You really love this guy?"

"Yes, Marcus, I really love him." Raven's voice telling Coyote she needed his help to throw off Fin's spell.

Marcus banked the hot coals of his anger and promised Raven he would bring powerful medicine. "I'll do your rings," he said. "Tattoo rings. It'll be my wedding gift."

Rook laughed.

"I'm serious."

"Why the hell would you want to do that? And why the hell would I let you?"

Marcus took a deep breath and smiled, warmly he hoped. "Like I said, you're special. I want you to be happy. I wish you could be happy with me, but if you can't, who am I to stand in your way? If I don't wish you happiness I'm being petty and that's not good for my spirit."

She seemed to believe the words he was saying. Raven was aiding his cause, guiding him to say the things Rook wanted to hear. Reminding him to smile. Raven understood his rage, but it had to be kept hidden from Rook. Rook had to think he was happy.

And he would be, soon enough. Coyote looked ahead to winning his Raven back, and that made it easy to smile.

"By giving you the rings I'll prove to myself that I'm the bigger man. And seeing you marry him will be absolute proof that it's over between us. It'll give me closure. If I don't see it for myself I'll always wonder."

Rook extracted an endless list of promises, demanding sincere assurance he wouldn't sabotage the wedding. But she never made him promise not to work his own magic into the design of the rings.

Raven didn't let it come up.

***   ***   ***

To say Bishop was surprised when Fin asked him to perform the ceremony would be putting it mildly. Fin remembered Bishop getting ordained to perform his sister's wedding and wondered if he could "really perform real weddings." Bishop assured Fin he could, all the while wondering what the punch line would be.

Belatedly realizing Fin wasn't joking, Bishop felt honored. And rushed. The ceremony was to take place the next day, Friday the 13th. The happy couple insisted the date didn't matter, that they'd already used up all their bad luck. The three of them were now discussing the details of the ceremony over Chinese take-out at Cinemopolis, specifically the guest list.

Rook downed the remainder of her beer in one gulp. "Not my mom, that's for sure. She'd jinx it."

Bishop and Fin quirked eyebrows.

"She's on her seventh husband." Rook tossed her empty onto the pile with the others. "Unless, of course, there've been recent developments. She doesn't approve of my relationship choices, so we don't talk much these days."

Both men said, "Shit."

"Yeah. It's embarrassing. Fucking ridiculous. What it comes down to is: I don't want her at our wedding." Rook looked defiantly at Bishop. "And no, I don't want my dad there either."

Rook opened another beer. After several swallows she took a deep breath, then looked sheepishly up at Fin and Bishop.

"Sorry." She smiled weakly. "Issues."

"Just proves you're human," Bishop said.

"I can think of at least one household item who would be prepared to debate that assertion," said Fin.

Rook laughed, her eyes and Fin's dancing to the beat of a private joke. She looked at Bishop and turned grave. Fin took her hands as she spoke. "I don't want to be Brook Brandymoon anymore. My name has always changed according to my mother's whims. Reflected her egregious choices. I want a name I have some say in. I want to be Rook Tanner."

"You are," intoned Fin. They looked at each other again, and kissed. It started as a peck, a discreet thing rehearsed between lovers for use in public, but they immediately forgot Bishop was there. Soul kissing, nuzzling. Resting upon each other, cheek-to-cheek. Holding hands. Bishop watched politely, or at least as politely as one can stare at an oblivious couple necking within arm's reach.

They stopped kissing with obvious reluctance but not a hint of embarrassment. Bishop wondered if they could jump right back into the discussion.

"What about siblings? Rook?"

She sighed. "I have an older half-brother and a younger half-sister. Wouldn't miss either one. Goes double for the temporary siblings. I lost count of them."

Bishop turned to Fin. "You don't want Kyle."

"Sadly, he left no forwarding address. I wish him well, in hopes he'll have less reason to come back."

Everyone clinked cans.

Fin looked at the metal ceiling of the projection booth. "Brad and Melissa can read about it in the newspaper. The only family I want there isn't going to be." He looked at Rook. "Willow."

"Your mother." Rook's voice was gentle.

Bishop felt a mixture of emotions. Sympathetic sadness for his friend, and a kind of pride. Fin's mom had always been a forbidden topic. Lurking behind these noble feelings were pangs of jealousy. Rook was the reason Fin could be this open, this strong about a painful subject. She was replacing Bishop in Fin's cosmos. Probably healthy for all three of them.

Fin became quiet, and Rook stroked his temple. He closed his eyes, tightly then more tranquilly. "Sorry," he said. Looking at Bishop, he said, "I momentarily forgot my cool demeanor of slacker detachment." He glanced at Rook and added, "Issues."

She grinned.

"So, Bish," Fin resumed, "do you have an entry for our dysfunctional family awards?"

"Some of my cousins married each other. Second cousins, mind you, but still."

"I'm afraid that doesn't top an Evil Half-Twin, but thanks for playing."

Bishop regarded Rook. "I guess we give him this award?"

"Well, Kyle is tough to beat," said Rook.

"But..." Fin waited alertly.

"But... Mom met Number Five because I was dating his son, so while they were married I was sleeping with my stepbrother for a while." Rook showed off, pincering a clump of fried rice with her chopsticks and popping it into her mouth with a flourish.

Fin said, "I think we should invite him to the wedding."

Rook quickly replied, "No, you don't."

Fin grinned. Bishop interjected, "So, do we have a winner?"

"My entry," said Rook, "despite its piquant whiff of scandal, pales beside a ripe dung heap like Kyle. Fin takes it."

"Which all translates to no family at the ceremony," Bishop said. "Just us."

"And Marcus," said Fin.

"Marcus?" Bishop exclaimed.

"He's going to give us tattoo wedding rings," said Rook. "Besides, we need a witness, right?"

Bishop shook his head in amazement.

"He's cool with it. Rook talked to him," explained Fin. "We think it will help him understand we're serious."

Bishop hoped they were right. "I'm a firm believer in letting people make their own decisions," he said, "and their own mistakes. But I don't like to actively participate in making those mistakes."

Rook and Fin nodded at Bishop and smiled at one another.

"Before I can agree to wed you, I need to know why you want me to," Bishop declared, hoping to get on to the next topic before the couple forgot he was there again. They turned to him, and Fin spoke.

"Because you're my best friend. And you'll let us do it the way we want."

"I meant, why do you want to get married? You share a pretty low opinion of marriage as an institution, and you've both come from very bad examples of how families operate. So, why?"

Rook considered for a moment. "It never occurred to me such a question existed. It's the kind of thing you know way down deep, below words. It's hard to explain."

"Take your time."

Rook continued, "I guess it seems, from the outside, like we're jumping to do the conventional thing. Like we want society's approval of us as a couple. But, it's the fact that we are willing to jump through these hoops. It's a statement. No — not a statement. A sacrifice. We don't care if society approves of our bond, but the bond is more important than our individualistic ideals. So, we'll do the conventional thing, but not in the conventional manner." Rook looked at Fin quizzically. "At least that's the way I see it."

Fin put his arm around her waist and pulled her onto his lap. He moved her hair aside so he could nibble her ear. They both started giggling and Fin moved down her neck.

Bishop said. "What about you, Fin?"

"Ditto," came the muffled response.

"Nope. You can do better than that."

With a sigh, the lovers slid back to their previous positions. As Fin spoke, Rook kissed his fingers.

"I do agree with Rook. Who wouldn't?"

"Good boy," Rook cooed.

"I mean, being together, forever, is all that matters. That's the ideal of marriage. We're idealists. It's sensible to marry the woman I love. That's what marriage is for."

"More than that," Rook added, snaking her arms around Fin's neck, "all through time, while people have married and done their thing, it's been leading up to us. Ours is the reason marriages exist."

"So, by ceremonially sacrificing a bit of your idealistic freedom, and creating something eternal and beautiful, you will be, in effect, fulfilling the destiny of connubial arrangements." Bishop paused. "Did I miss anything?"

"When we're together, I am complete," Fin said.

"Making it official is a way of protecting us. No one will dare to pull us apart."

They faced each other, Rook straddling Fin's lap. They began kissing again.

"Okay, you pass," Bishop said. "Run to your subterranean love-nest before I have to dare to pull you apart."

Fin carried Rook out the door, kissing her.

*** *** ***

The buzz of the tattoo needle filled the small room. Fin sat beside Rook on the edge of Bishop's bed. Marcus sat on a stool while he worked on Rook's left hand, having finished Fin's already. Bishop sat cross-legged on a large pillow. Vesuvius undulated beside him on the floor. Incense burning on the windowsill lent the proceedings the scent of spice cookies baking in an opium den. Their one nod to tradition was Rook's white dress, in actuality a nylon slip with a lacy bodice that she picked up at Goodwill for a quarter.

Bishop had been talking for more than half an hour about love and its cross-cultural importance, traditions, legends, lore, manifestations and beauty. Fin felt uncharacteristically content and alert.

Several minutes later Marcus indicated he was done and sat back to watch with an amused expression, his arms folded across his chest and his boots on the stool. Bishop wove the final thread back into the verbal tapestry of his marriage benediction and fell silent.

Fin looked at his left hand, at Rook's, and into her eyes. When he'd first seen her, her eyes reminded him of snow and shadow. They were much warmer now, like tropical waters. She smiled and Fin knew they were doing the right thing.

Sinking to one knee, he held the tattoo needle the way he'd been shown, and completed the circle around her slender finger as he pledged his love, devotion, support and protection. Marcus handed Rook the other needle, and she completed Fin's ring and made her pledge.

Bishop said, "By the power vested in me by the Natural Order, and certain legal entities, I now pronounce you Husband and Wife. Congratulations. Now kiss."

*** *** ***

After anointing the wedding bands with antiseptic ointment and signing the papers to make it legal, Marcus left.

Fin and Rook lit a joint and passed it around. "We didn't get a cake," Rook explained.

Lounging on Bishop's bed with Fin she felt perfectly content. She concentrated on Fin, the feel of his body next to hers, the smell of him, the sound of his breathing, his gentle thrumming in her head. Her eyelids drifted closed.

Rook saw herself in a long, heavy dress of black and white, many layered, regal. A crown rested light upon her brow and she stood alone by the edge of a flat, gray lake. To her right was a small, oval table, waist high and glossy ebony with mother of pearl and ivory inlaid inside the lipped edge. The six legs of the table were twisted copper, green with age. The air hung dank and still. Her feet were cold. Wiggling her bare toes, she felt the damp, rough grass.

When she looked back at the table she noticed a small velvet bag, black on one side, white on the other, drawn with a braided silk cord. She cupped her hands and breathed on them, then rubbed them together to warm them. Her wedding ring had healed, and there was a similar one on her right ring finger, still raw.

Once her hands were warmed, she reached into the bag and pulled out its contents, a single silver coin, large enough to fill the palm of her hand. Slippery smooth and brutally cold, it drew heat from her hands as she turned it over and over to examine it. On each side was the likeness of a knight's head. Similar, but not identical. One side shone bright in the dim sunlight, the other, dark with tarnish, glinted dully.

She tucked the velvet bag into her sash and contemplated the coin a moment longer. There were neither words nor numbers, just the two faces. The crown on her head felt heavy now, but she knew she couldn't remove it, could not abdicate. The coin was drawing all the heat from her fingers, her hands. It would rob her of all warmth if she held it much longer, would kill her, and when she fell it would land on the table and the decision would be made. Heads, or heads? Rook was unable to make the decision, but it was her destiny, so with numb fingers she stood the coin on edge and spun it.

The coin twirled on the table's glassy surface. As Rook held her breath and watched, awaiting the decision, the two knights melded into one regal face, complete with crown. Rook gasped. She couldn't let a choice be made of one or the other. It must be both.

The spinning coin started to slow. Rook dropped to her knees by the table, grasping it to steady herself and getting her gown muddy and wet. She blew at the coin in a desperate attempt to keep it spinning, but knew she couldn't continue for long. She grew colder as the coin began to wobble.

***

Rook's head cleared and she wanted to get Fin alone. Being an understanding sort, Bishop kicked them out of his room and wished them a happy wedding night.

As all newly married couples are wont to do, the two of them spent the walk back to the bomb shelter where they planned to honeymoon calling each other Mister and Missus and Husband and Wife and marveling at the newness and wonder of it all.

As Rook's wedding gift to Fin she finally pierced his right nipple, and placed the silver hoop from her navel in it.

Fin closed his eyes while he played his bass and quietly sang Rook his first song. After exchanging gifts, they spent the remainder of the night making love and sleeping cradled in one another's arms.

Chapter Seventeen

Limousine

Party tonight (Saturday) at Sanderson Park.
Kegs and a variety of chemically interesting party favors arrive at
8:00 and you should, too. Bring libations or victuals to share. Or
more party favors.
Nicotine plays at 9:00, and probably again later. Unless the cops
show up.
Come meet my new wife! Her name's Rook and she's awesome.
email invitation to Fin and Rook Tanner's wedding
reception

Pay dirt.

"A signal has been identified as this 'Fin Tanner.' He dropped out
before a geographic fix could be obtained, but he's in the Webster area."

Kyle sat up straighter, then slouched a little to conceal his eagerness.
"Let me hear it."

The technician, Rodriguez, placed a laptop on Kyle's desk and
tapped a few keys. "I assigned several of the newer guys to scan through
the recent archives, listening for keywords. We're running out of
storage and we hope to purge the system of the unnecessary
information. One of the grunts found this. I'm afraid there's not much.
It starts with ambient noise, but shortly we get this exchange."

Rodriguez tapped one more key and Kyle heard:

"Mr Tanner? Hello. I'm Leaf. I'm very happy, and honored, to meet
you."

Who the hell would be honored to meet Fin? Or call him Mr
Tanner? Must be a different Tanner. Fin's tinny voice assaulted his ears.

"What do you want?"

"We want you, actually. You are very special," said the other guy.

A crackle of static interrupted, followed by several seconds of feedback. The guy talking to Fin cut back in, "—elling predestination here, Mr Tanner. That's superstition. But like many superstitions, it grows from a hidden truth. Our actions are part of a larger pattern, and free will is limited."

Kyle was bored with this guy already. It was time for him to say something important or shut up. Instead of doing either, he said, "Would you say I was talking about fate if I predicted this pebble will fall to the street when I drop it?"

"Wow. You're good," Fin said.

The man sighed. "Humor me."

"I am the pebble. I g—"

Rodriguez said, "Unfortunately that's all."

The maddeningly inconsequential snippet revealed nothing of Fin's plans or whereabouts. 'I am the pebble'? What the fuck did that mean?

"With his frequency isolated," Rodriguez continued, "we're searching the archives to see what else we have."

"Good," said Kyle. "What about the girl?"

"If they're together, we'll be able to determine her frequency. Then we can begin a search for her, too."

"I want to hear anything with her voice on it."

They were still in Webster, his brother and this woman. They could not be allowed to slip away. After ordering his men into civilian garb to prepare for reconnaissance work, Kyle told his driver to get him to Webster.

The techs in Donner sent updates at regular intervals. He listened to each recording with interest, though they lacked anything concrete to base a plan on. When he got his first fresh taste of Rook, his tongue quivered where she'd bitten him. He listened again.

She said, "I had a family emergency, Roger."

"Yeah, well you still should have called!"

"I think you'll stop yelling after you read the story. It's great stuff."

Roger made some harrumphing noises. There were several moments of relative silence then Kyle heard a grudging chuckle. More laughter. Roger said, "I don't know where you come up with this shit. Dream control. Fanatical alumni sports fans. It's vintage Brandy Moon."

"Thanks."

"It doesn't excuse your unprofessional behavior."

"Can it, Roger. You can print it, or not. I don't care. Give me my check if you're gonna use it though. I lost my other job."

"I'll print it."

"Thanks."

"For your next assignment—"

"I have to go now. You wouldn't believe me if I told you why."

"Now, don't get all cr—"

Kyle shivered. Her voice went right to his groin. She sounded sultry and playful when she said, 'You wouldn't believe me if I told you why.' And the way she disrespected her boss. Delicious. She was strong. She didn't take anybody's shit.

Kyle wanted her.

His phone rang.

"Tanner."

"Sir! We've acquired the targets. Both of them. They're together and we're beginning triangulation."

"Fantastic." It took work to keep his voice neutral. "I want the live stuff patched through. Once you have a fix on them, send in the plain-clothes. Keep the trucks out of sight. No one moves until I give the word."

"Yes sir."

It took several minutes for the live patch to be up and running. Kyle waited impatiently until he heard loud music and lots of people talking. A party. Good. Easy to infiltrate.

All the hubbub made it difficult to pick out any single voice, but then he heard Rook.

"Tanner," she said. And again, louder, "Tanner. Rook Tanner."

More noise. Rook said, "The wedding was yesterday."

Kyle's blood roared in his ears, drowning out everything else. Sweat beaded on his temples. He looked down at his phone, now a mass of ruined electronics in his hand. Sounds of fevered revelry poured from the laptop's speaker.

***   ***   ***

Mercury vapor street lights lit the park with an eerie blue glow, modulated somewhat by the oranges and yellows of a bonfire. All the kegs had been kicked, but more were on the way.

This wedding reception was shaping up to be fodder for legends.

Nicotine's equipment was set up in the back of someone's old green pickup. The first set went over well, and the guys were taking a break to drink and mingle. Fin and Rook were making the rounds, meeting each other's friends, getting congratulated. They took frequent kiss breaks, one of which escalated into a quick sex break inside the cold green plastic tunnel of the park's twisty slide.

The arrival of the replacement kegs brought cheers. The small parking lot overflowed and people were parking on the street, now drawn by the crowd more than any desire to wish the newlyweds well.

Bishop tracked Fin and Rook down and said, "The crowd's gonna draw the wrong kind of attention."

Fin agreed.

Rook said, "If you want to play another set, why don't you do it now so we can split."

Fin gathered the rest of Nicotine and they climbed onto the truck. Rook and Bishop stood near the bonfire, away from the majority of the so-called dancers. Fin's new song thundered out and made small talk impossible.

Rook closed her eyes and let the music wash over her. The heat from the fire felt good at first, but became too much and she drifted forward a few steps. She noted with pleasure the slight changes this made in the connection she felt with Fin. As their proximity to each other increased or decreased, it caused swirls and eddies in the vibrations, or whatever they were. With time she'd probably learn to tell a lot from them, but for now it was an unknown language: pleasing and melodic, but relatively meaningless.

A hand on her shoulder brought her back to herself. She knew Marcus by the rough familiarity, even before she opened her eyes. His face looked spooky in the flickering light, full of shadows, but she knew him well enough to recognize his state of mind. He felt wronged, cheated. They had gone through this before. Rook realized Marcus still considered this an infidelity on her part.

Transferring his grip to her elbow, he tried to lead her away. She refused. They stared at each other. Rook watched, fascinated then frightened by the emotions storming on Marcus's face. His carefully constructed beliefs were cracking and falling away. Rook saw pain and anger, growing into fury, fleetingly supplanted by awe, finally resolving into hate. She refused to drop her gaze, to give him an opening. Her heartbeat accelerated and she struggled to keep her breathing smooth, not wanting to show fear. She let it sink in that she had, in his parlance, out-tricked him. That he had performed the act that bound her, his ultimate prize, to Fin, his ultimate foe.

Good thing there were a lot of other people around, especially Bishop. Fin still had the fading bruises from his last run-in with Marcus.

With a shriek and a boom the amplifiers blew out.

Rook became aware of people all around her screaming, of colored lights flashing. Her first thought was of police cars, but the lights came from overhead. Wave after wave of subsonics made it impossible to form any other thoughts. Marcus let go of her and grabbed his head with both hands.

Rook sidestepped and looked around for Fin or Bishop. On the truck, Fin flung his bass to the side and scanned the audience. She yelled to him, but of course he couldn't hear her. Everyone was screaming, the subsonics were ungodly. Feedback whines, loud popping sounds, and a buzzing hum drilled her ears. As Rook watched, the truck lurched and started drifting backward through the crowd, toward herself and the bonfire. People scrambled out of the way. The lights flashed faster.

A hand grabbed Rook's elbow and she turned to see Marcus. He pulled her through the panicking crowd, picked her up and slung her over his shoulder. She couldn't see anything, couldn't think. Marcus skirted the fire and broke through to open ground, hurrying toward the parking lot. Rook knew she couldn't let him get her into his van.

She struggled and twisted free, landing hard on her back. Winded, she scrambled to her feet and watched in horror as the pickup rolled into the bonfire amid sounds like gunshots. The gas tank ignited in a concussive fireball, throwing her to the ground again.

An insinuating blackness invaded the perimeter of her vision. For all the noise of the crowd, Rook noticed a profound silence. An emptiness where Fin should have been. Fighting the blackness back, she scanned the crush of people. The light was all wrong, illuminating nothing. Her eyes watered with the strain and she closed them.

Where was he?

Throbbing vibrations pummeled her. So much confusion. Rook frantically reached out for Fin with her mind. She knew, felt, just where to look for him. His frequency remained blank. Her fright mounted as she scanned.

Dead. Fin was dead.

The blackness swarmed her barriers and Rook collapsed into it.

*** *** ***

Marcus's vision swam in a poisonous green haze. He had to get Rook again, but couldn't find her. The world around him melted in acid flashbacks, she made it better. Stumbling, he fell hard to all fours. Crawling, away from the fire he hoped, his hand brushed something hard and smooth. Black leather boot. Marcus's gaze traveled up and discovered Rook attached to the boot, sprawled in the grass. Marcus pushed unsteadily to his feet, wanting to carry her to the van and get the hell out of here. He bent to lift her, but she was gone.

The light show ended, as did the hallucinatory effects. Pandemonium reigned in the aftermath of the explosion. Marcus took this all in as his head cleared. The side of his face felt wet. He touched it. Blood. His jacket was sticky with it.

Turning full circle, Marcus caught sight of Rook. A man in a black jacket carried her in both arms like a child. Marcus staggered after. The man placed Rook in the back of a waiting limousine and climbed in with her. Marcus steadied himself on a car, leaving a bloody smear on the roof. He read the license plate as the limo sped off. SHAWMIN. Shaman.

Marcus got to his van and put a rag over his wound to slow the bleeding. The possibility of another Shaman being involved changed everything. He had a hard time imagining a real shaman riding in a limo with vanity plates, but he'd seen it himself.

This was his real calling. Fin was nothing. Marcus needed to claim his woman from an equal, a shaman.

*** *** ***

Kyle said, "Lock the doors. Give me your phone. Close the privacy panel."

Once alone with Rook, he relaxed and checked her pulse. Steady. Her breathing, slow and shallow. He straightened her clothes and smoothed her hair back from her face, then plucked the blue stone from her nose. Haltingly, almost reverentially, he lifted her black tank top, revealing her taut, pale belly. Her skin was silky and incredibly sexy, and he kept finding more tattoos, like these birds all over the side of her torso. A tiny empty piercing hole capped her navel. After tracing his finger around it for a few moments, wondering what her jewelry looked like, and where it went, Kyle slid her shirt up to expose her glorious tits and enticingly erect nipples. He removed her silver nipple ring and placed it and the nose stud in a small steel box.

He ran his hands over her naked flesh.

Her skin felt smooth and warm, the paleness a vivid contrast to the hunter green leather of the limousine's upholstery. She smelled of plums and exotic spices. Her neck looked so delicate and inviting, Kyle had the urge to kiss her throat and feel her pulse with his mouth. Her eyelids were almost translucent in their paleness, rimmed with smudged black. Kyle could do anything he wanted. She couldn't stop him, wouldn't even know. Her slate-green miniskirt rode low on her hips. It flared invitingly, and Kyle ran his left hand up her thigh. She wasn't wearing stockings, but she was wearing panties. Cotton. Damp.

He stopped because he wanted her to want him. When he'd rescued her at the factory, she almost gave in to him. Would have, if that lumbering oaf Marcus hadn't barged in. Given time, he would have anything he wanted from her.

Bending, Kyle licked the pale skin between Rook's tits, and took each nipple between his teeth for a second, swirling his tongue. With a force of will he sat up and replaced her shirt. He rearranged her so her head rested in his lap and he could study her face. Lovely. No wonder Fin and Marcus had their undies in a bunch over her. Once he got her hair fixed and bought her some real clothes, she would be worthy of his plans for her. Using a tissue he wiped off her lipstick and kissed her. Nice, but he wanted her to react, to wake up. He considered going into her mind, but not knowing what in particular made her special, the last thing he wanted was to screw himself by breaking her.

The drive to Shaw Ministries headquarters in Donner would take an hour. Kyle fixed himself a drink and called Dr Clark, the late Reverend Shaw's personal physician, now Kyle's own. He got the old fart out of bed so he would be ready to examine Rook as soon as they arrived. Make sure the ill-timed explosion hadn't damaged his prize.

Better remove her wedding band, so she would have one less reminder of his wayward brother. He could always blame the theft on Marcus. The only thing on her left ring-finger, though, was a tattoo, and he wasn't equipped to remove that.

Rook twitched and mumbled something, on the verge of consciousness. Kyle poured them each a drink. When her eyelids fluttered, he bent and kissed her. She responded reflexively, kissing him back. A volcanic surge ran from the base of Kyle's skull to his balls, but then Rook realized she wasn't kissing the man she thought. She struggled against him, but Kyle refused to stop until she bit his lip. He sat up, grinning, and took a sip of his vodka tonic.

Rook sat up too quickly and made herself dizzy. She leaned on Kyle for support. He chuckled and helped her, handed her a drink.

She stared at it uncomprehending, then looked up at him.

"Kyle?"

His smile broadened. "I've missed you, Rook."

"Me?" Rook sounded muddled.

"Take a drink. It will help."

Mechanically she obeyed. She looked at him wearily. "Are you kidnapping me again?"

"Why would you think that?"

"Well, you did it once before."

"A misunderstanding. You're perfectly safe now. You weren't when I found you, you know."

"The truck exploded," she said dispassionately.

Kyle gave a grim nod.

"Oh, Fin!" Rook started to shake. Kyle took the glass from her to hold her hands in his.

"He's gone isn't he?" she asked.

Kyle put on an air of regret. "I'm afraid so."

She sobbed. Kyle held her and relished the feel of her, her scent. He acted consoling. Many minutes later she calmed somewhat and wiped her eyes and nose. Her blue eyes were bright, her cheeks damp and flushed. She finished her drink.

"I don't know what to do," she said.

"You don't have to do anything. I'll take care of everything."

She searched his face. "But you didn't like him."

"We may not have gotten along, but we were brothers. That means something, doesn't it?"

Kyle could tell she didn't know whether to believe him. He poured her another drink, stronger this time.

"You'll be safe. I saved you from the fire and the stampeding crowd.

I even got you away from that old boyfriend of yours."

"Marcus."

"Yes. I'll protect you."

She wanted to believe him, he could tell. The depth of her attachment to Fin surprised him. Her grief helped him though; she wanted to not think. He wanted to make it easy for her to let go.

"You're part of the family now. I'll keep you safe."

She downed several more drinks in quick succession and looked drowsy. She wept sporadically and eventually allowed him to comfort her. As he held her, it seemed the most natural thing in the world to kiss her again.

Kyle eagerly moved things along and found Rook pliant enough. His urgency grew as he undressed her and he didn't bother stripping completely before he took her, there, in the back of his big black limousine.

Chapter Eighteen

BONES

Female voice: I don't feel well.
Male voice: That's good, Little Raven. Breathe deep. Go past it.
(gulping breaths)
Male: Good, Raven, good. Do you see?
(pause)
Female: Oh! (panting) Swirling. All pulsing. Help me. Oh, fuck,
Marcus!
Male: I am Coyote. You are Raven. Say it.
(vague sounds of discomfort)
Male: Say my name so I can help you.
Female: Coyote.
Male: Drink this.
(gagging sounds)
Male: Good. Now, look. See. You see the energy.
(pause)
Female: Yes.
Male: You're doing well, Little Raven. Very well. Let me guide
you.
Female: Yes.
Male: We must join our flesh. The energy demands it.
        excerpt from SSA Surveillance recording W22.4-083199-X

Kyle was finally sleeping.

Rook stared at him and tried to feel something. Hate. Revulsion. Pity. Love. Passion. Interest. There was nothing. She'd hoped she left the emotionless sex behind when she left Marcus.

"Old habits," she murmured.

Kyle had moved up in the world since she'd seen him last. He'd said something bizarre about going to the top of the food chain, and he seemed to have done it. Limousine, armed guards, private elevator, spacious, austere apartment: all spoke of wealth and power. What the hell did he want with her? Besides sex. And how did he come so far so fast? Two weeks ago Kyle lived in the same crappy house as Fin.

Fin.

Rook shuddered with suppressed grief. She needed to wail, but couldn't risk waking Kyle. He would want to rut some more. She shuddered again.

The pain was too fresh to assimilate. Fin couldn't be gone. She scanned for him again. And again.

In the limo, it became like a mantra. She'd barely been aware of anything outside her own head. That overwhelming emptiness in her heart, and the alcohol Kyle was so generous with, made it easy for him to take advantage of her and manipulate his way into her pants. And the whole time he was fucking her, once in the limo and again and again here on the bed, she searched the aether.

Now she must stop, must lock Fin away until she got out of here. In the bomb shelter she would feel closer to him, and she and Vesuvius would cope together. She wouldn't leave it until... Until what?

If only she and Fin had stayed there.

Maybe she would never leave.

Keeping an eye on Kyle, Rook crept out of his bed and scooped up her clothes. He was breathing heavily, drooling on his crisp white pillowcase. The digital clock on the nightstand read 5:48 am in fierce green digits. She hurried into the hall, her bare feet silent on the muted sage Berber carpet. One entire wall of the cavernous, sparsely furnished living room was glass. Earlier, when Kyle's sycophantic doctor examined her, the lights had rendered the whole thing a minimalist, bland hall of mirrors, but now the dimness afforded her a view. While dressing and pulling on her boots, Rook tried to figure out where the hell she was.

She was about seven or eight floors up, the top floor. Beyond all the glass a wide, plant-strewn balcony overlooked an atrium. It reminded Rook of a hotel. Maybe it was. That could be the rather mundane explanation of Kyle's apparent meteoric rise. The area around the building, lit by several streetlights, reminded her of a campus. There were lots of trees and green space, also an empty parking lot and a long, snaking driveway. No people in evidence. She'd have a long hike if she couldn't get a cab or bus.

The front door let her out into the elevator vestibule and she pushed the down button. After only a few nervous seconds a 'bing' signaled the arrival of her escape pod. The doors hissed open. Empty. Rook breathed a sigh of relief. Inside she looked at the buttons. *Parking, Office, Private, Roof.* The express, apparently.

Rook reached for the button labeled Parking, but stopped. Office? Was this not a hotel after all?

Kyle's office.

The doors began to shut.

Fin wouldn't want her to live out her life in fear, in the bomb shelter. He was the one to first go outside. He knew they couldn't hide forever. Rook would let her reporter instincts guide her. She would find something in Kyle's office to protect herself. She would destroy her enemies. She would smash this Hydra with a boulder before it sprouted any more heads. She would do it to honor Fin.

After a short ride the elevator let her out in another anteroom. A sleek, dark wood door opened into the promised office. About an acre in size, it held only a single desk and a long conference table. The lights were off, but a little illumination came from the large window. Rook blinked several times as she took in the new vista.

A short distance away across a manicured lawn stood a huge church with a soaring spire of glass, spotlighted against the night in greenish white, a laser-like beam shooting from its tip up into the cloudless sky. It was by far the tackiest thing Rook had seen in a long time, and she recognized it from the news. The Shaw Ministries Cathedral.

Not long ago, Kyle kidnapped her on Shaw's orders. Now he seemed to have stepped into the dead man's life. How fucking creepy!

With varying degrees of horror and nausea, Rook contemplated whether Kyle killed the reverend or just moved in opportunistically upon his death, because clearly the fancy penthouse upstairs had been Shaw's. Which meant the limousine, guards, and personal physician had also been Shaw's.

She'd just been thoroughly fucked in Brian Shaw's bed.

Please, please let Kyle have changed the sheets when he moved in.

Rook whimpered and blinked back tears. Time to make a hasty search for damning evidence and get the hell out of this freak show.

A large wooden cross edged in gold hung beside the window. The other walls held framed documents and pictures. Rook turned on the desk lamp. The pictures were all of Brian Shaw glad-handing. One picture in particular drew her attention. It showed the reverend with his arm around Kyle, both of them grinning. Something about the lighting didn't look right. It reminded her of the pictures they sometimes ran in *CTP*, the ones they created in PhotoShop.

Rook gave herself ten minutes to search. She wanted to be gone before any ministry personnel could show up and start asking questions. They might believe that 'early to bed, early to rise' crap, and today was Sunday. Presumably their busiest day.

The desk was a mahogany behemoth. Its polished surface held no stray papers, no sticky notes, no gilt-framed photos of an adoring wife and children, no name plate, no computer. The doodles on the blotter offered nothing significant. An appointment book lay beside the phone, open to this week, with notes in two different hands. Several public appearances had been canceled. Rook flipped back through the preceding weeks and deduced Kyle took over from Shaw shortly after the eventful day she first encountered them both. Of those events nothing in either hand indicated anything unusual had been planned. The desk drawers were her last hope.

The long center drawer held the typical pens and paperclips, other stationery shit. There were two drawers on each side. They were locked, but using a letter opener from the first drawer, Rook pried them open. The bottom drawer on the left contained a half-empty bottle of whiskey, a bottle of vodka, several unopened bourbons and a pack of chewing gum. The top drawer held a bible, a dictionary, and a bunch of religious pamphlets.

The bottom drawer on the right held an interoffice mail envelope addressed to Mr Tanner, the previous recipient one Carl M. The contents disappointed: a report on the ministry's demographics, a budget report, a hefty document titled 'Justification of Budgetary Allocation and Proposal for Upgrade of Tertiary Equipment per your request' and a single sheet labeled TEF. TEF? What did the Threshold have to do with Kyle? No time to figure that out now. Rook decided to take the papers.

The top drawer contained a box of tissues, a small tape player, and a cigar box. Rook put on the headphones and started the tape player. She laughed when she heard a woman moaning, wondering what sort of kinky audio book Kyle was listening to, but then she heard Marcus's voice and her own reply. Anger, horror and bafflement battled for supremacy of her emotions. Kyle had a recording of her having sex with Marcus, but she hadn't met Kyle until after leaving Marcus. She ejected the tape and put it in the envelope. Later she would figure out how he got it.

Rook opened the cigar box and found the green panties she threw away in Fin's room. Now she knew why Kyle kept his tissues in this same drawer. She didn't want to touch the panties after what Kyle had done with them, but wanted even less to leave them for him to do it again, so she scooped them up and added them to the envelope. Underneath rested a small, moleskin notebook.

Aha.

But it only contained religious ramblings in Shaw's handwriting. The title page called them New Revelations. She riffled through the pages, which were filled with revisions and margin notes. The book fell open to a section near the middle. This part talked about some kind of 'Divided Child,' the second coming or something. A loose page of lined paper covered with notes marked the page. Kyle was trying to map this hokum onto real life. She put it away in disgust.

This was getting her nowhere. Time to get the hell out.

Looking around for a weapon, Rook settled for the big gold-trimmed cross from the wall. At least she could clobber someone with it if she needed to. The elevator took her down to the garage level.

As the elevator doors opened, the guards stood there, pointing pistols at her.

Rook dropped the cross and tried to look sheepish. The smaller guard took her by the arm and escorted her back upstairs. He didn't seem like your typical religious zealot, or rent-a-cop. He seemed dangerous. He wore the same black uniform she had seen on troops at the factory.

Kyle awaited her in the open doorway, wearing black silk pajama bottoms and a wryly amused expression.

"Thank you for returning her. I'm sure she just got lost, isn't that right darling?" He took her from the guard, roughly pulling her to him and kissing her. "Lock the elevator once you've gone back down," he said to the guard. "I'll call when I need it."

Kyle led Rook back into the apartment. Without an audience his demeanor grew gruffer. Rook could tell he was furious with her but trying to hide it.

"Now, what have you found?" he asked as he took the envelope from her. He frowned when he read the label. Sitting her on the deep green leather sofa, he stood over her, glaring down. After several moments, he said, "I forgot you were a reporter. My mistake. It won't happen again. Will it?"

Rook shook her head.

Kyle's expression softened. "You're going to keep me on my toes, I can see that." Tossing aside the envelope, he flipped through the papers he pulled from it. "I don't suppose you made any sense of these?"

Rook shook her head again.

"Ah, well. I can't make heads or tails of them. I was hoping a smart girl like you could explain them to me."

"I didn't read them yet. If you'd like to let—"

"You won't be offended if I say no." He picked up the envelope from the coffee table. "What else did you find?"

Rook said nothing.

Kyle slid out the panties and cassette. He ran his fingers over the silky crotch before dropping the panties onto the cherry coffee table. A sly smile slithered across his face. "Did you listen to it?" he asked, indicating the tape. "I found it very informative. Very enjoyable, Little Raven."

Rook's tenuous control snapped. "Don't call me that!"

"Calm, calm, darling."

"I'm not your darling. And I'm not Little Raven!"

"Very well. I'll think of my own pet name for you."

"Don't bother. I'm leaving."

Kyle raised his eyebrows. "Oh, really? Where will you go? You have no home now, except with me."

"Fuck off. You're a stalker pervert."

"Didn't seem to bother you the first four times you fucked me."

Rook stood and brushed past Kyle, heading toward the phone on the end table. She didn't know whom she expected to call but she wanted to show Kyle he couldn't keep her against her will.

He watched with placid green eyes as she lifted the receiver.

No dial tone. She heard a ring followed by, "Yes, sir?"

Kyle moved past her in the direction of the kitchen, chuckling.

"I'd like to leave now." Rook knew it wouldn't work. "Please send the elevator up."

"Certainly ma'am. Let me confirm that with Mr Tanner."

Rook glanced at Kyle, busy at the counter with his back to her.

"He's unable to come to the phone right now, but he said it's okay." She knew she sounded lame.

"Sorry, ma'am. I need orders from Mr Tanner."

"Oh come on! What if he were dead or something? Would you leave me up here to starve?"

"Is Mr Tanner dead, ma'am?" Rook detected a note of aggression.

Kyle took the phone from her. "Return to your duties." He replaced the handset, but held onto Rook's wrist.

"I hoped it wouldn't come to this, babycakes," he said. Rook scowled. Kyle held up a syringe. "I don't want to use this, but I will if I have to. You're a smart girl. Is it really so bad, being here with me? I can give you everything you want."

"I want to go."

Kyle nodded and sighed. He jabbed the needle into her hip. Rook felt woozy immediately, felt Kyle lifting her.

*** *** ***

Kyle tossed Rook onto his king-size bed, amid the jumble of sweaty sheets, and regarded her. By pure luck his alarm clock awakened him at 6:00. He trusted his guards not to let her walk out, but without explicit instructions to the contrary, they may have been talked into it.

The feather tattoo on her collarbone drew his attention. It and the ones on her arms were covered when they'd first met and he hadn't noticed them or the one peeking out over her shirt in the back, a weird tower made of birds, until last night. She had quite a collection of tattoos, he had discovered. Not surprising since she'd been dating a tattoo artist. The other girls he'd known with tattoos all had small, cute, colorful things like flowers or hummingbirds, hearts, stars and rainbows. Like they'd chosen them from a box of Lucky Charms. Rook's were different, bold and black and strong. They weren't an accessory. They were her and they delivered an erotic charge. Except the wedding-ring one.

With the dim lighting of the limo and the darkened bedroom here, he had yet to get a good look at any of her markings.

Kyle removed Rook's tattered boots and briefly examined the chess pieces on her feet and the birds around her ankle. He ran his hands slowly up her legs, searching for anything he had missed. Her inner thighs were sticky with the smell of sex. He rolled her onto her stomach to unzip her skirt and spent several moments studying the enormous flock of crows spewing from the castle tower on her side before tracing her bird tramp stamp, first with his fingertips, then his tongue. He slipped her skirt down and off, her panties with it. The scent intensified. The whisper of the fabric across her skin promised sensual surprises still to be uncovered and Kyle urgently pulled her tank top off. In the process, he exposed her neck and stopped short.

The tower there unnerved him. He hadn't seen it before. There was something deeply wrong about it. The person who chose this image for this spot must be fundamentally unhealthy, declaring to the world that the root of her mind, the core, was this shattered, flaming structure of stone.

Absorbing Shaw's knowledge afforded Kyle power, wealth, and Rook. The downside was thoughts like those. Talk about a mood-killer.

He wouldn't let it beat him. It was just ink. After staring at the tower until the creep-factor was gone, he rolled her onto her back.

Her eyes were closed, her jaw slack. Her nipples were standing up. And she had one more tattoo, right down by her pubic hair. He trailed his fingers from her breasts down to it and leaned in close to get a good look. Another black bird. As he studied it, her smell engulfed him.

Kyle slid his pajama pants off.

***

Kyle showered and dressed. He would need to brief the guards on expectations regarding his new girlfriend, and push off his Ministries meetings until afternoon so he could deal with Rook thoroughly. Make sure there weren't any more incidents. He would talk to Markowski about handcuffs or other restraining devices, as a last resort of course. Or maybe just for fun.

Over breakfast Kyle made his phone calls, waking people up. He didn't let it bother him though. The calls would seem that much more important coming before seven in the morning.

Rook was still out cold when Kyle went back to her. He had never gone into an unconscious mind before, unless Shaw counted, and was uncertain how to proceed. Usually he would listen to what someone said and follow an unspoken thought in, but right now Rook had no thoughts at all, didn't even appear to be dreaming. Kyle sat beside her on the bed and lifted her head in both hands. Pressing his fingers against her temples, he concentrated on letting his will flow out through his fingertips, and found himself in unfamiliar territory. Cold moonlight on shaggy evergreens, silence.

Kyle observed Rook's mind as she idled. A shiver ran through him as he absorbed her slight vibrations. The subtle electrical impulses underlaying everything around him were exquisitely sensuous, like her scent. Incredibly intimate, something he hadn't felt with anyone else. Erotic as hell.

The chaotic architecture of her mind consisted of derelict facades, rotting, half-completed walls like a ghost town. Things Kyle thought of as the usual cues to a person's psyche weren't where he expected them to be, or were missing altogether. When she woke up he would observe the workings and should be able to make better sense of things.

A large, pulsating mass drew his attention. He'd never seen anything like it in anyone else's mind. The dull surface looked like moldy elephant hide, but prodding it with his toe split it open and the noxious innards seeped out. Within the rancid film festered a Pandora's box of negative emotions, a green-black sludge of everything she suppressed upon learning of Fin's death. The little that escaped when Kyle poked caused Rook to stir. Kyle felt overwhelming sorrow, and fanned the oozing tar of despair with his hands to try to make it skin over again faster. He needed to vent all the unpleasantness or it would spill into her conscious mind and make her unmanageable.

Exploring further, Kyle discovered the source of the green-black stuff. Rook indeed had a tower in here, though it bore little resemblance to her tattoo. The slime seeped out where a gaping hole had been battered into one wall. But there were no flames. Not right now, anyway. Kyle remembered the bad shit that went down in Fin's head and was reluctant to expose himself to that sort of thing again. The tattoo could be a warning.

The tower was the root of something, many things. Maybe everything. She was supposed to be special, to Complete him. Whatever made her special was probably locked up in this tower. There might be constructs representing Fin. If he could find and alter them, he could change her mind about his dear departed brother.

Kyle talked himself into entering.

Inside, he found a layer of the green-black ooze several inches thick. It covered the floor and a collection of ramshackle lumps against the far wall.

Recoiling a bit, Kyle scraped some of the algae off the largest of the lumps and uncovered a ribcage. Further exploration produced five mostly complete skeletons and three additional skulls. Obviously they were important.

Carting the skeletons back to his own mind proved challenging. They were information he couldn't assimilate because he didn't understand it. Instead, he opted for brute force, and it left him reeling.

As his headache subsided, Kyle retrenched in order to take care of the pile of Fin-trauma before Rook woke.

Kyle knew he couldn't disperse that much ugly emotion all at once without leaving signs. Best to hide it for now and deal with it more thoroughly later. Locating the empty foundation of a tiny cottage, he drew his entire will down through his fingertips and into Rook's mind. He pushed the pile over to the gaping foundation. Feelings seeped into him. A sorrow, a longing filled him. Kyle sobbed involuntarily, aching for Fin. Pain like an icicle in his heart threatened to overwhelm him. He lifted the leading edge of the mass over the lip of the foundation and shoved. The pile slithered over and landed with a splat. The foundation, weak and soggy, caved in as the mass of black gelatin shifted over it. Kyle felt somewhat better. It wasn't pretty, but it would do. He struggled to rid himself of the foreign emotions that leached into his soul.

He needed something to throw over the top so Rook wouldn't experience this. She would thank him if she knew.

Rook turned her head and made a soft noise. She would be awake any second now. Knowing it would cost him, Kyle peeled the top layer off a section of his own mind. It hurt like hell, like mental rug burn. He laid the strip over the emotion pit in Rook's mind. Quickly he tucked away the loose edges of worry so she would be less likely to trip over them, and scattered a few rosy thoughts about himself. Kyle let most of his consciousness drift back into his own head, but left a small portion with Rook to monitor the modifications after she woke up.

Tendrils and wisps of faintly green light, like static electricity, flitted over everything, including Kyle. It felt wonderful and prickly and made him shudder. His handiwork attracted the sparks. Kyle feared they might expose him, but they rocketed away.

Rook opened her ghostly blue eyes and laboriously focused on Kyle's face. She smiled weakly. "You win."

Kyle grinned. "There's a good girl." He lifted her head and kissed her, plunging his tongue into her mouth. She complied without enthusiasm, but from his internal vantage point Kyle detected stirrings of arousal.

Intriguing ideas about how to exploit his newfound mental abilities brought a chuckle, and a different kissing technique. In a matter of seconds Kyle determined that what really got Rook's motor running was an alternation between sucking on her tongue and nibbling her bottom lip. He knew he had it dialed in when the lighting shifted inside her mind, making everything both clearer and softer-edged at the same time. She was hyperaware of her body's responses but was fighting them. Still kissing her, Kyle traced her arousal to its source. Rook's libido was like a black fox; wary, alluring and ready to pounce. Kyle scratched it behind the ears.

Rook brought her hand to the back of his neck, pulling him to her, returning the kiss.

That was more like it. With help from the glossy libido creature,

Kyle continued to refine his technique, using his insider knowledge to guide his hands and mouth and play Rook like a fully immersive, x-rated video game. He was well on his way to the high score when the black fox scampered playfully away and disappeared into a large berry bramble. The part of Kyle's attention that wasn't focused on Rook's body followed the sleek animal into the thicket. Deep, glossy foliage and voluptuous white berries surrounded him with the smell of female arousal. Kyle breathed deeply. It was thrilling to know that, in spite of herself and her ridiculous loyalty to Fin, she wanted him, and had since their interrupted kiss at the factory.

The fox peered out of the undergrowth just long enough for Kyle to spot it before darting away again. It was playing with him, as Rook was now, too, in his bed. He followed it, ignoring the scratches inflicted by the thorns. Their game of hide and seek continued, ratcheting up Rook's physical participation and Kyle's enjoyment. He wanted to catch the creature before he fucked Rook again, to be fully in control of her pleasure. The fox stopped and looked back at him with golden eyes, daring him. Reaching for it, Kyle brushed away a tangle of dark vegetation and discovered something far more interesting than the libido-fox.

On a large flat rock like a pagan altar, stood Rook. She was magnificently nude, except for tendrils from the berry thicket encircling her wrists and ankles. A black velvet gown lay at her feet like a puddle of ink. Her shimmering blue eyes watched him intently, a sultry smile playing at her lips.

Lust coursed through Kyle as he took her in, mitigated only a little by curiosity. He had never encountered a representation of Self inside someone's mind, and from his stolen knowledge he knew Shaw hadn't either. Another sign that Rook was special.

The black fox leapt up into her arms and licked her cheek. Rook stroked it, smiling, her pale fingers disappearing into the downy-soft, ebony fur, emerging to plunge in once again. The animal swished its bushy tail languorously across her breasts and stiff nipples as it reveled in her attentions. Rook bent her head and nuzzled the fox between its ears, sparking unaccustomed jealousy in Kyle. He set aside all intellectual concerns about what she might represent, and stepped up onto the stone slab to stand beside her. Around him he saw torn vines and creepers, evidence that until recently this Rook had been bound. That thought made him even hornier.

He took the vixen from her, tickled it under the chin, and set it down. He swept Rook into his arms and laid her down on the flat stone.

Kyle's senses were overwhelmed. Simultaneously he entered the Rook in the physical world and the mental one as well. The fox circled them as they fucked, rubbing its warm, sleek fur against them sensuously, licking them with its hot velvet tongue. The mental Rook, a sort of offshoot of her libido he decided, was a direct conduit to the physical Rook's pleasure. By using this copy of her he dictated what the real Rook enjoyed, and in that way remade her. No longer would she be a hesitant lover, inhibited by her ideas of decorum, her own likes and dislikes, or even her lingering hatred of him. She could hate him all she wanted but would be unable to resist him.

Through manipulation of her pliant double, Kyle planted further seeds of desire for himself throughout her psyche. He made her eager to please him and easy for him to pleasure. To prove that last he brought her to a rapid series of orgasms that left her limp in his arms before allowing himself to finish.

Now she was truly his.

Once he had recovered he sat back and studied her face. "We've got to fix your hair and get you some clothes."

Kyle took Rook to the shower and kept tabs on her mental state while they cleaned up and she shook the last effects of the sedative. His fix was holding. She hadn't thought about Fin since waking up. She was confused about her feelings toward Kyle and the events of the past day, but wasn't wasting any energy trying to work things out.

The slippery bliss of lathering her body came close to another roll in the hay, a distraction Kyle couldn't afford. Like it or not, he was head of a corporation that required a lot of hand-holding. To keep the gullible masses eager and willing to finance his lavish lifestyle here in the penthouse with his new pet, he'd need to spend the afternoon holding the proper hands and nodding sagely at the proper times. After his trip to the mall with Rook, of course.

He dressed her in some of his own clothes, making sure she left the shirt open down to the fourth button. She didn't have a bra, and easily acquiesced to going without her panties.

Kyle's head felt like a frat-house carpet, and he gave up monitoring her on the way down to the parking garage.

*** *** ***

Rook sat on the sofa, surrounded by shopping bags containing all the new clothes Kyle bought for her. He spent about twenty five hundred dollars all told, with the clothes, shoes and salon bill. Lunch cost another hundred. Rook had never been spoiled like this, except it wasn't really spoiling because she didn't like any of the stuff she got. It was the sartorial equivalent of a mullet, demure dresses over Victoria's sluttiest secrets. And the hair! The stylist stripped out the dye and managed to get it pretty close to its natural color, a reddish-brown, and cut it to look like some sitcom bimbo. Kyle liked it, but Rook thought it was stupid. She looked like everyone else. Kyle assured her she didn't, that she was special.

Now here she sat, in a luxury apartment with a grinding headache and Gary, her 'bodyguard,' while Kyle took care of some business. He couldn't take her along, but wanted to be sure she wouldn't do anything stupid. She might have been tempted to try, but didn't see any options. She couldn't get an outside phone line. With the elevator locked, the only other way out was off the balcony, which let out into an atrium. Even if she jumped the eight floors or managed to climb down a palm tree, she'd still be trapped. Down the hall from the bedroom was a locked door. She couldn't hope to get in without Gary noticing, and found she didn't want to. Snooping had lost its appeal. She settled into her new life with a shrug.

There were worse places to be held prisoner, she supposed. A rerun of *Cheers* came on and Rook let her attention be drawn to the TV.

*** *** ***

Halfway through a bottle of whiskey, Kyle got his headache under control and was left with a warm tingle near the base of his skull that felt just like Rook tasted. He examined the damage he'd done to his own mind in his rush to smother Rook's memories of his asshole brother. It didn't look bad, just itched and seeped. Next he turned to Rook's skeletons. Beyond noting that touching them felt like touching her delicious, warm skin, not slimy dead bones, he had no insights. Later, when he was better able to focus, he would try to figure out what to do with them. So far she was functioning well enough without them.

They weren't what he needed to Complete himself, because he was still the same. Fucking, though greatly enjoyable, didn't do it either. What did that leave? Did she need to consciously decide to Complete him? If so, why hadn't she done that for Fin?

A thought occurred to Kyle. He dismissed it out of hand, but it nagged at him. Maybe she had Completed Fin. His brother never struck Kyle as the marrying type, and yet got hitched to this girl he hardly knew, this Completer. Kyle seethed at the thought of his Rook being used by Fin. That damn tattoo on her finger was a symbol of it he had to look at every day. So did she. It would remind her of Fin.

He buzzed his secretary. "Eleanor, get Spitz on the phone."

Kyle was unsure how Spitz would react, but anticipated some kind of judgmental rebuke about impropriety and impulsiveness. Probing questions about the lack of a license, why they must get married the next day. But Spitz went on at giddy length about being so honored, although he seemed disappointed over such a small ceremony. The paperwork didn't worry him. Pronouncing them in the cathedral would make it "legal in the eyes of the Lord."

Kyle was pleased. The ceremony would allow him the freedom of having Rook with him without raising eyebrows. It was for show. Additionally, "in the eyes of the Lord" they'd be married. Hence, he would be Complete.

What if the powers governing this whole Completer business were sticklers? It might be necessary for him to perform the ritual, down to its last detail. Besides, Spitz might ask awkward questions if never asked to sign anything.

Kyle made a call to Documents and ordered new ID for Rook. Kyle didn't want to lose due to a technicality. He'd get her ID, and they would get a license.

In the meantime, he would go ahead with the ceremony. If it did the trick, he might skip the rest. But probably not. Kyle liked the idea of having a legal claim to Rook.

Chapter Nineteen

Asteroid

Alien abductions have become quite common in otherwise tranquil Webster. Abductees looking for help dealing with the abduction experience should contact a newly formed group on campus, the Abductee Support Society. The ASS is sponsored by the Buck U Student Union and staffed by alien abductees, and volunteers from the psychology department. I recently attended a meeting (Mondays at 7:30 in the Abernathy Hall cafeteria) and spoke with several abductees...
        from *Local Phenomenon* by Brandy Moon, *CTP*, 09-01-2000

The white noise felt like someone attempting to create a sand painting on Fin's brain. A steady chaos of sound granules trickled through his ear canals and ricocheted off his eardrums.

Couch and television in their familiar places, but Fin didn't remember there ever being a chalkboard in the living room before. Rows of empty desks surrounded him. No one else had signed up for this class, probably because there was no teacher but the TV. The show was some educational thing about neural nets, but the sound wasn't coming in. Loud static over an image representing how brain cells interconnect. It looked like gooey wads of damp lint, with frizzy strands of snot linking them all.

That he must be dreaming had occurred to Fin several seconds ago, but he didn't feel asleep. The weird classroom tableau wavered, but the noise persisted.

Fin opened his eyes. Some kind of pale green veil blocked his view. He tried to evade it by moving his head, but discovered a spiraling sensation of vertigo. And that he was tied up.

He waited for the dizziness to subside. It was mild compared to the disorientation caused by some of his favorite pharmaceuticals, so being tied up quickly became the more important aspect of his situation. His arms were pulled away from his sides. He felt suspended by his bonds.

The restraints proved rather feeble and Fin easily worked one arm loose. Using the freed hand, he pulled the fuzzy material away from his face.

He was swaddled in the stuff, cocooned in filthy pistachio cotton candy. Several taut lines led off to other cocoons like his, all strung on a huge web filling a gigantic chamber.

When he dropped the torn hunk of shroud it didn't go anywhere, floating where he released it.

The situation now far exceeded the effects of anything Fin had ever inhaled, injected or ingested.

The hissing grew harder to ignore. It reminded Fin of a modem, scratchy and echoey. He completed the task of freeing himself, careful to retain a handhold on the web so as not to drift away. For the moment, he would take this experience at face value.

Fin clawed through his memories. The gig. His wedding reception.

His wedding.

His wife.

Rook was there of course, during the performance. They had dispensed with all formalities and lunged into a party. Nicotine converged in the bed of someone's pickup. The invited guests numbered about fifty, but as soon as the music started at least 200 more people showed up.

The first set went smoothly, unusual but not enough to base a conspiracy mythology on. Things went wrong during the first song of the second set. He remembered people running and freaking out, some unscheduled light show effects, and a weird kind of interference coming through the amps...

The white noise. It wasn't quite white. It had reverby qualities, and subtle risings and fallings. It started during the first song.

Where was Rook at that point? Fin could recall people drifting away from the pit area up front and congregating closer to the picnic tables. Rook had been back there with them. Ever since their sabbatical in the bomb shelter he'd felt a pleasant little tingle that gave him a fair idea of how near she was, and in what direction. At the time, he'd thought it was the feeling of being in love.

Where was she now? The tingle-signal was silent. Fin looked despairingly at the gangrenous cocoons. There could be a thousand. Was everyone from the reception here?

No. Fin didn't know why, but he knew that most of the concertgoers weren't here. It was like a voice in his head, and he habitually trusted the voices in his head. There was a furtive aspect about this, though. It felt like eavesdropping. Fin concentrated and began to trace it to the irritating hissing noise. Imagining it as a babble of whispers, he could detect even more patterns in it.

Was Rook here? No.

Was she safe? Unknown.

What was this place? An asteroid.

Fin couldn't be sure if this information came from some outside influence, or if he was just making it up. The asteroid thing didn't seem like something he would come up with. And it *would* account for the lack of gravity.

But it was impossible.

That assertion drew heavy fire. It was certainly possible. Moreover it was accurate.

There was that sense to the protest, 'accurate' as opposed to 'true.'

Fin struggled with such an enormous revelation, couldn't accept something so shocking on sheer sincerity. There could be simpler explanations. He needed proof.

A cacophony of proof flooded his mind but he got none of it. The surge was too strong, an overload at first painful then numbing. Instinctively, Fin let himself go with the current rather than fighting it.

Fin came through the brief spike with continuity and recall, but it skewed his sensory matrix. Sight and sound traded places somewhere in his head, which had happened to him before. He'd done it on purpose a few times. Rather than freaking out he patiently started trying to put things back in order.

With the hissing noise channel-shifted into his visual cortex, things made a bit of sense. The tail end of the information surge showed him a lingering image of Gaspra, the asteroid he now inhabited. The asteroid's orbital distance, mass, composition, surface area, temperature and uncountable further bytes of useless trivia were also in there, like a hangover from an astronomy exam.

Fin took care not to revert all this incoming data to auditory irritation as he put his head back on track. A strong flavor of approval, a warm kind of pride, now permeated the images. He was learning to understand.

Now that he could see the images, he started picking up on ways to focus on the ones he especially wanted to study. He could navigate, find what he needed instead of asking questions. Encouragement came from an unknown source.

It was thrilling. He found exhaustive compilations about every significant orbiting body in this solar system, and in others. Comprehension of space and time, matter and energy — Air and Water, Earth and Fire. It was that simple. Wondrous crystals of biological and psychological insight.

Too much.

Fin crashed back into the moment. He had just been told he was on an asteroid. In an asteroid, he corrected as he looked around at the cocoons. And not alone.

But he was very special.

That was another thing. The voice in his head seemed quite fond of him, bordering on smarmy. Fin's trust for it weakened as his innate cynicism weighed in about all the positive regard. The voice told him so much, but nothing about itself. He was being watched, being led. Accuracy wasn't the issue for him anymore. He wanted truth.

Which meant, evidently, he would need to go back to asking questions. The data he could readily peruse seemed limitless at first, and it was huge, but finite. A set of facts expressly tailored for Fin, for this moment. Something lurked outside the boundary, regarding him intently. It was of this evasive presence that he demanded his answers.

Why was he here? Nothing comprehensible.

Who was responsible? Again, the answer didn't make sense. No sensible answer would be possible if he insisted on such provincial notions.

Okay. Fin decided to start with something more concrete. Who or what constructed the webs? A spider image, but with something indefinably askew about it. It felt hedged. It wasn't the whole answer.

Let's go out on a limb, Fin thought. Were they aliens?

They had been waiting for that one. He triggered another gusher, but was much more ready this time. There were landscapes and cityscapes and vibrant mother-of-pearl skies and milky seas. Postcards from a slew of worlds. With the images came reams of incomprehensible statistical and navigational data. The spider forms were not dominant. There were as many shapes and sizes of aliens as habitats on all those worlds. In addition to the many that were grotesque and unlike any life Fin could compare them to, there were slugs, worms, shrubs, squid, penguins and throbbing exposed brains. These many shapes, and himself as well, were One.

The forms of all these alien organisms were diagramed in glowing green silhouettes, with lines connecting them. The layout had a general correlation to the arrangement of their homeworlds. It became more complex, growing and increasing in density. Layers accumulated rapidly, and the individual details shrank as the whole thing zoomed out. Positions of the various races began to shift, and the interconnections took on greater prominence. Little clusters tended to twirl, twisting their strokes into lazy spirals.

The whole thing arranged itself into a pinched oval, a new image built from all the others. The critical thing. How all of these disparate forms of life had been united. It was a microorganism.

The germ divided over and over again, the new cells arranging themselves into smooth, glowing lines. The multiplying microbes created another image of an alien being, soon joined by others, all interconnected.

Comprehending that infection with these microbes brought different alien races together was another significant step, and earned Fin more praise. More comments about him being special.

They were trying to tell him the microbes were, collectively, the true self. They wanted to give him a place with them. To give all humans a place, but humans were simply unresponsive. Except Fin.

Yeah, I'm very special, Fin thought. Get a lot of that.

Absolutely, his secret admirer confirmed. A phenomenal and unique individual. Fittingly outlandish for his world, a place presenting more challenges than any other.

With the inscrutable societal structures and opaque minds of humans the project might have been hopeless. Recently though, humans began tagging themselves with minute transmitters, a logistical godsend for collecting subjects for study. And it allowed them to find Fin!

Fin became offended at the implication he would help them with their project. He reached past the edges of the supplied information, grasping for anything being kept from him. Hoping to poke someone in the eye.

There was no one there, but his reach grew as he lashed out. He got loose, into the next layer of data. It was like a kelp forest, a swaying maze filled with diffuse verdant light and occasional trails of bubbles. Little of it made any kind of sense, but he could move through it at will.

He dug through the information woven all around him, weeding out anything that wasn't whatever was watching him. He felt it trying to elude him, trying to look like just facts, just knowledge, and chased it. Picking up on his game, his quarry played with him. Didn't try too hard to escape. It would let him have a peek.

Now totally cut off from the physical world, Fin concentrated on the mental hide-and-seek. His maneuvers became increasingly fluid and quick, until his playmate was pressed to sustain the game. It was pleased, admired his skill in adapting to this pure-information environment. He was uniting with the…

Floating Wisdom.

Fin's eyes snapped open, but the image that concerned him was inside his head. An intelligence within the rush of data, made up of it, had just introduced itself.

Fin backpedaled to establish a little personal space. It tried to hold on, to embrace him, but he could pull away. The Floating Wisdom didn't like that, hadn't expected it. All of its responses were broadcast like emerald fireworks for Fin to see and decode. It knew nothing of privacy or reserve and was frustrated that it couldn't pry the lid off Fin's feelings and scoop them all up. He was an anomaly, a puzzle. An enigma.

It explained the situation to him. *You're the first of your kind we've been able to reach. We can't yet embrace you, absorb you. We'll figure it out.*

"Who's 'we'?" Fin asked without speaking aloud.

The Floating Wisdom. Trillions of united minds. We span most of the galaxy, all in glorious unity transcending space and time and matter. We have been at work here, Earth, for decades. Your brains have been deaf to us, keeping you from joining the Floating Wisdom. His ability to communicate with them made Fin special.

"You need to clarify this whole 'special' business. I'm having skepticism."

We could never before communicate directly with a solitary mind. Your case is all the more remarkable because your body does not house the True Ones, the microbes, as you say.

Keep talking, Fin thought privately. Addressing the Floating Wisdom, he said, "How is that remarkable?"

The microbes are analogous to neurons in many ways. They form a channel into the host brain. In the case of humans, the True Ones cannot equilibrate to the immune system and perish. Sometimes, the host does as well.

"Oh, that's too bad."

Regrettable, indeed. Of course, your arrival means an end to such problems.

As it spoke, Fin concentrated on pinpointing the Floating Wisdom. There was an impression of tentacles, or a heap of serpents. Although the number of its discreet thoughts went off Fin's chart by a wide margin, he could follow along with the main threads. It didn't appear to own a thought that could be called private.

"Has it occurred to you some of us might not want to join?" Fin demanded.

Everyone wants unity. No one wants to be alone.

"Wrong. I happen to like being alone, prefer it most of the time."

That is an illogical belief. Being alone is being lonely, and you can't want that. In the Floating Wisdom there is no loneliness.

"Bullshit," Fin retorted. "You're fucking made of loneliness! Who else is there for you to talk to? Just me, apparently, and no sooner did you meet me than you want to make me disappear. You're the illogical one."

It tried to pull him in again. *Don't think of it as disappearing. You will be part of the Floating Wisdom.*

"Let go of me." Fin had to fight harder to hold his ground.

The Floating Wisdom practically salivated, recalling the harvests of other worlds. With the creatures purified by the True Ones, their Floating Wisdom could guzzle them effortlessly. The scenes of various life forms twitching, writhing, howling, spewing fluids, and otherwise exhibiting symptoms of unspeakable agony stirred no remorse in the alien collective. What concerned it was breaching Fin's defenses.

"So," Fin tried to think casual, bluffing he was made of far harder stuff, "is there always this much wheezing and vainly striving?"

The body goes into shock, and there are typically chaotic

verbalizations. Decoding these noises linguistically, what emerges is a statement not unlike your own. Pain, fear and unwillingness.

"Why don't you listen?"

Uneasiness flickered, staining the Floating Wisdom's confidence. Its grip tightened. *All traces of fear inevitably vanish after uniting, when we can be one with the mind. The aberrant sounds made by the body are just a side-effect of the transition.* It bore down hard, and Fin screamed, raw fear pouring out of his throat.

Yes, intoned the Floating Wisdom calmly, *like that.*

The collective coiled down, constricting. Like Shaw multiplied a trillion times. Fin concentrated on blaring his terror and desperation at the Floating Wisdom on its own plane, drenching as much of it as he could with those emotions.

It recoiled as if burned. It eased up on Fin, throbbing with frustration bordering on anger.

"That," Fin admonished, "is what triggers those sounds! That's how all those creatures felt as you were slurping them up."

No, it protested.

"Yes. You didn't mean to, but you hurt them. For all intents and purposes, you killed them."

No! There is no death in the Floating Wisdom. Fluttering imagery of harmonious and elegant function in the collective. Notions of transcendence, of escaping from physical mortality. The uncertainty faded as the Floating Wisdom reminded itself of its own marvelousness. It had so much knowledge, there was nothing it couldn't figure out. It would spread like a soothing balm across all the pain and chaos everywhere. This was the great work.

Fin knew he would need to shake it again, and hard. Once it regrouped he wouldn't be able to hold it off.

He understood the way it saw things. The ends justified the means. Individuality was a small sacrifice for what it offered in return. He scoffed. "You don't understand. The fear disappears with the individual. Death does that. You don't embrace them, you smother them! You ignore their screams and you squash them! You must stop!"

The Floating Wisdom was becoming troubled, but it would pull Fin down if only to make him be quiet. It squeezed, trying not to listen. It dreaded another overflow of caustic emotions, hesitating to clamp down.

"That's right, you're afraid."

The Floating Wisdom backed off again and tried to gather a persuasive argument. Fin could plainly read that it hoped, by getting him to relax, perhaps he wouldn't spray his irrational fear on it this time.

You are the one who doesn't understand. The transition only looks painful because you can't comprehend it from your side. Think of it as a holy experience.

Fin laughed aloud. "You lost me. Where does religion enter the picture?"

It is everything. It is us. We are missionaries. Images of the microscopic life form, arcane polypeptide skeins and helixes that were the true seat of Wisdom. Thousands of species, all infected with this zealot bug. Once they understood what made Fin different, why he could hear them, they would reengineer this sacred plague so it would finally work on humans. That's what they had been attempting for more than twenty years, to adapt their contagion to human hosts. They meant to use Fin as the key to achieving this goal.

The Floating Wisdom showed a degree of smugness over Fin's reaction, or lack thereof. He wasn't broadcasting animal panic anymore.

When Fin's rage and indignation flashed out and scorched it, the Floating Wisdom merely smoldered in mute amazement.

It tried to let go, but he seized it and twisted. Saturated its billowing folds with his fury. "Maybe now I'll assimilate you, instead! But don't be afraid — it'll only hurt until I stop."

The Floating Wisdom wrenched itself loose. It wanted a place to hide.

"Just a fucking side-effect, remember?" Fin pounced almost

playfully, grabbing the Floating Wisdom again.

A shrill acidic scream reverberated throughout the alien collective as a billion billion overlapping voices wailed in fear and agony. The harmony was disrupted, and what had been an elegant interlocking system began shredding itself. Fin tried to pull back to safety, to stay out of it, but was unable to tear himself away from the hideous collapse.

Constructs emerged within the roiling nebula of alien thoughts, things trying to become personalities. They voraciously swallowed up all they could reach, growing until their edges met.

Fin thought they would simply merge and reconstitute the whole of the Floating Wisdom. Instead, wherever two constructs collided they further destabilized one another. The entire thing rapidly evaporated in an inferno of green tie-dye fire.

With a psychic boom, the collective imploded.

*** *** ***

Rook's head wasn't right. She felt disoriented, like she shouldn't be trusted to make important decisions. Most of it was probably due to lack of sleep, but the accompanying dull throb couldn't be explained by mere exhaustion. Kyle made her prepare breakfast for them, and, cooking not being one of her more-developed skills, it wasn't a raging success. Maybe she just needed a good cup of coffee.

Kyle took several phone calls from someone named Spitz and always hung up agitated. He told Rook he had some errands he couldn't delegate and left her alone with Gary several times, but never for more than an hour or so.

The first time he left, Rook's nagging little headache dissipated and she fell into a dead sleep on the sofa. She woke with a start some time later.

Kyle sat in the dark green paisley armchair, looking at her. And she had known. A faint throbbing vibration in the base of her skull told her. He smiled lasciviously and scooped her up. She struggled, but could tell he liked it by the shift in the vibration, so she stopped. Undaunted, he carried her onto the wide balcony. Hanging plants and a half-wall of rosewood obscured her view to the ground.

"Don't make a sound," he said as he spread her out on a chaise lounge and lifted the skirt of her modest floral dress. Rook could hear a crowd below her: people chattering, shoes ticking on the atrium's tiled walkways, children laughing. Kyle pushed her cherry-red lace thong to the side. A macaw shrieked and flapped through her field of view.

"They call this the Garden of Eden Atrium," Kyle said. "I like that."

The frequency of the throbbing in Rook's mind oscillated, slowing until it matched the rhythm of Kyle's grinding thrusts. His mouth was on hers, his hand inside her red lace bra. A line of emerald parrots perched on the balcony railing. Below her everything hushed, and a choir began to sing.

The hymn lasted many minutes and clashed eerily with the lewd, atonal Kyle-theme ebbing and flowing in Rook's head. When it ended, a round of pious applause reverberated under the glass roof and startled the birds. Kyle came with a grunt, and the presence in Rook's mind receded. She could still feel it, though.

His signal.

Him.

A part of Kyle stayed with her now, even when he left.

Their connection was the crude flip side of the warm reassurance she used to get from Fin's signal, back when he was alive. It told her she was Kyle's possession and could never truly escape him. He would always be with her. Confirmation came when he left on another of his errands. The connection became tenuous as he descended in the elevator, but a trace remained — the faintest itch.

In one corner of the living room was a credenza that held a silver tea service and a sleek marble chess set. On the wall, a glass case displayed an assortment of antique chessmen. Seeing her interest, Gary asked if she wanted to play. The thought made Rook unaccountably sad and she declined. Instead she watched TV.

At 7:00 Kyle came back with a hairdresser, but refused to explain beyond, "I want you to look nice." Rook tried not to think about why and let the woman do her job. After the hairdresser left, Kyle sat Rook down at the dining room table and said, "We're getting married tonight."

Rook stared back, uncomprehending. "Why?"

Kyle watched her carefully as he answered. "Because I want to. Then you'll really be mine."

Her brow furrowed. "But I married Fin."

Kyle kept staring. "That doesn't matter now. Does it?"

Rook felt she was missing something important. "I guess not."

Kyle nodded. "I'll have the ladies come up to help you dress."

"Who?"

"My secretary, and some old biddy from the Cathedral Decoration Committee. They feel bad that your family can't make it for the ceremony. You will behave for them won't you?"

Rook wondered why she wouldn't behave. "Sure."

"That's my good girl. The next time we're together you'll be mine forever."

Whatever.

Chapter Twenty

Honeymoon

Princess Brook ran because a wolf was chasing her. She climbed up a tree and threw apples at him. He ran away. She would be in trouble when she went home because her mother told her not to go in the woods. Her dress was dirty. The queen would know she was bad. Princess Brook cried and cried.

She tried to climb down but her shoe fell off. It landed in a berry bush. Princess Brook would be in even bigger trouble if she didn't find her shoe. She crawled under the bush. It had jaggers. It scratched her. She found a girl all tangled in the bush. She was sleeping. Princess Brook touched her because she was so pretty and the girl woke up. Then Princess Brook knew that the girl was her twin sister. Princess Bramble was kidnapped years and years ago. And now Princess Brook found her. She helped her sister out of the bush and they went back to the castle. Princess Brook knew that she would not be in trouble now.

The Twin Princesses by Brook Webb, age 8

Fin landed softly on something hard, and woke up. Reflexively putting out his hands, he encountered rock and bounced back up like a balloon. Too groggy to kick or flail much, he didn't make the situation worse. As he descended once again he noticed he wasn't alone.

A small group of strange beings stood around him. Six of them. Initially Fin didn't think he could be awake yet, because they looked too classic to be the real thing. They were about four feet tall, with gray-green skin, slender limbs, oversized heads and exceptionally large, unblinking eyes.

Fin managed to stand up in the slight gravity. He stared for a few minutes, the aliens content to let him get adjusted. In the early part of his conversation with the Floating Wisdom, when it revealed so much detail about the many forms the aliens took, he was not shown any creatures such as these. So what were these guys?

"Hello," Fin said tentatively.

Hello, came the reply. He hadn't seen any of their lips move. Or seen their lips, for that matter.

Another idea arrived. Their form was not important.

"Okay." Fin looked at each one. The faces had some slight individual character despite the general lack of expressiveness. He didn't know what to say to these creatures, and they were waiting for him to run the conversation. "Great. Look, I really don't have time to chat. I need to get back to Earth. Can you help me?"

The aliens radiated distress. They could help him, but it was unthinkable. Let him leave? Now?

"Now would actually be excellent. No offense guys, but I don't know how much more of this I can stand."

The members of the group all moved a little closer together. After a few seconds, they spoke to Fin without sound. The words came through clearly, not just detached thoughts or images but complete sentences in his head.

We are ready.

Fin guardedly replied, "Ready for what?"

To be assimilated. We will not resist.

"Now, wait a second," Fin began, but they interrupted.

We see you cannot be opposed. Only we ask, please, do not abandon us. There was more than a hint of desperation.

"No, no. That was rhetoric. I can't absorb you. I wouldn't if I could. My whole point was assimilation sucks."

We see.

"I doubt that."

Sincerely, we understand. They were waiting for Fin to say something.

"Well, good. Behave."

Of course. We will not harm the creatures of Earth.

"Great. Can I go now?"

Please restore the Floating Wisdom.

"Sorry. I don't think so."

The aliens' words were now laced with fear. *Why do you mean to leave us like this? If you will not engulf us, you must give the Wisdom back. We will perish without it!*

"I can't. Look, I don't even know what happened. It broke. It's gone, and good riddance. Now you can all think for yourselves."

No! This suggestion horrified the aliens. *You can't leave. You must stay and help us.*

"Oh give me a break. What do you want from me?"

Gather us up, make us whole again. The wholeness was good. With it nothing was hidden from us. Now it is lost.

They were becoming edgy. Fin could feel their fear. The thing they were most terrified of seemed to be themselves.

"I can see this whole independent-thought thing is new to you. I understand. But you can all be like the Floating Wisdom, or like me. I mean, it said I was 'novel' but it wasn't afraid of me."

It feared you.

Fin gritted his teeth. "I imagine it did, a little. You'll just have to get used to a small amount of fear and doubt. Get some perspective. It's normal."

Fear is the result of disunity. The wholeness was holiness. We never knew this fear until you shattered our faith.

"Shattered your faith? I only stuck up for myself." Fin shook his head. "Believe whatever you want."

We believe we must be whole. You must restore us. We knew you were unique, but failed to understand what that meant. It meant you would purge us of our flaws and remake us as a better Wisdom. We tried to use you, and that was wrong.

"Is that supposed to be an apology?" The aliens backed up a step.

"And you're full of shit. How could the Floating Wisdom fear anything, if fear comes from disunity? I come along and shatter this thing for you and you refuse to let go of its double-talk anyway!"

The aliens backed up farther, huddling as close together as possible. Fin's attitude softened a bit. The poor things thought they were being scolded by God, personally. He still needed to know how to get home, and arguing about religion and philosophy looked like an unlikely way to achieve that.

"Look," he said, extending his left hand, "I can't solve your problems for you. I didn't ask to be here, and what I did was in self defense, but I'm sorry about the mess. Now send me home and we'll all muddle through."

No. We will not be without you.

Fin's attitude hardened again. "Then go FUCK OFF!" he bellowed, waving his arms.

As he let out his roar they all toppled backwards, as if they had fainted. Before they hit the floor their arms and legs split lengthwise into pairs, and the knees and elbows tilted upward. They suddenly sported eight legs apiece, and he saw, before they spun away and scuttled off in six different directions, small glistening eyes on their true faces. They were gigantic spiders. What he had taken for faces were in fact their gray-green abdomens, the huge black eyes merely spots.

The scritching noises of their flight diminished and stopped, leaving Fin alone. He remembered spiders being mentioned, but it was a jolt to meet them close up.

Fin stood still for a few minutes, contemplating. There had to be some kind of transportation system or they never could have brought him here.

Searching for the means of transport would give him an excuse to leave this creepy chamber.

Fin craned his neck looking for some kind of landmark in the expanse of undressed rock. There was enough concavity to tell him he stood on the inside surface of a sphere. Although the dim light and tangled network of cocoons thwarted his attempt to look across to the other side, he could see a glow coming from a distant point on the wall, maybe a third of the way around from where he stood.

It was like learning to walk all over again to keep from bouncing up into the webs. The curvature fooled his eyes, making him expect to be moving uphill all the time. The minuscule gravity made it necessary to walk very softly and slowly, exhausting because it required so much concentration.

Fin squinted up at his bright patch to determine if he was on course. He could see it much more clearly now with less of the webbing in his way, a circular opening in the rock wall, letting into a bright corridor. A promising target.

Soon he drew close enough that he didn't need to look up to see it.

To his right, not ten feet away, a spider with a six-foot leg span descended with eerie slowness on a silken strand. Fin's skin temperature dropped, but he reminded himself this was not really a spider. He recognized it from the group he had been talking to a few minutes ago.

"You scared the shit out of me. What do you want now?" The spider reached stone, and pawed the air with its front legs. It clicked its mandibles and advanced a step.

Perhaps it really was a spider.

As it sprang at him, Fin jumped away. His jump carried him high above the rocky floor and into the outskirts of the web. The spider followed a much flatter trajectory and was far below, but it began climbing rapidly through the web. If Fin snared himself he'd be easy meat.

He had risen almost a hundred feet, getting farther away from his intended escape from this hellish chamber.

Pretty sure the structural lines of the web weren't sticky, Fin grabbed one. With some amount of awkward tumbling he arrested his flight and braced his feet against the line he held in his hand. There was nothing else within reach, making it difficult to control his position, to aim himself at the exit. The spider moved toward him efficiently and quickly. Fin forced himself to take his time aiming, twisting his wrist while counter swinging his right arm, gauging the springiness of the webbing.

Close enough, he decided, meaning both the rushing arachnid and his aim. He jumped, launching himself headfirst at considerable speed.

Fin saw the faint glint of something in his path, and jolted to a painful halt with a fine strand across his throat. This nearly invisible thread was sticky, and much stronger than the cocoon material. While he spun around the taut line, he became tangled. His twirling slowed and he was granted periodic glimpses of two spiders squaring off. The one chasing him faced another, even larger, who apparently set this ambush.

As Fin watched, the newcomer overwhelmed his original pursuer. It bent the smaller arachnid's legs aside and administered a single gruesome bite.

Fin wished he knew how to get the monster to act civilized. It turned away from its ruined opponent before the twitching stopped, and advanced with mechanical calmness toward Fin.

He screamed at it and struggled against his bonds. They were stubborn but not unbreakable. By the time the huge spider neared him he had use of all of his extremities. That left him outnumbered eight to four, but he was going to put up a fight. He tried to keep himself aligned for a kick and kept shrieking. The spider paused, considering its next move.

Don't hurt it, Fin heard. *Just a moment.*

Chancing a quick look away from the monster to locate the source of the thoughts, he saw more spiders, at least a dozen, streaming into the web in a tight group.

We're coming.

Fin couldn't stop screaming.

The arachnid rescue squad surrounded Fin and his would-be assailant and stopped. The big creature dropped back a little. Simultaneously, the entire group rearranged their limbs and tilted their bodies so they lifted their abdomens toward Fin. They looked like they were seated on the web with their legs dangling, all staring at Fin with eyes that weren't eyes. When they spoke to him again it seemed the voice in his head came from the largest, the same one that had been about to attack him.

These are confusing times. We think it would be best, for you and certainly for us, if you left.

"Amen!" Fin yelled.

We will take you to our transport system now, and return you to Earth. Please climb down along the new webbing we will create for you.

"Finally, some reasonable creatures. You got it." Fin looked over at the dead spider. He felt responsible for it, for the unkind way he'd treated that group. Had the thing attacked out of spite? He opened his mouth to ask about the violent events, but the answer came immediately.

Without the Floating Wisdom, old instinctual ways take over. In small groups we can function, but we are cut off from the Floating Wisdom—the calm knowledge of trillions of beings. Unfortunately, two is too small a group to overcome the violence of our instincts.

The work on a ladder for Fin proceeded while he received his explanation. The spiders always kept themselves arranged such that none strayed too far to remain part of the group. Fin followed the aliens down the makeshift ladder toward the glowing circle.

They were not embarrassed by their disapproval of Fin's presence. He could sense some general ideas about how his example meant there must be evil in freedom, but mostly he picked up blame and resentment. They clearly wished to see the old order restored.

Fin was getting steamed over the aliens' attitude that he had destroyed their wonderful religion. He paused before he entered the corridor, a tube fitted with many rungs and handholds.

"You do realize I didn't ask to come here, right? I mean, if I damaged your society you literally brought it on yourselves."

The past is done. We will send you home. We need not argue matters of blame.

The aliens all entered the corridor, standing upright, and waited for Fin. He moved forward by means of the handholds. The tunnel's apparent orientation fluctuated with each foot he traveled. It was all in the fractional-G scale, so Fin didn't get thrown around. Just a bit nauseated. An image appeared in his head, showing a 3D cross-section of the asteroid, meant to explain the complex gravitational issues here. Fin gathered that the insanely advanced mathematics that should have accompanied the diagram were part of the Floating Wisdom and therefore not accessible right now.

They moved along, through two junctions and past several doorways, before stopping at an open door. The aliens walked in, and Fin pulled himself after them by grasping the edges of the doorway. It shut behind him.

The room was featureless except for a pedestal protruding from one side, which might as well have been the floor. The pasty green aliens stood around this, and Fin asked, "How does it work?"

You must lie down here so we can prepare you.

Fin wanted more information before trusting a group that so openly loathed him. The situation looked too compromising. He could still access the cutaway map they showed him. Some of it was labeled...

He dug the information forcibly out of the group consciousness of these aliens. They showed distress as he exacted more detail, located his present whereabouts. He looked up the real purpose of this ominous chamber and saw how right he was not to trust them.

They panicked, scuttling around the room, losing their cohesiveness. As a baker's dozen separate bugs they were far more dangerous and they would lack the sort of information he could exploit.

Fin addressed the collective mind, pinning it and refusing to let it disintegrate. "You have lied to me, the One Who Shattered the Wisdom! You see now how such deceptions anger me!" He pulled them back together before any of them could operate the door and allow the group to scatter.

"Now, send me safely back to Earth!" he commanded.

Yes! We can! We will! A clamor of explanations about how their technology worked filled Fin's head. He comprehended little of it, except that it was a way of pinching space. It could be used from virtually anywhere, even this laboratory.

He visualized his room at the boarding house. "That place. Now."

The walls moved in irrational ways, concave corners splitting to reveal hidden space — all curves. It engulfed Fin and surrounded him with a spherical shell of non-space. He could feel it moving, the pebbly surface undulating as his bubble in the continuum glided toward its destination. The slippery feeling lasted for several minutes, then the sphere unfolded into a dark, stale room distinctly lacking in Rook's presence.

***   ***   ***

Eleanor and Mrs Swenson had no end of nice things to say about Mr Tanner. He'd been so understanding in the wake of Reverend Shaw's sudden passing. He ran things so well. He was such an honorable man, so handsome, so dashing, so kind. Rook must be very proud to have made such a fine catch. Rook stayed quiet while the ladies prattled on and answered their own questions.

They dressed her all in white: white bustier with way too many hooks, white silk panties, garter belt and stockings, trimmed with pale blue bows. Rook had never been one for lingerie. She felt like old-school Madonna. Mrs Swenson helped her slide her blue garter into place. The women clucked disapprovingly over her tattoos, but concluded that they must have been a youthful indiscretion, and it wasn't their place to judge. So unfortunate the dress didn't cover them all, but what could be done at this late date? Maybe she could wear a shawl? Rook declined.

The wedding dress fit well, with a sleeveless bodice, sweetheart neckline, and skirt of gauzy netting that fell to the floor like an overgrown tutu. The veil hung to her elbows and obscured her quill tattoo. The only ones on display were her ring and the rooks on her wrists, and Kyle hadn't provided gloves. Low white heels and a bouquet of blood-red roses completed the ensemble.

The old ladies got weepy over how lovely she looked, then scurried off to the cathedral, leaving Rook alone with Gary.

Gary took her downstairs to the limo and rode with her along a private lane and across the empty parking lot to the cathedral. It was an impressive structure, all glass and chrome in an impossibly intricate pile.

Gary led Rook through big glass double doors and into a green velvet nightmare. Hundreds of pews, all upholstered in bright kelly green, held twenty or so people clustered together at the front. The television cameras placed at strategic locations around the church added to the surreality.

The Wedding March played on a pipe organ. Gary walked her down the aisle to where Kyle waited in a severe black suit. The preacher nodded and smiled.

Kyle lifted Rook's veil and she felt his eyes crawling over her as his oscillations in her mind fluctuated in impatient counterpoint with the music. She suddenly understood that her getup enabled some sexual power trip of Kyle's. He wanted to pretend she was a virgin so he could take pleasure in deflowering her, soiling her.

The preacher began his religious ramblings, but Rook didn't listen. A mercifully short time later she heard something about richer and poorer. She paid attention then.

"Do you, Brook Bramble, take Kyle to be your lawful wedded husband, to love, honor and obey 'til death do you part?"

"Whatever."

The preacher looked at her, puzzled. Kyle nodded, indicating he should continue.

"Do you, Kyle Robert, take Rook to be your lawful wedded wife, to love, cherish and protect 'til death do you part?"

"I do."

There was only one ring. For Rook, of course. A wide gold band with several moderately large diamonds. Tacky. Kyle wore a self-satisfied expression as he slid it onto her finger.

"With this ring I thee wed and proclaim to the world that you are mine."

Rook blinked. This was one weird wedding.

Next thing she knew, the preacher pronounced them man and wife in the eyes of the Lord and all mankind. Kyle pulled her against him, one hand in the small of her back, the other on the back of her head, under her veil, and inflicted a voracious kiss that lasted at least a minute and took her breath away. Her mouth filled with the boozy taste of Kyle, her body pressed tightly against his. She couldn't breathe. He held her possessively, his hand creeping toward her ass. Rook had no strength. Kyle supported her now. Her fingers tingled. Her eyes fluttered closed. All she knew was the pressure of his hands and body, the feel of his lips and his teeth, the taste of his tongue, the surge of prickling rawness inside her skull, the rush of her own blood.

He was whispering in her ear, "They're giving us a reception. We won't stay long. Be good."

In another wing of the cathedral the newlyweds were photographed and toasted with fake champagne. Neither of them wanted to be there. Mrs Swenson brought out a small, flowery wedding cake for them to feed each other while more cameras flashed. Rook didn't know she had frosting in the corner of her mouth until Kyle leaned in to lick it off.

He held both her hands in his and bent over her. His tongue lingered and the lick became a kiss. With dread, Rook felt the awakening in her crotch, her nipples, her lips, the quickening in her tummy. Euphoria flooded her and made her hips quiver, her knees weak. Rook submerged in guilty horror and everything about her that was Brook burst joyously forth.

The little girl who watched with envy as her mother married time and again reveled in her chance to play dress-up with real wedding clothes. She made a low noise in her throat, and opened her eyes to stare into the hard green of Kyle's. Would he want to play house, too? She hoped so, and kissed him back.

*** *** ***

The relief Fin felt at escaping from the giant space spiders was acute. So was his emptiness at Rook's absence.

The trek to the bomb shelter in his father's back yard took Fin about an hour, and when he arrived, the padlock was in place, meaning his wife was not going to be inside. He climbed down anyway.

"Hey, Vesuvius. Miss me? I've been in outer space."

"Welcome back. Did you have a good trip?"

"Not so much. Have you talked to Rook?"

"She hasn't been here. Was she in space too?"

"No."

"Well, maybe she couldn't get the day off."

Fin smiled, and they sat silently for a few minutes. Fin decided to permit himself some optimism, to hope Rook might be waiting elsewhere. He bid his lava lamp farewell and went to find her.

The exploding truck at the reception dominated coffeehouse debate, although most people fell silent when Fin appeared. He learned Bishop was in the hospital. Worry sprang in full bloom. Rook hadn't been seen by anyone, and he couldn't locate her signal. He wished he understood it better, knew its range or if there was any way to block it. Then its hollow absence might be a useful clue and not just a source of despair.

He rode the bus to the hospital, spent almost a day roaming the wards and disrupting doctors' rounds to describe her, over and over. The doctor who treated him after the *Sycamore* disaster finally convinced Fin they had no unidentified patients. Rook wasn't there. He was too chickenshit to visit Bishop.

Yellow police tape cordoned off the entire park. Fin ducked it and walked all around the charred pickup and the picnic tables where he thought she'd left her jacket. She'd want that back soon because it was getting colder. He found nothing, figured the cops had her jacket, and probably his bass if it survived the festivities. That seemed like a safe place to leave them for a while. Asking the police for help finding Rook would hit a major snag when they asked him to account for his own whereabouts since the ill-fated party.

The next day he went to the *CTP* office. They wouldn't tell him anything, didn't believe him when he told them he'd married Rook. Rather peremptorily they assumed he was a psycho stalker fanboy. When the secretary threatened to call the police, he left.

The *Sycamore* site was also roped off. Nothing remained standing now. The few remnants that survived the blast had been pulled down. Fin stared across the rubble heap, recalling his mad dash with Bishop. He'd been looking for Rook then, too. In the end, she found him instead.

Hearing his name startled Fin, and he blinked a few times. The person who knew him was a receptionist, seated behind her desk in a cramped office with tacky paneling. He turned to leave, alarmed at his apparent wandering. The place registered in his memory and he spun back again. *Sycamore's* temporary location, the place where he worked. Rook might have asked about him here.

No?

No.

Fin gave the receptionist a detailed description of Rook and made her promise to keep an eye out for her before he left.

He asked around. Lots of people knew her. No one had seen her. When he asked at the battered women's shelter if she was staying there, they wouldn't tell him anything.

He revisited the hospital in case she had arrived since he checked. Still nothing. He went back to his job to check for messages. When he got there they talked him into staying for his shift. He rationalized that if she showed up while he was there, they'd be reunited immediately. The first hour or so went quickly, but the longer he sat in one spot and Rook didn't appear, the more depressed he became and he left halfway through the shift.

Fin spent the night hunched against the chill, sitting motionless, staring at every passerby on Linden Avenue. At six in the morning, he wandered down the block to The Shamrock but couldn't eat any of the breakfast he ordered. The bulletin board by the door inspired another tactic for his search, and he put up fliers in the places he knew she frequented.

*** *** ***

The wedding ring finally started Rook thinking again. It was ugly and uncomfortably tight.

She had the vague knowledge that something like a week — an entire week! — passed while she left her body in the hands of her inner child. Unfortunately, her inner child was twins.

In fifth grade, during her mother's third divorce, the school counselor recommended Brook see a psychologist. Her mother embraced the idea, treating therapy as an extra-curricular activity — something to keep her little Brook Bramble occupied after school. To heighten the competitive aspects, she'd signed up Dragonfly Bay and Junebug Spring too. Who's the most screwed up? Who can get better the fastest? Who might need medication? Go team!

The psychologist said Brook suffered from a depersonalization disorder. She shielded herself from the pain and confusion of her real life by inventing an alter-ego, the perfect Princess Brook. When Princess Brook was unable to stay out of trouble, a second alter-ego developed to take the blame. Princess Brook was the perfect one: complacent, eager to please, loved. Princess Bramble was the naughty one: bold, devilish, mischievous. Young Brook increasingly watched her life unfold from a third-person viewpoint, her world hazy, her actions not her own. She began to burn herself with matches and poke fingers with sewing needles just to feel something, to be in control. That's when she started therapy with Dr Wymbol.

Princess Brook embodied everything the real Brook thought she ought to be, Bramble everything she feared she was. Rook knew it was Bramble who enjoyed being fucked by Kyle. While Rook cowered in denial, Brook cooked and smiled, Bramble gave blowjobs and had orgasms.

Rook shuddered.

She considered the ring again. If she kept it on she would develop a dent in her finger where it would nest and become like an extension of herself, mostly not considered and difficult to remove. Kyle would insist she wear it, she knew. It symbolized his hold on her. But he wasn't home right now, and her finger itched.

She started wiggling the ring, trying to take it off, for a little while at least.

It had all been so simple when she was a child. Slipping into the role of Princess Coping Mechanism made perfect sense. Princess Brook never had any problems. Who wouldn't want to be her? And if reality intruded, Bramble was waiting to take the heat. The real Brook could ignore everything and stay safe. At least until the disconnection became overwhelming and she had to hurt herself to drive the fog away.

Slowly Brook had learned how to deal with her real life. On her last day of therapy she symbolically locked the Princesses away. Princess Brook lay in an orchid-scented glass coffin on a bed of smooth, white stones, under briskly flowing water. Princess Bramble stood on a rough slab of lichen-encrusted rock, arms bound above her by thorny vines, ankles by whispering creepers in a glossy, black-green berry thicket of epic proportions. The fact that she could vividly picture their prisons and the serene aspects of their sleeping faces should have been a sign to somebody she wasn't really cured.

There were times throughout her life, her term with Marcus being a good example, when she pretended to be someone besides herself. It was easier to be Raven for him than to insist she was Rook. She had outwardly sublimated her identity, but the Princesses stayed asleep. Until now. Maybe the Kyle vibration in her head had weakened the foundations of their prisons.

Rook went into the bedroom and got the Astroglide from the nightstand drawer. She lubricated her finger and the link of gold slipped off. Underneath, the skin was wrinkly and mottled black. Rook thought for a moment she had gangrene, but then understood. Her other wedding ring, the tattoo. She had forgotten about it.

After wiping her hands and the ring clean, Rook studied the tattoo. It wasn't healed and needed to be exposed to the air. She liked it so much more than the gaudy gold monstrosity Kyle had claimed her with. Elegant and simple, the delicate black lines twining around and around. She could never pawn it and it could never be stolen. It could only be obscured, which is what Kyle had done. He didn't want her to be reminded of Fin. Didn't want to be reminded himself. Who would want to think about his wife in bed with his brother? Rook felt uncomfortable, like she had betrayed Fin.

She wished this were a betrayal, wished he was alive to be betrayed.

Her karma must really suck. How else to explain finding such unexpected love only to have it stolen and replaced with a shoddy replica? She and Fin were happy together, but now she was compelled to go through the motions of a marriage with Kyle instead. Since her husbands were half-twins did the universe assume she wouldn't notice the difference?

Rook curled up on the bed, hugging her pillow and trying to call up memories of Fin. Her lack of success confounded her. What had they even had together? Perhaps it was pheromones and nothing more.

But he must have loved her. He wore a wedding ring like hers, painful to acquire and impossible to remove.

Her mother hopped from husband to husband, never giving herself time to figure out what she wanted, what she hoped to find in these men. Rook always swore she would never marry, never be like her mother.

Yet she was already on her second marriage. One mistake could be forgiven, but two?

Fin was not a mistake. If he had lived, things would have been different. Rook laughed humorlessly at the understatement.

Kyle was the mistake, not Fin. She could still be forgiven, just needed to get away from Kyle and start over. Not make any more mistakes.

Getting away from Kyle could prove difficult since he took no chances with her 'safety.' If her behavior changed or she let on she felt discontented, who knew what he would do? Rook didn't relish the thought of being drugged again or locked in a closet. Best to keep him happy.

Brook certainly liked playing house with Kyle. She enjoyed the idea of status, of being married to a rich, powerful, handsome man. Bramble, on the other hand, reveled in the naughtiness. Kyle had an endless supply of degrading fantasies to act out, and Bramble loved them all. Rook resisted the idea of handing her reins over to the pair of them, but what choice did she have?

Rook uncurled herself and stretched. She felt better, almost fully awake. The idea of forming a truce with Brook and Bramble was daunting, but Rook would grant them rights to her body while retaining her intellectual property.

The rook tattoos on her wrists would remind her every day who she really was. Rook Tanner. At least her name hadn't changed again.

Hearing the elevator brought her mood down again. Kyle's low vibration in her head strengthened. What to make of that? It must mean something. Did it signal a deeper connection than she wanted to accept? Reaching for the ring, she noticed lettering on the inside. What sort of romantic notion did Kyle deem worthy of inscribing on a wedding band?

PUT IT BACK ON, ROOK

Chapter Twenty-One

PENTHOUSE

The unprecedented wave of missing-persons reports continues
with another eight individuals added to the roster as of press time.
Neighboring communities are also affected, although the main
locus of the phenomenon appears to be Webster.

Historically, the Webster/Donner region has seen a higher-than-
typical rate of disappearances over the last three decades, but
virtually none of the affected people remain missing for more than
two days. The current surge is especially alarming because some of
those who vanished have not been seen in over a week, signaling a
darker turn in the pattern.
from *Webster Daily Press,* 10-23-2000

Fin knew that Rook's sister went to Buck U. Their relationship was
strained by Rook's discovery that her sister slept with Marcus, but Fin
was counting on lingering familial warmth to help him out.

When the dorm room door opened, Fin's heart lurched and
foundered in a pool of adrenaline. It was Rook. Only it wasn't. Maybe
Rook four years ago. Naive, happy, puzzled, and very, very young.

"Are you looking for Celine?" asked the girl who could only be
Rook's sister, in a close approximation of Rook's voice.

Fin stared.

Rook's hair, the same black and red. A little taller. A little thinner.
Fresh tattoo on her collarbone. Nose stud on the wrong side, the wrong
color. Dressed like she'd raided Rook's closet and nothing was quite the
right size. She was a poorly made copy. Depression flooded him. Rook
wouldn't have gone to this little girl who so obviously worshipped her

big sister. That he came here looking for her shone a spotlight on the depth of his desperation.

With a start Fin noticed her eyes were light brown. Not at all like Rook's.

Junebug laughed nervously, about to shut the door.

"I'm looking for your sister," he said belatedly.

"Who do you think my sister is?" Junebug asked.

"Rook. Maybe you call her Brook. Brandymoon. Except now she's Rook Tanner. We got married a little while ago."

Junebug arched one eyebrow in an exact replica of Rook's incredulous look. Fin couldn't decide if Junebug was a good thing or a bad thing. He wanted to shake her. To get her to stop aping Rook, or to get her to do a better job? He wasn't sure.

"What's your name?" She purred, sounding more than merely curious.

"Fin," he replied warily.

"I never heard her talk about you. She lives with M—" She stopped herself.

"Marcus. Yeah. Not anymore." Fin saw what he had been avoiding, doing useless things like looking up Junebug as a distraction. In all his snooping Fin hadn't run across Marcus or heard any mention of him. His absence was a most unwelcome clue.

Junebug's not-blue eyes crawled over him and she licked her lips. She opened the door fully and stepped aside, motioning him to enter.

Fin wanted to escape. Junebug was a bad thing. Possibly a wild thing. She couldn't help him, would just pump him for information about her idol. Fin had the distinct impression there was more than one kind of pumping on her mind.

"I'll see you at the family reunion," he said, and left.

From Rook's laptop he obtained the address of the apartment she'd shared with Marcus. Nothing. The air was stale, ashtrays empty. Like no one had been there for a week. Which was how long ago the reception was.

One week since he'd seen his wife.

Fin filled a garbage bag with all the girl things he could find. Rook would appreciate having more than his old clothes to wear. Sobbing, he carried her recovered belongings to the bomb shelter. He'd taken to leaving the padlock off in case she came back when he was out looking for her, and subsequently lost it, so now his dad's snooty neighbors were on the honor system. Those fuckers better not steal Rook's stuff.

He patrolled his flyers, tearing down lost cats and bar bands that overlapped some of them. At the bookstore a balding man commented on the rudeness of Fin's actions.

"Do you think so?" Fin challenged. The man quailed a bit, but nodded, held eye contact.

Fin barged into the stranger's mind and rifled all the cabinets looking for a connection to Rook's disappearance, went back again looking for a coincidental meeting, even brushing elbows in the street. He dug fiercely for any glimmer of recognition. He found nothing.

Fin released his victim, feeling ill over what he had done. The man looked dazed and horrified, but not permanently harmed. Fin rushed out the door seeking fresh air.

His hope crushed, Fin collapsed into a frenzy of self destruction. He had only been on the wagon for a short time. When he fell off, there was nobody around who noticed.

He plunged into the deviant candy store of his personal stash and cleaned it out in a single binge. Adept with self-medication, he knew how his chemistry would react to mixtures of hard drugs, could tweak the blend to achieve subtle degrees of psychosis, shades of being fucked up. With the aloof air of a sorcerer he could cast a spell over himself but never give up control.

Tonight he gave up control. He made no pretense at seeking pleasure, or enlightenment, or looking for the edge of the world. This was the unceremonious consumption of a shitload of toxins. This was seeking oblivion.

The shakes and a mammoth headache told him he'd nearly found what he'd gone looking for.

Before the disappointment even fully registered, Fin was planning his next score. Without Rook, he reverted to his instinctual behaviors. Some people owed him, some others were not good at saying no. No one had much luck saying no to Fin this time. He was preternaturally persuasive.

*** *** ***

Besides the ring and the marriage license Brook eagerly signed, Rook decided another symbol of Kyle's hold on her was her own willingness to be held. Kyle slept soundly, and they were alone in the apartment at night. It didn't take a genius to see night was the time to snoop. It galled Rook this had not occurred to her before. She couldn't just walk out, but she could try to learn something in the locked room at the end of the hall. Or maybe figure out a way to climb down from the balcony.

A quick look over the railing confirmed Rook's memory. No easy way down. Her aerie-prison perched well above the tops of the palm trees and the tame little waterfall. She knew from the sex field trip Kyle took her on a few nights ago that the koi pond at the base of the waterfall was only knee-deep, so a swan dive would be her swan song. There were no other balconies to climb to. She assumed offices made up the rest of the building. Apparently god didn't see fit to parcel out prime real estate to the entire flock, just the shepherd. Damn.

Rook thought about picking the lock on the door at the end of the hall, but had a better idea. Kyle would have the key.

Their creepy mental connection should act as an early warning system if he woke up, so her position needn't be too compromising.

The keys were easy to find.

Rook crept down the hall and knelt in front of the door. After several wrong guesses, a key turned in the lock. She allowed herself a smile of satisfaction as she opened the door and slipped into the dark inside.

With the door closed behind her, Rook flipped on the lights. Her eyes adjusted to the low wattage and she looked around, suddenly conscious of her nudity. A large den. With the business office right downstairs, this place must be intended for more private activities. Personal. Secret.

Bookshelves lined the walls. The majority of the books were religious tomes. There were some biographies, some historical studies, a few Classics of Western Literature and a smattering of art books.

The only window shared its view of the horrible illuminated cathedral with the office downstairs. In the center of the room, on an Oriental carpet, a dark walnut desk patiently waited to be plundered. Covering its surface were papers, open texts, religious objects, and a portrait of a sickly looking young blonde woman wearing a honeydew-colored pantsuit, its frame inscribed, 'Molly Oliver Shaw 1952-1981.' A leather armchair with a reading lamp dominated the far corner, flanked by an old-fashioned console radio and a pipe stand full of pipes. All of it left over from Brian Shaw. To one side of the door sat several office supply boxes. Kyle boxed up all the things he didn't want to look at on a daily basis and stuck them in here. That meant he wasn't likely to notice if she snooped around, but it also meant there wouldn't be much, if anything, pertaining to Kyle himself.

A door along the right wall caught her attention. Maybe Shaw had a hidden arsenal. Inside Rook saw a small altar, complete with wooden chalice and leather-bound prayer book, and a lock of long blonde hair tied with twine. To each side she spotted something much more interesting. A narrow flight of stairs leading up and another leading down. Rook felt a flutter of excitement in her belly. What would she find on the roof? Maybe a fire escape!

Rook raced up the carpeted stairs and came to a tiny room with one metal door and one shatterproof window. Out the window she saw a helipad. Lights defined the perimeter of the roof, and a helicopter silently waited. Beside the door Rook saw a small keypad with a display blinking 'armed.' Damn.

Well, there were the other stairs. Which hopefully didn't lead straight to the sentry station.

Rook retreated, passed by the altar and descended the other flight. These let her out in the anteroom off Kyle's office, near the elevator, and disappointingly went no further. The elevator buttons were dark and mocking, but she jabbed the Down arrow anyway. Nothing happened. When she'd been here before she hadn't explored beyond this office. There must be another elevator for the rest of the staff to use. And stairs. That was fire code, wasn't it?

Rook crossed the expansive office, the parquet floor cold under her bare feet, and another armed alarm pad confronted her. What demanded all this security? Maybe Kyle didn't want some rival religion to come in and steal his deluxe leather bible with the word of god highlighted in red.

If he was so pious, shouldn't he believe god wouldn't let anyone in here who He didn't want in here? Kyle only pretended to be religious in order to keep control. There was something else going on. If she couldn't escape, she might as well try to figure out what it was.

Was there any point to searching this desk again? Rook slumped into the overstuffed leather chair and pouted. Everything looked the same as on her first night here. She flipped through the desk calendar again, and again found nothing of interest. She stopped, hand hovering beside the phone.

Would it work? Or would it call the guards?

This was a business office. There was no way all the phones were routed through the guard station.

Right?

After five agonizing minutes of internal argument, she made up her mind and lifted the receiver to her ear, ready to hang up and dart back to bed if it rang through to the guards. If not, she'd dial 911.

There was a third option she had not anticipated. A robotic female voice stated, "The phone system is currently on Night Mode. If this is an emergency, you may override Night Mode by entering your six digit personal identification code, followed by the pound sign."

Fuck.

Rook climbed the stairs back to the apartment, resigned to a long, tedious search. But not tonight. If she slept all day, Kyle would get suspicious.

The desk had four drawers full of files, plus there were the boxes by the door. Rook decided to pace herself and start with the desk — one drawer each night. Not only would that interfere less with her sleep, it would also prolong the distraction the investigation provided.

*** *** ***

Marcus spent several days locked inside Talisman, fasting in preparation for a vision quest. When every cell of his body screamed with hunger, he nourished himself with peyote. His body was clean, empty and receptive to a message. The mescal slammed into his system and transported him to another realm.

The Great Spirits of that realm treated Coyote well. They smoked with him and shared their women. Coyote was honored and pleased, but not content. He needed Raven. The Great Spirits agreed, and told him of a plan to defeat the other shaman and claim her. They put a mark upon his hand so Raven could know the truth of his words.

He knew what to do, now he needed to find out where to go. The gods of the DMV were pleased with Marcus's monetary gifts and agreed to help him. The SHAWMIN plate was registered to Shaw Ministries in Donner. Marcus recognized Brian Shaw as his mental tormenter from Rook's rescue at the factory, but not as the man who carried her away. News of Shaw's demise confirmed that.

Coyote knew he was ready to face his adversary, whoever he might be. This one final test and he and Raven would begin their reign of chaos.

*** *** ***

After a day spent burning batch after batch of peanut butter cookies due to Brook's distracting obsession with soap operas, Rook slipped out of bed as soon as Kyle's breathing became deep and regular. The keys were once again on top of the dresser, in a pile with spare change and

Kyle's wallet.

Until now Rook hadn't considered rifling the wallet. If she was careful he shouldn't notice.

The contents were disappointing: Shaw Ministries corporate credit card, less than a hundred dollars cash, frequent flyer loyalty card from a Webster sub shop, a condom. Nothing that looked like a security pass, no cheat sheet with alarm codes. Rook memorized the credit card number and put everything back the way she found it.

Before starting her search of the den, Rook trotted down to Kyle's office and checked to see if the alarm was armed and the phone on Night Mode. Suspicions confirmed, she went back upstairs and sat on the oriental carpet in front of Shaw's desk.

The first drawer held correspondence, chronological within each alphabetical listing, mostly concerning the finances and 'good works' of Shaw Ministries. Rook went through all of it, looking for anything out of the ordinary, anything tying the ministry to the mysterious factory.

A *Real World* marathon kept Rook occupied the next day. Kyle came up for lunch and watched an episode with her. He took her out onto the balcony to fuck before going back to his office.

Rook checked the alarm pad that night. If she ever found it unarmed she would need to remember to get dressed before running out of the building.

The papers in the second drawer all pertained to old sermons and the New Revelations. The sermons were filed chronologically along with notes and bibliographies. Shaw had subtly been wording things to prepare his audience for his Revelations. A bunch of religious bullshit, but at least a change from the dry financials of the previous night. The writings were dense and Rook struggled to keep everything straight. Eventually she admitted she couldn't stick to her original schedule and saved half for the next night.

Rook couldn't take any notes during her research because Kyle might find them. While Brook watched *The Price Is Right*, Rook mentally reviewed what she had learned, which was not much.

Hopefully the rest of the papers in the drawer would fill in the gaps.

By the time she replaced the drawer that night, Rook's brain was so full of useless theology it almost drowned out Kyle's oppressive drone.

This stuff veered wildly off the map of generally accepted scripture. It was ridiculous of course, but Rook could see how someone could draw parallels from the story to Fin, Kyle and herself. She would be the Completer, the Tanner brothers the Divided Man. In some nebulous and undefined way she was meant to, what, be a bridge between the halves? Did Kyle step so neatly into her life the moment Fin died because it was foretold? Bullshit. Prophecy could go fulfill itself. She hoped this wasn't being preached from the Shaw Ministries pulpit. It would be utterly embarrassing to get away from Kyle only to have people regarding her as some sort of icon.

At lunchtime the next day Kyle came upstairs, pulled her into the bedroom and callously fucked her twice, then went back to work, all without saying a word. At dinner she caught him glaring. This was how things were with Marcus.

At least with Kyle she felt she had a good excuse for not leaving.

The third drawer held staff reports, employee records, resumes. Nothing about Kyle. No reason to think he had even worked for Shaw, let alone been the heir apparent.

All the next day Kyle was agitated. It was Saturday, so he spent the whole day in the apartment making Rook nervous. His signal came through skittery and intense.

Shortly after dinner Kyle announced he had some pressing business. Gary was needed elsewhere tonight, so Mitch would be staying with Rook. She must stay out of the bedroom so Mitch could see her. If she needed to use the bathroom, she was to use the one in the hall and not take too long. Mitch knew how to keep her safe. She shouldn't worry. She should, as always, behave.

Mitch turned out to be less personable than Gary. He sat in the armchair where he could see the front door and the glass door to the balcony. He had a hefty handgun which he kept in plain view, and a little thing in his ear like a secret service agent. He told her to keep the volume down on the TV. He called her Mrs Tanner. Rook didn't like Mitch.

The evening passed slowly. Mitch did not falter once in his duties. Rook hoped he would fall asleep like the guards in movies, but he stayed alert the entire time. She actually wished Kyle would come home.

At midnight, Mitch stood and stretched. Rook arched her eyebrows at him.

"Mr Tanner is on his way."

Rook felt Kyle's vibration increase and a moment later heard the elevator rumble. Mitch approached the front door. Rook heard the elevator bing and the doors open, lots of male voices. Mitch looked out through the peephole, opened the door, and holstered his gun. In swaggered Kyle and four other guys, including Gary, dressed all in black and wearing bulletproof vests. The boisterous gang smelled of gunpowder. Mitch and several of the men high fived, some let out war whoops. It was like downtown Webster after the Buck U Broncos won a football game.

Kyle grinned like a madman. He trotted over to the sofa where Rook sat, tossed her over his shoulder and did an end-zone dance. He stood her in front of him and kissed her. The other men cheered and hollered.

"We did it!" Kyle explained.

Then he was off to the kitchen, passing out beers.

Rook stood in the living room, wondering whether any of them would notice if she slipped out the open front door and into the elevator. She started walking in roughly that direction, which was also roughly the direction to the kitchen.

"Hey, Mrs Tanner," one of them yelled. Rook looked up in time to catch the beer he tossed.

Kyle removed his vest and handed it to Mitch. The others handed theirs over too and Mitch tossed the pile out into the vestibule and shut the door.

Amid the revelry Rook pieced together a small amount of the story.

This commando squad had just returned from a successful attack on a cult's headquarters. There was a lot of gunfire, but no serious injuries "on our side." They hadn't recovered the whole batch, but got most of it. They were the dudes! They were awesome! They kicked ass!

After two beers, Kyle gave the guys five hundred dollars to celebrate with and booted them out. He celebrated naked with Rook, then had her bathe him to wash away the scent of brimstone aphrodisiac.

In the hot, frothy water of the whirlpool bath, a memory blindsided Rook, of sharing the small bomb shelter tub with Fin. Her heart clenched painfully and tears threatened to spill down her cheeks.

They had the same shoulders. The same wisp of hair curling around their navels, the same arch to the eyebrow, the same toes.

She could not allow herself to be fooled by the similarities, lulled. There were differences. Rook set out to enumerate them all, to keep the two men separate in her mind. She owed at least that to Fin.

Fin had tattoos, and a pierced ear and eyebrow. Kyle was circumcised, had extensive surgical scarring on his right knee, and short hair...

***

Sunday morning Kyle was up early to watch Spitz's broadcast. The high from the previous night's revels had worn off and he was in a surly mood. He said sarcastic and ugly things to the reverend on the TV.

That night in bed things came to a head.

"Why, Rook?" Kyle's voice came out of the darkness, startling Rook.

"Why what?" Rook hoped she sounded innocent and sleepy.

"Why are you doing this?"

"Sleeping?" In fact, she had been about to get up. How long had he known? What would he do?

"Don't be stupid."

Rook kept quiet.

Kyle rolled on top of her, pinning her hands to the pillow above her head, looming.

"Fin's dead, you know."

Rook nodded.

"I'm the only one left. It's not like you have a choice."

"You've got me!"

Kyle used his knee to part Rook's legs as his vibrations rubbed her mind raw.

"Please, Kyle, tell me what you want!"

"You know," he said, starting to thrust. "You know exactly what I want and you won't give it to me."

"Kyle, I don't like this game."

He let go of her left hand and slapped her. She yelped in surprise and pain.

"This is not a game. This is everything. This is fate. You have to Complete one of us. Fin's dead. That leaves me! Do it!"

Rook felt fear rising into panic and confusion. "Do what?"

"MAKE ME WHOLE!"

Tears slid off her cheeks onto the pillow. Kyle kept thrusting. She realized, distantly, he was talking about the New Revelations.

"I... I can't. I would. I don't know how." It all tumbled out together.

Anger rolled off Kyle. Rook could smell it.

He growled, "A Completer, an Unknowing angel with Shadowed Wings, shall heal the Divided Man and restore Light upon the Earth!" He came. Rook held still.

Kyle got out of bed and left the room. He returned less than a minute later and turned on the lights, spreading out several file folders beside Rook on the bed, along with the little journal from the cigar box downstairs with her underwear. She recognized the files from the desk in Shaw's den.

She looked up at him, tried to keep her voice calm. "What's this?" She didn't want Kyle to know how badly he had scared her.

The anger had left him. Now he was desperate. "This is the future. It's all here. Read it and then tell me why you refuse to help me."

Rook read the journal first, while Kyle paced naked. When she set it aside, Kyle said. "Well?"

Rook shrugged.

"Don't you see yourself?" he demanded.

"Maybe. It could be anybody."

Kyle refused to believe that. He saw clearly the key individuals were the Tanner brothers and their wife. Divided Man and Completer. The New Revelations also frequently mentioned crows. Crows were rooks. He'd looked it up.

Rook asked why he believed this stuff when he didn't believe in the bible. Kyle explained this was more like Nostradamus. Rook told him Nostradamus could be interpreted any number of ways, and so could this, but Kyle was already convinced he was right.

"I can't figure out why it's not working. I saved you. I fucked you. I married you. I fell in love with you." He held her with his flat green eyes while she cringed inside and tried to decide if he believed what he'd just said. "You have to want me to be Complete. It's the only thing left. I even went..." Kyle stopped and looked thoughtful. Rook almost laughed. He looked like a dog trying to understand something. "Tell me, Rook," he said finally, "what's the significance of skeletons?"

"Skeletons?" Was Kyle threatening her?

"What do they mean?" he persisted.

"They're bones," Rook said slowly.

"What do they symbolize?"

"Please, Kyle, you're scaring me. I'll help you if I can."

"What do they symbolize?"

He wouldn't be happy until she said it. "Death," she said quietly.

"Well that's pretty obvious." He sounded impatient. "What else?"

"Um. Secrets."

Kyle's eyes lit up. "What kind of secrets?"

"Bad ones. You know, skeletons in the closet."

"Like what, specifically?" he prodded.

"I don't know!"

Kyle noticed Rook's agitation. He sighed and smiled. "Hey, calm down." He moved the papers and sat beside her, putting his arm around her. "You're so tense."

I wonder why, Rook thought.

Kyle took her left hand in both of his, playing with her wedding ring. He raised her hand and kissed the ring, kissed her forehead. Sitting with his back against the oak headboard, he snuggled Rook up against his chest with one arm around her, the other still holding her hand.

"You know, we never talk," he said.

Rook choked back laughter.

"You're a smart girl, aren't you?"

"I like to think so," Rook said. *But somehow I ended up in this situation anyway.*

"I'd like to find out. Let me get to know you." He almost sounded like he meant it.

Two weeks after the wedding and they were already getting to know each other? Wasn't that rushing it a bit?

"Tell me everything you know about skeletons," Kyle said, like he was asking typical first date, get-to-know-you questions.

"Why?"

"I'm just curious. I want to know what you think."

"About skeletons."

"Yes." He kissed the top of her head.

*** *** ***

As Rook spoke, the sexy purr that lived in Kyle's head settled down to its normal level. It always flared up while he fucked her, tonight more so than usual. Kyle soon remembered why he didn't usually spend his time in intellectual conversation with his lays. Several times he needed to drag his gaze away from her tits in order to follow what she was saying. All she knew about skeletons was a lot, it seemed, and most of it symbolic. Kyle tried hard to pay attention. Something she would say would enable him to decipher and utilize the slimy bones he dragged out of her head and forgot about.

She went from obvious things like death to more subjective things like mortality, secrets, buried things, to the downright abstract. That's where Kyle paid the most attention. The way Rook saw it, skeletons could symbolize very personal things since they were the innermost part of the body. They were also a lasting record of the past. Being the most enduring part of the body, they were the most likely part from which a resurrection would occur. That's why Egyptians made mummies, why burial started as a practice worldwide.

"Of course, by nature they like to be hidden. That's why they're easy to forget about."

"Are they?" Kyle thought that might explain why he hadn't thought about Rook's bones since he took them.

"Can you remember exactly where your childhood dog is buried?"

"Point taken." Kyle never had a dog, but he didn't want to slow her down.

"If you ask me, a person's skeleton is a sort of key, a Rosetta Stone. If you can control the skeleton, you can learn anything about them. You can control the person," she concluded.

Kyle liked the sound of that.

"How?"

"Ask Marcus, he's the one who thinks he's a shaman."

"Is that like a voodoo thing? A witch doctor?"

Rook laughed heartily. "No, more like a medicine man."

"But he didn't explain the zombie thing to you?"

"Skeletons are one of the few things he didn't preach about. He thinks we're going to live forever, being gods and all."

"Everyone?"

"No, where's the fun in that? Just him and me. We have a sacred duty, you know."

"Yes." How could Marcus hit upon the truth about Rook's importance, yet be so wrong about his own?

"Anything else I can help you with?" The fear had gone out of her voice.

He kissed her hair. He'd told her he loved her, and right now that didn't seem so far-fetched. The tingle in his head suggested a deep connection, but so far it hadn't touched his heart. Hopefully he would figure out what he needed from her before that happened. It might complicate things.

"No, that's all. Go to sleep."

Maybe that was the key, not the skeletons. Maybe they had to love each other. Kyle decided if the skeleton zombie thing didn't work, maybe he'd give love a try.

Kyle tucked Rook in and gave her a goodnight kiss. He pulled on some pants, gathered up his folders and left, too excited by this new lead to sleep. He commandeered the desk in Shaw's den.

Chapter Twenty-Two

VAN

Repairs to the workshop area will begin tomorrow, now that a final determination has been made not to report the incident. Loss of nearly all of the devices has been confirmed. Those few specimens still under our control must be kept secret. For the foreseeable future, we will not pursue any of the initiatives related to them, in order to keep the lowest possible profile and forestall further incursions.
TEF internal memorandum 10-30-2000

Fin sat gracelessly on the cold cement and leaned against a dumpster. He lit a smoke and made a face. Not his brand.

He'd probably stolen the pack from someone.

In the week since meeting his sister-in-law, Fin had tried to balance his time between searching for Rook and corrupting his brain chemistry. Searching occupied ever fewer of his waking moments, as his waking moments diminished. He knew vaguely that he'd been fired from the job he stopped going to, which only made sense.

This was the alley behind Nero's.

Was he really so low he'd get tossed out of a bar for stealing a pack of menthols? Even clove cigarettes would be better than this. He took another drag.

"It's not like I have anything better to do."

His head lolled around until his eyes came to rest on a staccato flash of lightning-green neon.

IS TOO!

Fin groaned and banged his head against the dumpster three times.

"She's not there."

IS TOO!

"If she is, then Marcus —"

IS TOO!

"There's nothing I can do."

IS TOO!

Fin sighed.

"Okay. But I'm going to finish my smoke first."

TA   TA

MAN

!

The Talisman Tattoo! sign made a crackling buzz and went black. Fin concentrated on his cigarette.

No activity in the alley. Must be late. All the bars had closed up and the revelers staggered home. Fin stood and pulled Rook's keychain out of his pocket. He studied the key to Talisman for several minutes, crossed the alley, and descended the stairs.

The door wasn't latched. There were no lights inside. Fin nudged the door with his toe and it inched silently inward. The feeble alley streetlight did little to illuminate the depths of Marcus's lair.

Fin's will to live was in remission. He shoved the door open, stepped inside and flipped the light switch.

The smell hit him before his semi-pickled brain decoded the images. Vomit.

A rather large puddle soaked the rug. Footprints led to a heap of clothes by the bathroom. The clothes were saturated with the stuff. Fin could tell from where he stood that they were Marcus's, not Rook's, so he felt no compulsion to examine them more closely.

Treading with care, Fin moved further into the room. He might not care if he died, but he sure as hell didn't want to do it while wallowing in someone else's puke. The speakers played one of those nature sounds CDs, only instead of whale songs this one had wolves howling against a backdrop of tribal drumming.

Moving on, Fin checked the bathroom, finding nothing except more puke. Rook's piercing room was free of bodily waste, but a small wooden doll with black feathers tied to it hung over the door. Fin pulled it down. Where Rook had tattoos the doll had reddish marks that looked like blood.

Well, that was creepy.

Fin strode boldly into the last room — the tattoo room — hoping to provoke a reaction.

Empty. Fin spat on the floor. What good was Marcus if you couldn't even count on him to put you out of your misery?

A notebook lay on the counter in here. Fin flipped through it. Sketch after sketch of ravens and coyotes. The design for the wedding bands. The words 'RAVEN' and 'SHAMAN,' sometimes misspelled 'SHAWMIN.' Lastly, several bile-fingerprinted pages of abstract and unsettling images and the phrase 'claim her from an equal.'

*** *** ***

Kyle hated all the thinking. In school it was never required of him. He was the star quarterback in high school, which earned him a great amount of slack. The football scholarship to Buckminster ensured continued neglect of his studies. Even the accident that blew his knee didn't really change anything, at first. The university's attorney got his breathalyzer results tossed, and he'd ridden the wave of goodwill all through surgery, rehab and several semesters of reinjury and bench warming. Once it became clear his knee wouldn't stand up to a sack, he was cut from the team and dropped out of school. Soon after, the Samaritan Security Agency recruited him. They didn't care about his academic career and were satisfied with his physical shape. He advanced through the ranks at SSA on the charisma and attitude he had always possessed. There were no written tests. Now Kyle found his brain rusty after a lifetime of disuse.

Rook's skeletons were important, obviously, but Kyle still wasn't clear on what they symbolized or how he should use them. He spent a great deal of time working with them lately, and they didn't tell him anything, even with all the inside information he'd gotten from her.

Sometimes while working with the skulls, Kyle felt a flicker of understanding, always instantly gone. Like having a word on the tip of your tongue and losing it. That in itself was proof he wasn't Complete yet, no matter how far he had come.

While it was clear the sultry throb in his head came from Rook, that it was evidence of her connection to him, it was not a symptom of Completion. Probably just a pleasant side effect of her skeletons being in him. Possibly a tantalizing taste of what true Completion would feel like. If that was the case, Kyle wanted to be Complete more than ever. To have the full-grown version of that tingle would be worth all this trouble.

*** *** ***

Fin prowled the streets, looking for more drugs, but daylight made such endeavors fruitless. The freelance pharmacists didn't keep bankers' hours. The only controlled substance he could find was Shamrock coffee.

He sat in a booth, staring at the inky fluid in his mug, tuning out the world, until he heard his name.

Fin looked up, but there didn't seem to be anybody paying him any attention. He looked over his shoulder, swept the whole place with his eyes, and sat glowering. Nobody made eye contact but a few people were kind of clumsy about avoiding his gaze. He took a sip of his lukewarm coffee.

Fin, we must speak to you.

"Oh, fuck!" Fin muttered not entirely under his breath, "Will you just go away? Please?"

Our thoughts have become much more ordered.

"Whoopty shit."

We are now operating as a few large groups, and there are no more stragglers. You have shown us humans are not a lost cause. The largest group has continued the research. The web chamber is nearly full. Their experiments are breaking many minds, but they hope to have the answer soon.

"Super. Fuck off."

In the booths around him, a few people called for checks, or simply gave Fin uneasy looks.

"Do you mind?" Fin said loudly, "I'm trying to talk to the aliens."

We, in particular, wish to apologize to you. We are the ones who tried to mislead you about the examination room. We regret the deception. We see how wrong it was.

Fin kept silent. He was in no mood to accept an apology and he doubted he could believe them when they told him they had learned their lesson.

You're quite right to remain suspicious. We are truly sorry, and we urgently need help with freedom, individuality, accountability, purpose, and mortality. All of this has been thrust upon us.

"Sucks to be you."

You have lived with knowledge of all these things. You can hear us.

"No, you're a residual side effect."

Should we follow the example you provide?

"No, no. Pick anybody else." Fin reflected a moment. "I think that's all you need to know."

But no one else could have shown us what you have. We have felt your strength. No one else is worthy.

Fin drank his coffee in unpleasant gulps. He stood and muttered, "Go to hell," as he tossed a few quarters onto the table and made for the exit.

The voices accompanied him down the street. They pleaded. They bargained, offering technology to make him rich and mighty. They threatened.

Fin knew that as an isolated population this group of aliens could barely sustain the basic functions of their base. The kind of advanced stuff they tried to bribe him with didn't exist without the Floating Wisdom, so there was no way they could deliver.

As for the threats, he knew they were terrified of having him among them against his will again. They didn't care to know what else he might break. They didn't have the balls to try anything on him.

That left begging. They were genuinely afraid, of themselves and of the whole universe. Why shouldn't they be? Stranded in the asteroid belt, cut off for the first time from the warm ocean of their Wisdom. Each one treading a line between consciousness and monstrousness, under constant threat of becoming a mindless predator—and prey for other mindless predators. Doze off for a second, you're a cannibal.

Sprawled in heroin-induced catatonia that evening he could still hear them. He'd returned to the house to be alone, to avoid the crush of remembrances in the bomb shelter. Even Vesuvius. Through the night Fin lay awake, ignoring the aliens' pleas.

***   ***   ***

Now that Kyle spent time in Shaw's den during the day, Rook took pains not to leave any trace of her nighttime activities. Both alarm pads were armed as usual, so she settled down on the floor and opened the last desk drawer. Maybe she would go through the boxes tonight too, since she lost two nights of search time to Kyle's unpredictability.

First in the drawer was a sheaf of foreign bank statements. Large sums of money were involved, but with no name attached to the accounts. Moving on Rook found folders dealing with secret divisions of Shaw Ministries. There were several, but the one that interested Rook was Samaritan Security Agency, with a payroll listing for Squad Leader Kyle Tanner.

Kyle went from covert division mercenary squad leader to CEO of the parent company overnight, following the death of the head honcho. Pretty non-standard career trajectory.

Along with the payroll information was a wealth of other useful facts. 'Reverend Wash' received a letter eight months ago:

```
We have recently acquired some intriguing
merchandise that we are offering for sale
to the highest bidder. You have
demonstrated an interest in similar items
```

```
in the past. If you are interested, please
respond through the usual channels and we
will provide details.
```

Shaw's vaguely-worded reply came next, followed by the more descriptive response.

```
    The merchandise we are dealing with was
developed under a secret contract with the
United States Army. It takes the form of
listening devices hidden inside body
jewelry, nipple rings, etc., for use in
assorted wetworks.
    We are offering one semi-trailer of these
devices, as well as the equipment needed to
receive their signals. This is a one time
only offer. The bidding starts at $10
million.
    We will schedule demonstrations for
interested parties.
                    Your Associates at IOTA.
```

Shaw won the bidding war and distributed several cases into supply channels under the PierceX name in order to run field tests and develop protocols. The rest of the jewelry he stored at a safe location while planning modifications. There were sketches of little angels with nipple-ring halos, and crosses made from piercing barbells.

Rook felt sick to her stomach. She had been used. Had, in the course of her job, spread these malicious little things among all her friends and acquaintances, Marcus, Fin, even herself.

Everyone Rook knew had a piercing of one sort or another. She had done most of the work herself. The jewelry was bugged, and furthermore interfered with people's dreams. That's why everyone dreamed about the same stupid spaceship.

Horrified, Rook now knew how Kyle ended up with a tape of her in bed with Marcus, as well as why he removed her nipple ring.

It might even explain why the sweaterguys pulled her off the street. Her jewelry was switched around when she woke up. Foolishly she'd been concerned about rape. Awful as that would have been, this was far worse, a pervasive and insidious invasion of privacy. It led to everything, even Fin's death. She should have replaced the jewelry after noticing it had been tampered with, but that wouldn't have done any good. She would have replaced it with more bugged stuff.

Then why was it messed with? Obviously she didn't have the whole story.

The next document concerned the handling of the devices. Metal could shield the signals. That must be why she'd been wrapped in foil, why she'd found it in her bra. Maybe the sweaterguys tried to help her by blocking her signal.

The last file contained profiles of the other bidders. One group in particular warranted a lot of ink. The TEF. What her mother told Rook about the Threshold Elsewhere Following didn't match up with them bidding on these devices. For one thing, they were a nature cult. For another, they were dirt poor. The bidder's name was finally spelled out on the third page — the Technological Evolution Front, not Mom's old hippie collective at all. An equal and opposite acronym?

TEF members had stolen information and samples. That's when Shaw hired Kyle and the other mercenaries. The TEF continued to be a pain in Shaw's ass, necessitating further security measures and counter maneuvers of nearly Spy Vs Spy proportion. After a TEF member named Gregory infiltrated Shaw's organization, Shaw "neutralized the threat," replaced his entire technical staff, and moved operations to a new site: the factory outside Webster.

Rook pieced the next part of the story together herself. Fin stumbled onto the sweaterguys' little secret office and talked to her about it, and she'd gotten excited about her article. The TEF must have been listening in on the jewelry, too. They knew she and Fin would be taken to Shaw, so they kidnapped her and tampered with her jewelry. Some kind of homing beacon? They used her to find Shaw's new headquarters.

The files contained nothing else. Kyle, it seemed, was too busy to keep his paperwork up to date. Rook wished she had her Mac. She always found it easier to think while typing.

If the TEF were the ones who attacked the factory, they were also the ones Kyle raided the other night. He had recovered the tainted jewelry. What could he be planning to do with it? Shaw's Prophecy seemed to be the only thing that mattered to Kyle, but how did these government-issue bugging devices factor into it?

Rook had assumed Shaw's interest in modifying the jewelry had something to do with boosting his ratings, but maybe Kyle spotted something in the New Revelations that she missed. Some role the technology was to play. Whatever it might be, Rook didn't like to think about Kyle finishing the job. But she couldn't believe he understood Shaw's writings any better than she did.

She reopened the second drawer and walked her fingers along the tops of the folders, lingering whenever she got to something that sparked a memory. Some of the sermons relied on precious metals for symbolism, others made reference to "wearing faith like a badge." Shaw definitely wanted to pave the way for mass consumption when he started marketing his trinkets, but none of these pages contained an explicit reference to what they were supposed to accomplish.

Rook stretched and looked over the TEF pages again. What to make of those guys? Their interest couldn't have anything to do with the Prophecy. Could it? What kind of evolution did they have in mind? That probably didn't matter anymore, judging by the boastful remarks of Kyle's goon squad. She swallowed to suppress her nausea. Had she been used to perpetrate that violence, too?

The night was nearly gone. Rook tidied up, not letting herself rush the job. She crept back to the bedroom before Kyle woke up.

Maybe it was better that the bugs were in his hands than in the hands of the government, a religious zealot, or a technology cult.

Were those the only choices?

Rook's mind and stomach churned. She lay in bed, with Kyle's body pressed against her, his arm around her, his hand cupping her breast.

Assuming she managed to escape, who would believe her story? *CTP* would publish it, but that didn't mean shit. No reputable news source would take her word for it, and she had no proof.

If she could convince Kyle she wanted to Complete him, maybe she could earn more freedom. She could gather evidence, be a real journalist.

Kyle stirred and kissed her neck. He pulled her firmly against him, his mental vibration revving.

It should be easy to convince him. Brook and Bramble were ready to play. Rook rocked her pelvis.

Was this story worth prostituting herself?

It would be if she could get the evidence.

Kyle rolled Rook over so they were facing each other, his signal now an angry wasp inside her thoughts, thrilling Bramble and Brook. She kissed him.

Rook felt more divided than ever. The princesses pulled one way, the easy way. She had to pull the other. And hope she didn't tear herself apart.

*** *** ***

Marcus trained his new binoculars on the top floor windows. There were always lights on up there in the evening, after the workers went home. Somebody's palatial apartment, where Raven was being held. He wanted to know how well-guarded she was before he confronted the other shaman.

From the front he could only see into the atrium, which occupied all eight floors. Getting a good view of the side facing the cathedral was tricky because he didn't want to be exposed out in the open. The left corner windows looked into a kitchen, dim and deserted. The right corner was dark. Marcus crept along to the right, keeping inside the dense evergreen stand encircling the compound. There were guards inside, but he had yet to see any walking the grounds.

Along this wall Marcus could see a marble tiled bathroom and an opulent bedroom, a man moving around in the bedroom, his back to Marcus. He turned and Marcus's temples began to throb.

Kyle had Raven. Again.

Marcus was furious with himself for not anticipating that Fin's brother would share his gift of magic. He had been tricked again. A flicker of self-doubt ran through Marcus's thoughts and he snuffed it. Raven would be his forever after a contest of powers with this pretender. The spirits would help if he was worthy. If not, he had his pistol.

Marcus watched as Kyle put on a white shirt and began to button it. Where was Raven? Perhaps in that dark room along the back. Maybe Kyle kept her tied up. With equal parts fury and satisfaction, Marcus gave consideration to all the things Kyle could have done, almost certainly had done, to Raven. A bitter smile rested on Marcus's lips as Kyle walked to the bathroom. His anger was stoking nicely. This whelp stood no chance against Coyote.

Movement behind Kyle caught Marcus's attention. He swiveled the binoculars and saw Raven step out of the shower, her hair wrapped in a striped towel, naked otherwise. The rush of familiarity was strong, but the rage was stronger. She was smiling.

Marcus stood stock still and watched Raven dress. She put on a lacy white bra and panties, but Kyle had her take them off again. The slim-fitting calf-length white skirt would slow her down if they had to retreat in a hurry. The powder pink blouse just looked ridiculous. He would never mistake her body or the markings he gave to her, but she was almost unrecognizable in her new country club clothes. Blow-drying her new hair and applying a hint of lipstick completed the transformation. She had changed a lot in two weeks. Or been changed. Kyle was a stronger foe than Marcus had imagined. He had enchanted Raven.

Kyle led Raven out of the bedroom. Marcus moved back the way he had come. A few minutes later a limousine pulled out of the underground parking garage and sped off. The license plate read SHAWMIN.

*** *** ***

Rook was pissed. Things weren't working out as planned.

She talked Kyle into taking her out easily enough. Apparently she wasn't the only one chafing under their domestic facade. Now that they were out, though, she couldn't make her escape. After an awkward quickie in the limo while cruising downtown Donner, they arrived at a seafood restaurant. During dinner, Gary and Mitch took a table closer to the door. Nerves and the fishy smell stole Rook's appetite. When she excused herself to go to the bathroom, Mitch loitered outside the door, pretending to use a pay phone. The bathroom had no windows. They left without ordering dessert.

It was Halloween, even though the warm weather and Rook's mental calendar told her it was still early fall. Teenagers dressed as goths and vampires and dead things roamed the sidewalks in packs, making lots of noise so everyone would know they were cool. Rook wished she could join them. Her new hair and clothes felt like a costume.

They had time to kill before the movie. At every store they entered, Mitch and Gary flanked the door, one looking in, one out. They were pretty good at this bodyguard thing. Kyle held her hand incessantly. She didn't know what would happen if she made a break for it, just ran. She didn't think it would be good. They would undoubtedly catch her, the three of them working together could hardly miss. Kyle would know her true feelings and would lobotomize her, or something just as bad. It would be better to wait until she was more assured of success. Maybe during the movie.

They left the theatre at midnight, Kyle clutching her hand, Mitch and Gary in tow. The moon lurked behind a bank of clouds and the air was brisk. The teenage spooks had all gone to bed and the streets were quieter, littered with candy wrappers, black and orange crepe paper, and the occasional smashed jack-o-lantern. Rook tried to talk Kyle into going to a club, thinking the crowd and confusion would give her a chance to slip away. Kyle refused, claiming early commitments the next morning. He tried to placate her by telling her they would go to a club. Soon.

Returning to the Ministries compound, Rook watched out the limo window, reviewing the streets and landmarks she memorized on their way out. She wanted to know where to go if she ever did get out of the apartment. Gary drove, with Mitch riding shotgun. Kyle dozed, his hand on her left thigh. Approaching the turnoff for the compound, they stopped. There were no traffic lights along this stretch of road. The opaque privacy screen blocked her view out the front. Rook craned her neck, but couldn't see anything. She tried to put her window down, but the controls didn't work. There must be a master control up front.

Rook moved Kyle's hand and scooted closer to the door. Beyond the shoulder of the road, the ground dropped away to a wooded area. It was an overcast night and there were no streetlights. She heard the driver's door open. This had to be it. Rook pulled the door handle, but nothing happened. Locked. She looked for the mechanism. There wasn't one. Those controls must be up front too.

Rook wiped her sweaty palms on her white skirt. What should she do? Kyle stirred. If she couldn't escape, she might as well make points as the devoted wifey-poo.

"Kyle?" She prodded his knee. "Kyle, we've stopped."

Kyle opened his eyes and sat up, fully alert. He leaned forward and rapped on the privacy window. The back doors unlocked with a tiny sound. Kyle pulled a handgun from his shoulder holster and opened his door.

"Stay here." He stepped out, holding the gun behind his leg.

Yeah right.

Kyle's door shut and she watched him walk toward the front of the car. He stopped when he reached Gary standing at the open driver's door, and they conferred.

Rook slid over to her side and eased her door open. Hoping Mitch wasn't looking, she slipped out and closed the door as silently as possible, staying in a crouch.

Two gunshots startled Rook and she flattened herself on the ground, quaking. Looking under the limo, Rook saw lights and Gary on the road, bleeding. At least they hadn't been shooting at her.

Another round of blasts kept her pinned to the ground and she crawled on her belly toward the drop.

"RAVEN! I'VE COME FOR YOU!"

Oh, fuck! Rook's insides turned to water. She tried to block out all sensory input and crawl toward the drop. Behind her she heard scuffling sounds and a car door opening. He grabbed her. She smelled gunpowder, blood and sweat.

"Hey, Little Raven, where you goin'?" Marcus lifted her effortlessly. He looked down at her and clucked disapprovingly. "You've been defiled."

Marcus dragged Rook to the front of the car. His van blocked the road. Gary lay on the ground, dead. Through the limo's open driver's door she saw Mitch leaking his brains all over the passenger seat. Kyle sat propped against the side of the car, bleeding from a wound in his right shoulder, pressing his left hand against it. Rook noticed a lurch to Marcus's step and saw he had been shot in the side. His blood stained her clothes.

Marcus smiled down at her. He dipped his fingers into his blood and painted a stripe across her face. "Now you're mine again." He bent and kissed her.

Rook gagged.

"Get away from my wife," Kyle said weakly, struggling to his feet. "Before I kill you."

Marcus snapped his head to look at Kyle, then angrily at Rook.

Kyle plowed into them, knocking them to the ground. Marcus's gun flew out of his hand. Rook rolled clear and backed away awkwardly on her knees.

Kyle reached the pistol and Marcus pounced on him. They hit the ground hard. Kyle grabbed the gun by the barrel and slammed it into Marcus's head. Marcus howled.

Kyle staggered to his feet and pointed the weapon at Marcus. When he pulled the trigger, it only clicked.

Kyle turned and ran toward Rook and the limo.

Marcus gained his feet and started for Rook also. Rook backed away from them both.

Marcus reached behind his back, but Kyle spotted the move and gave up on Rook. He dove into the limo and slammed the door. Marcus raised Kyle's gun and fired. The bulletproof glass spared Kyle and he put the limo in motion. He tried to mow Marcus down as he maneuvered around the van, clipping the fender, and sped off toward the compound.

Rook laughed hoarsely, hysterically.

*** *** ***

Kyle tore his eyes away from Mitch's dead body in the passenger seat and called Perkins, standing guard in the garage.

"Yes, sir?"

"Shut the fuck up and listen. Mitch and Gary are dead. I'm hit. Get the medic. I'm bleeding a lot. Shit, this is bad. Get someone in a vehicle to go collect Gary. Someone heavily armed. They'll need to clean up the scene. Ministry Road, near the junction. On the double. And get me a pilot for the chopper."

Kyle hung up on Perkins and called the lab.

"Schwartz, it's Tanner."

"Yes, sir?"

"I want an immediate trace on my wife. The new signal, from the wedding ring. You added GPS like I ordered?" Schwartz made an affirmative noise. "Track her location. I'll radio from the chopper when I'm ready. Stand by."

Kyle felt lightheaded, but he could see the lights of the compound ahead. He accelerated and kept his hand pressed into his wound.

*** *** ***

Marcus was howling, head thrown back, eyes closed. Rook's rusty, hysterical laughter sputtered to a stop and she took several deep breaths, head swimming. Looking around she saw Gary splayed on the tarmac in a dark puddle. And Marcus. And Marcus's van. Oh, hell yes! The keys had to be in it. Had to be.

Rook ran to the driver's door and jerked it open. She slammed the door and shoved the lock button down. The window was open.

Marcus heard the door and swung around to look at her. He wore black jeans, a blood-soaked flannel shirt and a menacing half-smile. His hair was loose and wild. He started walking to the van, not hurrying in the least. Rook grabbed the crank handle and started to put the window up. Marcus got to her as it passed the halfway point and he reached in, trying to snag her hair. She evaded him and continued to raise the window. Marcus grasped the glass with both hands. Smiling broadly, he tugged on it and it shattered.

Rook reached for the ignition, but the keys weren't in it. Disbelieving, she fumbled for the visor, to check behind it, but Marcus unlocked the door and yanked it open. He didn't look mad and that was the scariest part.

"I'll drive, Raven."

He started climbing in. Rook dove to the passenger seat. Marcus grabbed her wrist and pulled her back before she even reached the door handle. He smiled at her and sat her in his lap, bleeding on her. He reached for the handcuffs he kept hanging from the rearview mirror.

Rook tried to kick them out of his hand, but he twisted her wrist and pulled her arm up behind her back. Rook gasped. Marcus chuckled, cuffing her left wrist to his right.

"We better get moving before your latest boy toy comes back with reinforcements. Comfortable, hon?"

Rook said nothing.

Marcus shut his door and took the keys from his pocket. Rook watched as he started the van, and spotted the handcuff key on the ring. At least he had it. Unable to reach the passenger seat while cuffed to him, Rook knelt on the floor beside Marcus.

They drove in silence for several minutes and got on the highway. Rook could see the prismatic glass spires of the cathedral looming above the treetops as they passed. Somewhere over there Kyle was probably planning her rescue. Whoopee.

"I thought I could trust you," Marcus said.

"What?"

"You were mine."

"I married Fin. It's not my fault you didn't understand that."

"You lied to me."

"Oh, come on Marcus! You wouldn't leave me alone."

"You're mine."

"No I'm not!"

Marcus gave the handcuffs a tug. "Yeah?"

"Fuck you."

"Now you're talking like yourself. What the hell happened to your hair?"

Rook didn't answer.

"We had an understanding, Raven! We're supposed to create the next world! Together. What the hell are you doing marrying this one, too? You're not trustworthy."

"Then let me go. I'll never disappoint you again."

"No. You won't." His tone was flat.

He was going to kill her. Great. She could use some down time.

With her luck it wouldn't be that easy. Kyle would show up in time to 'rescue' her and she'd be right back where she started. But Kyle abandoned her, so maybe he had decided she wasn't worth it. Maybe she could die in peace. No doubt Marcus had something elaborate planned, so it wouldn't be peaceful, but at least it would end.

Marcus moved her hand to his crotch.

"Unzip it."

He was already erect and she started to stroke him. Her fingers slid over the three curved barbells in his corona without noticing them, but her wedding ring clacked against the ladder of straight barbells along the underside of his shaft.

The bugged jewelry. That's why Kyle let her go. He could track Marcus.

"Take it off, Raven."

Rook brought her right hand over and started to fumble with the barbell.

"Not that."

"But..."

"No. The ring. Take off the fucking wedding ring."

"That's not important. The stud. Oh, shit, all your jewelry. Marcus, you've gotta take it all off. You have to get rid of it."

"Fuck you."

"Marcus, you don't understand! Kyle can listen to us through it. He can track us."

"I don't know what the fuck you're talking about. You're suddenly not into piercings anymore, got too used to your little golf player? Take off the fucking ring now or I'll do it when I break your finger."

"Shit, Marcus! He'll find us!" She tried to work the ring off.

"Raven," Marcus growled.

Rook dipped her finger into Marcus's blood for lubrication. The ring came off and she tucked it in her blouse pocket where he wouldn't see it anymore.

Marcus looked down, and smiled when he saw the tattoo underneath. He held his left hand up for her to see. On the ring finger glistened a fresh tattoo. It matched hers.

"You're *my* wife now. Those others have no hold on you. I marked you as I was marked by the spirits."

Rook whimpered. He had given her the ring. But not all of it. Fin completed it. In her heart, Rook knew she was married only to Fin.

He moved her hand back to his erection. "We'll usher in the next world. Now. Tonight."

"Please let me take these out," said Rook.

"No. And no more talking."

"Marcus..."

Marcus clubbed her. It hurt like hell, but she knew he could have easily broken her jaw.

"Shut up until I tell you to talk."

Rook kept her mouth shut, but she pictured the helicopter she'd seen on the roof. Now, if Kyle got her back, she was screwed. He would know what she'd told Marcus, that she knew about the jewelry.

They drove in silence for ten minutes. The blood Marcus smeared on her face itched, but Rook didn't dare rub it off. Her legs cramped from kneeling for so long. Marcus took the next exit and several more turns in quick succession. Rook didn't pay attention to where they were going. She didn't know this part of the state, and was about to die anyway.

A few minutes later Marcus stopped the van and smiled down at her. He stood and pulled her into the back where he kept a couch against the left side. The place was cluttered and dark. They sat on the battered old sofa and Marcus kissed her. Rook didn't respond. Marcus didn't notice.

"You have to get out of these ridiculous clothes," he said and started to unbutton her pink top. The handcuffs made it awkward, and he soon just yanked it open, popping the remaining buttons off and exposing her bare breasts.

"Please, Coyote."

"Yes, Raven?"

"Please take out your jewelry. It's interfering. With your, um," Rook struggled, "your magic."

Marcus was kissing her chest, her nipples, her belly. He wasn't listening. He unzipped her long, blood-soaked skirt and shoved it down. Rook's hand, cuffed to his, went through the motions of undressing in tandem with him.

When he finally killed her would she be complicit in that too? She tried to push him off, pulled his hair, struggled, screamed. Marcus smiled at her.

"No one can hear you."

Rook screamed anyway.

As Marcus pulled his pants down, Rook heard a thud on the floor beside her. Reaching down with her right hand, she fumbled around and found his gun.

Marcus pushed himself up and Rook brought the gun between them. He saw it and laughed, but Rook thought she saw fear in his eyes. She pulled the trigger.

The shot was deafening. Marcus collapsed on top of her. Blood gushing from his neck ran over her, warm and thick, drenching her hair and filling her mouth.

Rook wretched and spat, jerking her head to the side. Gurgling sounds came from his chest and his body spasmed. Whimpering, Rook tried to wiggle out from under Marcus but he was too heavy and she was still cuffed to him. With a burst of adrenaline, she shoved him to the side and landed on top of him on the floor. She picked the gun up again and aimed it at his head, but her hand shook so wildly that the first shot hit his chest and the second went through the passenger seat and shattered the windshield.

She let the gun fall and concentrated hard on breathing.

Kyle wasn't here yet. She could still escape.

Marcus's glassy eyes stared blankly at her as she yanked on his arm. Unless she could get the handcuffs off, she wasn't going anywhere. The keys were in the ignition.

He was so fucking heavy. The cuff cut into her left wrist and the chain bit her fingers where she gripped it. The bare metal floor was slick with his blood and Rook struggled toward the front for several seconds without progress, even after kicking off her skirt and flimsy, slippery-soled sandals.

She braced her back against the rear door and shoved him forward with her feet as far as she could reach. Once she climbed back over him, she grabbed the driver's seat support with her right hand and pulled.

Slowly she dragged Marcus to the front and reached the keys. As she unlocked the cuff from her wrist, she heard the helicopter.

Rook jumped out of the van and looked around. She was in the middle of a field, trees a couple hundred yards off in all directions. The helicopter sounded nearer now, but she couldn't see it. She sprinted toward the woods on her right because they seemed marginally closer.

The sky lit up. Rook tripped. She looked up, expecting the helicopter and Kyle.

It wasn't the helicopter.

Chapter Twenty-Three

ZIGGURAT

Those who go Forth in Chains will be called into the Firmament,
but fall and be Minions of the Pretender
from *New Revelations* by Reverend Brian Shaw, unpublished

Rook was gone. One minute they had her signal, were tracking right to her. A short blast of interference, and she vanished, even from his head. Kyle thought she was dead, killed by Marcus. They arrived at her last known position within a minute. No trace. Just Marcus's bloody carcass, Rook's skirt and sandals, and the handcuffs. The shooting took place on an old sofa in the back of the van, so Kyle could picture what transpired. The thought made him furious. But his Rook fought back. Good girl. Kyle just had to clean up after her, dispose of the body and the van.

The ambush was only one of the shocks Kyle received last night. His clever wife knew all about the program. No telling what else she had figured out and neglected to tell him. Once she was home with him again, they'd need to have another talk about the Prophecy.

The tech guys were going through the logs to see what they could find out about Marcus's movements over the past few days. So far they hadn't turned anything up.

Everett, the squad medic, wanted Kyle to rest. Kyle knew he should, but was filled with restless energy. The shoulder would be all right.

More fuckin' rehab.

Kyle felt like shit. He'd already had two meetings with the religious idiots and there was yet another scheduled for this afternoon. They needed so much fucking hand-holding. And he was sick of everyone asking him why he looked like hell, not in so many words of course.

After fortifying himself with a pull from his flask, Kyle went downstairs in his private elevator. He nodded to the guards as he passed, and walked down to the lowest level of the garage. There he unlocked a supply closet and went in, locking the door again behind him. He unlocked another door on the back wall and entered a pipe-clogged tunnel. Damp and poorly lit, it had several smaller tunnels branching off to the right. Metal doors lined the wall on the left. Kyle opened the second one and stepped into the cramped room beyond.

The techs all looked up when Kyle came in, but quickly bent back to their work. Brody walked over.

"Nothing on Savage?" Kyle asked.

"We know his frequency, but there's nothing recent. Nothing useful. We found two instances of him, but there's nothing there. Just silence."

"Was he blocking somehow?"

"No. It's not dead air. You can hear movement, ambient noise, but no speaking."

"Keep looking. He had multiple piercings. Go back and search the archives for other frequencies he broadcast on."

Brody didn't go back to work. He looked like he wanted to say something.

"What?" Kyle demanded.

"Sir. I don't know if you'll be interested in this. We have that other signal back again. The one we were tracking earlier, when we were tracking your wife. Before she was your wife, I mean. Sir."

"What are you talking about?"

"Frequency 29.1137612. The Fin Tanner frequency, sir."

"Fin? So?"

"He's back, sir."

Kyle had forgotten about Fin.

"Back? Where was he?"

"We don't know, sir. He stopped broadcasting, but now he's back. I didn't know if you still wanted to track him. You hadn't updated our orders after the raid."

"Isn't he dead?"

"He may be soon."

"What the fuck's that mean?"

"He's been on a bender for the better part of a week, sir."

"Shit."

"If you don't mind me asking, sir, is he a relative?"

"Unfortunately. Where is he?"

"Webster, sir."

"Send the recordings to my office. Keep tracking him. I think we'll need to bring him in."

*** *** ***

Fin vainly sought some release from the increasingly shrill beseechings of the aliens. He blew the last of his credit for a very dirty speedball from Max's supplier, Ron. Nobody trusted Ron. Ron preferred to be called Caesar. Fin said, "Kill me, Caesar." Sweating and vomiting later, he blamed the aliens for keeping him alive.

Refusing their pleas didn't deter the spiders, nor did Fin's most eloquent and descriptive curses. His rage and blame and condemnation seemed to be no less than they expected. Finally, he had nothing left but pain. Denied an end to his grief, he shared it. He couldn't speak, could hardly breathe, but they heard him.

He let the weight of his loss crush him, and the aliens were trapped. Smothered in the horror of being left behind, empty. They became silent, and withdrew as Fin wept. He fell into a black sleep.

He awoke in the trunk of a car, reeking of vomit. His own, judging by the dampness on his chin and chest. Good news, given the circumstances. His body was cramped, as much from his recent excesses as from his current predicament. He wondered who he pissed off, but couldn't think of anyone besides Bishop who owned a car.

Fin belatedly thought of wiping the puke off his face, and discovered the handcuffs. Well, that ruled out a clandestine trip to the drive-in.

Shaking soon overtook splitting headache as Fin's primary source of sensory stimulation. In a short time he passed out again.

This time when he came around, Fin was still handcuffed and covered in his own waste, but now he lay in a closet. Bare and dusty, it smelled of cleaning fluids. The concrete floor had a drain into which Fin relieved himself. Spasms wracked his body.

The drugs worked through Fin's system, and the lack of drugs did, too. After he kept a rudimentary breakfast down, his captors finally showed themselves. Two burly men in black fatigues removed Fin's handcuffs and led him out into a deserted parking garage. They made him strip and blasted him with a hose, periodically squirting him with liquid soap. When they decided he was as clean as he was likely to get, they tossed him a towel, and gave him fatigues to wear. Fin wouldn't normally wear these sorts of clothes, but the men were armed. As he dressed, he noticed his nipple ring was missing. Rook warned him the clasp was loose, promised to replace it with a new hoop after the honeymoon they never got to have. He rolled his eyes skyward and confirmed the absence of his black hoop as well. One less way to remember her.

***

"Do you like my office?" Kyle asked, sweeping his arms wide to encompass the stark white walls, ugly cross, and blinking alarm pad.

Fin shrugged, more confounded than impressed.

Kyle looked across his big, shiny desk at Fin. "I've accomplished so much in a short time, wouldn't you say? I have this place, this organization, money, power." He paused and fixed Fin with a smirk. "And a wife." He laughed.

Fin didn't know what was supposed to be funny. Or why Kyle put him through this radical detox. He didn't really want to find out.

"She's quite beautiful. I think you'll agree." Kyle took a double picture frame off his desk and looked at it for a few moments before turning it for Fin to see.

Wedding pictures, with Rook as the bride.

Fin felt rage and confusion. He tried to grab the frame, but Kyle moved it out of reach. Her hair was different, lighter, but it was her. White dress, veil. His wife in a wedding dress, looking lost and confused, standing with his smug brother at the altar of a grand, sterile church. The other picture showed the classic cake feeding scene, Rook's expression vacant, Kyle's wolfish.

The evidence contradicted everything he knew about Rook. Fin knew real pictures from doctored ones, it was part of his job after all. The one on the wall showing Kyle with Shaw was fake. The wedding pictures were real. She married him, but she didn't look happy about it.

"I told you she's lovely," Kyle drawled.

"Rook's my wife."

"Possession is nine tenths of the law, as they say."

"You bastard."

"Oh, but no. You're the bastard. Dad married my mother, after all, not yours."

"Fuck you."

"That reminds me, Rook is a little spitfire in the sack, isn't she?"

*** *** ***

Taunting Fin wasn't as much fun as Kyle anticipated, partially because Fin stopped playing along, but mostly because the taunting centered on Rook. Fin didn't know she was missing, but Kyle felt her absence strongly. Rubbing salt in Fin's wounds necessitated getting a little in his own. Kyle decided to let Fin stew, and try a mind reaming session later.

Let him assume the worst, from his perspective. Maybe it would make him easier to crack. Kyle looked forward to that. When Fin cracked, Kyle would sift through the rubble and take whatever he needed to Complete himself. Whether it was something innate of Fin's or something Rook gave him wouldn't matter. With all the pieces in his possession, Kyle would no longer be the Divided Man. He would be Complete. And light would be restored upon the Earth. Whatever the hell that meant.

*** *** ***

Fin's guard ushered him down to the lowest level in the underground garage, through a maintenance closet and a tunnel, and into a subterranean room. The room was overly bright and full of mercenaries. They regarded him with minimal interest before returning to their activities. The guard led Fin to a door off to the left.

The room contained a cot, a wheeled stool, a rolling lamp and a cart reminiscent of a mechanic's toolbox. Must be the infirmary. The guard and a colleague removed everything but the cot. They shut Fin in and locked the door.

No windows. Cinder block walls, painted institutional green. Cement ceiling. Fin took in that much before the overhead bulb switched off. The only light now came through a slit under the door. He felt around by the doorframe, but couldn't find a switch.

Fin sat on the end of the cot and waited for his eyes to adjust. He searched the room. About eight feet by eight. The light was a bare bulb inside a cage. He had a thin mattress, a thinner pillow and one wool blanket on top of clean, white sheets.

Now that I'm not interested in killing myself, he thought with grim irony, these bozos leave me with a complete kit. Bedsheets or bootlaces: it would be an agonizing choice.

Fin took off his boots and stretched out on the cot. He didn't expect to be able to sleep.

He thought about Rook.

She was alive. Fin tried to savor the relief that knowledge brought him, and not move on to the next thought. She was alive and married to his brother. In all the time he searched for her, he never once considered this possibility. It didn't make any sense.

Kyle said he was going to her, implied she was nearby. Fin scanned for her frequency and came up empty, but in a place this big she might simply be out of range. How did she end up here? Did she know he was here? Fin couldn't accept that. She loved him.

Her expression in the photos scared him. So lost. Did Kyle have her drugged? Had she hit her head? Maybe at the reception, which turned to shit with help from the aliens, and possibly Kyle as well.

Painfully Fin recalled Rook telling him of her unbidden physical attraction to Kyle. Had he aroused her so strongly with his explosives and flunkies that she ran off with him? Fin snorted. He only knew any of that because she told him. It was difficult for her, but she had done it to strengthen their relationship. He couldn't possibly hold it against her now. He loved her too much.

Knowing this obsessing was what Kyle wanted didn't make it any easier to stop.

Later, more guards took Fin to another room in the underground complex, a dingy cinder block office. Kyle waited, sitting on the corner of the utilitarian metal desk, perusing a file. He glanced up when Fin entered, and nodded toward a chair. The guards pressed Fin into the chair and stood behind him while Kyle finished his reading. The whole setup made Fin feel like he was in trouble with the gym teacher.

"Good evening, Fin," Kyle said, closing the file.

Fin kept quiet.

"You'll get over Rook soon enough. In the meantime, we need to spend some quality time together." Kyle rose and looked down at Fin. "I think if we'd spent more time together as children we wouldn't be in this situation now. We could have reached an understanding on this point long ago."

Fin didn't know what the hell Kyle was talking about. How could they have settled Rook a long time ago?

Kyle continued, "But you always were difficult. Always had to cause trouble."

"What do you want, Kyle?" Fin asked wearily.

"Just what is rightfully mine. You guards can leave now," Kyle said, eyes locked on Fin's. "My brother won't be any trouble."

The guards left.

Kyle and Fin stared at each other. Fin felt animosity rolling off both of them and filling the small room. Something hot and slimy covered his brain. He yelled. Kyle chuckled. The hot sliminess chuckled too. It was Kyle trying to get into his head. Fin shuddered.

Fin willed his mind calm. He had to stay in command of his senses and work out Kyle's game. If he could handle this like a chess match, he'd be fine. Kyle would have no footing.

As slime seeped into every crevice of his psyche, Fin summoned up a herd of giant chessmen. From mist and smoke they thickened and darkened into marble and onyx, scudding like clouds a few inches above the cattails and brambles. He assigned himself the role of black knight.

✳✳✳   ✳✳✳   ✳✳✳

What the hell was this chess shit? There'd been nothing like this the last time Kyle was in Fin's head. That time it was a hostile alien environment and a big fucking sand pit. Fin must have remodeled after the eruption. The knights reminded him of Fin's gay horsey tattoo, while the towers reminded him of Rook. Fin would be the black king. That's the one you were supposed to protect in chess, right? The king was useless, but the queen was powerful. Stupid. Kyle hated the game.

Kyle settled into one of the white knights. Let Fin assume he was using the king. That's where he would concentrate his efforts, allowing Kyle the opportunity to escape scrutiny and reconnoiter. Somewhere Fin would have something that could Complete him. Since it was something Kyle lacked, he decided to let himself be drawn to it.

Pieces drifted in all directions, more ballroom dance than chess game. The white pieces obeyed Kyle's direction, so he tried to keep all of them in constant motion to better distract and confuse Fin. He closed ranks with the enemy king.

✳✳✳   ✳✳✳   ✳✳✳

Fin marveled at the effectiveness of his ploy. The chess tableau consumed Kyle's attention, keeping him away from anything important. He had expected to at least have to orchestrate some semblance of a real game, counter a clumsy gambit or two.

One of the white knights rose several extra inches from the ground, and swiveled constantly as if monitoring the motions of the other pieces. Subtlety never was a Tanner family trait.

The black knight shadowed Kyle's purposeful but oblivious steed. A faint, tinny sort of babble came through, Kyle literally broadcasting his intentions and guesswork. He sought the key to Completion, whatever the hell that meant. His technique was nearly as unrefined as the Floating Wisdom's. Cocky bastard.

*** *** ***

Kyle noticed something bent and black jutting out of the weeds. It could have been a charred branch, but it twitched. He seized it, hungry to know what secret fears Fin tried to conceal. This remnant of recent memory, tinged with dread, could be a perfect weapon.

Floating Wisdom? What the fuck was a Floating Wisdom?

A disease.

A thought infection.

Whatever. It gave Fin the willies. Picking up on an image, Kyle projected thoughts of tiny specks invading Fin's brain.

Scattering specks as he went, Kyle circled the king. He expected some reaction when he got so close, but nothing changed. The chess pieces continued dancing, all except one. Kyle noticed one of the rooks didn't move.

Approaching in what he hoped was an elliptical and roundabout way, Kyle discovered the castle was much larger than any of the chess pieces, and quite distant. He left the chess-waltz behind and reached the tower unchallenged.

*** *** ***

Fin fought down his frustration, knowing it would show. He didn't want to compound his problems.

Overconfidence had led him to hand over a dark, private thought, and Kyle zeroed in on it immediately. Only the fact that Kyle didn't know what it meant spared Fin from a major assault. Which now looked imminent anyway, as his brother sized up the castle.

The white knight slowed as it drew near, and circled to the right. Kyle seemed reluctant to charge.

Perhaps Fin had nothing to worry about. Kyle still didn't know what he was looking for. The chess pieces were more effective than planned, so Fin's other defenses would certainly hold.

*** *** ***

No way in hell would he go inside, but Kyle examined the exterior of the tower with great interest. Its form echoed the sandcastle Shaw took him into, but more substantial. Taller than the original, it was made of large sandstone blocks. Along the bottom were bricks, which didn't match the rest. Kyle recognized them from Rook. The bitch had helped Fin.

The marriage, the sex, none of it mattered at all, because she hadn't woven herself into his core structure. Now it was too late.

But, was it?

Kyle eagerly clawed at the wall, trying to dislodge the bricks. Not only would he claim them for himself, Fin's whole fortress would collapse!

They didn't budge.

Kyle growled in frustration and tried sandblasting the wall with a stream of disease specks. Nothing. Ramming it with his horse head did no good either. When he paused in his assault he heard scuttling sounds behind him.

Whirling around, Kyle came face to face with a dust troll. It drew back and snarled, baring its teeth. One on its own didn't worry Kyle too much, but as he watched, the cloud of specks he had formed imploded and another dust troll landed behind the first one. They were joined by a third troll and a big, dusty bird. The bird swooped at Kyle, talons extended, beak open but making no sound.

Kyle flinched and sidestepped the attack. The trolls advanced.

*** *** ***

Fin's mind felt suddenly lighter. Kyle had retreated. What he lacked in finesse Kyle more than made up in brute power, shaking the castle so badly with each blow that Fin's skull rang and icy sweat ran down his back.

Fin slowed his breathing and tried to assimilate the knowledge he had gleaned from Kyle.

Rook wasn't here anymore. She had been, had in fact married Kyle, slept with him. Kyle convinced her Fin was dead in order to take advantage of her.

Fin's disdain for Kyle gave way to cold hatred. Kyle walked behind his desk, placing it as an obstacle between them.

"Where is she?" Fin asked.

Kyle didn't answer, only stared at Fin in what he hoped was a menacing way. An image came to Fin of Rook. Through a green filter Fin saw her with Marcus, felt tremendous pain in his right shoulder and knew he was bleeding. Rook looked terrified.

"You let Marcus take her? Asshole! He'll kill her!"

Kyle's eyes widened. Fin stood and reached across the desk, poking Kyle where he knew the bullet wound was. Kyle flinched and halfheartedly grabbed Fin's arm.

Fin saw another image, this one not as deeply green-tinged. Swooping down to a van. Marcus dead, shot. Rook gone. Profoundly gone. "Vanished off the face of the Earth" was the term in Kyle's mind.

Fin shook his arm free and sat down. He knew where she must be. And then Kyle knew.

Kyle grabbed his head and yelped. He wobbled and sat down heavily. Unsteadily he looked at Fin.

"Fucking aliens took her? Fucking space spiders? You're crazy. It was drugs, asshole. Just drugs."

Kyle ordered the guards to take Fin back to his cell. Fin felt him hoping like hell this telepathy shit wouldn't continue. Fin's perceptions were too much. Kyle pulled a flask out of his pocket and chugged.

Fin was glad to be led away. Kyle's thoughts were poison. Like a bitter aftertaste, he could still see Rook and Kyle together. Knowing her better than Kyle did, Fin could see she wasn't happy. And she certainly wasn't happy to see Marcus.

Fin hoped she'd be happy to see him. She once told him she didn't like heroes, didn't want anyone to save her. But the aliens were disorganized, and hurting people. Alone in his darkened cell, Fin rubbed his wedding ring tattoo and put out the call.

"All right, you fucks. You want me so bad, you get me out of this cell."

*** *** ***

Of course Fin was gone. The spiders opened a hole for him and he'd walked right out. Out of his cell, out of Kyle's reach, out to the asteroid belt. Probably up there with Rook right now, kicking back with a needle full of heroin or a Piña Colada, laughing. Fucking bastard always ruined everything.

With Fin removed from his immediate vicinity, Kyle sorted his head out and took a closer look at his new Fintelligence. Swiftly but reluctantly he concluded it was accurate. It even fit with the Prophecy. That whole bit about people being called up into the sky made a lot more sense if you took UFOs into account.

So, aliens existed. How could Kyle use them to his advantage? Without Fin around to exploit, he needed to rethink his plan. Again.

Kyle would call to the aliens and get them to transport him to their hollow asteroid base. He would destroy Fin, get Completed, reclaim his wife, and restore light upon the Earth. Or maybe just have some really good sex.

Kyle tried to call to the aliens. Unsure what technique to use, he settled on the one that worked with Travis. Pacing in his penthouse, he concentrated on them. They didn't answer.

How fucking galling that Fin could do it but he couldn't. They were half-twins! They were the Divided Man.

Fin had pieces of Rook incorporated into the structure of his mind. That Completed him, gave him the extra oomph he needed to surpass Kyle. It couldn't be anything innate. Kyle refused to accept there was anything, aside from getting fucked up, Fin was better at.

Rook was the answer after all. The bitch pretended not to know what Kyle needed. Wanted him to fail. But Kyle knew something Rook didn't. He had her skeletons.

Turning inward, he entered his own mind. Imagining her heat, he embraced one of Rook's skeletons. The lipless mouth exhaled that he was on the right track. It implored him not to be angry with Rook. This was something for Kyle to figure out, to prove his worthiness. The skull told Kyle he would soon be more powerful than Fin and would get Rook back. The skull was glad Kyle would win.

Kyle moved deeper into his brain, hauling the skeletons with him. For all the exploring and plundering he had done in others' heads, in his own Kyle was navigating without a map or compass.

Several false starts and dead ends later, Kyle found what he'd been seeking. Sort of. Some kind of pyramid loomed up before him. He'd expected a skyscraper. Fin's core was a dumpy old sandcastle, Rook's an academic building. Kyle expected this most inner representation of himself to be more impressive. Sleek, shiny. It disturbed him to find this bumpy stone pyramid.

Still, it was imposing.

Ziggurat. The word came to him from Shaw.

Whatever it was called, it was coming down. Kyle needed to tear the whole thing down and rebuild it with Rook's help. Since she wasn't here to participate, her skeletons would have to do.

Etched into the faces of the blocks were the now familiar words of the Prophecy.

The top layers came off easily and it felt good, like peeling off a scab. Underneath, the work quickly became painful, the stone blocks heavier. As they scraped against one another, the smell of burning hair choked him. He worked faster.

The pain became unbearable, like rock strata shifting inside his brain, or the plates of his skull splitting apart and grinding their rough edges. He was only halfway down. A nagging thought now demanded attention. If he ripped this entire structure down, how would he rebuild it? With nothing of himself left, how would he do it?

The solution came from the skeletons. They rasped that he need tear down only one side at a time, allowing him to rebuild with some of

Rook's bones in place before moving on.

Two skulls per side, and an assortment of other bones. The pain grew worse the further he went and he could distantly feel violent tides and currents in his blood as if his magnetic field were fluctuating.

Rebuilding was even more painful than the destruction. Each block he placed released an electrical charge. The rib cages and long thigh bones threw green-white sparks that left markings like a dead language on the blocks, which now resembled oxidized metal more than stone. He was writing a new Prophecy, a new future for himself. Soon he would know how to read it.

Each skull pulsed in his grip, and spot-welded into place when inserted into the sloping walls. The original ziggurat was flat on top, but this one would be taller. Kyle used the blocks displaced by the bones to complete the point.

The pyramid looked magnificently eerie, littered as it was with human skulls and other bones. It reminded Kyle of something. An oracle. He decided to ask it a question.

"Will I win?"

The skulls answered in unison. The spooky harmonics of eight voices reverberating through the cold structure chilled Kyle and made him smile.

"It is a sure sign you are destined for greatness, this ability to resculpt yourself."

Kyle agreed.

The ghastly chorus spoke again. "Now you must minister to the masses. Stand before them and show them the path. Restore Light upon the Earth. Fulfill this holy office, and She of Shadowed Wings will return to you."

Now that he didn't need Rook, Kyle wanted her even more.

Chapter Twenty-Four

TUNGUSKA

The pennyroyal worked. The relief is exquisite. Must be more careful. I dreamed that a tiny spark was growing inside me — bigger and brighter and warmer. My belly glowed. In the dream it was a good thing because I had someone kind to share it with. Certainly not Marcus. A me that is not me liked the dream. This me knows real life isn't like that.
from Rook Brandymoon's journal, undated

Fin looked into the dim, green web chamber from the mouth of a corridor. Rook was in there among scads of other abductees, her presence an invisible beacon. Feeling her signal again blurred his vision with tears of relief.

In the web, he guided his weightless body purposefully, homing in on Rook. He tore away the front of her cocoon and felt a perplexed terror. Blood smeared her face, coated her chest and hands, saturated her hair and the only clothing she wore -- the remains of a blouse. The ghastly light gave her face a waxen cast.

He could see her breathing. There was no way this could be her blood. It was Marcus's.

Fin tried to wipe the dried blood away from her face, and wondered what to do about her clothing. As he stroked Rook's cheek, she opened her eyes.

Rook smiled sleepily for a second, then her face convulsed into a grimace of anguish. She wailed and sobbed and tried to turn her face away. At first he thought she was injured, but the pain she suffered was purely emotional. Fin's desperate queries went unheard. No amount of gentle coaxing would get through. He cried along with her. Large tears soaked his eyebrows and leapt from his lashes when he blinked, wandered where they pleased without gravity to make rules for them.

Rook hugged herself and shook with spasms of grief, refusing to let him hold her face or kiss her. With all the cocoon stripped away she kept staring at the blood, adding a visceral reminder of her trauma to her torment. Fin knew he must clean her up and began to carry her toward the tunnel. Her total withdrawal made her an easier parcel to transport, curled into a fetal ball.

Fin carried Rook through the tunnel until he found a door, which he struggled to open. The room was packed full of ghostly, gray-green aliens, grasping one another's bodies. They did not address him, engrossed in themselves. Fin could pick up faint signs of their thoughts, with an overtone of melancholy.

He moved on.

The next bend brought him face-to-face with a familiar-looking group. The largest was Fin's height. It said, "We will guide you to a safe room."

Fin didn't argue. He could trust them this time.

Shortly they arrived at an empty room.

"Get me clean clothes for her, and some water. And send all those people in the cocoons home."

The aliens made bowing gestures and departed.

Fin cradled Rook until they came back. She had quieted, was probably in shock. He looked at what his servants brought. Water in a clear bag, and a plaid flannel bathrobe.

Before sending the aliens away, Fin asked them to explain what was going on in the other room.

"They are waiting. All the other groups have converged there. They have become overwhelmed by loneliness and tried to fix it by joining as tightly as they can. It has not helped, so we told them of your return and of your promise to help us. They wait. For you to help."

"You haven't joined them?" Fin was proud that this group stayed together. He felt he had cemented them.

"We didn't think it would help."

Fin murmured to Rook as he eased her out of her shirt. Something golden came loose and twirled across the room. Fin snatched it and examined it. Rook's wedding ring. From Kyle. Smeared with dried blood. Fin shuddered.

"Please get rid of it."

The whisper startled Fin. Rook stared at him, pleading, ready to melt into tears again. Letting go of the ring, he went to her. She tried to turn away, but he caught her and held her.

"I know everything."

Rook trembled, trying to pull away again. "No, no. You can't... I don't..." Her throat caught and she shook her head.

"It's all over."

"I gave up, Fin. I didn't want to, but, but I let you down. I don't deserve you."

"You thought I was dead."

Her face contorted and she shook her head again. "So weak. Sorry."

Fin gently held her face and tried to look into her eyes. She squeezed them closed.

He said, "No, I know all about it. I got the story from Kyle. You were strong. I'm weak. When I couldn't find you, I gave up too." He looked away for a moment. "You were stronger than me. But we're together now. It's all over. It's all over."

Rook finally opened her eyes. She seized Fin. They embraced silently for a time.

"I love you," Fin said.

"I love you." Rook wept.

Fin took off his undershirt and wetted it with water from the bag. He began to wash Rook, starting with her face. As she worked she calmed, and he began to feel her thoughts.

"I can tell Kyle did some damage to your mind," Fin said. Rook stiffened. "It's okay. Remember that dream you told me about, when you repaired my tower? It wasn't a dream. I think I could help you the same way, but only if you want me to. I understand you don't want anyone in there. It's up to you." Fin concentrated on rinsing Marcus's blood out of her hair, manifesting serenity he didn't feel.

Faintly he felt her nod. He looked into her sad blue eyes and she nodded again.

"Please," she whispered.

Fin entered Rook's mind, feeling like a trespasser. He was wary of touching anything for fear of hurting her, hesitant at first even to make a close study of his surroundings lest he read some private notion she hadn't chosen to share with him. His memories of violations at the hands of Kyle and Shaw made him loath to follow their example.

All around him dark, tangled pine trees towered. They and the ground were coated with a black slimy substance, like the aftermath of an oil-tanker disaster. The foul sludge was a toxic blend of grief and shame, which must have built up while Kyle had her. Being exposed to it was painful for Fin, so he couldn't imagine how she felt with her entire mental landscape drenched in it.

The forest seemed endless. The trees dripped, the drops making nearly silent echoes of actual splashes as they landed. The sludge seeped into the ground. Fin had to do something or all this blackness would be absorbed into Rook's mind and leave her permanently traumatized. Cleaning the acrid stuff off the trees proved impossible, as it clung tenaciously to every needle. He changed his focus, pulling back until he gained an overview of the scene.

A large clearing drew his attention, the trees flattened outward from a square pit too regular to be a crater. It was a basement without a house, and it was the source of all the black stuff. Something cataclysmic happened here and toppled the trees. The inner rows were held up by the ones behind them, which leaned a little less and were supported by the rows behind them. And on and on. Rook's own Tunguska.

Fin moved in to the site of the explosion and waded into Rook's emotional tar pit. The black oil weighted him down with bleakness, sorrow. It burned his skin with anger. The fumes were the worst, a powerful, flammable stench of guilt choking him and stinging his eyes.

Buffeted by waves of emotion, awash in full Sensorama replays of carnal acts with Kyle and the pleasure she'd taken in them, Fin stifled his own anger. They'd have to talk it through later, but for right now she needed him to heal her. Which meant he must put it aside.

But how could he? Frank justification for her self-loathing saturated everything, everywhere he looked. Stifled or not, anger pulsated through Fin. Just as she had reason to feel guilty, he couldn't help feeling there was reason for him to be furious.

And suddenly he couldn't be. In her horror over what happened she wanted Fin to lash out, to punish her for Kyle's crimes, as if he could erase them.

Even if she would be erased, too.

Fin had the power to take these memories away from Rook, but it would be exactly what Kyle did and it would ultimately bring about the same catastrophe. Nothing in his power could alter her past, but he didn't want to. It was part of her, and he accepted it. He longed to tell her, but would she be able to believe him? Believing she'd betrayed Fin was poisoning Rook's forest, and, tragically, it didn't seem to matter that she was wrong.

The sludge eruption was very recent, based on how fast it was soaking in. It happened when she awoke and saw him, when the lie she'd accepted to mask her pain was revealed. Fin wished he could have prevented this upheaval, her anguish. It was his fault she suffered, even though the sludge was of Kyle's creation.

Now his own appalling sadness threatened to overwhelm Fin. He wanted to sag down into the muck, let it engulf him, but that would mean failing Rook. He couldn't let her down, but that was precisely what he feared he was doing. He choked back sobs.

But he wasn't choking on the awful fumes anymore. He looked down at the sludge and saw it turning clear where it touched him, his acceptance a purifying catalyst. As soon as he saw what was happening, he waded into the deepest pools of contamination, spreading himself through as much of it as he could reach. The clarifying effect propagated outward from him wherever he went. Soon all of what the pit contained, and much on the nearby trees, sparkled like dew. He laughed and cried at the same time, watching the clarification spread over the next row of trees, and the ones beyond them.

Resuming his bird's-eye position, Fin watched as the trees shed their horrid coats and began to right themselves. Here and there, small pockets of the muck remained dark. Some displayed a slight cloudiness. Some formed glossy, greenish-black crystals like obsidian or anthracite. They would give Rook an occasional twinge of regret, but that might even be a good thing.

Fin slipped out of her head and concentrated on washing her body. She smiled at him. He smiled back.

*** *** ***

Fin approached the mass of pale spiders cautiously. Startling it would accomplish nothing good.

He moved up to the doorway and cleared his throat. No response. He said, "Hello?" but the spidermind was silent. It didn't want to talk, but it didn't want him to leave.

Fin said, quietly but sternly, "I'm not putting your Floating Wisdom back. So get over it."

Sadness overflowed the chamber. The mass-mind knew he would say that.

As long as it understood.

It did. This was futile. Fin couldn't help.

"Hold it. You're the one who wanted me to come. This passive-aggressive routine isn't going to sit well."

But what could he do?

"Probably live to regret this decision..." Fin sought an entrance to the alien mind.

It was all entrances, designed from the ground up for access. These portals were for new members. Not the kind of access Fin needed. He would need to get past the perimeter some other way. Make his own door.

He tried to be as gentle as possible.

Fin stood on a tiny island, a bleak hunk of basalt. A foaming opalescent sea undulated all around it, and hundreds of other islands like it. The level of the sea was falling fast, the shimmering surface receding so suddenly that at first he thought his gnarled tower of black rock was surging upward. He started studying the other lonely jagged monoliths but all hell broke loose.

The sea came back, in the form of the next cataclysmic wave. It hammered the island and hurled tons of froth and spray far overhead. The top was swamped and Fin only narrowly avoided being swept off. The sea began to withdraw, calmly preparing for the next blitz.

Fin wrung himself out and tried to focus on the symbolism here. The islands were token representations of the individual spiders, their present unity an approximation of what the Floating Wisdom had been. Not only was this smaller, it was looser. Vestiges of their separate personalities remained.

Some relic of each individual was a good thing in a collective, a safeguard against the kind of callousness the Floating Wisdom displayed. The group mind would feel some empathy for the unassimilated, but these were too imperfectly arranged. Their unstable formation contributed to the depression.

The next wave crashed through. His islet tilted a bit from the impact. He didn't bother trying to dry off.

The aliens still had partially understood memories of what it felt like to know everything, and were painfully aware of how much they had lost. This small collective wallowed in fear of the gaps in its understanding, when by human standards it was virtually omniscient.

The sea was something like doubt. Not uncertainty, not lack of confidence. There was a taunting kind of saltiness in this sea. The might of all the things it didn't know. So far, repeated drenchings with this exotic neurosis weren't harming Fin, but it was rather unpleasant.

If nothing changed, the surf would erode or topple all the protruding rocks. Those individual spiders would die, or perhaps detach from the collective. Eventually there would be too few to sustain even this stunted personality.

Fin wondered why it should be up to him to save it. Was saving it even a good idea?

He felt morally obligated. This was a person, by certain definitions, and although it was scared shitless of him it had given him its trust.

Even the Floating Wisdom had assigned religious significance to Fin, and the spidermind worshipped him outright. It saw him as a savior.

Might as well act the part.

As the next breaker crashed down, he stepped from his perch and strode off.

Walking on the sea of doubt was easy, because of the powerful countering force of his arrogance. Fin usually called it confidence, or resourcefulness, but why mince words here?

He made his way to open water where the waves were rollers, not breakers. Much quieter.

No land was visible other than the sad forest of volcanic crags. The sea looked like it went on forever, but there was something odd about the horizon. Venturing a bit farther from the island cluster, Fin spotted a rope stretched tightly at a set depth in the water. A wave took him upwards, so he waited until the next trough for another glimpse. As he bent to look closer he saw that it wasn't a rope. It was the bottom edge of a sheet of some tough material that reached upwards out of sight. The distant, featureless horizon and vivid sunset were painted on this canvas that encircled the islands. Up close, the brushstrokes were obvious.

A dim green glow infiltrated the water under the backdrop.

Fin looked at the islets. The spidermind clearly believed the illusory endlessness of their sea, knew nothing of this barrier. Fin hiked along it for a while, and determined that it was stable. It seemed to be a natural part of the construct.

Why shouldn't it be? The sea couldn't really be infinite, so this was a convenient bit of shorthand, just a way of saying 'and so on.'

He turned away from the boundary, heading back toward the islands. It had occurred to him that loitering near the perimeter might reveal its existence and bring the spiders a whole new existential dilemma. That wasn't likely to help.

But he thought he had an idea of what would.

Fin planned to rearrange these rocks, tying them into a stronger whole but preserving their separate identities. He would place them in a ring, to better withstand the waves. Fin wandered among the standing stones, rising and falling with the sea. Weaving between and around them, he hummed.

And nothing happened.

Fin thought about shoving on some of the rocks to get them moving, but he knew that would only destabilize things and make the situation worse. He stopped and surveyed the forlorn archipelago, studied the crags and the play of mist around them, and he saw the problem.

The spiders didn't believe it would work. His approach seemed too simple. They expected their salvation to be more dramatic. Although Fin now understood what they wanted, he tried to think of some alternative, something that wouldn't perpetuate their ridiculous deification of him.

"You're making this harder on both of us!"

It wasn't going to work any other way.

From the water, he drew an outlandish bass fiddle made of brazen speculation. It was all fluted, reticulated spirals, something especially tacky from Neptune's attic. It had tentacles like a jellyfish, stretched from an unsavory-looking orifice near the bottom to coil around the tips of the salt-encrusted trident at the top. Barnacles clinging to a nautilesque bulge controlled the instrument's voice. Fin hoped its absurdity lent the moment sufficient spectacle, because he wasn't sure he could top it.

He began to play. Eerie, reverberating sounds, like whales baying at the moon.

Now when Fin marched, the islets nearby followed. He had to admit this was fun.

His path described a spiral, working his way around the group in several passes, entraining more spellbound rocks each time. On the fifth lap he picked up the last of the stragglers. He tightened his curve and had them neatly packed in a perfect circle at the end of the sixth lap. The next incoming wave lifted him to the top of the wall.

It was impervious to the crashing surf now, and held a calm lagoon. Not wanting to leave this mind with a pool of gnawing doubt at its center, Fin hurled the bass into the lagoon. It sank, and the color of the liquid became rosier, spreading outward from the splash. For Rook he changed guilt into acceptance. Here he transformed doubt into wonder.

Fin decided not to transmute the rest of the sea. An ocean of inquisitiveness would get anyone into trouble.

Things looked good. Fin felt proud. His sour attitude about putting on an act softened.

He left the collective before he developed any paternal feelings for it.

With continued coaching from Fin over the next day or so, the aliens became able to coordinate across greater distances. They could now operate their base at almost the same level as before he broke their religion, even increasing the gravity in a small block of rooms so the lovebirds would feel more at home.

They readily agreed when Fin asked if he and Rook could spend their honeymoon on the asteroid to finish healing their relationship.

*** *** ***

Rook could tell Fin was trying to act solemn, but he kept snickering. She grinned at him and moved over to the bunks to root around for clothes, wondering what outfit would be most appropriate.

Fin gave up on seriousness and said to Vesuvius, "We're going to outer space. Wanna come along?"

"Again?" Vesuvius murmured.

Rook found a garbage bag full of her dresses and shed the borrowed bathrobe.

"For real this time," said Fin.

"Does Mars need more women?"

"You watch too much TV."

Rook chose a black and white harlequin-pattern miniskirt and a shaggy black sweater. As compatible with interplanetary travel as anything else she owned. A pair of white patent leather go-go boots completed the Barbarella look.

Fin told Vesuvius, "We'll get you later," and put on the black jeans and dark green shirt Rook tossed him.

Fin climbed the ladder and opened the hatch, and Rook followed him up into the late-afternoon sunshine.

As they edged toward the street, Fin touched her shoulder to get her attention and pointed to the front of the house. Vans from two local news affiliates flanked the driveway, their crews sipping from steaming styrofoam cups. A reporter in a long overcoat spoke into his cellphone.

A flock of tiny, furry-winged pixies began a bacchanal in Rook's belly.

Attention was directed at the house, not the woods. By keeping quiet, Rook and Fin slipped away unnoticed. The oppressive storm clouds on the horizon seemed beautiful after so much time in a cavern filled with giant spiders.

They shared a few guesses about what Kyle's folks could have done to arouse media interest, but only came up with juvenile scenarios.

Entering Walmart to buy supplies, they passed a newsstand. Rook's pulse jumped and the pixies stepped up the pace of their revels. There on the front page of the *Webster Daily Press* was Kyle.

"Mystery solved," she said. Of course it was an answer that raised plenty of questions. The headline proclaimed *Local Boy Makes Good*. The copy made a thin pretense of asking, "Who is this guy, really?" while failing to question any of his purported miracles. Local residents gave "remarkable accounts" of how photographs of Kyle could cure warts and speed up computers.

Kyle had stepped out from the shadows, Shaw's successor in full. Looking at him, even in pictures, brought a tickle of his vibration low in Rook's head, and she gripped the newspaper in her sweaty hands. Fin saw her distress and led her away, tossing the paper back on the pile.

"With any luck, this will all blow over by the time we're back from our honeymoon," he said.

"We're going for more than 15 minutes, right?" Rook joked, but couldn't quite shake the feeling Kyle was watching her from the newspapers. She had to stop staring at her ink-smudged fingers.

They filled their cart with canned foods, chocolate, and, since Rook's diaphragm was still at Marcus's apartment, condoms. Passing by electronics on their way to the toy department to look for a travel chess board, Rook asked, "Do you think we could pick up any TV up there? I've heard that the signals keep going forever."

"Maybe the spiders can set us up with pirate satellite. I bet they could descramble all the fun channels, too."

"We could pretend we're on Mystery Science Theater."

The rows of TVs were all tuned to the same channel, where a shrill commercial for some pointless kitchen gadget was ending. Suddenly, Kyle's face filled the screens. Icy, insinuating echoes of his signal accompanied his appearance, and Rook gasped.

A voice-over smugly welcomed everyone back to the special weekday Shaw Ministries broadcast, a new initiative of the flock's new leader, Kyle Tanner!

Kyle stood at the pulpit, wearing robes of black and deep green. "Set aside your burdens, my children," he said gently. "Let me ease that load for you. Calm your mind, and let the Spirit exult in my light." His voice weighed oppressively on Rook, rekindling the ember of his signal. Brook and Bramble slithered from their hiding places and smiled maliciously.

The camera showed a shot of the audience. The pews were packed, everyone staring at Kyle with rapturous joy.

"Place looks tacky," Fin said.

"That's where... where he married me," Rook replied. The Bramble part of her chuckled low and throaty.

Fin squeezed her hand.

When she'd been there it was nearly empty. Strangers had witnessed her most shameful moment. Certainly some of the things she perpetrated in private with Kyle were worthy of condemnation, even if you weren't religious, but the wedding was her nadir. To have willingly submitted to Kyle... Why hadn't she fled?

Brook and Bramble said it was because she hadn't wanted to.

"This is scaring me," Rook said. Low-voltage ghosts joined the pixies in her belly. Fin wrapped his arm around her shoulders and pulled her closer.

"I know of the confusion you experience every day. I do," Kyle assured his flock. "This world places many difficult obstacles in our way. The path is hard to see. The path is hard to follow. We welcome our tests, don't we? But still we need to see the path for what it is. We must not become lost."

"He's good at that," said Rook.

"It's almost like it knows what it's saying," Fin agreed.

"Now is the winter of this world, as we all see," Kyle continued, moving out from behind the pulpit. "The spiritual barrenness is all around. These are days of tests for the flock, but late in winter is just before spring's return! Soon the Kingdom will bloom for those who've not been lured away."

The audience made appreciative noises.

Fin watched with detached disgust.

"This is horrible," Rook said. Kyle's acid green words seeped into her, and she could feel Brook and Bramble getting stronger.

Kyle's eyes locked on the camera. His gaze, multiplied across a dozen screens, followed wherever she went. Rook turned away, but was compelled to cast furtive glances at him over her shoulder. Snaking his presence deeper into her mind, he seemed to speak to her alone. "Many have gone astray. We pray for them, we call to them." Each television screen was the bottom of a well. Rook steadied herself, clutching Fin's arm so she wouldn't fall in.

"Every day, the twisted illusions leap in all our eyes." Kyle turned his eyes upward, his voice quavering. "How can we keep to the path?" He locked his gaze onto the flock once more, and his tone became silky, sinister, seductive. "How can you know you are living with the righteous and just? How can you know you haven't been deceived?"

The camera zoomed in for an extreme close-up. Kyle's green eyes held a feverish glow that stoked something low and primal inside Rook.

"You shall know it through me. I absolve you of your thoughts. Through me you are assured, assured a place. Free, free of confusion. The peace and light of Heaven can be seen. I am the way. You only need to look to me, look away from the world. Look away."

Rook's jaw dropped. Tearing her eyes away and looking around, she saw that a small herd of shoppers had drifted up to stare at Kyle in a mouth-breathing stupor. Rook self-consciously closed her mouth.

Rook turned to Fin, still fixated on the television. He did not wear a sleepwalker's bland expression. His eyes were narrowed, his jaw clenched, his skin reddening. She wanted to pull him away from the target of his rage, but felt too much confusion and fear. She took a steadying deep breath and touched Fin's hand.

The bank of televisions went black with a muffled pop. Rook and Fin both felt a clarifying rush of surprise. Leaving their cart behind, they walked out of the store. Without Kyle's visage and voice to fuel their ardor, the princesses quieted.

"We have to go deal with him," Fin said.

Rook was frantic. "He doesn't matter to us anymore. Let's just leave!"

"No," Fin said soberly. "If we walk away, when we come back he'll have even more followers. We can't live in a world full of Kyle-ites. Look at what's happening back there, he's doing evil shit to their minds. It's not going to only be the few die-hards who always used to watch

Shaw's show, he's getting his hooks into normal people."

Rook gnawed her lower lip. Fin didn't understand how fresh it all was for her, how tenuous her peace of mind. He didn't know about her princesses. Without breaking down again, how could she convince him to abandon this idea?

"We can't rush in with no plan," she said. "We should go figure out what to do, first."

Fin shook his head. "Now's the perfect time, while he's on camera."

"The perfect time to do what?" Rook asked. She felt near tears.

Fin smiled. "I just want to talk to him."

She shook her head. "Fin, this is crazy!" Seeing the Cathedral of Shame of TV was awful enough. To return to it, with Fin? Unthinkable.

"If I can make him look stupid on the air, it'll show everyone. Everyone, Rook."

"Don't you see? It won't be that way. He'll fight you!" Rook's voice was shrill.

"Then let them see that. Let them see their messiah is all too human."

Rook knew Fin would relent if he could only understand how Kyle's hold over her felt. "Fin, please. I don't want to go there." Ally. Prize. Weapon. What part would she play? And if the worst came to pass? Kyle would never allow her to escape again. "Please."

"I know, but it's important. I won't let him hurt you, I promise."

A feeble residue of Kyle's signal clung to the inside of Rook's skull. In his presence it would amplify to its previous level. She couldn't imagine how it would feel to have both Fin's and Kyle's vibrations in her head at the same time. One welcome and soothing, the other harsh and proprietary. They might simply cancel each other out, but more likely they would clash and reverberate and—

"I have to do this, Rook. I have to stop him. I know you can feel it. He's pulling them in, making some sort of monster slave-mind. Maybe a Sinking Wisdom. Something far worse than we've seen." Fin paused. "You don't have to go."

Rook laid her head on Fin's chest. No one else would deal with Kyle. If they tried to run now, he would forever be between them. They'd faced him separately with inconclusive results, so together they might stand a chance. Even without a plan.

It would all come down to her. When standing face to face with Kyle, his malignant aura corroding her mental bastions and the traitorous princesses sabotaging her resolve from within, would she be able to repudiate him? Would she have the strength? She had to find out, because the doubt, however subtle, would undermine her relationship with Fin. Any life they tried to build together would have uncertainty for its foundation.

"We'll both go," she said. "For us." She hugged him ferociously. He tried to soothe her, murmuring.

If Fin was distracted worrying about her, he might make a mistake. They couldn't afford that. She must be strong so she and Fin could have a life together. This foolhardy mission might be Fin's idea, but she was damn well going to do her share. Her princess-in-the-tower days were over.

Rook pulled away from Fin and smiled grimly.

"Okay," she said. "Let's do this. I'll be all right. Concentrate on Kyle."

Fin looked her in the eyes. He nodded.

Fin contacted the spiders for transportation. After a few seconds of sliding and twisting against the grain of consensus reality, the parking lot around them was replaced by the center aisle of Shaw Cathedral. They arrived just inside the doors, to the accompaniment of a brief squawk of feedback.

Memories of her last trip down this aisle invaded Rook's mind. Her stomach clenched and she swallowed hard. Fin looked at her and she remembered how important it was to be strong.

Together they strode toward the front of the church.

Chapter Twenty-Five

CATHEDRAL

*A Murder of Crows shall pick clean
the bones of the Pretender and of his Legions*
from *New Revelations* by Reverend Brian Shaw, unpublished

Fin glanced around the interior of the cathedral. The roof was one huge skylight, arching over the crowd and soaring into a 20-story spire of plate glass above the pulpit. Two balconies. The pews were jammed. Fin was both amused and dismayed to see the camera operators trying to figure out why their equipment suddenly stopped working. It had to be interference from the spiders' teleporter. He'd wanted the entire viewing audience to witness Kyle's humiliation, but by coming here they'd already knocked him off the airwaves. At least the home audience was safe, for now.

Kyle stood on the white-carpeted stage at the front of the church, bathed in spotlights, pontificating. Fin tuned him out and continued down the aisle. No one looked their way. Rook veered off to take cover behind a pillar. The closer Fin drew to Kyle, the more uncomfortable he became, so he couldn't blame her. Kyle's words fell on him like acid rain, trying to etch his mind.

Fin advanced to the front row of pews.

"KYLE!"

Kyle stopped speaking and looked at Fin. At the same moment, everyone in the audience looked too.

Kyle broke into a broad grin and held his arms out in a welcoming gesture.

"My brother." He began to recite and the audience joined him,

"Divided Seed shall a Divided Child Beget…"

Fin felt insanity pooling around him, flowing over the audience. He shook off the effects and raced up the steps to where Kyle stood.

"What do you think you're doing?" Fin demanded. "You're less qualified than me to be up here. You don't believe any of this shit you're saying."

From the audience came a low murmur. Fin took that as a good sign.

"Brother," Kyle said silkily, "anyone can be saved, if he but chooses the correct path. I'm living proof of that, and there might even be hope for you."

The crowd's noises brightened, which told Fin he'd misread their earlier response. They clearly wanted to buy whatever Kyle happened to be selling. Shit, Fin thought, they're as crazy as he is.

"You're crazy," Fin said.

Kyle fell silent, a tiny smirk toying with one corner of his mouth. The audience sat expectantly.

Fin turned to the crowd and saw that Rook had left her hiding place and was coming to join him. Encouraged, he told the rapt congregation, "He's insane. Kyle Tanner is insane and he's spreading his insanity to you. It's contagious. Can't you feel it?"

No reaction.

Kyle chuckled and his smile broadened. "Rook. I knew you'd come," he said, his vivid green eyes never leaving Fin.

The audience turned to look at Rook.

"My wife," Kyle explained. "Come here, darling."

Rook took a faltering step.

"NO!" Fin yelled. "She's my wife, not yours!"

There were scattered gasps from the crowd when Fin uttered that blasphemy.

"Rook's my wife," Fin repeated. "She chose to marry me. You gave her no choice."

Kyle smiled beatifically.

"Why don't we let her choose now?"

Rook stumbled up the stairs and stopped halfway between Fin and Kyle. Panic ruled her face as she looked out over the audience. Fin reached for her, but his hand was buffeted away by some unseen force.

"No," Kyle said. "Neither of us touches her. She decides."

Fin watched Rook crumble into wretched tears. Towering, malignant forces stormed inside her. The delicate strands connecting him to her stretched taut, singing with tension. She'd known it would be this bad. This was a sacrifice to demonstrate the strength of her love. Fin ached.

"Rook," Kyle said soothingly, "it's time to decide. Which one of us do you Complete?"

Rook lurched and almost fell. She turned her eyes to Fin and he could feel her pleading. She stepped backward, away from both of them. Fin tried to send her comfort and encountered Kyle weaving a shroud of his insanity around her. Rook sank to her knees.

The audience was rapt.

Fin turned all of his will on them. He broadcast to them the way he had to the aliens when he broke the Floating Wisdom.

"Snap out of it!"

***   ***   ***

Kyle was unaccountably stronger now. Upon entering the cathedral, a full-blown voracious throbbing supplanted Rook's gnawing little Kyle vibration and fully awakened Brook and Bramble. Kyle barged into her head, wrapped barbed tentacles around her freewill, and lasciviously stroked her libido. His throb amplified tenfold and drove out thought. Brook and Bramble basked in the glare of his personality, pulling Rook up onto the stage and toward oblivion.

On her knees now, swaying, Rook fought off unconsciousness and watched the horrendous scene through her tears. Kyle was everywhere. She was drowning in him, swept downstream on his greedy currents. She could still see Fin, receding on the shoreline. Was he speaking? Did he see her? Distantly, she heard Fin yelling. The current suddenly let her go as a collective cry of anguish rose from the crowd, Kyle, and Fin. Rook felt something snap in her own head and cried out as well.

Kyle roared in fury and leapt at Fin.

Fin tried to dodge, but Kyle plowed into his legs and took him down.

Fin slammed his elbow into Kyle's chin and sent him rolling, vestments writhing around him. Fin dove after Kyle, colliding with him as he rose to a crouch.

They tangled together and blurred in Rook's vision. Their black and green garments fused them into one entity, bruising her perceptions. She closed her eyes, but her mind filled with the image of a spinning coin. Her gown was not so regal now, but still stark-hued, constructed of opposites and contradictions. The choice remained hers to make, but she couldn't tell one brother from the other. Chance threatened to step in and decide in her stead.

The haunted verdigris blur of her husbands continued to tumble, savagely struggling for the upper hand. Waves of heat and prickly static emanated from the brothers as their minds grappled as violently as their bodies, jerking her heart back and forth through emotional electromagnetism. Her vision swam from turmoil, and also from the shimmering heat generated by the battle.

The men stood, began circling. Their fighting stances were mirror images. Rook was disoriented. Fin or Kyle? Which was which? Both wanted her, to hide her away from the world. Both were fundamentally connected to her, needed her to be Complete. Both claimed her, married her.

Seasick, Rook dragged herself to the altar and drew her knees up to her chest, her traitorous eyes squeezed shut.

Inside her mind the connection to each man was strong, but nearly invisible. Blotting out the stars, swallowing the moonlight, they were like wormholes in space, with blackly glowing outlines. Their mingled emotions saturated Rook and her princesses with an overwhelming fusion of love and entitlement, jealousy and passion, fascination and fear. The sheer volume and intensity obscured their sources and Rook was no better able to tell Fin from Kyle.

If either discovered that his brother also shared a connection with her, the battlefield would switch to her head. They would tear her apart in their efforts to claim her. In a flash of self-preservation, Rook built a wall to keep them separated, then opened her eyes. The men became more distinct.

Kyle swung at Fin. Fin rolled with the impact, too late to reduce the blow's effect. He turned far to his right and dropped to one knee. When Kyle closed in, Fin drove his left boot into Kyle's gut, doubling him over. Fin came across with his right, standing to augment the uppercut. He hit Kyle on the nose and laid him out on his back.

Fin pounced. He landed atop Kyle, glaring.

Kyle spat blood at Fin and locked on with fierce eyes. Fin reared back and tried to scream. Only a small cracked sound escaped.

Kyle jackhammered Fin's mind. The surge of hatred penetrated Rook's confusion and her shriek blew out every speaker in the hall.

Fin rallied and drove back Kyle's psychic ram. He clawed at Kyle's mind, seeking loose areas and tiny cracks. He seeped in. Kyle convulsed, knocking Fin over and momentarily breaking the mental circuit. Rook sagged with relief.

Again, they both stood. They remained still, concentrating their assaults on the mental arena. They launched brute-force attacks, attempts to crush the other's will.

Rook turned away and vomited. She needed to end this, but didn't know how. Bramble and Brook could end it. They clamored to join Kyle, assured that with their help he would triumph. Rook recoiled from opening her reserves to anyone, too afraid of what would happen if she entered the fray.

The temperature rose. The deathly white carpet began to smoke. The nearest television camera shorted out in a shower of sparks.

A low moan rose up from the congregation, and Kyle leered at Fin. He tapped into his followers' minds, drawing power to throw at his brother. In the front row of pews, a middle-aged woman with teased hair silently burst into flames. She stayed primly in her seat and was instantly reduced to a pile of black ash.

"Stop!" Fin yelled. "You're killing them!"

"They like it," Kyle said. "Can I get an amen?"

"Amen," the flock said as one, the word trailing off into incoherency as Kyle increased his power grab.

Fin ceased his counterattack to focus on defending himself. The power surge from the audience was grinding away his defenses. Rook could feel him pushing to shore them up. She could feel the pulsing energy all around her. As Kyle increased his attack even further, she felt tremors in the floor.

Fin roared, and shoved against the stream of antagonizing force. More cameras erupted in smoke and sparks. The building shook, and the glass spire overhead shattered in a concussive crash. Tons of glass began the long descent toward the combatants.

Rook screamed and rolled under the altar. Kyle and Fin didn't move. The deadly hail of razors thundered down, engulfing the entire front of the chapel. The sunset playing among the cascading shards created glowing shafts like an image from a prayer book. Both men were untouched. Seven-foot slabs stood in a jagged forest all around them.

Kyle regrouped and assailed Fin again. Fueled by his pool of slave minds, he loosed a searing fusillade. The center section of the audience was now empty back to the fourth row. Fin fell to his knees, struggling to expel Kyle from his head. He slumped forward, clutching his face in his hands.

Kyle laughed and pressed his advantage, snaking deeper into Fin's brain. Flares of light from the pews told Rook more followers were combusting to fuel Kyle's offensive, driving Bramble nearly orgasmic.

Rook sobbed, staring horrified at Kyle. His reflection moved erratically across the towering shards of glass, creating a horde of demonic preachers. Now free of her earlier confusion, she tried to feed Fin's struggle with her waning strength. The princesses fought to aid

Kyle, but Rook furiously returned them to their prisons and concentrated what remained of her energies on Fin. It was enough to halt Kyle's slithering advance.

Fin felt the support and hungrily drew in as much as Rook could give. He thrashed on the floor, rolling in glass. He needed more amperage, couldn't drive Kyle out. Fin howled. He called out for aid, for more power, and received an answer.

With a sudden influx of energy from the spiders, Fin repelled the invasion. Kyle was furious, but even with his anger he could not stop Fin from pushing him out and resealing the fallen defenses. Fin stood and poured his full intensity onto one area of Kyle's shields. Kyle demanded more power to brace the weakening walls, and Fin focused his beam on an even smaller area.

The carpet was now smoking heavily. With popping noises, flames sprang up. The conflagration spread into a large circle, and the huge slabs of glass shattered in the intense heat. Neither man could be seen through the four-foot flames and thick white smoke.

The fire vanished, as the adversaries withdrew their all-out attacks and sized each other up. The smoke rising from the carpet turned black, a cloud of poisonous fumes expanding to engulf the church.

Fin and Kyle each gathered energy for a new gambit, attuning to the masses augmenting their powers. They had different polarities, different textures. The dividing wall in Rook's head rippled like a waterfall, threatening to collapse. As she shored it up, Brook and Bramble's prisons failed and they emerged wild-eyed and giddy. Rook slammed her mind closed. A dreadful anticipation and mental ozone, like an electrified fog, choked her thoughts and seized her lungs. She could no longer aid Fin, but the twins couldn't aid Kyle either.

As Fin and Kyle built up their strength, they built up auras around themselves. The gangrenous glow enshrouding Kyle gave him a corpselike aspect, while pulsations of unearthly emerald flowed around Fin. Rook's skin crawled with static and her muscles twitched. The polarization of their energies drove swirling eddies through the smoke filling the cathedral. Soon the roiling cloud parted down the center between them, splitting to the accompaniment of indoor lightning leaping from one hemisphere to the other. The entire central section of pews now stood barren, and there were empty pockets throughout the side sections and the two balconies.

Icy winds carried the worst of the smoke out through the ruined spire, leaving the brothers to regard each other. They paused, fully charged and locked on target.

Kyle sneered and said, "If only you had been carted off to reform school, or better yet killed yourself when your mother abandoned you. It would have saved so much trouble." Fin didn't flinch. Kyle continued. "I see you've had to look outside of humanity altogether to find friends, and we both know about your recent marital troubles. Nobody loves you, Fin. Not like they love me."

Fin coolly replied, "Yeah, they love you. Just like they did back in your glory days, before your knee went to shit. Remember who stuck by you in rehab? Remember who cared if you showed up? Nobody. That's who loved you then, and that's who loves you now."

Kyle said, "So nobody loves either one of us. Whatever."

"No," Fin said, "nobody loves you. Rook loves me."

Kyle laughed. "She's done all the things with me she ever did with you."

Fin renewed his heavy assault. Kyle blocked it easily, still laughing. He retaliated, carpet-bombing Fin's mind. Fin stood his ground, grimacing with the effort.

Rook emerged from her shelter and stared at the scene. Wind screamed between Fin and Kyle, and green-white tendrils of energy crawled across the floor around their feet. The walls of the cathedral were ready to buckle. The superstructure of Rook's mind was ready to collapse as well. If her wall fell, that would be the end. They would all die.

It was Fin's wall that cracked, though. He remained standing, frozen in place. Kyle had advanced deep into Fin's territory, and now controlled him physically. Controlled his breath, denied it.

Rook felt Fin's panic, the drowning pressure. Kyle's laughter subsided to a persistent chuckle as he turned to her.

Rook's vision constricted to a fuzzy halo surrounding Kyle, her own lungs rigid. Air rasped into her throat as Fin let her go. His connection remained, but she could feel him sinking away, steadfastly refusing to stoop to Kyle's level of depravity and sacrifice the aliens for more power.

"NO!" Rook wailed.

"Yes, you do love him, don't you?" Kyle deadpanned. "Well, then I suppose you're the one I should be talking to. Talking about love, or at least respect." The last word was a snarl, but he chuckled again. "I never really saw what was going on between us, but I do now."

Shuddering, Rook crumbled to her knees. Bramble's fires flooded her body, kneeling before Kyle. Brook raised Rook's arms toward the victorious side of the Divided Man. She moaned, and tears poured down her cheeks. Rook couldn't tell her own grief from Bramble's ecstasy or Brook's desperation.

"But no, that would never do." Kyle took a calm step toward Rook.

The princesses shrank from Kyle's gaze, astonished to find themselves under direct scrutiny. He always looked through them before, and they hadn't known the difference until now.

"All that time, when I thought I was missing something, that was it. I only had these useless shadows, not you at all. And that means even now I'm not truly Complete."

Bramble quivered with helpless lust. Brook overflowed with degradation. Both reached for Kyle, but he passed over them and his will fell upon Rook like a storm cloud.

"Love me. Complete me. Give me your true self. Do it, or I'll kill Fin."

He didn't know she could feel Fin already dying, didn't know her wall was there. Rook clung to her connection to Fin, pulling him back toward the surface, feeding him her waning strength. Distantly, she felt him kicking, told him not to give up.

Brook seized the opportunity to be wanted again, by showing Kyle what Rook hid. She gripped Fin's tenuous lifeline and screamed. Bramble saw that for once someone else would get in trouble, and clawed at the wall Rook fought to sustain.

Kyle toppled the wall effortlessly and a tight grin appeared on his face. Rook watched fires consume the remainder of the audience as Kyle charged himself up and reached for the tether to Fin. Rook's darkest fear would be realized, the annihilating collision inside her head. Kyle cackled in anticipation.

Rook raced to head him off, too late, a shrill cry of warning all she could manage.

The vortex of malice howled through Rook's mind, filling it to the edges, using her as a conduit to bypass Fin's defenses.

The roar of the attack was followed by roaring silence. Rook saw Fin standing on the stage, but felt nothing.

A clear tone of reassurance rang in her mind, thanking her for the warning. Fin had let go and melted to the side, using Kyle's blast to recharge the exhausted spiders.

Kyle raged, off-balance and mentally hyperextended.

Rook was already sprinting. Kyle would know, would have time to react, if she let herself think. She dove into his bad knee from the front, plowing right through it with her shoulder. It bent ninety degrees the wrong way, making a noise like a bowling ball dropped onto bubble wrap.

Kyle fell, his face frozen in a silent shriek of agony. His broken leg folded under him unnaturally as he toppled to the scorched and littered floor, arching his back and clutching at his knee.

Fin swept back upon him. Kyle was defenseless, drowning in pain and shame. Fin sheared through the landscape in Kyle's skull and zeroed in on the ziggurat. His blow shattered it, reducing all its blocks and stolen bones to swirling gray ash and a deafening, discordant cymbal crash.

Kyle slumped, suddenly limp. His eyes remained open, unblinking.

Fin took one step toward the ruined body and sighed. He shook his head. One side of his face toyed with a grin, the other tightened more grimly.

Rook stood and brushed herself off. Her head echoed with the crash of Kyle's defeat. The merest hint of a smile curled her lips. She was complete.

Fin and Rook looked at each other, and out at the rows and rows of empty pews. Kyle used up the audience entirely in his final assault.

Fin said, "Those poor fools trusted him."

Rook shuddered as she took in the aftermath of the carnage. "No more mental powers. Ever."

Fin smoothed Rook's hair back from her face and kissed her. They walked hand-in-hand down the aisle and out through the ruined front doors of the cathedral into a flurry of falling cinders and early November snow.

Free Bonus Chapter

Vesuvius Has Many Questions…

Being the only one who can hear him, Fin is his only source of answers.

Find out where it all started.

Get a dose of what Fin was like before he met Rook, before nanotech and prophecy found him, in a bonus chapter told from Vesuvius's point of view.

Available exclusively to my readers group, free for a limited time.

Sign up for the author's readers group and receive a free copy of the short story, *Shrugging Lessons*.

Visit runeskelley.com/shrugging-lessons

About the Author

Rune Skelley lives in a northeastern college town, and works as a web developer and small business owner. Two jobs, marriage, and raising two sons did not quite account for every waking moment, so Rune took up fiction writing to fill the hole where a social life should be.

Fun fact: Rune Skelley has 20 fingers and 20 toes, but doesn't type any faster than you do.

For a sneak peek at new novels, free stories, and other goodies, join the email list at: runeskelley.com/shrugging-lessons

Rune strives to set aside time every day to answer messages from readers. Say hey at heyrune@runeskelley.com

www.ingramcontent.com/pod-product-compliance
Lightning Source LLC
Chambersburg PA
CBHW072120250626
47159CB00007B/2516